TREY

SACHA BLACK

Trey - The Eden East Novels

Copyright © 2022 Sacha Black

The right of Sacha Black to be identified as the author of this work has been asserted in accordance with the Copyright, Designs and Patents Act 1988.

All rights reserved. No part of this publication may be reproduced, stored in any retrieval system, copied in any form or by any means, electronic, mechanical, photocopying, recording or otherwise transmitted, without permission of the copyright owner. Except for a reviewer who may quote brief passages in a review.

This is a work of fiction. Names, characters, places and incidents within the stories are a product of the author's imagination. Real locales, and public and celebrity names may have been used for atmospheric purposes. Any resemblance to actual people, living or dead, or to businesses, companies, events, institutions or locales is either completely coincidental or is used in an entirely fictional manner.

First Published April 2022, by Sacha Black, Atlas Black Publishing.

Edited by: Lori Parks

Cover design: Andrew Brown, **Design For Writers**

www.sachablack.co.uk

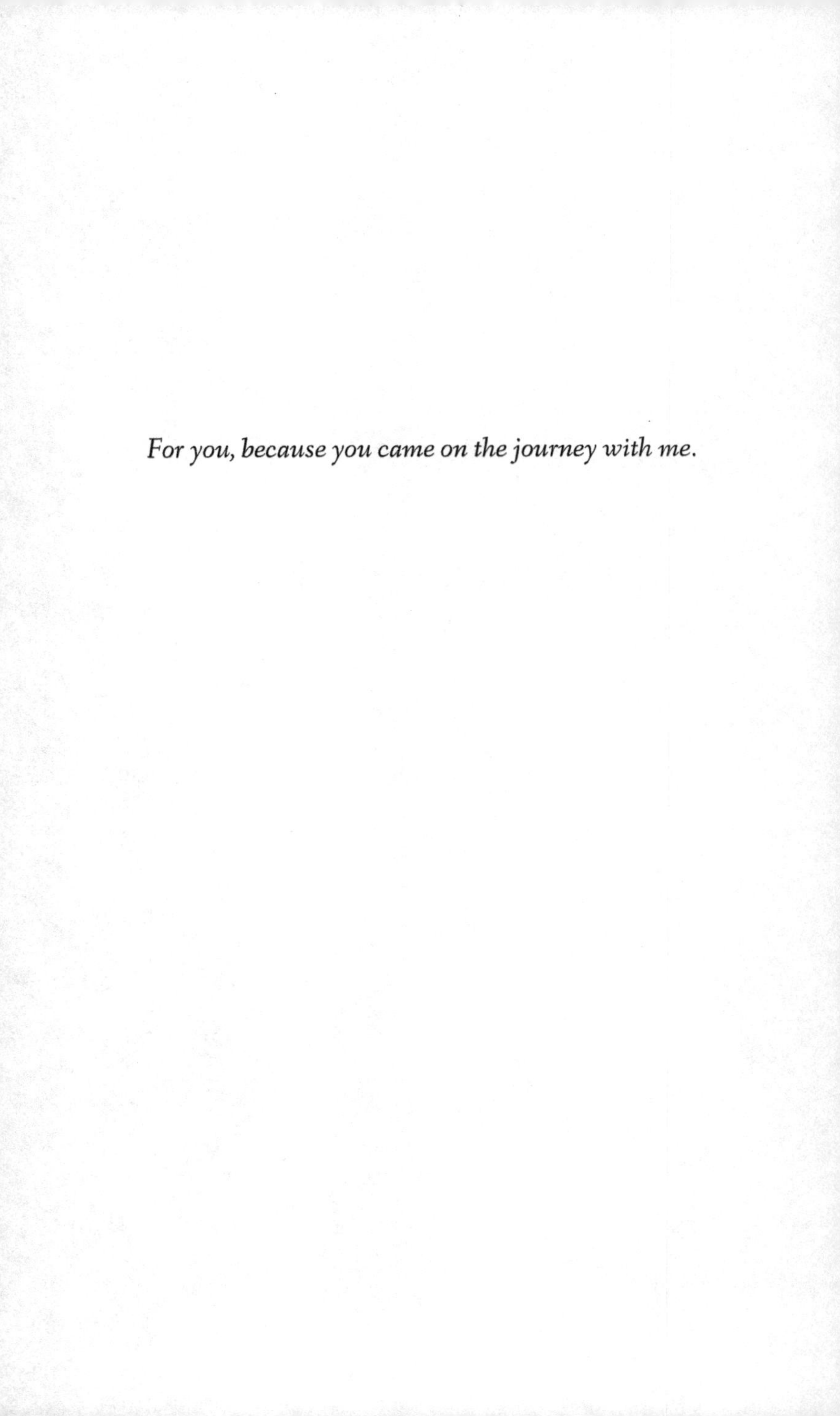

For you, because you came on the journey with me.

TRUTINOR
Houses of the North
NORTH STATE
The Dark's Castle
(1st House of the North)
Keepers School
Trutinor Council
EAST STATE
Ancient Forest
Luna Castle (Arden's)
Aurora's Cove
WEST STATE
Dryad City
& Hospital
SOUTH STATE
Eden's Tower
Stratera Academy
Trey's Mansion
Trey's Bar
Datch Prison
Rhys Davies

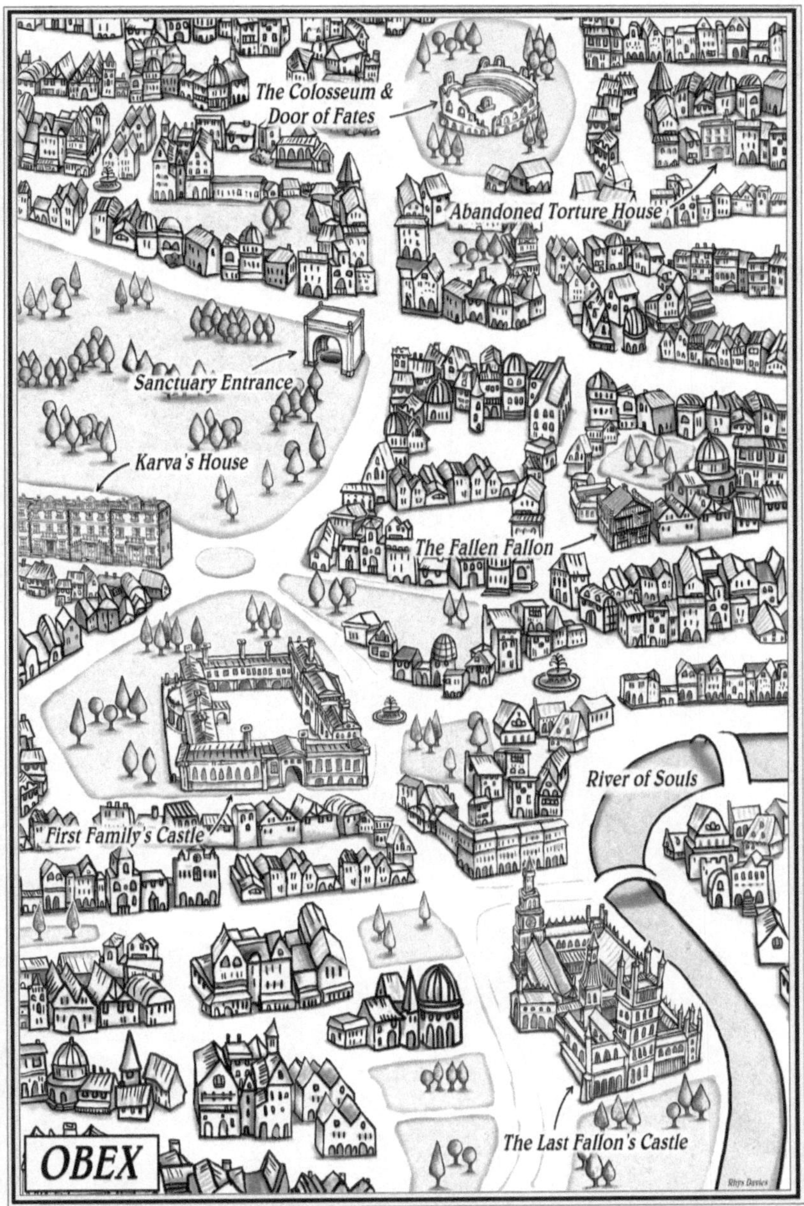

The Colosseum &
Door of Fates
Abandoned Torture House
Sanctuary Entrance
Karva's House
The Fallen Fallon
River of Souls
First Family's Castle
The Last Fallon's Castle
OBEX
Rhys Davies

BREAKING NEWS

"Good morning, Trutinor. This is Tarkin Tavas reporting for CogNews TV. We interrupt your regular viewing schedule to bring you an urgent broadcast."

Tarkin adjusts his tie and clears his throat.

"It is with a deep sadness that I have to report the death of a dearly loved Fallon. Trey Luchelli, Siren Fallon of the South, was tragically killed last night. Early investigations suggest there was a disturbance at Stratera Academy involving the mysterious Door of Fates. Eyewitnesses report the silver door was obliterated. There was movement in and out of the Door, but it's unclear who came through. What we do know, is that the Last Fallon did not return through the door, as myth and prophecy would have us believe was the

Door's intended purpose. However, rumors suggest another crossed.

CogNews interviewed several eyewitnesses who all report both the First Fallon and Fallon East were injured during the events. Reports from Dryad City Hospital suggest the First Fallon is already recovering. Fallon East was unconscious when she was taken from Stratera, and no one has seen her since."

Tarkin pauses as a hand reaches out and gives him a sheet of paper. Tarkin reads, fidgets and then looks up at the screen.

"It appears that a prophecy has been leaked to CogNews. We're running it across the bottom of your screen now."

Where there is Balance, there is Imbalance.

The oldest law of the universe.

Two sisters. Two halves. One of light, the other of dark. Sisters born to protect the universe, sworn to keep it Balanced; equal parts, Balance to Imbalance.

Where there is Balance, there must be Imbalance.

But the sister of light will fail; in her search for Balance, she will create disparity in the universe. Bringing with it, not utopia but the crumbling of fabric between worlds and universal destruction.

A new pair, one of the East and one of the South will be born, fated to be Bound and bring Balance to the universe once more: the First Couple, two halves of one soul. Equal parts Balance to Imbalance, light to dark, and able to Inherit power. Together they will unite with the sister of darkness and wage war on the sister of light.

But they will face a grave choice. Their decision will lead either to the defeat of the sister of light and restoration of Balance to all the realms or the end of the universe and all life within it.

"This, of course, raises alarming questions. Both for the safety of our dear leader and God incarnate, the First Fallon, but also the legitimacy of this prophecy. Surely, given the untimely death of Fallon Luchelli, it no longer stands? Well, Keepers of Trutinor, this is a mystery. One we will, of course, continue to investigate. That's it for today. I will bring you more information on the status of both The First Fallon and Fallon East along with any Dusting arrangements for Fallon Luchelli as soon as we have them.

This is Tarkin Tavas reporting for CogNews TV on this very sad morning. Back to the studio."

ONE

'Symptoms of Balancer Loss

Early Symptoms

- Loss of consciousness (temporary or permanent)
- Convulsions and seizures
- Acute, prolonged global pain
- Death in some circumstances

Prolonged Survivor Symptoms

- Torn soul for the remainder of the living Balancer's life until they pass and are reunited with their soul mate once more
- Depression, loneliness, feelings of emptiness
- Mood swings, poor judgement and self-destructive behaviors
- Substance abuse
- Abuse of Keeper powers, addiction to Siren compulsion—specifically, pain removal'

Excerpt—The Journal of Dryadic Medical Healing

EDEN

The darkness is violent.

For a while, there's nothing. The gloom slithers around me, a mass of writhing eels. It thickens to a pulp and coats my thoughts.

I'm drowning.

Sharp noises.

Cuts of panic.

Where fingers touch my skin, it burns like the kiss of a branding iron.

Something rips.

My insides pull apart.

Pieces of me sear and spit fire like solar flares. I reach for the molten torture, but it shifts and moves.

I float between moments of all-consuming agony and the solitude of nothingness. Time no longer exists. There is nothing and everything in an endless solitude. At some point, my body sinks into the soft sheen of silk covers and ambient warmth.

Movement stops—the torment doesn't.

As I draw close to full consciousness, a variety of smells

fill my senses. Spice, damp fabric, and the stick of generated heat. Later come the scents of smoking wood, hot broth and the cool, crispness of night air. I could be anywhere. But it doesn't feel like home, it doesn't feel like the Ancient Forest or the South.

I continue to fall in and out of lucidity.

Always alone.

Chunks of me are missing.

Hacked out.

Tattered fragments of memories float through the sludge of my unconsciousness.

Everything's wrong. None of me fits together.

My heart flutters; not with the tingle of love's wings, but with an icy realization:

I have to wake up, and when I do, Trey won't be there.

Somewhere out in the realm of the living, my name's being sung. It tugs at my mind, dragging me through the coagulated mess of obscurity.

I can't wake up.

I don't want to.

I'm not ready.

If I wake up, I have to accept that Trey is dead.

I push the tune of my name away until the voices grow quiet. I squeeze until the nothingness is complete; until eternity wraps its infinite arms around me and I stay in the last moment with him.

Sepia color runs through my mind, rushing and pulling me to that memory. The Obex colosseum ruins build themselves back together, brick by broken brick. This was our goodbye. I cradle the memory like oxygen, even though reliving it tears off a fresh piece of me every single time. This is all I have left of him. I need to keep it, even if it hurts.

Stone slabs and pillars fly over our heads and smash against the ruins. Twisted sisters—The First and Last Fallon —fight around us, destroying Obex and slicing each other up. We will die in their crossfire if we don't get out of the colosseum. Trey is staring at me with that crooked smile. Beneath his softness, he's shivering—it terrifies me.

"I love you, Eden. Only you. Always you," he says.

"Trey. Stop. You're talking like this is the end, that this is goodbye."

He closes his eyes and touches his forehead to mine. "It's time," he says. I can still smell him; the scent of frankincense and summer. I realize now, this was the moment he knew it was goodbye. He lowers the barrier, protecting me from his emotion—just a fraction—enough that the river of his love flows into my ribs and swallows my heart whole. Under the river is a trembling current. He's afraid, and so am I.

"Kiss me first," I say, gripping his shoulders till my knuckles whiten. "Kiss me like everything's going to be okay."

He does.

This is where I want the memory to stop. Where I want my mind to wrap me, safe in a single eternal moment: Trey and I, surrounded by flying slabs and exploding magic. One last blissful second of his lips on mine.

But it doesn't stop. The memory continues, even though I beg and plead with my brain to stay in his embrace.

"I love you, Trey, in this lifetime and all the lifetimes to come," I say.

Then the world shifts, tilts, and ruptures in red. My arms are suddenly cold, my lips alone.

Trey

is

gone.

My dream is coated in darkening rouge, my face splattered with his blood. The glint of silver protrudes from his neck. All of it ricochets like an echo.

Trey's body.

The knife.

Victor.

Blood.

So much blood everywhere.

The vision shudders, the memory fades. When it settles, I know I really am dreaming because Trey stands before me. I can't see his face, but there's no question he's staggering through cobbled streets. The dimness of twilight makes it hard to focus. Dark red crusts the side of his throat, shoulder and ribs. The knife has vanished. Trey stumbles, corrects himself, and pushes forward across a park and toward a set of abandoned houses.

My heart flutters, a faint breath of hope. Maybe I can reach him. As soon as I think it, I'm yanked back.

There's movement. A shadow passes over me, washing in and out of focus; it's following him. A sound beats, echoing around us. Loud, thudding roars. A heart thudding. I bellow Trey's name. No sound appears. The harder I scream, the further away he moves. My chest clamps, the final shred of hope extinguishing. The dream funnels into a pinpoint, vanishing as I'm dragged back to consciousness. I'm not ready. I can't wake up because if I do, the only thing I'll find is a heart full of shadows and a soul full of scars.

Trey is dead.

Victor killed him.

And now he has to pay.

My lids peel open. I expect to see an empty room. I don't. Pressed against my cheek is a set of bare toes. I recoil, wrinkling my nose. We're surrounded by tarpaulin, its muted colors ripple and shudder in the breeze. Muffled voices drift in from outside. I shift position. The foot shoves my face as its owner sits bolt upright.

"Eww. Jesus, Kato."

His head is on the end of the bed. One of his arms and his other leg hang off the side of the mattress. His remaining foot is still on my pillow. I smack it off, immediately regretting it as a sharp stab shoots through my hand.

Kato's blond hair is strewn across his face. He looks ridiculous, and I'm sure the crusty flakes beneath his lips are the remains of dried drool.

I blink, and giggle. I can't help myself. It bubbles up and over.

"Look at the state of you," I gasp between laughs.

"You haven't seen yourself yet." He dissolves into a snuffled laughter too.

We both sit there giggling. It builds and builds and

builds. And then it ruptures into hysteria. Instead of laughing, I'm crying. Giant sobs that cleave my ribs in two and squeeze my lungs until I'm suffocating.

Kato's eyes well up. He reaches out, pulls me into his arms, gripping so tight I'm sure he'll break what's left of me. No matter how tight he holds, or how loud I moan, we stay there clinging to each other. I scream and cry and whimper. Then I do it all over again. I hate myself for being so weak, but I plead between the sobs. I plead with Kato, with the Balance, even with myself. Three desperate words claw at my atoms.

Bring him back.

Every time I utter it, instead of bringing me comfort, it carves me into unfamiliar pieces; all of them with frayed edges and broken corners that don't fit together—that fall through my fingers like crumbs. I'm damaged, there's no fixing me. The missing parts are long gone. Lost. Dead.

No, they're not dead.

Trey is.

Kato stays quiet. Although, he too is crying. Drips of his salty tears coat my shoulder and leave it cool and damp. Eventually, my voice runs out of sound and I'm consumed by overwhelming emptiness.

I find my voice. "I'm sorry."

"For crying? Don't be stupid, Eden. Why do you think I'm here?" Kato clutches my hand.

"You've lost your brother, too."

He stares at the window.

"Are you okay?" I ask.

"Not really. But what am I meant to do? The Council has already instated me as Siren Fallon of the South. I've had some duties and all sorts of shit I'd rather not be doing."

He takes a breath and turns to me. "It was never meant to be me doing this stuff."

His expression glazes over. After a pause, he gives me a weak smile.

"Obviously my tousled blond locks and boyish good looks scream loved and adored monarch. But..." His voice fades.

"But it should have been Trey?"

He squeezes his eyes shut tight. We're silent for a while, then I frown. "What do you mean 'already' instated? How long have I been unconscious?"

Kato looks up, his expression soft. "Three weeks... We weren't sure if you would make it. It was bad. You were bad. The world outside is fucking bad. I've stayed here where I can in amongst Stratera and Fallon duties."

"I didn't realize it had been so long."

"You were in a coma. They kept you alive using some stasis bubble. The engineering behind it is actually pretty fascinating."

His face twitches like he wants to vomit engineering geek on me. He doesn't. I'm grateful.

"Two days ago, your vitals stabilized. The doctors were confident you'd wake up on your own, so they removed you from stasis." His eyes glisten. The tears make the blue sparkle just like Trey's. Mine are raw and burning, but no more tears come.

The fabric door ripples, a Keeper enters carrying a clipboard and a bag of liquid. "Oh, you're awake. Excellent. No need for this, then." She pops the bag into her coat pocket. "I'll just check your vitals and fetch the doctor. Good morning, Fallon Luchelli."

Kato nods to her as she fusses with a tall metal frame holding other bags of liquid attached to me via copious amounts of wires. The frame looks more like a hat stand than anything. She takes my blood pressure, listens to my chest, notes down some numbers and then pulls a needle out of my hand, disconnecting me from the liquids and wires.

It hurts. I wince. Rubbing my bruised hand. The longer I'm awake, the more I'm aware my entire body is aching. My muscles are on fire, my chest is tight. My head groggy. I glance around the room again and realize I've been here before. Everything is familiar. The strange fabric room. The rebels kidnapped and brought me here last summer.

"Definitely on the mend, Fallon East," the doctor says.

"Really? I feel about as far from on the mend as you can get."

"Yes, well. You lost your... But, anyway. It's going to take some time. The good news is your vitals are strong. I'll send the doctor in shortly. Do you wish me to notify anyone?"

"I'll do that," Kato says.

"As you wish." As she leaves, a cacophony of noise pours into the room, but it vanishes as the fabric door closes.

Kato squeezes my hand. "I should leave you to rest. I have to tell everyone you're up."

"Wait. Why here? Why are we in the rebel camp? You're not even freaking out. I didn't think you knew about the rebels."

"It's been a long three weeks. Things are... different now. After they took you in the mountains a few weeks ago, it appears the rebels continued watching you. You're important to them, it seems. And holy Balance, they have people everywhere. Literally everywhere. Their infrastructure is so much bigger and more established than the Libra Legion. It's frankly quite impressive. Their men were in Stratera when everything kicked off and they got you out. It's not like you could have gone to Dryad City Hospital, anyway. She was taken there."

Of course she was.

"Is she...?"

"Alive, unfortunately. The First Fallon is lying 'lower than normal' but she's been on CogNews spilling bullshit and lies. And we're all convinced she's causing bigger problems. But those are problems for another day."

"Problems?"

Kato hesitates. "The number of skirmishes and attacks has increased significantly since the Door of Fates. Like... It's really not good out there, everything is falling apart. We've not been able to attribute it to the First Fallon, but there are weather changes. Arden said the Guild is investigating, but things are rough. There's so much unrest, the Council are losing their minds."

"But you think it's her causing the problems?"

He nods. My eyes darken.

"I'm going to kill her," I say, putting as much venom in my words as I can. Kato raises an eyebrow.

Kato rolls his neck before picking up his CogTracker.

"I mean it, Kato. Trey shouldn't have died. And I don't mean that because we love him. If our fate is predetermined by the Balance, then he shouldn't have been able to die. Not with the prophecy."

Kato puts his CogTracker down, "Okay, I'm listening."

"If Trey shouldn't be dead, then it means Cecilia is lying. If our fate isn't predetermined or only determined in part, then she's got to be brought to justice. Victor might have been the one to stab Trey, but the First Fallon orchestrated it. Everything bad that's happened. She's behind it."

Kato rubs his chin. His gaze is off somewhere in the

distance. Then he nods, just once. "Okay. But not today and not right now."

And just as he says it, a wave of drowsiness descends over me. I yawn, all the venom and spite draining out of me. I'm exhausted even from the short chat.

"Big god-killing plans are great, but first you need to sleep. Rest. Get better. I'll be back in a bit." He kisses my forehead, and I slump onto the pillow.

When I wake next time, the air feels thicker, warmer. Speckled sunset light dapples the floor from a fabric window flap. I, however, am frozen, even under the thick duvet. I pull it tight under my chin.

"Good afternoon, sleepy," Kato says.

"You're still here."

"Obviously." Kato pinches the skin at his throat. "If you'd died as well... I..."

"I'm still here." I take his hand and squeeze it. The movement makes me wince. "I'm not going anywhere unless the pain kills me first."

Kato looks at the floor. "I know we shouldn't, but I can't stand seeing you like this. Do you want me to help?"

"With the pain?"

He can't meet my eyes and we both know why. "No... That's a bad idea," I say.

I shift, trying to reposition my body, but hot lances pour into my chest and I collapse where I am. It's a terrible idea. Every inch of me knows I shouldn't ask for his help. I've read the horror stories, the addicts who die from withdrawal instead of Balancer loss. Hell, I berated Trey constantly for what his Sirens did—removing or controlling emotions. But in this moment, I am weak; I am grieving, and I am in excruciating pain.

"Perhaps once is okay," I mumble into the covers.

Kato slides his hands under my armpits and hoists me upright, leaning my back against the headboard. I bite down to stop a scream.

"I think I need you to help more than I want you to," I say through gritted teeth. "I don't know if I'll ever be able to get out of bed without pain relief. Even breathing hurts."

"Whatever it takes, I'm not losing you, too." He reaches for my hand, pushing it out flat like I'm waving. "Ready?"

His eyes lock onto mine. I nod and flinch as my neck spasms in protest.

A spark of heat and power ripples between our palms. He slides his fingers through mine and a flood of cool energy washes over me. It's like the silk slip of cold cream gliding down my throat. Where his palm meets mine, a layer of ice smothers the burning inside me. My eyes roll back, my breath heavy and rapid from the sudden relief. Oh, god, it's euphoric. His hand slackens as if to let go. I grip harder, needing him to take more pain.

"Don't stop," I breathe.

I know it's wrong. But at this moment, swimming in relief, I want him to take it all away. The soothing coats everything, cooling pain, hurt, the aching emptiness. Everything numbs under a blanket of nothing. And it is glorious. My mind clears, the fuzz of discomfort evaporates.

I can't believe I used to tell Trey how immoral it was to take someone's emotion away. On and on I went at him. But this? Oh, I was wrong. So very, very wrong. This nothingness is ecstasy.

I'm snapped out of my thoughts as Kato yanks his hand away. The murmurs of ache return instantly, albeit dulled for now. Kato's eyes are wide. He's panting as much as me. The throb of magic and emotion still shimmers around his fingers. Flecks of violet and purple light the space around his nails.

He holds my gaze, "We shouldn't—"

"No. We shouldn't." But I don't mean it because what he's given me is everything. The air shifts between us. It's stiff, awkward.

"That was…" he starts. "You can't get addicted."

I lean away from him, my skin crawling with the wrongness, the intimacy of what just happened. But wrapped deep inside my aching skin, my soul feels the pure clarity of respite. Kato is like my brother, but this reprieve is… It's absolute. Is pain relief really so bad of a sin? Wouldn't I heal quicker and more effectively if he helps?

"I won't get addicted." The words trickle out, smooth and plump like a promise. Almost. "Half my soul has been severed. I promise not to ask often."

There it is, that word "promise." Golden, full of hope and shine. I mean it too. He mouths, as if trying to swallow my words. He shakes his head like they don't taste right.

"Fine. But we need to be careful. Pain relief doesn't last that long and I won't be on tap for you. You'll have to cope with some of this."

"Agreed."

"And whatever I take, I'm giving back when you're stronger."

I shrug and shut my eyes. He could tell me the price was an arm or my magic for all I care. All I want to do is sink into the covers and sleep.

"I mean it," he barks. But it sounds like a whimper.

"Mmm hmm. Agreed."

"You can't heal properly if you can't feel anything."

I peel open my eyes. He's rolling his hands around, the lilac and black sparks twirl and spin and form a wispy ball. I stop dead. My heart seizes. Trey kept a ball of my emotions. There's something unnerving about Kato rolling threads of my feelings around his fingers.

"Okay," I say.

Seeing my pain, the ball of my emotions so blatant like that, makes the relief he's given me a little less clean, and a little more dirty. I slide into the morsel of numb solace that's left and close my eyes.

I must have fallen asleep again, because when I wake, the room is dim. Kato is still on the end of my bed. His CogTracker is open, and he's tapping furiously at the keyboard. When he notices I'm awake, he pulls a tray of food over and places it on a stand over my lap.

"You should eat."

I pick at the food, chicken that's cooled and gone dry, some kind of neon liquid, fruit and nuts, but I start with the fruit. I still can't believe I've been gone three weeks. That means... Oh.

"I missed All Souls Night," I say.

Something inside me twinges, but I'm too numb to work out whether it was my heart or my body trying to heal.

"Did you...? Did anyone see him?" I ask.

All Souls Night happens twice a year during Trutinor's summer and winter solstices. As we pass from one season to the next, there's a small window of time where the fabric between all the worlds thins. If you're lucky, the souls of your loved ones—the ones who haven't passed on to their next life and still live in the Soul Sanctuary in Obex—

appear like shadowy spirits. You don't get long, a brief glimpse, and no one's sure how aware the souls are. But it brings comfort to those of us left in Trutinor. I like to think of it as the Balance repaying Keepers for not being able to search Obex for our dead soul mates. We can't find them till we die, but the Balance gives us a moment of connection, and comfort to keep us going.

Kato bites his lip, his eyes watery. "I looked. Spent all night trying. He never came."

My fists curl around the duvet, smoke hisses from under my fingers.

"Careful..." Kato says, pointing at my smoking hands. I take a breath and draw water into my palms, drenching the duvet and embers.

"Hermia visited while you were asleep. She didn't want to wake you, but she'll be back. She hasn't handled Trey dy—She's not doing so well." He jerks his thumb at the coffee table in the corner. There's an empty bottle of whiskey and a single tumbler. "She'd want to know you're awake."

"I can't wait to see her. Where's Bo?"

He stiffens. "Do you remember what happened before?"

I scan my memories, trying to put the scraps of events together. "We argued in Datch?"

"You did." He slides his CogTracker shut and discards it on the bed.

I pick at a few pieces of chicken, trying to pull the memories of our fight to the surface.

"I honestly thought she'd let go of what we did to Victor."

"You two never really talked about it."

"I can't believe I threw the fact she was partially responsible for my parents' deaths in her face." I rub my hands, my skin itches.

"She wasn't."

"I know," I breathe. "That was all on them."

"Eden darling, you made a mistake. Whether you thought she was okay or not, you weren't there for her while she was recovering from losing her leg."

The strain of remembering etches memories and hurt into wrinkles.

"You're right. I should have been there for her."

"You should."

"I was so wrapped up with Victor. And... And she looked like she had it together."

"She did. She's good at hiding how she feels. Even I have trouble working her out and I'm a bloody Siren Fallon." He pauses, his voice softens. "She's been here, you know. Spent almost as much time here as me, but—" He gesticulates, wafting his hand in the air.

"But she's still pissed at me?"

"Essentially."

My lips press together. I can't lose anyone else in my life, least of all Bo.

"She'll forgive you. If I wasn't Bound to her, I swear you two would be soul mates. You've been there for each other through everything. In fact, I should tell her you're awake and ready for visitors."

I have to make it up to her, no matter how angry she is with me. Kato is right, and I don't want our friendship to change now.

"What about Titus? Is he okay? What with Nyx...?"

Kato rummages around the duvet for his CogTracker. He opens it and a dozen messages ping in.

"Shit. I have to go. Siren duty calls. There's a bodyguard

outside if you need anything. Donald? Dennis? Do...
something?"

My chest tightens. "Hang on, if you're instated as Siren
Fallon, then... did I miss Trey's Dusting?"

Kato shifts position, leans against the bed's footboard,
and runs his fingers through his hair. How can two brothers
be so similar and yet so different?

Kato has the same jaw line, only softer than Trey's. In
fact, everything about Kato is softer than Trey. His hair a
smidgen fluffier, his skin a fraction smoother, his stubble a
shade lighter.

He gets off the bed and pulls the duvet up and closes
the fabric window flap. What evening light there was,
vanishes. I glance at Kato's back. Remembering the moment
I saw Trey standing in the same position in his bedroom.
The curtains were open and his scars—the ones the First
Fallon gave him—on display. The memory sets loose
another ache, another hole, another reminder I'm alone.
And another reason she needs to die.

Kato turns, his face narrows. I tilt my head, scanning his
expression.

"You need to sleep. Tomorrow we can go through more.
But today, you take it easy."

"Kato. Just tell me, did I miss the Dusting?"

He hesitates, his attention shifts to the door.

"You tell me or I'm getting out of bed to wallop you,
even if it puts me back in a coma."

His shoulders sag. "There hasn't been a Dusting yet,"
he says, and a darkness passes over his face. He hardens, a
rigid determination straightening his back.

"Why not?"

"There was no body. We never found Trey."

TWO

RIP Trey Luchelli, 11th April, 1998 - 1st October, 2017

TREY

I feel everything.

Eden used to joke that for a Siren king, I behaved like I was dead on the inside. She said I refused to feel things; I pushed them away. Sure, I might control my feelings, extract them, examine them, store them away for safe-keeping—but isn't that what Sirens are supposed to do? No, Eden was wrong.

I feel everything, I always have.

And dying is excruciating.

Where Victor cut my throat, heat coils around my neck like a fiery noose. Embers flake and lance hot spears into my skin. It's torture and makes what the First Fallon did to me as a child look like a cocktail hour in Siren City.

I'm dead, or I think I am. I'm lying in the colosseum ruins, my blood flowing between the rubble and cracks, my body tearing into a thousand fragments. Each one a shattered sliver of my life: regrets, moments not felt, hurt.

Eden.

Always Eden.

Every limb, cell, and ounce of me is in agony. But why am I still in pain? I thought everything stopped after you died. Victor nicked my carotid artery, I should be dead, but the burn of blood loss still tingles in my neck. In fact, if I'm dead, why is my blood oozing at all?

I fumble with my arms, trying to locate the sensations of my limbs. When my fingers twitch in response, I slip my hand under my vest to check for a beat. I'm greeted with silence. No thump, no rise and fall—quiet.

So, I am dead.

Moving makes my body burn hot like molten lava, liquid pustules of anger and violence spitting and cracking inside me. I want to use my Siren power to take out the pain.

I need to understand it.

I have to control it.

But I can't. It's buried so deep inside me I can't reach it. A scream erupts from my chest. I claw at my skin, trying to pull the monster out. But there is no monster, just my soul desiccating until all I am is another broken slab in amongst the decayed colosseum.

I'm splayed across the dust and stone of Obex's ruins long enough, the icy stone leeches the warmth from my skin along with the blood. Long enough, the unstable ground in Obex shifts and moves beneath me. Long enough that sandstone and concrete slot together, creating new, foreign ground. When the assault is over and our Binding is broken,

I'm delirious. But more than anything, I'm empty. I can't feel her—Eden's gone. I'm carved up. Nothing left but scraps and bone shards.

An awful realization crawls into my consciousness—I'm stuck in Obex—the world between. Home to the lost, broken and dead. Isn't that what Rozalyn said? I died, so now I wait for Eden to live out her life until we can move on to our next life together. Aren't I meant to be in Obex's Soul Sanctuary? I thought that's where Keepers went to wait until their Balancers can meet them. My body shakes in prolonged juddering convulsions, a dull throb settles over me. I try to move, but my neck convulses and warmth oozes over my collarbone. Nausea rolls around my stomach like a cannon waiting to explode. I try to lift myself up, but my head is thick with the woozy swim of death's hangover.

Knots form in my chest as images of Eden's lilac eyes, her curves, and her desert-olive skin float through my mind. I squeeze my eyelids shut and do what I invariably do when things hurt; block it out, push it away and bury it where I can't sense it... Okay, fine. Maybe Eden had a point.

No matter how much I push it away, though, my heart can still sense it. Despite its stillness, emotion screams and thunders inside my torso like a vicious hurricane.

The thud, thud, thud grows more insistent until it crescendos to a roar and ricochets around my body. Groans escape as I roll into the fetal position; I need to move; I can't stay here forever. Obex is full of nightmares and darkness. I don't want to become one of them.

When the aching eases, I haul myself to my feet. Every movement is greeted with searing spasms.

I puke, though it's more of a retch as there's nothing left to throw up.

The shadows between the pillars and surrounding

buildings wriggle with things I can't see. My skin prickles and my hand slides to my throat, instinct kicking in. I have to find something to cover the wound. While it weeps blood, I'm in danger. There are far too many demons that would find a freshly severed artery, a delightful snack. I scan the area for a weapon, something—anything—I can use to defend myself. It's inevitable—I'm dinnertime, Obex's freshest meat.

My head is dizzy, my vision glazed. I don't understand why I'm still in pain. Is this what happens to all dead people? Do I have to carry my fatal wounds around for eternity?

I walk—although it's more of a stagger—out of the colosseum; I have to grip pillars and slabs to steady myself.

Progress is slow, labored, and full of stifled moans and bitten down screams. Anchors of loss tether my limbs in reluctance. But slow as I am, I eventually leave the colosseum and after a glacial age, I reach what I think is the outskirts of Obex city.

Stained cream and white townhouses stretch down mile-long streets. Once, these towering streets were decadent, marble columns support generous porches. But all the Imbalance Keepers send here has decayed Rozalyn's world. In front of the porches, iron railings stand guard, their filigree spikes a warning to outsiders—outsiders like me. Covering the decadence is a thick coating of mold, blackened marks pattern walls, and the iron railings are flaking and rusted. A pungent stench fills the air and the further I walk, the stronger the aroma gets. Obex stinks of decay mixed with something so strong and metallic it clings to my tongue: blood. I didn't smell it when I came here with Eden. But I suppose I was still alive then.

I wander for what seems like hours, but could be

minutes, and with each step, I'm a little more uneasy. Every so often, the ground shifts and moves underfoot. Streets I'm certain I've walked past reappear, making my grasp on reality slip further away. Hermia told me that Obex was a maze designed to disorient and confuse the dead; make them submissive and compliant to the Last Fallon—she was right.

I lean against a set of railings. This street looks just like all the others. I swallow hard. The first flutter of panic simmers in my gut. Taking a breath, I push it away—I can do this, I just have to stay in control.

Emotions have their own scent—fear more so than the rest. The blood dribbling down my throat is enough to attract demons; I need not add a bitter reek on top.

I glance up, looking for the moon or the sun, anything to help orientate me. But the sky is just as treacherous as the earth. Smoky oranges and dusty pinks streak the perpetual twilight. I have no idea if it's morning or evening. I grip the railing hard. The skin on my palm pulls against the metal, but the pinch calms me; almost like being alive.

Time, too, it seems, is as fickle as everything else. As the streets move, they elongate into eternity. Another trick, one of Rozalyn's delightful reminders of your fate. Every second that drains away, her message beats:

You can't escape.

You're trapped.

Alone.

Your only comforts are the memories of the things you love most. Things that are gone.

A line of cold sweat slides down my back. I need somewhere to rest. Halfway up the street, I spot a darkened patch. As I inch closer, I realize it's an alleyway.

Only an idiot would walk through a dark alleyway in a world LITERALLY filled with monsters.

I step forward and topple. The ground shifts, the alleyway vanishes, and I'm left standing in a quiet street.

A park with corroded climbing frames lies empty. On the other side is a row of equally empty houses. Outside, one is a sign that creaks and swings over the door. It's too faded and filthy to read.

I head toward it. If it has a sign, maybe it sold things once. There might be some old supplies I could use. As I reach the door, I'm aware the air has stilled. Even the shadows seem silent. It makes me uneasy.

As I push open the door, it creaks and cries with neglect. The walls in the entrance hall thrum. Dodgy electricity, I assume. The thought reminds me of Eden, the way the air is alive around her. The place is empty except for the darkness that shrouds the walls like a cloak. I throw a last glance behind me. When I'm certain I'm not being followed, I step inside. On the right is an enormous round desk littered with papers, some notebooks and a couple of rows of seating. I grab one of the notebooks and a few half-blunt pencils and shove them deep into my trouser pockets. Nothing else is useful, so I continue along the hallway and roam deeper into the darkness.

Debris decorates the floor like a mural: iron bars, flails, handcuffs. The deeper I go, the more torture devices scatter the carpet.

Fuck.

The buzz of electricity fades, leaving the crunch of glass under my boots. As I move through the hall, the air stales; even the ghosts have abandoned it. I shiver, but keep going. No matter what, I need to stitch my neck so I can find somewhere to hide without being eaten.

A door hangs off its hinge. I push it open. Unlike the front door, it's silent as it yawns wide: death has already taken it. There's a switch on the wall. I hesitate before flicking it. Can you electrocute a dead man? Nothing can be as painful as having my soul ripped in two; I turn it on.

This room is more of a mess than the hall. There's a long chair with handcuffs on either side. I pause, tingles fill my gut. This is not a room I want to be in.

Patches of black and brown smear the chair's ripped plastic fabric. An ominous round light hangs from the ceiling, its half dozen eyes all struggling to blare to life. I stare at it; I swear the bulbs size me up, wondering if they can devour me like they have everything else.

The rest of the room is empty except for a set of drawers and a sink against one wall. I turn the tap on. It judders and splutters, spitting out brown liquid. I open the drawers, searching for something to close my cut. But most of them are empty apart from rust-crumbs and unidentifiable scraps of something that once lived. The next set of draws have dozens of metal knives and sharp objects.

What the hell is this place?

I pull open the next drawer and smile. A single needle rests inside, rusted and blunt, but a needle nonetheless. I take it and keep searching. My scavenging leads to a half-opened bandage that's not even remotely sterile and a short piece of metal thread. Not ideal, it will hurt like a bitch, but better than being a demon appetizer.

Attached to the ceiling light is a mirror on a long arm. I pull it and the light and perch on the long chair. When I'm convinced it won't collapse, I shuffle onto it and position the mirror in front of my neck.

My gut twists at the sight of my throat. Layers of skin peeled back, wine-colored muscle and sinew mangled from

Victor's knife. Crusts of black and red paint the wound's edge and a lazy flow of claret oozes out. I focus on the wound instead. My fingers skim over the shredded skin. The edges are soft compared to their grotesque appearance. A strange desire to poke the inside of my neck makes my fingers twitch. I leave the wound in case the bleeding worsens.

I grab the pillaged needle and shove the metal thread through the eye and tie the end. I take a deep breath and plunge the needle into my skin. Sweat instantly pools on my forehead as I suppress a groan. My breathing races as if I still had a heartbeat. My fingers stick against each other as blood oozes around their tips. Gray spots smatter my vision, but I continue to sew stitch after stitch, each one burning like acid.

As I tie the thread off, I notice the heart scar on my wrist. A remnant from an ancient Siren ceremony Eden and I took part in to protect the source of all our power: The Heart of Trutinor.

I let my index finger slide over the scar. My eyes glaze over. The thudding I heard in the colosseum roars back to life. My finger attaches to my scar. Then, whatever breath I have left in my lungs vanishes.

I feel her—Eden.

Our connection, our Binding, I think. It's weak, like a veil, but it's there. It throbs, beat after beat, each one stronger than the last.

I try to reach out to her, but the connection is so fragile, I'm afraid to break it.

"Eden? EDEN?" I shout. But she can't hear me.

For a split second, the connection twitches, a soft static buzz, like she can sense me. My wrist burns. The heart-shaped scar each of us received swelling with heat.

In my mind, I stretch out, desperate to touch her, to grasp her; to be whole. But like an illusion, the harder I stretch, the further away she gets.

And then she's gone.

My eyes snap open, hot and stinging. Although my heart isn't beating, my chest squeezes so tight it smothers my lungs. I can't do this. How can I survive decades waiting for her here? I'll drown in my own emotions.

I shove the mirror away and flip my hand over. A speck of Dust appears in my palm. It grows and expands until it's the size of a golf ball. The Dust ball spins and pulses, like it's alive, and I guess, in a way, it is. It's filled with memories and emotions, little slivers of life, some stolen, some given willingly. The memory ball was lilac for a while. I stole Eden's memories to protect her. Now it's maroon with only a hint of her lilac spinning through it—the only piece of her I have left are my memories. My breathing slows, calms and matches the ball's slow, rhythmic spin. She will always be my anchor, even though our Binding is broken.

My finger hovers over the top of the ball, coaxing out a speckled Dust-ribbon until it dances around my hand. It ripples and shudders, forming two figures. They spin atop the ball like ballerinas in a music box. Around them are Dust-trees and tiny flowers that blink in and out of focus as the ball spins. This is my most precious memory. It's also my most painful one: our first kiss. I hold up the ball as The Pink Lake crystallizes. Dust-me places my hand against Eden's cheek.

"Wait..." she says, and places her hand on mine.

"No. I don't want to wait anymore; I love you. Only you. Always you." I lean in, our breath mingling together, then I kiss her. The perfect memory, in the perfect place. The perfect kiss.

Until I ruined it.

Our figures spin on, she tells me it has to end, that we can't keep this relationship going when I'm Bound to Evelyn. Her Potential announcement is in the morning—we both know it's going to be Victor. My free hand balls, remembering the ache and shivers that bled from her heart into mine. My Siren powers are a gift poisoned by a curse. If I know what other's emotions are, I can help them, heal them, or if I have to, hurt them. But that's when I wish I couldn't feel their emotions—not when it's pain, and definitely not when I've caused it.

I didn't tell her, but I felt everything that night; she was in agony trying to say goodbye—to let me go. I knew before she said anything. Of course I did. I always know because Keepers, humans, people—they're all the same. Their emotions leak out of them even when they try to hide it. It pours out of words, and chests and body language.

I couldn't bear it. So I did what I always did; I took it away.

"This... Us... We can't..." she says. She doesn't finish the sentence, but she meant "love each other." Back then, we didn't know our fates connected. We were still the First Fallon's puppets. We thought we'd won when we remade our Binding. What a fucking joke. We were always her puppets, and we still are—she won. We're separated for who knows how many decades.

Dust-me says, "I know, but I don't want to be without you." Then presses his lips to hers, kissing her with such intensity I remember thinking my heart would rip from my chest and crumble in my hands.

"I'm sorry," Dust-me whispers, and then I close my eyes and steal her memories.

Every CogMail, every night at the Pink Lake, even that

kiss. All of it. I recall the throb and flow of her memories into my essence as I drained her of the knowledge of me. Her Dust-face slackens, the hurt I'd caused dissolving into darkness.

The memory is almost over. Dust-me slips into the trees behind Eden. She drags herself toward Keepers school, sobbing; her heart knows why, but her mind has forgotten. As she disappears into the tree line, the ball of her memories presses as heavy in my hand as the tears in my lids.

I shut my hand, making our Dusty figures disappear. Breathe deep, shut off. Push the hurt, longing, and love away, pouring everything into the familiar black hole: the vault. I carved it inside the innermost reaches of my mind; it hides the Imbalance. It also hides the things that hurt the most.

Something clatters in the hallway. My blood turns to ice. I snap the needle off, shove the bandage over the wound, and move toward the door. I place my back against the wall. Why didn't I notice any emotions creeping in? I should have paid more attention.

I inch my head around the frame and freeze.

Millimeters from my face are a set of eyeless sockets staring at me. Before I have time to react, he yanks his veiny skull back and smashes his head into mine. I fly backward, crashing against the chair and scattering debris everywhere. As my vision spots, the demon marches in, robes fluttering around him, and grabs my ankle, dragging me out of the room. I cling to consciousness and push myself up as he hauls me down the hall. I grab his wrist. He stops and snaps his head around. His skull-face is skinless and eyeless, and yet, I am certain; he rolls his eyes at me.

"Rozalyn wants a word," he growls. His mouth and jaw don't move.

What the fuck?

Then he punches me in the temple.

As I lose consciousness, he throws me over his shoulder and grumbles, "Fucking Breathers."

Then the darkness takes me.

THREE

'*After the Mermaid-Siren war was over, it is said the First Fallon cradled the lifeless body of her daughter Karva on the sandy shores of Siren beach. She cried for seven days and seven nights, praying to Balance for her daughter to breathe again. When the eighth day dawned, and Karva was still limp, the First Fallon grew vengeful. As punishment for killing her daughter, she cursed Aurora and all her kind from Trutinor soil— never again to roam the land. Aurora, scorned, banished and wounded from war, vowed to slay any Siren that dare trespass in her waters. For centuries the sea was filled with danger and the hushed whispers from sailors of screaming Sirens and bloodthirsty Merpeople. Fishing routes changed, lost, or ruined. Trade deals soured. Until one day, the ocean, sick of swallowing so much loss, bled red. The sky blistered, the sand and the waters all burned ochre, claret and crimson. And so the Blood Ocean was born and no Siren ever set foot in the waters again.'*

Excerpt—*Myths and Legends of Trutinor*

EDEN

The next morning, I wake and spot Kato asleep on the armchair in the corner.

"Morning drooler," I say.

He rubs his face, and moves to the bed, clasps my hand and removes a slither of my pain. We stare at each other, breathless, awkward. Uncomfortable.

"I have to go," he says and vanishes before I can appease the situation.

I lie back, trying to recall the night. Charlie, the Chief Dryad doctor usually found in the Ancient Forest, popped in periodically to take bloods and do various tests. Seemingly, he too is a rebel.

For the most part, I slept and with no dreams of Trey. I'm not certain how I feel about that; at least when I was unconscious, I had fragments of him with me. Last night, I had nothing but blackness.

Bo never appeared. Despite Kato saying he'd tell her I was awake. I'm not certain how I feel about that either.

I sit up. The room is claustrophobic. I need to get out.

There's a wheelchair next to my bed. The doctors must

have left it there. I haul myself slow and wincing into it and thank Balance the chair is Cog-driven. I flip one cog and it shunts toward the door. My torso flies forward, but I grip the chair and stay seated. My arms spasm for a minute, but when I've caught my breath, I'm ready to leave. Thank goodness Kato took some of my pain away or I'd never have made it into the chair, let alone to the door.

"Okay, nice and steady, then."

I open the door and discover a man. "Oh." He looks fresh, full of sun and energy, and his hair is wet. I suspect he's only just come on shift. This must be who Kato meant.

"Good morning, Fallon East. My name is Klein. I'm your temporary guard this morning. Dorian is in physio."

Not Dorian then. Klein is more meat than man. He's a giant slab of a Keeper. Shoulders as wide as a train, face buckled and scarred. If he weren't here to protect me, I'd be terrified. "I was just going for a walk... well, a wheel."

"Not a problem. I'll stay a couple of paces behind."

I maneuver the wheelchair out of the fabric room and into the main thoroughfare. Window flaps are open in the fabric roof, and midmorning light streams through and onto the flooring, dappling the patterned carpets. Outside my room, there's a collection of flowers, element orbs, and gifts. They stretch further than I can see, right to the end of the corridor. They must be from Elementals in the East. I wonder how they got here. Hermia perhaps, or maybe Kato. I crane my head up and breathe in the Eris mountain air. It's cool and clean—city air is always thick and there's a stale taste to it. This air is alive with wind crackling across craggy rocks, chilled snow flurries in the distance and the sharpness of air devoid of people breathing it.

I glance left and right. Klein keeps a couple of paces back. Close enough to react quickly, just far enough I still feel free. I give him a tense smile. I'd rather be completely alone.

The fabric corridors weave and stretch for miles through the mountain valleys. I find the central square. It's bustling with stalls and food and people singing. A girl with raven dark hair spots me and waves. I squint and realize it's Rita.

She bounds over with open arms. Klein is on me in an instant.

"It's fine," I say, waving him off. "She's a friend."

Rita gives him some vicious side-eye and then grins at me. "Eden, you're awake, thank Balance."

"Hey, Rita. How are you? I'd heard you made it here, okay?"

"I did. Thanks to you and Bo. I can't tell you how much I appreciate what you did for me. Giving me the supplies and staying quiet."

Just before the fight with Victor by the Pink Lake, Bo and I found Rita battered and bruised in the woods—her Balancer was beating her. She asked us to let her go because she wanted to find the rebels.

"I'm just glad you're safe. I know it's completely your choice, but I'm here for you. If you... you know..." I say, unsure quite how to broach the subject. I don't want to push her into anything that would make her uncomfortable.

She smiles, her eyes light up. "Oh, don't you worry. That bastard is going to get a very particular shade of come-uppance."

She leans in, hugs me, and then someone catches her eye on the other side of the square.

"I have to bounce, but it was good seeing you, Eden. I'm so deeply sorry for your loss."

"Thank you," I say and she leaves to meet her friend.

I veer right back into the hospital wing, Klein silent on my heels. I can sense his presence in the air, the way it flows like water around his body, but he's so quiet that if I wasn't paying attention, I'd have forgotten he was there. Anatomical artwork adorns the corridors and rooms. Pictures of Keepers, essences, and even long-lost creatures like Mermaids. One Mermaid picture catches my eye. Her face is silvery, long shimmering hair the same sheen of metal down her back. Neck down, the artist has drawn skeleton and organs. It's strange and morbid, but still beautiful. It's titled: Matriarch of the Ocean.

I continue down the walkways. The hospital area, while isolated away from civilization high in the Eris mountains, seems fully functional. I exit the patient ward and enter a longer corridor with various larger wardrooms peeling off.

There's a CogTV hanging on the wall. News broadcasts are pinging through and, shit, things are bad.

Tarkin Tavas, infamous newscaster, appears on screen. His hair is slick, his teeth enormous and his ego ballooning over the screen.

"Skirmishes have broken out on the borders at multiple locations. The North and East are suffering the worst outbreaks. But additional Alteritus outbreaks have been reported at the Southern and Western borders. Elana will bring you the details in a moment. Last—"

I can't bear to watch anymore. I had to deal with Alteritus outbreaks in the East not so long ago. It's an illness of the Balance. Keepers, once infected, turn wild like chaos and fire. It's ugly and, while treatable, can cause a lot of harm. I turn away and scan the corridor. At the end, is an enormous open area with apparatus and doctors and patients. I wheel down and into the space and watch for a while, realizing it's a physiotherapy area. Most apparatus are made of woven wood and metallic cogs. There are patients on mats doing stretches, other's arm exercises and some using odd bits of equipment.

The scent of roasting chicken drifts into the room and the place clears almost at once. Recovery is grueling, I'm exhausted and all I've done is sit here and exist, so I turn to leave and join them for lunch, but there's one Keeper left, myself and Klein who's stayed at the door.

The Keeper is on a set of what looks like parallel gymnast bars. Arms locked straight, he's upside down. His arms are enormous, bulging through his top. He swings up and down, over, hops—still upside down onto one bar, then the other. A black walking cane rests next to the bars.

I hesitate, wondering if it's rude to watch. But I'm curious. He's stayed behind when the others have left and I want to see if he makes the landing, so I drive the wheelchair a little further into the room.

He brings his legs and feet to rest on the bars and pushes off to flip for landing, but one foot slips. My gut clenches. I want to leap out and stop him from falling, but I can barely keep myself in the chair, let alone help him. He catches himself and makes the final spin, before the same foot slips under him and he collapses on the foam mats.

I wheel the chair to the mat to see if he's okay.

"Fallon East," he says, smiling up at me from the floor. His accent is delightfully precise. His teeth are straight and blinding white and his grin so perfectly wide, I reluctantly find myself smiling back. He's wearing a shirt and green pants, so dark they're almost black, but there are flecks of shimmering emerald in the fabric. They reflect the smoldering green of his eyes.

"Hi," I say, uncomfortable that he knows my name and I've no idea who he is.

"Sorry, let me introduce myself. I'm Dorian Oswald, the bodyguard that's been assigned to you. When I'm not on duty, I'm in the room next door if you need me."

"Oh," I say, glancing back at the door. Klein is standing, arms folded, scowling at the hallway.

"Morning, Klein, I'll take her from here," Dorian shouts.

Klein nods at Dorian, then to me, and leaves.

"You've got quite the ballooning shrine of flowers and gifts now."

"Ha. Yeah. I guess you already know I'm Fallon East."

He smiles.

So this is who Kato meant. "Nice to meet you, Dorian. I suppose if you're my guard, you can call me Eden." I twist a cog and shunt the chair forward a foot to reach down and take his hand. He doesn't take it. Instead, his face creases as he shuffles to his knees and staggers to his feet. Once he's upright, I notice how much taller and broader than me he is. I also notice how unreasonably attractive he is and just quite how bulging his shoulders and arms are. It makes me swallow. Hard.

He takes my outstretched hand. His skin is tanned, cheeks and nose brushed bronze, like the tan of a sailor always exposed to the sun.

I don't smile or move. I'm not sure I even breathe. Holy Balance, he's like some sort of demigod level of beautiful.

He leans down and presses his lips to my hand and this, too, makes me swallow and my cheeks flame red.

His eyes flick up to meet mine, his lips slip into a half smile as though he can sense the adrenaline threading through my stomach. I snatch my hand away and scold myself. I'm Trey's in this lifetime and all the lifetimes to come. He straightens up and flashes me a grin that lights up his entire face the same way the sun streams across the sky after a downpour.

There's a rigid silence. I shift in my chair, trying to think of something to say. "So... physio? How's that going?" Jesus, you're awkward, Eden.

He glances at his feet and grabs his cane. "Ah, yes. Despite appearances, it's actually an old injury. I occasionally require top up surgery. But I do regular physiotherapy as a preventative. It's a bodyguard's prerogative to stay in shape."

"Of course." I can't bear to look at him, or say the words, or admit what's happened. If I do, it makes it real.

"I guess you know why I'm here," I say.

"I do."

The silence returns, thicker, stagnant, filled with poisoned memories and my failings.

Dorian softens, "I'm sor—"

"Please don't."

He nods and rests his hand on my shoulder and smiles. "Hungry?"

"A little, actually."

"Well, Ms. East. As your assigned bodyguard, I feel it's my utmost duty to escort you back to our rooms for a spot of luncheon. Shall we?" He picks up his cane and leans on it.

I hesitate. But I've forgotten how I even got here and I'm frankly exhausted, so who am I to refuse?

"Sure, thank you."

I know I'm asleep because Bo is in my dreams. I've had this dream before. We stand outside the Council in the Ancient Forest. Structurally, the world is the same, but the color has leeched white. I've seen this before. I saw it in Obex when I touched the Last Fallon's bracelet. But this isn't her doing. It's her sister's. A world bleached of hopes and dreams and fueled by extreme Balance. The five towering roots signifying the entrance to the Council aren't made of wood as they should be, but twisted bone. The trees are ash white instead of the billowing green canopy they used to be. Their leaves missing, skeletal trunks and spindly twigs are all that remain.

I turn to Bo and stumble back. She too looks the same except instead of black, her eyes are green. Her hair, too, has changed. Instead of white locks, it shimmers silver.

"What happened to you?"

"You did this," she says, and grabs me by the shoulders, digging her nails in. "Don't you see?"

She shakes me and the dream rattles away, replaced with choking smog. I'm in Luna City. Fire blazes through the streets. Thick smoke pollutes the air, floating strands of flaming straw drifting on breezes. Everywhere I turn, bungalows burn and charred carcasses litter the ground. Sheridan, my dream weaver, doesn't appear. Maybe she's not asleep. I'm on my own this time. When she sleeps too, she helps protect me.

The Last Fallon stands a few paces ahead of me observing the mess her sister has made. I run to her, pull her around. "You're meant to stop this."

"Not me," she says. "Us."

"There is no us. No prophecy. Trey is dead."

She vanishes as Bo appears to our right. She scans the horizon, tears welling in her eyes.

"Do you trust me?" she whispers.

I step toward her, slide my hand in hers. "What do you mean?"

Her head snaps to face me, her expression as sharp as it is hard. "There's no time, Eden. Do you trust me?"

"I—"

"This is the only way..."

She raises her arm, and the dream goes black.

I wake in a cold sweat. I can't have slept long. It's still dark out. There are two trays of cold food next to me. I pick out a roll and ignore the rest, reaching for my CogTracker instead.

I'm alive.

I didn't doubt it. You're far too stubborn to die.

I smile at Sheridan's response. No pity, no sympathy. She's carrying on where we left off—I think I love her a little bit for it.

I had those dream-visions tonight.

Tell me more.

Bo was in them. That's new. Also, she was different. Her hair and eyes had changed color.

Interesting. I'll investigate. We can meet when you're back in Stratera.

Deal.

I finish the roll and nibble a small piece of fruit and push the tray away. Chewing makes my jaw ache. Even reaching for the food hurts.

It takes several minutes, but I get out of bed and hobble toward the wheelchair. Kato's pain removal from earlier has worn off. Every inch of me protests.

Once I reach the chair, I pause, realizing there's a notification on my CogTracker.

So relieved you're awake. We were praying to Balance you'd come back to us. Alas, I'm the bearer of official news. There are several East State Council officials wanting to see you tomorrow for lunch. I've tried to limit them as Hermia and I will be around in the morning to see you, too. But please make sure you're back here for them.

Arden

There's a rustle followed by footsteps outside. I close the notification down and crane to see out the window. Someone mumbles in a posh accent, Dorian my new body-guard, I assume. I glance at the CogTracker and frown. It's 2:30am. Where's he going so late?

Every ounce of my body just wants to go back to sleep, but I am so bored with sleeping, I clamber into the chair instead.

My limbs scream, my arms shake from the pressure of pulling myself into the chair, but I make it and drive the chair to the door. I wait a minute, then ease it open. Klein is there. Shit. Dorian must have been changing shift.

"Fallon East," he says.

I glance at Dorian, who's already at the end of the corridor. I'm up now, so I figure I should go for a walk, anyway.

"I need air," I say.

"As you wish."

I don't mean to follow Dorian, it just sort of happens. I move down the fabric walkways. But when I turn the corner, he's vanished. There's a rustle of fabric a short way ahead, the clink of porcelain, and then chatter. I'm so sick of my company that the lure of unfamiliar voices tempts my curiosity. The chair moves like a ghost through the corridor. There's some more artwork on the walls. I glance at Klein who walks a few paces behind. I stop at the picture, pretending to examine it as I strain to hear the conversation. One sounds like Dorian, but I can't quite hear. I drop my hand down the side of the wheelchair and tilt and curve the air until it makes a funnel and pulls the sound waves through my essence. It's a bizarre way to hear, but it works. I was right. It is Dorian. What oh what are you doing out here, Mr. Oswald?

Klein realizes I'm intensely fascinated by this anatomical art, so he paces the corridor and checks the adjoining halls.

"It's your job to protect her, and not just from Cecilia. She's vulnerable to addiction, and you know as well as I do the issues that can cause," someone says. The voice is familiar but I can't place where I know it.

There's shuffling, more porcelain clinking.

"No thank you, the caffeine keeps me awake." Dorian pauses, hefts a deep sigh and says, "I understand your concern, but forcing her to heal with no pain relief is brutal and not going to win us any favors."

"Don't you understand the importance of the role she

needs to play? Without her, I don't know if we can win. She must join us because she has to—"

"Then let her choose to work with us of her own accord."

"What would you have me do, Dorian?"

"Wait."

"Don't be naïve. We don't have the luxury of time. Haven't you seen CogNews? The world is falling apart around us. Rozalyn says we're talking days and weeks, not months anymore."

There's a pause. "I see. Did Gabe find another route to secure the comm channels with Rozalyn?" Dorian asks.

"Yes. But Cecilia keeps intercepting and killing our Obex runners. We lost Thorn and Samson last week. And our supply of barrier pills is dwindling, so we're keeping comms to a reduced minimum for now."

"Shit."

There's silence. I lean forward, straining my essence harder, racking my brain, trying to fish through memories and conversations. My breath catches. I slip forward and out of the chair with a thump. *Shit.* I freeze. They're still talking, so I think I got away with it.

And now I know who Dorian's talking to. Klein rushes to my side and helps me back into the chair.

"We should get going and get you back to your room."

"Could I just have a few more moments? The artwork in this corridor is fascinating..."

Klein scowls, thick blond brows bunching in the middle. "Fine, be quick, please."

I turn to another painting. Mmming and aahhing at it while I curve my hand around the air again.

"What of the weapon? The last I heard, no progress had been made in sourcing it," Dorian says.

"I'm waiting for a report, but the last update was they think they may have located it."

"Well, that is something." Dorian pauses, footsteps shuffle. "Don't lose faith. We've come this far."

"It's going to happen, whether we like it or not. It's already happening. Look outside. Have you seen the state of CogNews? We don't have long. The weather is declining in each state, there are skirmishes everywhere. The Balance is destabilizing. My concern is we won't be ready. We need her. She has a pivotal role to play, and she needs to be ready."

"So noted," Dorian says. "You know I've seen your daug—"

"No. Not here. We're not discussing that."

"As you please, Sir."

"Your job is to protect Eden, no matter what. She needs to heal and then, when she's ready, I will explain what is to come and the role she must play. Understood?"

There's a pause, followed by a sigh.

"Yes, Sir," Dorian says.

"Good. Dismissed."

There are footsteps.

"Okay, time to go." I don't wait. I shoot off down the corridor before Dorian can catch me eavesdropping. Klein huffs and, Balance knows how, makes his tank-sized body run to keep up with me. I wheel around the central area, kill a chunk of time, then wheel back to my bedroom door. I pull it open and an almighty scream erupts from my lungs. Standing in the doorway is Dorian.

"She's your problem now," Klein says and leaves.

"Care to explain why you're eavesdropping? You'd make a terrible spy, Ms. East."

"I wasn't spying... Or, at least not at first."

"But then you decided to?"

I open my mouth to reply but nothing comes out. There's literally no defense, I really was eavesdropping.

"Yes?"

He smirks.

"Give me a hand?"

"This should be interesting, one cane and a chair between us. Lean on me and wrap your arm around my elbow."

I do as he says. His body is warm. He grasps me and pulls until I'm upright; we're so close to each other, I can smell his aftershave. My cheeks heat, but as he eases me into bed, I pull myself together.

"Thanks," I say. And then add, "So we're going to have a little talk about the fact you're working directly for Castor and apparently I have a job to do?"

He smiles. "I knew you were there. If I wanted to keep it secret, I'd have stopped him speaking. Eavesdroppers tend to emanate strong emotion."

"I see. So you are a Siren then?"

He smiles—sort of. It's tight and even though it reaches his eyes, they're just as tight as his lips. He doesn't respond, but I take it as confirmation, especially if he can read emotions.

"And it's your job to what? Be my bodyguard or convince me to work for Castor, because that's what it really sounded like. Weapons and comm channels and secret roles."

"Are you finished?" he says.

"No, actually. You know he kidnapped me a few weeks back?"

"I think kidnapping is a little extreme. It was more like a casual chitchat at midnight."

Dorian's lips squeeze tight like he's trying not to laugh.

"You bastard. Was that you? Did you help kidnap me?" I want to be mad. But the ridiculousness of it all tickles the corners of my mouth and a bubble of laughter blurts out.

"No comment."

Castor's the leader of the rebels. Dorian's right, maybe Castor did just want to introduce himself and the rebels' ideology. I was treated great aside from the fact that when we were done talking, he drugged me asleep in order to put me back where I came from.

"And what exactly makes you think I'm going to work or do anything for the rebels?"

"Aside from our fabulous hospitality, fantastic medical team and dashingly charming bodyguards?"

"I mean it. Enough games. I heard what Castor said. War, *the* war, is coming. How do I know you weren't just saying those things and making out like I had free will because you knew I was listening?"

I glance up at him. His face is serene, I want to believe him.

"I knew you were listening, but I stand by what I said. I meant every word."

"Then I have questions. A lot of bloody questions in fact."

"And, Fallon East, when the time is right, I promise to give you answers."

FOUR

*'**Soul Death**—**The absolute and final destruction of a soul, thereby preventing it from resurrection and severing the eternal tie with its Balancer forever.***

*****N.B. Performing a soul death is treason under the jurisdiction of The First Fallon Law.'***

Excerpt—The History of Forbidden and Lost Magic

TREY

I rouse from unconsciousness still draped over the demon's excessively bony shoulder. I wonder if I could grab his throat or yank his skull-face clean off his neck. But before I can consider doing any of those things, we reach a crossroads. The demon halts. I shunt on his shoulder as he looks down at two cobbles and then stamps on one of them.

The ground shifts, the street splits in two, and the town-houses that towered above us a second ago vanish.

A grin peels across my face. This place might be a maze, but if he can make the streets move, then surely there must be a map or instructions somewhere?

When the street-puzzle pieces back together, the demon takes a sharp left and moves down a set of steps. Then he flings me to the ground and cuffs my wrist to a chain he holds.

I rub my arm and my stomach, the imprint of his boney shoulders still sore.

He pulls me but I'm caught, motionless. I know this street. I came here with Eden and Hermia. On the right is the park that had giant rocks in it. Rocks that turned out to be demons. There aren't as many in there now, but they're no less creepy. Their demon backs shudder and twitch, and one raises its head. Hollow eyes and jowls with rows of teeth leer at me. My neck spasms in response and my hand reaches to cover it.

"Come on, sunshine," the demon growls.

He yanks the chain and I stumble after him as we march toward the alley entrance to Rozalyn's castle.

"Will you at least tell me your name?"

"Pest."

"As in Pestilence, like the disease?"

He halts so fast I almost bump into his back. He turns his head, slow and steady. I crane up to see him. It takes every ounce of strength not to flinch at the sight of his skele-tal, eyeless features.

"I'm only a disease if you're dead or a demon."

He smirks, and I'm not sure if that's a joke or not. He

doesn't wait for a response, just continues down the stairs and into Rozalyn's darkened alleyway. Rifling through his robes, he pulls out a thin brass tube that looks like a flashlight and presses a button. Light showers the lane. The device is just like the one Hermia used a few months ago.

Broken bodies and corpses clutter the ground. Moans and whimpers slip from their chapped lips. The air is thick with the sour throb of their pain. My skin prickles in response.

As Pest walks toward Rozalyn's door, I'm transfixed by the poor souls lying like roadkill on the pavement. Their ribs are split open, there's no blood, but what's left of their innards spill over the street like a sloppy dinner. The souls of long dead insects and rodents gnaw at the juicy pink tissue and although bile rises in my throat, I can't tear my eyes away. Whatever these Keepers did to Rozalyn, it annoyed her enough she ate half their insides and discarded the rest to rot outside her palace. I guess being dead doesn't mean you get to rest in peace.

One of the bodies shudders. I can't tell if it was male or female. There are only sparse patches of hair and some of its face has been eaten away. Its half-chewed fingers reach out to me. A plea I can't answer. As Rozalyn's front door hisses open, I flick my wrist, and throw them some temporary relief, not enough to stop the moans, but enough the relief eases the tension in what was left of its face.

Pest steps inside and seals us into darkness. He yanks the cuff so hard and fast I drop to the floor like a swatted fly. The stones are damp and the chill sends a shiver over my skin. He grabs me by the chains and yanks me upright. My entire body shunts forward as he drags me through the darkness. My neck pounds, hot throbs sear deep inside my throat. After a few paces, he halts, uncuffs me, and disappears into the smoky walls, leaving me alone. Something moves in the misted, twisting walls. There's a flash of blonde hair. A thin girl steps between the shadows. I blink, but she's gone. Too fast for me to see her face.

From the floor, I scan the area. The room is lit by hundreds of candles. I've been here before, of course. I recognize the semi-opaque glass walls; the smoke playing with the shadows and the chair in the heart of the room. Rozalyn's throne is ivory and speckled with tiny fissures. I squint, my eyes roving its surface until I remember it's made of bone. Darkness curls into the room from every angle, thick folds of blackness that slither and squirm with creatures. The familiar tingle of being watched spiders down my spine. I observe the room, checking the corners and when I turn to the throne, my blood curdles. She's standing right there.

"Good evening," the Last Fallon's rasping voice trickles into the room. She extends a long, thin arm which, to my surprise, I take. Slow, and with screaming muscles, I stand. She helps me to her throne, not to sit on, but to lean against.

How merciful.

She steps back, watches, her maroon eyes studying me, hovering at my throat. Her hair is as maroon as her eyes, pulled back severe against her scalp and slicked down. She's wearing a white corseted dress splattered with blood—the remains of her dinner, no doubt.

"Your Majesty."

"Rozalyn, dear, call me Rozalyn. I think you've earned that, given your brief outburst of control in the colosseum."

I suppress a nervous laugh. Just before Victor stabbed me, I used my Siren power to control both Rozalyn and her sister Cecilia. It gave everyone else enough time to escape.

I stiffen, waiting for the punishment I know will come.

When Cecilia looked after me shortly after my mother died, she didn't take disobedience well. My back bears the scars as proof.

Rozalyn's face is placid, smooth even. And unless she's masking her emotions, I can't sense anger. No punishment comes. Maybe she's not as similar to her sister as I thought.

"Am I dead?" I ask, changing the subject.

Her head tilts to the side, her eyes narrow as she examines me. "No."

A burst of hope trembles in my chest. But when I notice the deep ridges furrowing into Rozalyn's forehead, the hope expires.

"So I'm still alive?"

"No. Not alive either."

"Then... Then, what am I?" My fingers hover near the wound in my neck. The bandage has gone, fallen off en route. The metal thread itches and throbs as though it's infected. But to have an infection, you need to be alive, right? And although it's slowing, blood is still oozing between the stitches.

Her mouth peels open, a grin of silvery spikes on display. Her tongue skitters over her lips. I inch back.

"I'd say you were something of an enigma, Mr. Luchelli."

Like Victor. My knuckles whiten where I clench the throne.

"So you lose an anomaly and gain an enigma?"

"It appears so," she says. Her grin widens. "I'm rather fond of a new plaything. So. Much. Potential."

"You're becoming quite the collector. What happened to your other anomalous pet? Shouldn't Victor be here instead of me?"

"'Should' is a strong word. I *should* be in Trutinor instead of that little brat niece of mine."

Karva is Cecilia's daughter. We found her with Victor… dating Victor when we got here before the big fight. She slipped through to Trutinor using the Door of Fates—the same door Rozalyn had planned to use.

"You want to be in Trutinor, but you are *meant* to be here." She leans into me, her mouth of spikes millimeters from my face. "Looks like neither of us got our way."

"For now."

My chest warms, a tumor of venom and vengeance ballooning inside me.

Her eyes glint. Hundreds of candle flames flicker in the depths of her pupils. "Jealousy and bitterness suit you." She pauses and picks up a goblet, taking a sip. "I like you."

"What do you mean, I'm meant to be here?"

She shrugs, picks her nail. "Cecilia always was short-sighted. You've read the prophecy. My dear sister is terrified of you and the girl. You will be her downfall. So what did she do? Tried every which way to separate the pair of you." She's grinning, her eyes wild and bright. "She's a fool. In her quest to separate you, she played right into my hands. She's given me the one thing I needed."

My mouth opens, my expression widens. "Because the prophecy says we're meant to work together?"

"Exactly," she says, clapping her hands together.

I frown. "Well, I'm not a lot of bloody good to you dead. I might be here, but how the hell are we supposed to defeat Cecilia now?"

"Oh, don't worry about that. Trivial details. Dead, alive, in-between, we're going to help each other just fine."

She leans close, her head slides into the crook of my neck.

She inhales the scent of my festering wound. Her head snaps back, tongue flicking across red-stained lips. My jaw flexes. She's baiting me, or about to eat me. Either way, I refuse to show fear. When I don't answer, she takes a seat in her ivory throne.

"Come," she barks at the shadows. A short, crouched figure scampers out of the gloom. His hair is fiery orange, his eyes are mismatching, one maroon, one ocean blue, both skirt in feverish movements around his sockets. On his forehead are two horns, as mismatched as his eyes. One is long, thin, and hooked like a crooked branch out from his brow. The other is a broken nub that pusses a green liquid from the fractured splinters. There's a gnaw of familiarity about him, but whoever the creature is, he's seen better days because every jerky movement is followed by a wince. He's dressed in pants and a pale long-sleeved top. The cuffs are stained red and brown. As he draws closer, there's a waft of stale meat emanating from him. He reaches Rozalyn and stops.

"Fix his neck. It's making me hungry."

She wafts her hand at the creature, who bows and retreats. His eyes locked on mine the entire time. Just as he melts into the shadows, I suck in a breath, realizing who he is: Bellamy—Hermia's husband. No wonder Hermia never found him.

"I assume you want to return to Trutinor?" Rozalyn's willowy nails skitter over the arm of her throne, clattering against the bone.

"With all of my soul."

She nods. "Good, that makes two of us."

"The Door of Fates—"

"The Door of Fates was just one way to break the banishment. There are other more..." She pauses, a glimmer of something passes through her expression. "Permanent solutions."

"So, there is a way back? A way to restore..." I throw my hands up gesturing at my body. "Myself back to life?"

She smiles, waves a dismissive hand at me. "But of course. There's always a way."

She doesn't elaborate, but the way her eyes are probing me tells me everything I need to know. "There's a catch, isn't there?"

"There's always a catch, Mr. Luchelli. Your return doesn't come for free. We have a prophecy to fulfill."

Bellamy appears, and with him is a trolley. It's covered in pots of ointment, bottles of liquid and what looks like an array of medical tools. He pushes me into a chair that definitely wasn't there a moment ago and unthreads the metal wires in my throat. I bite down with every tug, my throat burns hotter. He pats the line of sweat on my brow with a rag and hands me a jar of something orange. I raise an eyebrow, but he nods and tips it up to my chin.

I drink the lot; It's cold and tingles all the way to my gut. Everything glazes. The room softens and blurs. He shoves a hard strip of wood between my teeth and plunges his fingers into my neck.

White erupts through my vision, followed by nothing.

When I wake, my neck pulses. I'm in the same chair I passed out in, and Bellamy has gone. The Last Fallon hasn't. She observes me from her throne of bones. Her eyes tracking my every movement. She will always be a predator. My fingers skim over the gash in my neck. It's stitched neat, and the skin, although swollen, is dry. The oozing has stopped.

"You're much less appealing now your skin's not rotten or weeping blood."

I let out a nervous laugh. "Ha, well, yes, perhaps this is better for business." My voice is husky. No surprise given the ache in my throat with every syllable I utter.

She smiles, razor pin teeth on display, and I have to shove down a shudder.

"What is the price for my return? Your sister's head on an Obex-shaped plate?"

She jerks back, a low rumble of laughter billows from her chest. "Are you in the god-killing business now, boy?"

I don't answer because frankly, there's one I'd love to kill.

"No heads. Not yet. But soon. The time is coming when you, me and the girl will take Cecilia's head. Imbalance is seeping into Trutinor. The Guild won't be able to hold it back for much longer, and then... Well, then we'll rip the world in two."

I laugh. It judders, staccato out of my mouth. Her face remains stoic.

"What do you mean, rip the world in two?"

She folds one leg over the other. "All in good time. Besides, you're hardly in a fit state to be waging war."

My fingers brush my neck. "You sent Victor back. Can't you just send me home the same way?"

She stands, walking behind me and leaning down to my ear. The trickle of her breath over my skin makes my stomach curl. It smells sour, like hatred and raw meat. I can't help but wonder who she was eating before I got here and if the smell is them or her.

"Victor was different." She stands and moves through the shadows and darkness. When she reappears, she's holding a goblet and a piece of something fleshy. "I control the dead. Victor was actually dead. You're only half dead."

"But you will send me back?"

Her eyes roll onto mine. "Obviously."

I search her face, trying to work out what she's scheming. She wears a blank expression, so I lower my guard a fraction, stretch out with my power, and probe for a hint or clue. I find it. Smooth and warm, slick almost, and ruffled with a tangy sweetness—hubris. My eyes narrow. Something is off.

"Can you get me back to Trutinor or not?"

Her lips press shut, thinning into a tight smile. "You're much more fun than Victor. So bold. So confident. A little arrogant..." She perches on her throne, drips of red splatter her white dress. "I like it."

"Thanks?"

A full row of serrated teeth glare at me. "Yes, Mr. Luchelli. I'll send you back. But first, we're going to work together. I need you to do something for me."

BREAKING NEWS

"Good evening, Trutinor, this is Tarkin Tavas reporting for CogNews TV. I'm on location at the border of the North and Ancient Forest. I have some troubling news to bring you this evening."

Tarkin moves aside and gestures to the border field behind him. There are several officials, Guild Sorcerers, and Council members in the area.

Tarkin's expression is grave as he turns back to the camera.

"As you can see, Trutinor is facing unprecedented levels of Imbalance. So much so, the land is now infected. I'm standing at the border of the North and Ancient Forest, however, we're seeing similar land infections at the borders of the East and Ancient Forest and there are early reports of issues in the South too. Let's try to talk to one of the Guild Sorcerers…"

Tarkin runs after a Sorcerer, who stops and gives him a skittish look.

"Excuse me…?"

"Jacobs."

"Yes, hello Jacobs, I'm Tarkin Tavas, you're live on CogNews TV. Can you tell viewers what's happening?"

Jacobs glances from Tarkin to the camera.

"I… Um…"

"What are the domes and why are there so many blackened crop plants?"

"They're stasis domes we're using to prevent the infection from spreading."

"Trutinor is infected?"

"I… That's not what I meant. At this stage, we're unclear what the issue is. But we're trying to prevent spread further than the borderlines."

"So, whatever is happening to the plants here is infectious?"

"At this stage—"

"Should the Keepers in the North and Ancient Forest be worried? Will this impact the Dryads?"

Jacobs' skin flushes.

"We don't know at this time."

"I see. What do you say to the farmers rioting outside the Guild? Should they be panicked?"

"Now listen here, Mr. Tavas, there's no need for exaggeration or alarm. We don't want a mass panic on our hands."

"So, we should be panicking, is what you're saying?"

"No, I di—"

Tarkin turns to the screen, blocking Jacobs off.

"Well, Keepers of Trutinor, you heard it here first. Even the Guild of Sorcerers is worried about the sporadic crop deaths appearing at the borders. Imbalance is spreading, and it appears no one knows what to do about it. This is Tarkin Tavas reporting for CogNews TV."

FIVE

'While there are limited numbers of Soul Deaths, the impact on the Balance has been debated throughout history. With such intensely varied consequences on the Balance, no conclusion has been reached. Three cases in particular are known to have had such severe consequences they resulted in the law passing to make Soul Deaths illegal. These Soul Deaths caused catastrophic consequences to either Earth or Trutinor. For more detailed information on the consequences to the Balance, historical records can be found in: The Lost History of Balance: a longitudinal study.'

A short history of the most significant Soul Deaths

Victim: Known only as N
Perpetrator: Mitchell O'Neil
Reason: unknown

Consequence: fault line created on Earth which led to a catastrophic eruption and subsequent tsunami that killed 40% of the Earth's population.

Victim: Thomas Thornton
Perpetrator: Janella Thornton
Reason: revenge for adultery
Consequence: the seasons shifted in Trutinor. The permanence of weather was eradicated for three seasons. Crops were lost across Trutinor. Thousands starved as food shortages reached their peak.

Victim: Broc Fawcett (Human)
Perpetrator: Hermilda Endlesquire
Reason: Assassination
Consequence: the creation of Obex'

From the History of Forbidden and Lost Magic

EDEN

It's been a week of chaos—visits from Arden, Sheridan and Felicia, Kato, and Hermia. Members of the East State Council came to finalize membership and a deputy. They're giving me a year to recover. I'll still have some decisions to make and papers to sign, but mostly, they're going to do the heavy lifting so the state doesn't fall into any more chaos than it already has. Doctors visited me multiple times a day, and each time a trail of juniors followed in their wake. All of them poking and prodding at me or drawing blood samples.

Dorian dutifully stood guard. Sometimes at the door, sometimes inside—usually when people arrived and occasionally when I was on my own. He's polite, charming and quietly funny. At first, he irritated me with his presence. Two nights after I met him, I barked at him to leave, get out of my room. But then he did, and I was more alone than I'd ever been. On my own with nothing but pain and memories and an aching soul with a giant hole in it, suddenly I didn't want to be on my own anymore.

I struggled out of bed and pulled open the fabric door flap. To my surprise, he was standing there, on guard, silent.

"I—" I started, but looked at the floor, unable to find the words to apologize. There was a pause, then he tipped my chin up to face him.

"It's okay," he said, and stepped inside. "How about I sit there, and we can just be quiet together?"

A tear rolled down my cheek. He didn't have to do that. I didn't deserve the kindness. He wiped his thumb over my cheek, smearing the tear away.

"Thank you," I said.

He helped me back into bed and, as he promised, sat in the armchair in silence. The one exception to that was when Kato visited. Dorian would leave. I think he knew what we were doing, given Castor's and his conversation.

Kato draws off small pieces of pain to enable me to function with some semblance of normality. It's helping, and he's trying not to take too much, so we don't get addicted. I know I promised him it would only be once, but I literally can't function unless he helps and I have too much responsibility not to function right now. Healing is the priority, right? I have enough that they're releasing me later today. Back to Trey's mansion.

Dorian's head pops around the curtain just as I'm trying to clamber into the chair.

"Morning. Here, let me help," he says and grabs my arm and waist to support me down into the chair. "Where to?"

"I was just thinking I'd sit in the communal square. It's busy, and I'm sick of staring at these walls."

"Well, it's almost home time. But communal square it is. I'd stay with you, but I've got some business to attend to. I'll stay till Klein arrives and then I'll be back with you as soon as I can be."

"Yeah, don't rush."

"Oh, Ms. East, don't pretend like my delightful company is a burden instead of a pleasure."

I bite down a grin as he wheels me into the communal square. Klein arrives a minute later. They greet each other and Klein drifts a few feet away, giving me space while staying close enough. Once I have everything, he leaves for his meeting. I'm captured by how many people are here. How many rebels are hidden beneath Trutinor society? I wish Trey could be here, to see how big the rebellion really is.

CogTVs hover, the news blaring from them. It's bad. Worse than the other day. More skirmishes, public killings. Borders on fire. Outbreaks of Alteritus—a disease of Imbalance. That buffoon Tavas, whatever his name is, appears then runs after Jacobs the Guild Sorcerer. Poor bloke looks traumatized.

I'm staring at the news when a figure goes still in my periphery. Castor. I flag him down. He nods, finishes a brief conversation and then approaches. Klein stands, Castor waves him off and he settles back in position.

"Fallon East, I hope you've found your stay with us accommodating." He scans the square.

"Dorian's gone to meet someone. But yes, he's... umm, he's very good at his job. Anyway." I pause, unsure how to ask my question, but knowing I shouldn't waste this opportunity. "I wanted to ask you something."

Castor tilts his head at me. "Okay, but first, I wanted to discuss what happened in Stratera. I'm sure you're aware it wasn't Rozalyn who came through the door."

"Karva. I saw her. But Victor too."

"Victor, though, is dead. And Karva had already used the door to restore herself. Our Obex runners have let us know that because Victor betrayed Rozalyn, she's shut off the connection she had to Victor. He's dead, or dying again or... We'll, it's complicated. But we wanted to let you know because we're tracking him as a matter of priority. Until we've established what he's doing in Trutinor and why, we're treating him as a high-level threat."

"I see. So he's dying again?"

Castor rubs his forehead. "I'm unclear about the exact magical bonds of Rozalyn's Obex magic. But the runners have assured me he will end up back in Obex before long. We suspect he's going to search for any magic he can get his hand on to prevent that."

"Okay," I say.

"We want you on alert. I will, of course, be sending Dorian with you as a permanent guard."

My mind scrambles into fog, words, thoughts, magic jumbling.

"Look, I just want to know what you want from me," I say.

"Well, we want you to recover and—"

"No, enough pleasantries and bullshit. What do you really want, Castor? Seriously? We both know something is coming. You only have to watch mainstream CogNews to know there's Imbalance leaking all over the place, something is brewing and you wouldn't have gone to all the trouble of rescuing me from Cecilia at Stratera unless you wanted something. And lest we forget about the minor kidnapping incident in the summer. And now we have a dead and re-dying Keeper who's probably after me, let alone the fact Cecilia is doing Balance knows what."

He opens his mouth and then closes it again, straightens himself up and then faces me square on.

"Okay, Ms. East. Ultimately, we need you to fulfill your prophecy."

My chest heats, making me want to lash out. How can he think about the prophecy now? I try to measure my tone out of respect. "The prophecy is redundant. I can't fulfill it without Trey."

Castor pauses, purses his lips and then continues. "I understand your concern, but we must continue trying to end the fate system. The only way to do that, unfortunately, is to start a war. Cecilia has to die for us to be free."

"And you want me to fight for your side in that war?"

He nods. "Yes, but it's more than that. In order to fight, we need Rozalyn. But to have Rozalyn, we need to open the barrier. Cut a hole in the world big enough and stable enough so she can return. It's what she was trying to do with the Door of Fates."

My mind drifts back to a conversation I had with Arden and Hermia in the library before everything kicked off with the Door of Fates.

"I asked Arden once whether allowing Rozalyn through the door and letting Trutinor merge back with Obex was such a bad thing. I mean, if they were together once, why not again?"

"And what did he say?"

"He said that the barrier is really some kind of scar tissue. That if you reopen a scar, it doesn't heal well. That the scars only get bigger and more damage is done."

Castor's lips press together and he wipes his mouth. "He could be right. No one knows what will happen when we tear open the barrier. But we know what will happen if we don't. Cecilia is leaching Keepers of hope and happiness. She seeks to control us to the point of destruction."

"I know," I say because I do. "I've seen it in dreams. The land bleached white, bone trees, Keepers devoid of emotions."

"Then you know what has to be done."

"But that's the thing, Castor. I've also seen what happens if you let Rozalyn free to reign over us, too. Trutinor will burn. Neither option is appealing."

A Keeper with the greenest eyes I've ever seen interrupts, leans in, and whispers in Castor's ear. He straightens and says, "On my way. Excuse me Fallon East. I have something to attend to."

He drops his head in deference and leaves. I'm on my own for a while until I spot a familiar face on the other side of the square.

Bo.

Between the numerous doctor visits, East State Keepers with reams of paperwork, Arden, press releases, CogNews broadcasts, carts of gifts and flowers from Elemental Keepers and Fallons from other realms, I realize how long it's been since I saw her. Kato said she knew I was awake and that while I was in the coma, she'd stayed with me. And yet, despite all those visits, Bo never came. Each day that's passed with no sign of her made the slick of fear inside me spread. The last thing we did was argue.

I tried to message her, I really did. I opened my

CogTracker a million times. I even wrote a few words. But nothing came out right—it all sounded wrong. So the silence between us continued.

Bo doesn't notice me at first. Her back is to me and she's staring at her CogTracker. Some rebel Keepers obscure my view, and when they pass, I spot her marching next to Kato and gesticulating aggressively enough. Kato's eyes are focused on the floor. I'm not sure what possesses me, but I tilt my hand, making a funnel shape, and reach out to the air. There's a pocket of heat. I bend and curve it until the air shapes like a funnel. I angle it toward them. The click of her prosthetic leg and the mumble of their voices comes into focus.

"Do you have any idea how dangerous what you're doing is?" she barks.

"I get it, but what am I supposed to do? She's family and she can barely walk, let alone function. I can't stand seeing her like that. If she died... Besides, where's your compassion? She's been family to you for your entire life, or are you still pouting?"

"I resent that."

"I resent your accusation."

Bo halts, folding her arms. But this time when she speaks, her voice is softer.

"God, Kato. It's not an accusation. I'm just worried, okay? I love you both so much I don't want either of you hurt. Look, I'm not exactly in a position to call her out right now, but you... You, I can say something to."

They continue walking across the main square in silence. When she lifts her head and notices me, her expression freezes. I release the air funnel. I've heard enough.

As they near me, Kato takes her hand and pulls her to a stop. He buries a dozen kisses on her lips and then leans his head on the opposite side and whispers something in her ear. He lets go, gives her a long, soft kiss, and then smiles at me. "I'll get coffee." He glances between us, hovering as if trying to decide something. He decides to shuffle away.

There's a pause. Our eyes meet, and a single, thick beat passes between us, unraveling the last three months.

"I..." we both say, then stop, waiting for the other to continue. She's stiff, her back rigid. Her appearance, as always, is immaculate. Bo has the whitest hair and palest skin of anyone I've ever met. Her signature red lipstick is ever so slightly smeared in one corner. She used to wear red gloss when we were younger and before she and Kato were Bound. But Kato would moan that he couldn't kiss her without being caught. So she swapped to a matte color and had some Sorcerer enchant the lipstick. It's meant to be smudge free. But I guess when someone loves you that much, no amount of magic can hide a kiss.

I lean forward, groaning and wincing as I try to stand up to her level.

"Oh, sit down you idiot," she says, grabbing my arms and helping me back into the chair.

She wheels me to the edge of the square and sits down on a bench next to me, our knees, my skin, her cogs almost touch. The gap between them is so small and yet it still feels like an ocean.

"Eden..." she starts.

"No. Me first," I interrupt, picking her hand up. It's as rigid as her back was, but after a second, she relaxes. "I'm so sorry. I should have been there for you after the battle with Victor. It was selfish and I was wrapped up in myself, and I, of all people, should have seen you weren't coping as well as you seemed."

She pauses, her lips tight. Then she nods. "Yeah, you should have been there..."

The pause that follows is awful. She takes a slow breath.

Oh god, she isn't going to forgive me. I've lost her too. My chest clamps and I swear my heart stops beating.

"But," she says, "I should have been there for you. We both messed up. We've both done horrible things to each other's families..."

"I don't want to lose you."

"You haven't lost me. I was just angry."

She leans in and wraps her arms around me. I squeeze her and a single shuddering sob bubbles over.

"I'm so sorry," I breathe into her shoulder.

"I'm sorry too," she says, rubbing my back.

Kato appears, holding three coffees and dishes them out. Then he pulls a sausage roll from his back pocket and hands it to me. "Eat, you're looking scrawny."

I take a bite, it's delicious.

"Mmm," I say between mouthfuls. "It reminds me of the sausage rolls Nyx and my mom used to make on the weekends." Which reminds me, *bloody* Kato still hasn't told me how Titus is. I put the roll down. Kato freezes. A glance passes between us.

"You tell me right now," I say.

Kato's eyes flit to Bo's. "In my humblest of defenses, Arden forbade me from telling you."

"He said you needed to concentrate on getting better and weren't in a fit state to travel, anyway."

"I don't care. Tell me what happened to Titus."

"We're using a Stasis CogPod to keep him in an induced coma. We knew you'd want to..."

"To say goodbye?" My voice is quiet.

Kato nods, his eyes never meeting mine.

Bo reaches for my hand and clasps it in hers. "I'm sorry."

"What happened?"

Kato sags against the bench. "Titus was outside Datch prison and saw Victor being taken inside by the guards. It was before you found Nyx, so I guess the worry and fear got to him. He lost it and attacked Victor. Of course, the prison guards couldn't just let him get away with brawling on prison grounds. Even if it was a prisoner he was beating. So they locked him up in a cell for the evening... The evening Nyx died. As soon as Arden realized, he rushed to Titus's cell. But he wasn't quick enough... They got him to Dryad City Hospital as soon as they could. Charlie tried every-thing. But..."

"But souls once Balanced never part, unless one half is strong of heart," I whisper. It's one of the oldest Balance proverbs. I squeeze my eyes shut, pushing thoughts of Trey away. I should have died like Titus.

Dorian appears, slicing the atmosphere. He walks with his cane, but he's a little straighter, leans a little less on it today. Kato nods to him. "Hey big D," he says.

I raise an eyebrow. "Big D?" I wonder how many conversations they've had while I've slept or healed. Bo raises an eyebrow and glances at me the nearer he gets. Dorian holds out his free hand to Bo.

"Dorian Oswald," he says, smiling that perfect smile.

"Pleasure is all mine," Bo says, giving me a pointed stare.

"I'm the rebel assigned bodyguard."

"I can see that," she says, her eyes rolling slowly over his muscled arms, shoulders, thighs. She glances between me and Dorian, and I have to suppress a smirk. I glare at her, wishing we were telepathic—Yes, Bo, my bodyguard is smoking hot.

"Well, it's lovely to meet you," she says. Kato, having seen her practically undress Dorian with her eyes, is no longer smiling. So I decide to break the tension.

"I want to see Titus."

"Eden," Bo starts, raising her hand, "I think you need to res—"

"It wasn't a question."

There's a thick silence.

"I'll call Magnus," Kato says.

SIX

'No living Balancer shall seek their departed soul mate until they too pass.'

Fourth Law—The Book of Balance

TREY

I fall silent. Of course she wants something. Her eyes roam my face, watching, assessing, waiting to see what move I'll make next. This is a game.

Her lips draw open. Most people should smile more. I wish she'd smile less; her grin is filled with ghosts and nightmares.

"I have nothing to give you in exchange for sending me back."

"Oh child," she says, her face softening, "there's always something you can give."

"And what is it you require?"

She walks to the back of the room; her figure almost floating across the damp stone. Her fingertips brush the back wall. If I remember right, it's not a wall. It's where the Book of Imbalance is kept. A light behind glass turns on, and there, resting on a plinth, is the book. She's quiet for a moment, contemplating the book, or perhaps the contents. Then she glares at me.

"I can get you home," she says, walking toward me. The light in the wall dies, plummeting the book into darkness as she returns to her throne. "And alive. But what I want in return is significant."

She has the upper hand. She could ask for anything and I'd have to give it to her if I want to get back to Eden.

"Okay...?"

She comes to me, her hand traces the outline of my head, then she presses her fingers to her mouth. "You must sense it... the Imbalance? The growing weakness between our worlds."

I think back to being in Trutinor, the border fields, the rift that opened in the sky. "What does it mean?"

"It means that the banishment magic Cecilia used to tear Trutinor in two and imprison me here is growing weak. That presents us with an opportunity."

"The prophecy. The war?"

"Exactly. No one wants to be separated from their Balancer, but I believe you were brought here for a reason. It's prophesied that together we will bring down Cecilia. But in order to do that, we need to tear the world open again. Which brings me to what I want from you: an army."

An army? We're in Obex where the hell am I going to find an army?

She glides back to her throne, picks up the goblet and drinks. Her tongue slides across her lips, mopping up a droplet of red. "What say you, Mr. Luchelli? Time is short. The fabric between our worlds is thinning. And whether my sister likes it or not, the barrier will fall. If we're to defeat her, then we will need an army."

I laugh. "You've had millennia down here. Why haven't you built one already?"

She hisses, spitting each word. "You think I haven't tried? You take me for a fool. I've tried. A thousand times I've tried. But these demons cannot be threatened. They have no way out, no way forward. Stuck here for eternity. What leverage do I have to convince them to fight for me? Sweet requests, torture, threats, none of it has worked. They care not because I have nothing I can give them."

"If you failed, what makes you think I can? How do you propose I build one?"

"That, boy, is your problem." She wafts a hand at me. "It's a fair price for a life with your Balancer. Besides, I'll assist where I can. But I, too, have preparations needed before I can return."

"Where am I supposed to get soldiers? Obex is full of dead people and demons."

She leans into my face, her expression hard. "Then, dear, build me an army full of dead people and demons."

I fall silent, my lips pressing together as she watches me watching her. After a time, I speak.

"It would take months."

"You don't have months. When the barrier is thin enough..." She points a long nail at my chest. "And it will be soon. You need to have an army ready because we are going back and Cecilia will not take kindly to it."

There's more to this, I can feel it, it's making the air thick, claggy. Everything tastes like secrets.

"What are you not saying?"

She sits on her throne. A quiet, thin smile pressing her lips and eyes narrow. She cocks her head at the back wall where the Book of Imbalance sits.

"Your role in this whole grand affair with my sister... You and the girl are the ones who bring the barrier down and enable my return. When I send you back, you will tear our worlds in half. You'll open the floodgates and rain war down on Trutinor. You will start a war to end all wars."

She rotates her glass in a circular motion, her eyes closing, as if she's smelling the aroma of her drink. Eventually, she looks at me.

"And you're going to do it quickly because that thing that's keeping a piece of you alive isn't going to last forever."

I swallow down a hard knot in my throat. "What is keeping me alive?"

Her lips curl, but she doesn't answer. I rub my wrist and consider making a run at the wall, stealing the Book of Imbalance, and finding the right piece of magic to send me back. But I wouldn't have the right skill, magic or tools to do it. Even if I tried to run for the wall, she'd rip my heart out and swallow it whole before I was halfway across the room. Where I rub my wrist, my fingers brush my scar. Her eyes dart to the bobbled shape. There's no thud, no roar through my head, only the shiver of something that once was. The heart. The magic. The ceremony. *Oh.*

"It was the blood I ingested. During the ceremony?"

Eden and I took part in an ancient Siren ceremony, bonding ourselves to The Heart of Trutinor as its protectors.

"It was."

"How long will it keep me alive? How long before I die for real?"

"Maybe a few weeks. You're a Fallon, so that's in your favor, I suppose."

Prickles radiate from my spine. A few weeks to create an army. It's an impossible, colossal task. And if I don't? I never get home to Eden? We never have a war? Cecilia reigns forever. There's no way I'm going to let that happen.

"Well?" she says. "Why are you still here? Go build me an army."

BREAKING NEWS

"Good afternoon, Trutinor, this is Tarkin Tavas reporting live from Dryad City Hospital. We've had word that the First Fallon has come for a follow-up appointment here at the hospital and we're going to try to sp—"

There's a rustle. The camera wobbles.

"Ladies and gentlemen, as you can see behind me, the First Fallon is exiting the building now."

Tarkin and the cameraman both hustle through the growing crowd to get in front and next to the First Fallon.

"Your Majesty? Your Majesty? A moment of your time, if you will?"

The First Fallon turns to the screen, a serene smile plastered on her face.

"Yes, Mr. Tavas?"

"Have they given you a clean bill of health, Your Majesty? Trutinor is worried."

She tilts her head, the smile deepens.

"But of course, Mr. Tavas. I'm the First Fallon, a picture of health, always."

"Can you address the rumors that you were injured during the battle of Stratera?"

There's a hesitation, a fleeting flicker in the corner of her eyes.

"Just rumors, Mr. Tavas. As you can see, I am in perfect health. This was nothing but a routine checkup. And I think 'battle' is a little exaggerated for the headlines. Don't you? That's all. Good day, Trutinor."

She waves and turns away.

"Wait, Your Majesty… Your…"

Tavas returns to the screen.

"As the First Fallon said, she is in great health and dismissed the alleged rumors of a battle at Stratera. But it remains to be seen whether there's any basis to these allegations. I will, of course, continue to investigate on Trutinor's behalf. This is Tarkin Tavas reporting for CogNews TV."

SEVEN

'Souls once Balanced never part, unless one half is strong of heart.'

Balance Proverb

EDEN

I'm discharged from the rebel hospital a few hours later. Dorian is assigned to me as a rebel bodyguard—though honestly, I'm convinced he's just there as a pair of eyes for Castor. I'm standing on one of the North State train stations waiting for him to put his case on the train and grab coffees. Then we'll leave for Titus.

Kato and Bo were finishing up packing their things at the rebel camp and then following behind us. They should be here shortly. Magnus is up at the front end of the train inspecting something and preparing for the journey.

The station is virtually empty. There's only one or two

Keepers and Steampunk Transporters milling around. I'm cold. So I shrug the fur cape the rebels gave me tighter around my shoulders. I'm also exhausted, as I left the wheelchair in the hospital wing. While I tire easily; I can be on my feet for short periods now.

The air bites, a crisp breeze whips around the gaps in the cape and I shiver. My senses automatically reach out, roaming deeper into the atmosphere. Something is amiss, wrong. It's too quiet. The temperature drops further, motion in the air stills like necrosis and rot. I probe the oddity; it's sharp and acrid, too much like death.

A chill splinters down my spine. It can't be him.

I inch a foot forward. "Dor—"

He snaps around, lunging for me. Our fingertips brush, but it's too late. I'm sucked into crushing darkness.

When the world reappears, hatred so dark it smothers my soul in a thick tar of Imbalance pours through my body. A red haze drops over my vision like a veil. The vault snaps open. Ribbons of darkness slide into my body, so easy, so fast. It's like this is where they're meant to be. I shut my eyes and take a slow, deep breath. I'm far too comfortable having Imbalance in my veins. It feels like the power has returned home.

"Victor," I snarl.

I stiffen, ready to fight. My insides spark, a boiling rage floods my chest with flames. I'm vaguely aware I'm surrounded by rocks. Back outside the station, then.

"Hello, Eden." Victor's scratchy drawl drifts through the dissipating darkness.

I bristle, static pops of electricity pulse over my skin. It builds hard and fast, pumping into my fingers; a surge so strong it takes my breath away.

I turn to face the voice, my skin ripples with more violet

power than I've ever pooled. Burn, burn. I fire every molecule of electricity that I have in the voice's direction. I blink, but Victor's nowhere. Instead, Karva is standing before me. Her white mass of curls is stark against her bronzed skin. The maroon catsuit she's wearing clings so tightly to her curves I'm convinced it's painted onto her skin. The bolt blasts into a rock, a rumbling explosion erupts from the stone. As shards splinter into the air, pebbles and fragments rain down around us. I use the cape to shield my head.

Behind her, Victor pulls a stray sliver of stone from between two of his ribs. He doesn't bleed or flinch. I frown, stumbling back. *This is fucking weird.*

"Advantages of being dead," he sneers. "I'm hard to kill."

"I seem to remember fire worked pretty well on the dead." Or it did on the Lost Soul Demons Victor brought from Obex last summer.

"No, no, sweet thing," Karva says tutting, her white curls bobbing in time with her tuts. Everything about her is so much more vibrant than it was in Obex. But then, she's alive now thanks to the Door of Fates.

And Trey isn't.

My insides harden.

My other hand rises automatically. If I kill her, Victor suffers. But an invisible force clasps my throat. The red Imbalance veil vanishes and a white searing sensation digs its claws into my brain.

Images, memories, emotions pour into my head: my soul tears in two all over again. There's screaming. Disjointed, hollow, familiar. Mine.

Karva's face appears millimeters from mine, her hand on my throat. "Hello sweets, it's better if you play nice."

Her voice is high and soft and childlike. It makes her words so much worse.

"Fuck you," I spit.

She sighs. "That's a shame."

The memories intensify, the swirling blackness, the empty void, the tearing. She shoves me onto my knees, her hand tightens around my throat. The memories whirl, fracturing parts of my mind and soul that are still so fragile, still healing. Somewhere deep inside, I'm laughing.

The laugh bubbles over, blood and spittle spraying down my chin.

"Is pain funny?" she asks. There's an innocent tone to her voice, like she's genuine and wants the answer. It's unnerving.

"What are you going to do? Kill me?"

She tilts her head as if examining.

"Do it," I snarl.

I have nothing to lose. She can't win, but I can. "You kill me and you'll give me exactly what I want."

I push one leg up, standing. It's agony, but I refuse to cower beneath her or Victor. Electricity pools in my fingers.

"You wanna play?" I say and wipe the blood and saliva from my mouth. "Bring it, bitch."

"Karva, wait." Victor's voice snaps me out of the fog. For the first time, my eyes settle on him properly.

"Fucking hell," I breathe.

He looks frail, his wolf hand shriveled. His skin sallow and death-gray, the maroon scar that tracks from his temple down his face and under his shirt collar has withered and parts of it have blackened. He's wearing black pants and a t-shirt, but as he stumbles toward me and Karva, I notice they hang off his thin frame. There are a few necrotic patches on his arms. They flake as he moves. My face scrunches.

"Don't look at me like that. You're not exactly fresh yourself," Victor snarls.

I breathe deep, refusing to rise to the bait. "What's happening to you?" *Not that I give a shit.*

"I'm decaying," he says. "Rozalyn cut me off from her power."

Well, that much I knew, thanks to Castor. "I should think so, too, you traitorous piece of shit."

"Please, you think I had any choice in what I did? I was just as much a pawn as you were."

"YOU KILLED TREY."

"Yes. And you killed me."

"Well, you don't look very fucking dead."

He rolls his eyes. "I'm not dignifying that with a response."

"What do you want?"

Karva grabs my wrist and bends it around, displaying my heart-shaped scar.

Victor glances from my wrist to Karva. "You were right."

She smiles. "Told you, baby."

I snatch my wrist back and he steps toward me, close enough his putrid stench clings to the inside of my nose.

"I'm going to kill you," I say, every word laced with acid.

Victor's top lip curls into a sneer that makes the heat in my chest erupt into flames—I try to draw on water elements to dampen the flames down but it only fuels the flames harder and embers flicker in my palms. Now is not the time to fight him. Not with his pet Rottweiler guarding him and me barely recovered. His eyes meet mine. The same hate-filled fire in my chest reflects back at me through his stare.

"Don't be unoriginal, Eden. You're better than that. We both know you tried to kill me once..." He pauses, straightens, and slides his hands into his pockets. "That didn't work out so well for you, did it?"

His thin smile stretches across his face. I bite the inside of my cheek so hard I draw blood. But it stops me from ripping the smile clean off his face.

"Now, now, sugar," Karva hums, her fingers tiptoe over my chest, leaving a cool trail in their wake extinguishing the rage in my chest. I slap her fingers away.

She smirks at me. *I'm going to destroy them both. I'm going to kill her mother, her fucking aunt, Victor. They're all dead.*

"We have a deal for you," she says.

"I don't want shit from you."

"I wouldn't be so sure about that," she says. "This deal means we all win."

"What if I could help you take down Cecilia?" Victor says.

I falter. An insidious worm of hope burrows into my brain. *He's lying. He's always lying.* It's always a game with him.

"All I need is a vial of blood from the Heart of Trutinor," Victor says.

I laugh, then step right into his face. "You think I'm going to trust you for one second?"

"It's not me you need to trust. I can't do anything. But Karva," he looks at her. The scent of decaying flesh hovers between us and I have to suppress a gag.

"Karva can bring her mother down."

"I don't care if you stake her to a plate and drop her at my feet. I. Will. Not. Give. You. Anything. Victor. You're a pathetic excuse for a Fallon. I'm going to destroy you. Slowly. Piece by piece, until even the maggots won't touch your rotten remains."

He sneers. No comeback this time.

I laugh.

Victor wavers. "What's so funny?"

"Because even if I can't end you. It doesn't seem like you have long left in Trutinor, anyway. The minute the last piece of you decays, you'll be right back in Obex with a violently sadistic Last Fallon. And I hear she doesn't take too kindly to traitors."

I shunt forward and he cowers away. I can beat him. He will perish and I will swim in the ash of his soulless, nonexistent form, right after I ash Cecilia and then Karva to boot.

"Leave," I say through gritted teeth. "You're not getting shit from me."

There's a soft tap, tap, tap of footsteps.

Karva's eyes widen. "Someone's coming. You go. Take her back, or this was all for nothing."

Victor's dark wings expand outward. They're decaying like the rest of him. Little holes and thinning patches make light speckle through them.

"Give me your hands," he says.

"Go fuck yourself."

He growls and grabs me.

"I'll prove we can help," he whispers in my ear as everything darkens, and a crushing blackness presses into my body. For a split second, I wonder if he's taking us to Obex until I remember Rozalyn's cut him off. A second later, we pop back into existence a short way outside the station. I spin, shooting fire behind me, but it's too late. He's already vanished.

"The only thing that's a matter of time is me figuring out how to Soul Death you, you son of a bitch," I shout into the air. But he's long gone.

As I hobble toward the station doors, my legs scream

and buckle every other step, Victor's words echo around my mind. I want them to be true. But no matter how much I wish he was telling the truth, I will never trust him again. Besides. The prophecy says it's Rozalyn's help I need. Not his.

After a few meters, I can't walk anymore. I'm hot and my muscles burn. So I sit on the rocky path, sweat pooling on my skin, panting.

Cheers, Victor, you prick.

The station doors fling open, cracking against the wall.

"What the hell?" Dorian shouts. He walks over fast, barely using his cane. I bat him away.

"What the hell happened? You disappeared."

"It's fine. A long story involving an undead demon-corpse and a resurrected demigod and a rather unladylike bout of sweating. Can you help me? My legs hurt?"

He hands me his cane, wraps his arm around my waist and lifts me into his arms, and takes me back to the platform. This close to him, I can smell his aftershave. It's fresh, breezy like oceans and beaches. I resist the urge to lean into his shoulder.

"Am I going to get any more detail?" he asks.

"It was Victor. He was trying to get me to help him in exchange for supposedly helping us bring Cecilia down."

Dorian's arm hardens around me.

"I see. So he didn't die when the Door of Fates was sealed?"

"It seems he is still dead, but whatever residual magic Rozalyn was using to enable him to wander Trutinor is fading."

"You going to help him?"

I wriggle out of his arms and drop to the floor, wincing

as my ankles jar. "You're aware Victor is the reason Trey's dead?"

"I'm aware."

"The only help I'll be giving him is a swifter return to Obex."

We amble back onto the platform and find Bo and Kato waiting for us.

"What happened?" Bo says, running to help. She offers me an arm, which I take.

Should I tell her?

"I umm."

"Everything okay?" Kato says.

"It was Victor. He did that thing with his wings and whisked me just outside the station."

Bo's face falls. "What? What do you mean it was Victor? He was here? Why didn't he...?"

Kato's face darkens like thunder and shadows. The lines of his jaw are sharp and flexing. I don't blame him. Victor killed his brother, and I want revenge as much as I imagine Kato does. Fine line though when your brother's murderer is also your Balancer's brother.

"I don't know. In the battle, he scooted through the Door of Fates. I guess because he was already dead and Karva had used the restorative magic he could go through. Cecilia threw me through too, remember. Anyway... he's... he's not doing so great. He's decaying. No matter what happens, he will end up back in Obex. I'm sorry, Bo."

Her face crinkles, her lids fill with water. Kato slides his hand into hers. My chest twitches. His show of affection reminds me Trey is gone.

"But you didn't... What did you do to him?"

"We'll give you a minute," Kato says and gestures for Dorian to follow him.

"Did you hurt him?" Her voice is so small it makes my chest ache.

"I didn't touch him. I might've said a few choice words, but I didn't hurt him."

She chokes out a sob. "I know he's a complete jerk. He's done awful things for Balancesake. But he's also my brother and if he's... if there's a chance he can come back to us... I still want that not just for me, but for Mom and Dad too. I should call The Six."

Her words fuel a war inside me. I want vengeance. He deserves to die for what he did to Trey, and yet, he's somehow still here, still clinging to whatever shred of existence he has and Bo still loves him. My mind wanders back to his words. *All I need is a vial of blood from the Heart of Trutinor.* I should tell her he thinks there's a way.

But I don't.

"Bo, he's not alive. There is no coming back for him, he's a demon. But the magic Rozalyn used to get him here, it's fading."

The words stumble out, half-truths, avoidances. If I tell her, she'll make me give him the vial and I'm not going to do that. Even if he rots before I can kill him, I'm certainly not about to help him.

Her bottom lip wobbles, and it breaks another piece of me.

"Let's make a promise, here and now," she says.

"Sure," I say, knowing how fragile our freshly repaired friendship is.

"No matter what happens, we never hurt each other's families again."

I blink at her.

How can she ask that? Victor killed Trey. Victor is still roaming around Trutinor, half dead, while Trey is dead-

dead in Obex. Can I really promise her that? Can I swear I won't go after him?

"I want your word. I need you to promise," she says, holding my shoulders.

I stare at the floor. How can she make me promise that? Victor is an infection. A worm carving a path of destruction wherever he roams.

"Eden. Please?"

"I... pr—"

"You ready, Eden? Magnus says it's time to go," Kato says.

I glance from Bo to Kato, and she pulls me in for a hug.

"Thank you," she breathes into my ear. "Meet me tomorrow when you're back in the South?"

I nod and give her a limp smile as Kato helps me hobble up the train steps and into the carriage. Dorian follows behind and Bo waves from the platform.

The whole time the only thing that runs through my head is, I never said "I promise."

The train East is faster than normal. Perhaps because I'm so desperate not to say goodbye to yet another person I love, or maybe because Magnus drives differently to Titus. My body still aches in places I can't describe. The only relief comes from the occasional snippets of pain Kato draws away. I get comfortable in the main carriage, but the chairs are hard and the leather cool under my legs, so I give Kato and Dorian my excuses and leave for a private cabin on the top floor of the train.

The stairs take far too long to climb and by the time I collapse on my bed, I'm sweating and feeling sick. The rebel doctors told me the pain would pass, but they couldn't tell me how long it would take. I can't stop thinking about Victor. He's a liar and a bastard. But he could always manipulate me with hope.

"Every Binding is different," Charlie said, as he checked me over one last time before allowing me to leave.

"The strength and complexity of the Bind is only an indicator of how long the post-loss healing might take. As a Fallon, you are far more powerful than a Keeper. Unfortunately for you, the more power you possess, the stronger the Binding. On the upside, as difficult as it is to hear, you weren't Bound for long. That will, at least, decrease the healing time. These Bindings are like weeds. The longer they exist, the more rampant their roots grow."

The creak of stairs breaks me out of my memory.

Kato's head pokes around the door, carrying two glasses. He hands me one.

"I need to tell you something," I say. "Victor said he needs blood from the Heart of Trutinor."

Kato hesitates. The same wash of vengeance and rage flickers across his expression that I feel every time I think about Victor. But then he snorts. "Hilarious. Because we'd totally give him blood that has healing properties. After what he did. The only thing I'll give him is a knife in the back."

"Neither of us are going to do anything. Bo wouldn't forgive us."

Kato takes a deep breath, the muscles in his neck loosening, his face softening. "Let's not talk about that asshole. I came to see if you were okay?"

"Not really." Even less so now. "But I'm bored with saying no. So yes, I'm fine. Just tired. Would you mind...?" I'm not sure when I stopped saying "compel" the pain away.

But neither of us say the word anymore. It's not like we're doing anything wrong. He's helping me survive. Even if it's weird and awkward and strangely intense. How the hell else am I supposed to get through the days?

Kato looks out the window, and after a pause, he nods and perches on the tip of the bed.

"Hand," he says, and I slide my fingers over the duvet and raise them until our palms meet. He loops his fingers between mine. There's a moment of hesitation, and then the watery coolness of relief washes from him into my hand, to my shoulder, and down into my body. My lids lower, a smile passes over my lips. Then I lie back, the rocking motion of the cabin lulling me into sleep.

When I wake, Kato is snoring in a chair over in the corner. His blond locks are messy as usual. I pull a thick blanket off the top of my bed and lay it over as much of his body as I can. I notice his CogTracker is open to a string of messages from Bo. I reach down to close it and stop.

I catch sight of the first message. I don't mean to read their private Cogs, but as I scan the first message, I can't help but read the rest of the screen:

… Look, I've done some research, addiction is common after a Balancer loss. I know you're trying to help. I want to help her too. But we only just made up, and I'm afraid to ruin it. But YOU need to be careful too.

I harden. There's no way I'm addicted. I'm sick, and

broken, and in constant pain. My chest pinches. How could she think I'm addicted? Does she want me to suffer? He's helping me heal quicker. That's what Kato and I agreed. He'd continue to help until the daily pain reduced and was manageable. My eyes skirt back to the message.

She's not addicted… I don't think. She's in a lot of pain. I've got it covered. Don't you trust me?

Of course I do. But someone needs to talk to her. Whether she is or isn't addicted, you're enabling her. You don't need me to tell you how addictive Siren power is. I've read that in situations like this, the Siren can be as addicted as much as the Keeper. You need to protect yourself. You're the only Fallon left in the South. You can't ignore your State…

The rest is cut off. I consider scrolling down to the end, but I don't. My throat is thick and I just want to get out of the room. I grab my own CogTracker and tiptoe as quietly as my aching legs allow down the stairs. I pause and glance back when the wooden steps groan underfoot, but Kato stays asleep. So I escape into the main carriage and head straight to the private bar.

Dorian is at the end of the cabin, his head buried in his CogTracker, typing away. He nods to me as I come in, gives me the visual once-over but must decide I'm fine as he wiggles the tracker at me and mouths, "Just got to make a quick call." He doesn't go far, just into the next carriage. But he stays by the glass door, his eyes on me, or scanning the carriages.

There's a tumbler, and a bottle of something dark purple on the side, which I grab and slide down behind the bar and out of sight. I'm not dealing with him, or the rebels, or Kato and Bo. Just want to drink in silence.

There's a click of the door. Dorian's head pops over the counter. His lips purse flat, but he nods and vanishes again.

I lean against one of the fridge doors and slop some of the liquid into the glass and swallow a huge mouthful. It burns as it goes down and leaves a sparking sensation in my gut. It tastes like cherries and almonds. I let a long, heavy breath out. It's been well over a week since I regained consciousness and I've been praying for a moment alone ever since. But now I am. The isolation is like a thick concrete wall: suffocating, dark and utterly endless. I grip the neck of the bottle harder and bite down on a sob.

There's a twinge in my wrist. I pull my sleeve up. The heart-shaped scar I got in the Siren ceremony with Trey itches and stings. Karva showed Victor my scar and his response was *you were right*. I scratch at it, my fingers brushing over the rumpled edges, wondering what the hell they were talking about. Maybe I should go to the library and research or... My heart hammers to life, beating in my chest. It thuds through my ears. Gallops out of time, and I swear for the briefest moments, I can hear the beat of a second heart: Trey's heart? I let go, shaking my head.

Don't be an idiot, Eden. You're just grieving.

My eyes drift up to the new splodge birthmark tainting my skin. This one the First Fallon gave me when she turned me into a lock for the Door of Fates. A door that allows a single soul to return from Obex and regenerate back to life—the life sacrifice needed to open the door. A life for a life. Nyx for Karva. A door that could bring Trey back, but only if I'm willing to die in his place. I slide my sleeve down and pour more purple stuff in my glass, and take a huge gulp. In seconds, my eyes glaze and my body feels lighter. I pick the bottle back up and examine the label. It's called Mind Numb. I smile. I think I just found my new favorite drink.

There's a pop, and a puff of dark navy smoke plumes over the counter followed by muffled swearing.

"I'm behind the bar, Hermia."

A swath of orange curls appears before she does.

"What's that and why don't I have a glass of it?" she says snatching a tumbler off the counter and plonking herself down next to me.

"I struck lucky. It's good."

She turns, and with pointed precision, raises a single orange eyebrow.

"Stop looking at me like that." I pass her the bottle.

"You sound like me. I'm not a good look for you."

"Not you as well," I moan.

"What's that supposed to mean?" she says and takes a gulp of her drink.

"Just Bo. Things are better. We're talking. But—wait, I need more of that first." I take the bottle back and pour another half a glass. I swallow three large mouthfuls and turn to her.

"I happened to see some messages from Bo to Kato."

"Happened?" Hermia snorts, her second eyebrow rising to meet her first one. "This should be good."

I lower my voice. "He's passed out in the chair upstairs. Before I came down, I put a cover over him and caught sight of his CogTracker. Bo thinks I'm addicted to Siren pain relief."

Hermia glugs what's left of the tumbler and takes the rapidly diminishing bottle of Mind Numb from me.

"Well," she says, pouring herself another glass, "are you?"

I swill my glass, watching the liquid lick up the side. I raise it but pause. "No."

She cocks a frown at me.

I take a sip and when I can't bring myself to look at her, say, "Fine. Maybe. I don't know."

"It's a slippery slope. Trust me."

I reach for the bottle, but she pulls it away.

"And I, for one, will not let you replace Kato's abilities with booze. You're in pain. But at some point you're going to have to choose to do something about it."

"Did you come here just to berate me?"

"No. I came for Titus. And maybe to talk business with Kato. And to see how you are... And... Er... to let you know, the First Fallon made her first public appearance this morning. She did a fake flyby interview with the guy with the teeth." She makes a strange gnashing expression, digging her teeth into her lip. I chuckle but she tuts at me, so I swallow the laugh down.

"Anyway, she was on CogNews. Total bullshit, you understand? Appearances for the sake of Keeper morale."

"Have you seen what she did to me?" I yank my sleeve up, showing her the splodgy birthmark on my arm. A mark identical to the one Nyx had on her cheek. Hermia winces and pours herself another drink.

"Definitely not reopening the Door of Fates to get Trey, then?"

"Not unless I want to die and still be separated from him. I swear to Balance I'm going to kill the First and Last fucking Fallon. Give me that..."

This time, she relents and lets me take the bottle. The Last Fallon—Rozalyn—conspired to open the door by manipulating Victor into kidnapping and killing Nyx, the old lock. But unlucky for Rozalyn, Victor's a double-crossing Judas and made a deal with Cecilia, the First Fallon. Together, Victor and Cecilia sabotaged the plan by bringing Karva—Cecilia's daughter—through the Door of Fates instead. Oh, and replacing Nyx with me as the lock.

"I spoke to Cassian," Hermia says. "Lani fled to Paris. Are you going to tell Kato now that Trey...?"

I try to process her words. Cassian is Bo's oldest brother, the one that her parents had before they were Bound. Lani, though, is Trey and Kato's mom. A woman who was suppos-edly dead until I found her in London. "I don't know. Trey forbid me, but... I guess that doesn't matter now. I just need to find the right moment." We're both silent. We both have reasons for telling Kato. We both have reasons not to. I change the subject.

"Victor came to me," I say.

"So the scrotal sack stayed in Trutinor then?"

"He did. He also told me he could take Cecilia down if I gave him a vial of blood from The Heart."

Hermia stands. Then sits. Stands again and paces behind the bar mumbling something obscene. Then she glugs her Mind Numb, snatches the bottle back and pours another glass.

"You're not going to give it to him, are you?"

"Not if Trey himself rose from the dead and asked me to. Have you found a way of tracking him yet? Because the rebels are also trying to hunt Victor down." I sip my drink.

"Not yet, but no one escapes me for long," she says.

My eyes widen. The train judders beneath me and it dislodges a thought. Hermia is right. No one escapes her for long.

She raises her hand. "No."

"Oh, my god..." I breathe, trying to grasp the enormity of my idea.

"Absolutely not. Don't even think about asking. I won't. I probably can't, anyway."

"Please, Hermia. I'm begging you. I need closure. Kato said they haven't found his body. What if... What if..." I glance up at her. "Either I'm going to do whatever it takes to bring him back, or I need to lay him to rest. You're literally the best tracker I know."

"No."

Oh god, please say yes. I give her my sweetest puppy dog eyes.

She folds her arms and sits down, then tilts her chin at me. "I'm not just the best tracker you know. I'm the best tracker that ever lived."

"Is that a yes?"

She rolls her eyes. Relief washes over me.

She spins the bottle on the spot, her eyes gloss over and relax. "Even if I attempt to track him, no matter how good I am, even I can't bend the laws of Obex. Why do you think I haven't found Bellamy? I highly doubt Obex would let me find Trey. While he's not my Balancer, he was like a very annoying but deeply treasured son. I don't know what the Balance will do about that."

My eyes flit to my wrists, the small heart-shaped scar on one arm and Binding Scar on the other. The shadow of the heartbeat I felt earlier still lingers under my skin.

"But technically he's not a blood relative, and he's not your Balancer... So there's a chance. It might work... Please, Hermia? Can you try?" I breathe. "If there's the slimmest chance we can find his body... I just need to know for sure he's gone."

"Guilt-trip me, why don't you," she grumbles and bats

me away. I smile inwardly. She'll do it because she can't resist a tracking challenge. Standing up, she glares at me, then at the bottle and guzzles the rest of the Mind Numb. She gives me a sharp stare and drops the bottle in the trash.

"Let's just get one thing clear. I'm also the greatest drunk." She staggers as she leans forward, pointing an accusing finger at me. "So get yourself another gimmick."

She heads toward the stairs, punching a few chairs on her way and grumbling, "Fucking Fallons. All the same. Demanding little bas..."

I don't hear the rest of her sentence, but it makes me laugh, anyway.

EIGHT

'The four soul categories are:

Lost Soul—*categorized as demon—A soul that died from Alteritus—the disease of Imbalance in a living Keeper, or failed to be Bound before death.*

Obex Soul—*Obex inhabitant—A soul waiting for its Balancer in order to pass on to the next life.*

Absent Soul—*A soul that has passed into the next life without its Balancer.*

Deceased Soul—*A soul that has been destroyed.'*

The Dictionary of Balance

TREY

The Last Fallon pushes me into the street past the moaning bodies littering the path and onto the main road.

"Careful of the bald demons," she says. "The piece of life still beating inside you is poisonous to them."

"Isn't that a good thing?"

"For you, maybe. But I suspect it might piss them off somewhat. Nobody likes a gourmet meal wafted under their nose if they can't eat it."

"That's a joke, right?"

She just laughs at me. I turn to leave, but she calls me back.

"Don't forget that piece of life won't last forever."

"But I have some time?"

She shrugs. "If you're lucky." She descends the steps, leaving me in the street.

So I walk. A tumultuous cocktail of fears and hope buzz through me, pouring adrenaline into my system. The air is thick with my emotion. It's sweet and sour and edged with a sharpness all rolled into one. I can get back to Eden and still have a life with her. I just have to build an army.

I scan the road. I have no idea where I am or where I should go next. But I do know that if I want to go home, I have to work fast. I need shelter, somewhere to sleep, and an army-building idea. I wander, thinking, turning ideas over but with no clue of where I'm going or how the hell I'm actually going to pull this off. The longer I walk, the more cross I get at myself. A thousand questions I wish I'd asked Rozalyn pop to mind. What if I need resources? How do you kill a demon that's already dead? How do I contact her? I don't know how many questions she'd answer, but I make a promise to myself to be more prepared next time I see her.

Everywhere I walk, it's quiet. I don't understand where all the dead people are. There must be thousands of

Keepers down here waiting for their Balancer to die so they can pass on to the next life, and yet the streets remain silent. The only movement is in the darkness, just out of sight. There have to be people here. But the only creatures I catch glimpses of are demons.

I look up. The constant twilight creates a strange twisting wrongness in my stomach. I cling to that feeling. It reminds me of my goal; that I shouldn't be here, and that I have to build a sodding army.

When I open my eyes, I realize there's no cut in the sky. It's been pieced back together. Another escape route gone. I slouch down against a set of iron railings in front of a house and open the notebook I found in the derelict building. I write. Thoughts, memories, ideas and schemes for building an army, potential negotiation methods for the demons. None of it seems like a workable solution. But getting it on the page helps.

When I'm done, I continue walking, a hardness resolving in my gut: I will build this army and get home to Eden. No matter what it takes. First, I need to find shelter.

After an hour of walking, I stop. It's like I've gone in circles, derelict street after derelict street. Everything is too cracked, too broken to be safe enough to rest in. But I can't wander around Obex aimlessly, trying to find somewhere to stay for much longer. I shift my footing and a cobble wobbles underfoot. I hesitate. Pest just stomped on it, but then he knew where he was going and I haven't got a clue where it will take me. What if I end up on a road full of demons? I suppose I have nothing to lose?

I slam my foot down, and the street responds. It bends and peels away from its position like it's made of flimsy rubber. The cobbles fuzz and blur. I reach down to touch the road, curious to see if it is permeable. But as my fingers meet the cobbles, the road slots back together and it's solid under my touch.

I notice the tall townhouses that followed me for the last few hours have vanished. Instead, I'm in an eclectic street. The buildings are short, stubby, almost. Thatching covers most of the rooftops, though some are made of patchwork tiles. None of them are straight. They lean against each other like drunk men trying to stagger home. I move further down the road and peer into some of the windows. Most of the curtains are open, unlike the other streets. As I strain through the darkness, I realize they're empty: abandoned to the demons and darkness. My fist balls. I slam it against the wall in frustration. Where is everyone? How the hell am I supposed to build an army, be it of dead Keepers and demons, if I can't find a single fucking soul?

I turn my back on the building, but something sizzles through the air, fizzing and snapping at my senses. It's emotion. And a lot of it. I stop and close my eyes, letting my powers reach out and zero in on the sensations. When I'm locked on, I jog through the streets, hunting. Left, right, over a T-junction and into a street overflowing with emotion in the air: at last I've found people. Hanging above the front of a building on the other side of the street is a sign:

The Fallen Fallon

It's a pub. Holy shit, there's a bloody pub down here. I race to the side of the building and place my back against the wall and peer inside the dust-covered window. It's full of people.

Correction: it's full of demons.

For the first time since being trapped here, I smile. If there's one pub, there has to be more. I must be reaching civilization, if you can call demons that. I wipe the dust away with my hand and peer into the gloom. An array of demonic creatures sit in chairs of varying disrepair. Strewn across the floor are glass splinters and filth, and there's a film of grime so thick across the bar I can see it from out here. None of that matters. It's a bar. I know bars and bar culture. I've grown up in them. A bar I can work with. I'll introduce myself, join in the banter, offer to help serve drinks, make myself "one of the locals" and then... well, then I'm not sure, but we'll get to the army. First, I need to make contact with some demons. How hard can it be to make friends with a demon? They were Keepers once, right?

I move to the door and try the handle—it's stiff. As I shunt the door open, it cracks, and a plank falls to the floor, blowing up billows of dust that shower me in a filmy spray of fluff and glass shards.

The pub falls into an awkward silence. Every set of eyes turns to face me. I attempt a smile and wave of my hand. But no one returns the gesture.

Shit. Maybe this is going to be harder than I expected.

I turn around and scan the road. The shadows seem closer, as if they're crawling through the streets and coating the pavement and walls in a dark slime. There's movement in my periphery.

"My mistake," I breathe, and inch my foot out of the pub, my breath rattling in my ears. I force my lips shut to still the rasping.

"I'll leave you all to it." I give a lame wave, pull the door to and edge toward the street. A skittering, like nails clacking against the cobbles, echoes from inside. Gooseflesh shivers down my arms as I pivot into the street and back away as fast as I can. I watch every step, every inch of movement, so I stay quiet. There's a swell in the air. Hot, urgent and undulating like clouds of sticky smoke. It smells like desire and iron. A trickle of sweat beads across my forehead. *This isn't good.*

Behind the bar door, there's a tapping of nails. It grows erratic. Stops. Starts. As if it's darting from spot to spot. Like a bloodhound sniffing. Hunting.

I swallow and peer down the street, assessing how fast I can run. This was a mistake. I should have found a more discreet way to introduce myself. It's too late now. Something pulls the door off the hinges and steps into the street.

It's ash white and deformed; skin mottled with the same purply veins as the bald Lost Soul Demons that Victor brought into Trutinor. The more I stare at it, the more I think it might have been a Lost Soul Demon once. But not now. Now it's something else. None of its limbs are the right shape. Even its head is partially caved in. Its jowl gapes a foot lower than its top lip, much more disconnected than the other demons. Slathers of red coat its lips like paint and every few seconds another line of spittle dribbles to the floor. From its back, dozens of thin spindly arms rise outward. What makes my chest spasm, are the pincer-like claws at the end of each spindle. They click and snap together like whips, promising a laceration to come.

It hobbles forward and then halts in the street. Behind it, the remaining pub-goers spill onto the road. Dozens of demons run, crawl and skitter outside, forming a ring around us. Blocking me and it inside the circle.

Fuck. This is not going to plan.

Its head tilts, something red and wet slips from its mouth and splashes on the Road. Blood. Or maybe tissue. My heart doesn't pound, but I can hear the shadow of a throb in my ears.

"What do we have here, Little Breather?"

It takes a step forward. The click-clack of dozens of its claws reverberates through me. I take a step back; the demons inch closer together, blocking any chance of escape.

I can either stand here and wait for it to eat me or I can try to fight. Either way, I'm not getting out of this circle. So I inch forward to where I was. As my feet fall still, there's a click, click, scrape against the cobbles as it moves toward me. Its pincers dance around the space between us, as if it's testing the air, or me, or god knows what. I can smell the decay peeling off it. The rotten, putrid stench of flesh and iron. I want to throw up, but I steel my stomach.

"What's the problem? I just wanted a drink," I say with a confidence I really don't feel.

"You don't belong here, Breather," the Demon says, his voice is hollow and crackles like a smoker.

"Isn't this where the dead live?"

"You're not dead."

"True, but I'm not alive either."

The demon falters, glancing at another tall spindly demon in the crowd who shrugs at him.

"You should be in the Soul Sanctuary with the other Keepers waiting for their Balancers. Only dead people are allowed in my bar. Unless you're dinner, that is?"

Maybe Rozalyn wasn't joking? There's a snigger around the circle and I figure if he was going to eat me, he'd have charged right out the bar and tried to munch my thigh immediately. I stand taller.

"Come on, man, make an allowance for a weary half-dead guy?"

Its jowls pull up into a ghastly smile.

"I don't like your attitude. But I do like the smell of you. Roasted Keeper anyone?" The crowd cheers and growls.

"I meant no offense. I'm just trying to find somewhere to sleep for the night."

"That ain't my problem."

"I just stumbled upon your bar and it looked like a... umm, reasonable establishment. Give a guy a break?"

The demon's eyes narrow. "Reasonable? This is the finest demon pub in Obex. Who are you calling 'reasonable?' The only way you're getting in that bar is over my ashy carcass or inside my gut."

He turns to the crowd, walking around with his arms up in question. "What say you?" he says. "Shall I eat the Breather?"

A roar explodes from the demon circle. At first, I think it's anger at me for trespassing. But the more I listen, the more I tune in to their strangled cries. They're neither cheering for the demon, nor for me. They're singing a song for blood, for a fight and for death. If they're not even loyal to each other, building an army is going to be impossible.

The demon's smile slides higher, and a shiver crawls down my back.

"I'll tell you what," he says, "prove yourself worthy and you may enter."

"And to be clear, by 'prove' you mean...?"

I blink.

The demon examines me. I hold my nerve. *Wait, Trey. Just wait.* All of its arms rise behind its back. All of them aimed at me like arrows.

There's too many arms and if I miss one, it will tear chunks out of me. I need to put the demon down before it has the chance.

"Fail, and I'll eat you."

Its head twitches left, then right. Then focuses on my

eyes. A long thin tongue, split at the end like a snake and colored white like its skin, slithers out and over its jowls.

It shunts forward, but I'm ready. I lean back and launch a kick straight into the demon's chest. He's light, hollow almost.

His eyes widen as he clatters to the floor, his spindly arms and claws ricocheting off the cobbles. The echo bounces around the street as he skids to the other side of the circle.

He lets out an almighty shriek, then he's up lumbering forward. Click. Clack. Gaining speed.

Ten feet.

Five feet.

Snip. Click.

Three feet.

I drop to the floor and barrel into his legs. It falls and smashes to the ground, but not before three claws catch hold of my back and pinch together. I groan as it slices through flesh and muscle. Warm blood oozes over my skin. The demon screams so loud and so shrill I have to cover my ears. Spittle and blood flick in a thousand directions. But while it shrieks, it's distracted.

I shift and roll out of its grip. But it hauls its body upright and comes after me. Thin arms reaching forward, pulling its skeletal figure closer to me. One of the arms is broken. Hanging down, limp.

It can be injured.

Two arms lunge out and grab at my ankles. As the demon's pincers bite into my calf flesh, my breath bursts from my chest. I crash to the ground, and it clambers on top of me. Blood and blackened saliva speckle my face and cheeks. It takes everything I have not to gag. Its mouth is ashy and necrotic, but empty of teeth.

Instinctively, my hands reach for its jowls. They're slimy and cold, but my fingers find purchase and I yank, hard. A pitchy roar bursts from the demon's throat and five pincers plunge into my chest.

There's a disjointed scream. Mine. I grip as hard as I can and tug, severing the demon's jaw from its face. Then everything is quiet and the demon's limp, twitching body slumps to the floor, dark blood seeping into the street.

I pluck the demon's remaining pincer from my chest and shove its arms off me. It shivers, swells, then explodes in a puff of decaying ash, and the crowd erupts in cheers.

No loyalty, no care. It's going to be impossible to form an army, let alone one loyal to Rozalyn. No wonder she hasn't already built one.

A tall, thin demon steps out of the circle and toward the pile of demon ash.

"Is he? Did I Soul Death him?"

The thin demon snorts, "Don't be ridiculous. The ash is temporary. He'll heal eventually."

"Looks pretty permanent to me."

"I didn't say it would be quick." He shrugs and kicks the pile of ash flat. After some fingering of the remains, he pulls out a set of jangling keys, which he promptly shoves into my chest and cocks his head at the door.

I take the keys, raise an eyebrow and open my mouth to ask a question, but the demon steps through the ash, leaving a footprint. He parts what's left of the circle of demons and vanishes into the bar. The demons left give a mumbled cheer, then peel into the bar behind the thin demon. I stare down at the keys in my hand and smile to myself, wondering if this was some sort of cosmic joke. I never wanted the Fallon life, just me and Eden and a bar full of customers. Now I have a bar and no Eden, and a monumental task ahead of me. What if I can't do this alone?

My Siren senses bristle. I can smell something rich, like longing mixed with a strangled sweetness. It tastes like stale sugar and sour berries, like love and anger.

"Guess that makes you the new landlord," a girl's voice says.

I recognize that voice. My blood runs cold.

"Eve?"

"Hello, stranger."

BREAKING NEWS

"Good afternoon, Trutinor. This is Tarkin Tavas reporting live from the East-North border, just outside Terra City. There are increasing reports of skirmishes, battles and growing political tensions between the East and North state councils. Both Fallon East and Fallon Israel Dark have refused to comment other than…"

Tarkin pulls out a piece of paper and reads from it.

"To claim they're both committed to upholding the treaty set in place shortly after Lionel and Eleanor, sadly, passed. When pushed for comment regarding the Houses of the North and whether they were initiating a civil war, CogNews was escorted from the Dark's premises."

Tarkin throws a glance over his shoulder.

"But as you can see, there are clearly

Shifter-Elemental battles happening as we speak. The Trutinor Council is yet to meet on the topic, but it's safe to say political tensions will be high. One can only imagine how distressing this must be for the First Fallon and what regulations or laws might need putting in place to bring this civil war under control and return Trutinor to Balance. W—"

There's an explosion behind Tarkin. The camera shudders, static rolls across the screen. Tarkin ducks. His eyes, big as the moon, glance back at the cameraman. There's a crack of lightning. A fireball burns dangerously close to where they're standing.

The camera cuts out.

NINE

'The line of Fallon heirs must descend from the First and Last Fallons.'

Sixth Law—*The Book of Balance*

EDEN

I must have fallen asleep because when I wake, Kato's CogTracker is blaring out a news report from Tarkin Tavas. The two of them are standing staring out of the train window.

"What's going on?" I ask.

Dorian glances at Kato. "News report said there were skirmishes outside Terra City. We're umm... passing through it now..."

I frown, then haul myself upright and out of the chair, trying not to moan as my muscles rebel against me. A gasp escapes as I clasp my hands to my mouth.

The city is on fire.

As the train rattles over the city's high tracks, the view below is devastating. Buildings are on fire, thick columns of smoke billow into the sky, orange licks the horizon like sunset, only it's lunchtime, but ash shrouds the sun. I can just make out swarms of ant-sized Keepers on the ground. Some are running, while others are massed in giant groups and crowds. But what makes my skin rise in a fleshy coat of goosebumps are the occasional ant forms that are motionless in the streets.

"I've alerted Bo. She's taking The Six and some of the army to stop the fighting. The East State Council has sent an enormous group of fire and water Elementals to prevent any more of the city burning."

"How did it happen?" I ask.

"Imbalance. It's leaking out from Obex and causing chaos."

We all fall into silence. Kato picks his CogTracker up and turns it off before sitting in an armchair. Dorian tugs me away from the window. "Don't watch," he says before sitting opposite Kato. "Castor thinks Cecilia is actually fueling some of this."

I frown. "But why? She's all about Balance. That doesn't make any sense."

"Doesn't it?" Kato says, picking up a sandwich from the table between us. I join him, suddenly starving, and eat one of the chicken ones left on the platter.

"Think about it," he says around his mouthful of sandwich. "What she wants more than anything is control, right? So one way to convince everyone that we need more control is to let chaos reign. Then she can swoop in with her restrictions and laws and masquerade as the good guy as she instills regimented controls on us." He takes another bite and mumbles around the bread. "It's frankly kind of genius."

Dorian picks up his CogTracker. "While you were sleeping, I read a report from Castor. He believes the prophesied war is coming. A rebel task force has been tracking Imbalances and found thinning patches of the fabric between Trutinor and Obex. Rozalyn's failed attempt to return using the Door of Fates has only further fueled her desire for war. If we don't open the barrier, I swear Rozalyn will tear it down with her bare hands. And before too long, the veil will be thin enough she can. We have to be ahead of this or a lot of people are going to die. We need to capitalize on the prophecy's power."

I snort. "There is no prophecy. Not anymore. Not without Trey."

Kato stares out the window. I join him, unwilling to talk about the fucking prophecy any longer. The scenery is changing from the densely packed skyscrapers of Terra city to the sand dunes of the East's deserts. Miles and miles of undulating yellow. On the horizon, I spot a dark speck— Element City—the capital of The East State. The major cities in the East were designed for Keepers of different Elements. Terra, Caelum, Ignis and Oxonia: Earth, Air, Fire and Water respectively. But Element City is different, home to all the elementals. It's a menagerie of people, families and power. I stand up and slide open the train window a notch and inhale the dry desert air. It's dusty and choking, and still coated in a lashing of smoke. But under the ash, the air smells like warm skin and sand; like home. I close the window and sit down, flipping open my CogTracker.

When I was in the coma, Kato programmed my Cog to divert most of my mail into a set of folders so I could go through them when I was stronger. The number on the "condolences" folder makes my brain weep. I can't deal with them yet. There are literally thousands of messages. I ignore them and go to my main inbox. There's a few from Arden. One from Israel, one from anonymous, and another from Professor Astra.

From:anonymous@FallonCogMail.com
Subject: Blood
To: Eden.East@FallonCogMail.com

I need the blood.
I swear Karva will help.
Meet me in Siren city at the back of Trey's bar and I'll prove it.

My jaw tightens. I want to watch him rot in the fear and knowledge that Rozalyn's wrath will devour his soul. He isn't getting shit from me.

I flick back to the emails and scroll to Astra's.

From: Professor.Astra@strateraacademy.com
Subject: Academy Attendance
To: Eden.East@FallonCogMail.com

Dear Eden,

I won't profess to tell you how to feel at this deeply sad time. But I do want to express my sincerest apologies at the loss of both your Balancer and our Siren leader. There has been too much loss of late, and I fear we may not have seen the last of it.

I appreciate that Trey's death will still be raw at this time, which is why I don't expect you to decide right now. The

Academy will welcome you back when you're ready. That said, as a Fallon, there will undoubtably be additional pressure from the Council to return to the Academy as soon as possible. While I don't wish to add to that pressure, I think it's necessary to explain that the pace of Stratera is significantly different to Keepers school. I'd like to propose that you skip the rest of this year and return in September for the new academic year.

In order to ensure a smooth transition back into Academy life, I have spoken with the Board of Examiners. They have agreed that all work completed already can, if you wish, be used next year, to save you from redoing similar assignments. Last, we are removing the Door of Fates from the main foyer, and in fact, from the campus entirely. It will be stored at an undisclosed location.

I want you to know we, both myself and the entire academic staff at Stratera, are here for you.

Yours in deepest sympathy,

Professor Astra

I falter, unsure of how I feel. Do I want to go back to Stratera this term? If I was strong enough to study, it would be a welcome distraction. But then I'd have to live in the apartment Trey and I shared with Bo and Kato.

My fingers hover over the keypad. I reply, a brief message, stating I'd like the option to return this academic year to be left open and thank her for her kind words.

I skim through a selection of other emails. One from Israel and Maddison—Victor's parents—offering their condolences. There's a few from Stratera classmates, three from Sheridan, with a ton of attachments and what looks like dream research. But before I can go through them, the train slows and pulls into my home tower's underground station.

"I'll escort you to the corridor, but wait outside while you go in and while the dome is over you. If you can wait for me on the platform, I'll be right there. I just need to pack some bits, as I guess we'll be a couple of hours. I take it you can keep her safe for two minutes?"

Kato raises an eyebrow at Dorian. His jaw flexes and then relaxes. "Obviously."

I don't need the chair anymore, but movement is still hard. Kato offers his arm. I glance down, his Binding Scar is poking out of his sleeve. My eyes skirt to my arm and the streaks of maroon and violet essence: pieces of Trey, of us, and our memories. All of them torn away. The scar is bitter-sweet. It's a reminder of what I had, what I'll have in my next lifetime. But also what I've lost. How can something so precious be so painful?

Kato must sense me looking. He glances at his arm and pulls his sleeve down. But I push it back up, my fingers brushing over the striations of his and Bo's Binding Scar. When you're Bound, it's for eternity—your scar for life. Even if your Balancer dies, you're still Bound. Balancers wait for you in Obex until you can both move on. I bite my bottom lip. *I'm still Bound. She can't destroy a Binding.* But even as I think about it, the emptiness in my mind closes in. The isolation. The gaping hole in my soul that no amount of healing is filling. I scream silently. But nothing comes back. Not even an echo.

"Let's go," Kato says. "Dorian will catch up."

Most people would ask me if I was ready, and I'd say no so I could put off watching the last trace of family I have die. But Kato doesn't ask if I'm ready because he's lost as much as I have and he knows I never will be.

Looping his hand around mine, he tugs with just enough force I have to follow. He guides me up the underground station's stone steps, retracing the same path Trey and I took a few weeks ago. Everywhere I go, I see Trey, in the stone and brickwork, in the paintings and smells. If memories are all I have of him, I pray they stay fresh forever.

Kato puts his hand on the door to my tower, but in the corner of my eye, there's a poof of blue smoke. *Hermia?*

Only it's not Hermia.

It's the First Fallon.

My back goes rigid, Kato's stiff under my arm. Dorian rushes to join us.

Her face is placid, the serene white of fresh snowfall and void of any emotion. The vault thunders. I dig my nails into Kato's arm. What I want to do is slash out her eyes and tear pieces of her apart until her soul is left tattered and shredded. But in my state, I'm barely able to walk unassisted and attacking the most powerful Fallon alive is a recipe for death.

"Fallon East, Luchelli," the First Fallon says, nodding at each of us.

"What do you want?" I sneer.

"Merely to offer my condolences. First your parents." She examines her nails, flips her hand over, but doesn't look at me. "Then Trey, and now Mr. Kilburn. Such a significant loss to Trutinor etc etc and whatever else one is supposed to say."

I wrench around, take a step. But Kato's hand is on my shoulder, moving me behind him.

"You're not welcome here, leave."

She purses her lips into a paper-thin line. "Dear boy, I'm welcome everywhere."

I push forward, step into her personal space. "You think we don't know what you did? I know you manipulated Victor into killing him. You won't win."

This makes her laugh. It's a huffy sort of laugh. She leans in, staring down her straight, milk-white nose. "And what could possibly give you the idea that I haven't won already? Where's your soul mate, Eden?" Her eyes darken. "Too bad about your prophecy. I hear they don't work when one half is dead."

The vault cracks, splinters, threads of temptation, darkness, raw untapped power flow into my veins. I grab her throat. Despite how hard I'm gripping, she doesn't even flinch. Her head tilts, her lip curls. She grips my wrist, squeezing and turning until I have no choice but to release her or let my bone snap.

I glance at Kato, who's frozen, one arm extended out as if to grab me. Cecilia's other hand is clenched—she's controlling him.

"You forget about that little prophecy nonsense. It's over now. Do you understand? You're going to step in line and under my law."

"Or what? You've already taken everything that means anything to me."

"Oh, really?" Her clenched fingers flex. Kato sucks in a breath, a soft whimper escaping his lips. "I think there's always something else that can be taken." She smiles a thin, twisted smile as she stares down at me. The door to the tower opens, and she snaps out of it and releases Kato. The Keeper who enters gasps, bows and fawns over The First Fallon.

"Yes, well, I just came to give you my condolences. I am truly sorry for your loss, Fallon East."

She erupts in a puff of navy smoke and vanishes. The Keeper bustles and flusters away through the foyer door, but I'm not listening. Neither is Kato. We're staring at each other, our expressions equally dark.

"I'll fucking kill her," he barks and then paces up and down the underground station.

"How fucking dare she. She's a joke. A fucking plague. She killed him."

He's babbling. His face growing redder. He stops suddenly, both hands on the platform wall. He screams into the wall and throws a punch at the concrete.

"THAT IS ENOUGH. Jesus, Kato, what the hell has gotten into you?"

I touch his shoulder, and he slumps, as if all the fight and energy has drained out of him.

"I... I don't. I'm sorry, I don't know what that was. I'm fine now."

"What were we supposed to do? It's not like we could wage war on her in an underground station. She's testing us."

"You really think that's all she wanted?"

I nod. "She wanted to see me and see the damage she'd done. It's pathetic."

Dorian's head appears at the train door. "What's going on? Did I hear shouting?"

I shake my head at Dorian. "It's..."

I consider telling him about Cecilia, but I don't want any additional security or fuss. So I tell a white lie. "It's fine. Kato is all cool now, right?"

I scan Kato up and down, as if that might give me clues. It doesn't. But he seems fine, so the three of us enter the foyer. On the other side is a memorial. An enormous banner hangs from the ceiling. It looks like the banner's made of the same elemental magic as the ones that hung behind my parents' Dusting ceremony stage. Except instead of all the elements, this banner is made of sand: the earth element. The sand falls in one long waterfall-like motion until it hits the checkered tile flooring and cycles back up to the top. I focus on the banner, and my breath catches. Nyx's and Titus's faces ripple in and out of focus; moving sand sculptures. They're smiling and laughing at each other. Almost as if it were a film projected into the sand. When Nyx leans in and kisses Titus, my throat locks. I tear myself away before I crumple in the foyer.

"Lift?" I say to both of them.

Kato nods and guides me through the foyer and into the lift. When we reach Titus's floor and the lift door pings open, my eyes trace the ceiling. The floor above—the penthouse—is home.

"Is this the floor?" Dorian says.

"Yeah," I breathe.

"I'll keep guard out here. Kato, please ensure you sweep the room on entrance."

Kato nods at Dorian, and we walk up the hall. We draw to a halt halfway to Titus's door.

"I can do this bit if you could..." I say, squeezing Kato's hand.

"I... We need to be careful. I shouldn't keep..."

"Today is not the day to take away my primary source of pain relief," I growl. But hearing myself say those words makes my stomach lurch. I don't sound like me. Is Bo right? Am I addicted? What other choice do I have? Dorian's eyes bore into me from the other end of the corridor. He can keep his judgmental opinions. I need this.

Kato's brows knit together. Though the blue of his eyes softens, his lips pinch, he's going to protest.

He doesn't in the end. Instead, he raises his hand. His forearm undulates and throbs as everything I feel feeds into his veins like a current. The cold pull of his compulsion makes my eyes roll shut as the aches and stabs plaguing my muscles and heart siphon away in one long silky ribbon from me to him.

Kato does exactly what Trey did: keep my pain. But Trey used to keep pieces of me like they were priceless treasures. This isn't the same. Kato stores the ribbons like he's a locker. It's so transactional, so cheap. Every time he takes a piece of me, I feel dirty. He's told me a thousand times that when I'm ready, he will open the door and give it back piece by piece. His words replay in my head: "You can't heal if you can't feel."

His eyes flash violet as my emotion surges between us. It makes his mouth drop, and I wonder if it's as awkward for him as it is for me. A twist of guilt loops through my chest, but it's as fleeting as the rest of the emotions being drained out of me. The grip between our hands tightens as power surges. It's glorious. Pure. An unadulterated relief mingling with power and magic and... a sigh of relief escapes.

Ribbons of emotion burst from me. Violent threads of black, lilac and sparking lightning. All of them hissing and spinning as they attach themselves to the growing ball Kato's creating.

When it's over, we're left standing in front of each other. Lines of sweat coat our foreheads. Our lips parted, every inch of me feels as filthy as it does relieved, a strange concoction of bliss and shame. The silence is thick, palpable. He still grasps my hand, but his shoulders and jaw are loose, his eyes ablaze, and I know he's struggling with his own uncomfortable mix of emotions. At the other end of the corridor, Dorian coughs, but I ignore him.

I shake Kato off. Nausea rolls around my stomach. Bo was right. I shouldn't be asking him to help me. But then, I'm standing straighter, my body is lighter, everything, however brief the relief, feels better. Kato can't, or maybe won't, look at me.

Why are unspoken words so loud?

"Thank—" I start.

"Don't," he says, and walks toward Titus's door.

I try to keep up, but after a couple of paces, it's obvious I can't, so I stop trying. After a few more paces, he slows and stays by my side, eventually offering me his arm for support. Which I take, even though there's nothing wrong with my legs; it's my heart that's in pieces.

We reach Titus and Nyx's door, my eyes already cloudy with tears. I can barely speak, let alone breathe. My fingers trace the gold brass numbers.

Then my hand slides to the door handle and unlocks the door.

"They brought him here last night," Kato says as we enter the living room. Teacups litter the kitchen cutout hatch in the corner of the room. There's a pungent mold smell and under it, something sour.

Photo frames that hurt to look at, sit on the side table.

"Arden didn't tell you. But Titus has a nasty cut above his eye. It won't heal because he's... Well, anyway. When Arden found him, he was convulsing and fitting. He hit his head on the prison bed. They still don't know why he was fitting, possibly because of whatever happened to Nyx."

"What happened? She exploded."

Kato flinches. "She could still be in Obex."

"She fucking exploded, Kato. She's not in Obex. Cecilia

killed her the minute she made the fucking lock. She's gone. And now we have to send Titus to Obex, where he's going to be trapped forever because he doesn't have a goddamn Balancer."

I'm shouting, my shoulders heave. When I glance at Kato, his muscles are flexing, his eyes focused on my hands.

I glance down. My fists are balled and on fire. I shake the flames away. He grips my face in his hands.

"Listen, princess. You're going to have to suck your shit up and get a grip. Yes, you've gone through the worst thing that can happen to a Keeper. You've lost everything—almost everything," he corrects. "But what are you going to do? Poison those of us that are left and give up? Let Cecilia win? Are you really going to let Victor get away with killing Trey?" His voice hardens. He spits Victor's name and I wonder which one of us hates him more.

There's a long silent pause. Both of us giving each other a hard stare.

"You said yourself, there was no body... What if he didn't? What if Trey is still..."

"Eden..." Kato pauses and I plead silently for him not to say the words I hate. But they don't come. Instead, he looks away. His thumb rubs the top of my hand and he says, "Don't give me hope, darling. It's cruel."

My eyes sting, my tears are sharp and bathed in the acidic reality of the truth. "Okay," I whisper. "Okay."

He wraps his arms around my back, squeezing tight. When he pulls back, he leans his forehead against mine. I shut my eyes and remember the way Trey used to do the same. Is it hereditary? Or just another Siren quirk? For the briefest moment, I let myself pretend he's Trey. I want him to be Trey, but he smells different. Kato is sweeter, like spring buds and clean mountains. I guess the mountains must have rubbed off from Bo. Trey smelled deeper, like heady summer evenings and the comfort of home. Then Kato speaks and what scant illusion of Trey I had, shatters.

"He needs to die."

I open my eyes and frown. "Who?"

"Victor." Kato's face is hard, drawn deep with lines.

"I hate to be pedantic, but Victor's already dead... he's a demon or, I don't know what he is, but he's not alive."

"That's not what I mean."

His blue eyes smolder with a ferocity that makes me recoil. Kato is never serious, never angry. Not like this, anyway.

I lower my voice, and check behind us to make sure Hermia and Magnus aren't about to walk in. "You want to Soul Death him?" I whisper.

"Don't you?"

I stand back. "I... I..." I stammer because I hadn't even considered it because Victor's already dead. How do you kill the dead? Besides that, no one's committed a Soul Death in centuries. I'm not even sure I could name a case. The First Fallon outlawed it centuries ago. And what about Bo? Didn't I just promise her I wouldn't hurt him? Or... I almost promised.

"He can't just go back. Obex is too good for him, and more to the point, Soul Death is permanent. There's no coming back. He would simply cease to exist." Kato's words are ice cold.

I stiffen. Thoughts roll around my head until my eyes harden, and a slow steady smile spreads across my lips. *Victor would cease to exist.*

I meet Kato's gaze, my shoulders sag. "Yes, I want to. But I won't. And neither will you. We can't. Victor has wronged us. But Bo didn't. Do you really want to do that to her? After how mad she was at you when you took her blood?"

He hesitates.

"I want Victor dead as much as you. But killing him will only damage those of us left here. Don't you see? It was never Victor. Yes, he's done some awful shit, but he's just a puppet. It was never him…"

A tear rolls down Kato's cheek. I brush my thumb over it and wipe it away.

"Cecilia?" he asks.

"Cecilia." I grip his shoulders. I need him to understand how serious I am. "Why do you think Cecilia came to the underground station? To rub it in our faces. Promise me, Kato. Promise me you won't go down this path. It's not you. I think these dark thoughts are stemming from me and the pain you're holding for me. And if anyone deserves that, it's Cecilia."

He rubs his face, and as his hands come away, the lines in his skin are smoother, his jaw softer, more Kato.

"You're right. I'm just—"

"Angry? Yeah. Me too. But this isn't the way. It would cause too much damage. She would never forgive us."

I take his arm and pull him toward Titus and Nyx's bedroom door.

***

Hermia, Magnus, Kato and I stand huddled in Titus's bedroom. Hermia and Magnus clink glasses and take a sip of whiskey. Both of them have wet eyes and tight expressions. Everything about this is wrong. Titus shouldn't be dying. He doesn't deserve it.

"It's okay to let it out," I say to Hermia as she clears her throat for the third time in as many seconds.

"Don't know what you're talking about. The whiskey burns," she growls.

I want to point out that there's no way a hardened alcoholic—who can drink any man, beast or creature under the table—struggles with a twelve-year-old single malt. But I remind myself we all deal with goodbyes differently; no one likes them. I close my mouth and let her grieve in peace.

She dips her finger in her tumbler. "I made sure it was your favorite." Her voice cracks and she falls silent, sweeping a whiskey-covered finger over Titus's lips. Then she squeezes his hand. "Couldn't let you go off without one for the road. See you in the next life."

There's a shuffle in the room as the air thickens. Unless Nyx's soul somehow survived exploding into light, Titus won't be able to move on to the next life. We might see him as we pass through Obex and on to our next lives, but he'll be stuck there. Alone. For all eternity.

Hermia turns to us, scowling, "He's coming back. He's a good man and doesn't deserve this. Neither of them did."

I want to shout at her. Scream that we're supposed to stop bad things from happening to good people. But we failed.

I failed.

And now there's nothing any of us can do about it. But I don't say any of those things because there's an iron lump in my throat. Instead, I wonder who says we can't change our fate? The First Fallon? Well, fuck her and her sister. I'm done letting everyone I love die.

"He's coming back," Hermia says, angrier this time.

She downs the rest of her whiskey, slams her tumbler

onto the table, and pushes past me. As she walks out of the room, she vanishes in a puff of navy smoke.

I turn to Magnus. His giant figure towers above me. But there's something small about him in this room. Sadness has dulled his skin, his navy Steampunk uniform out of place. A button loose, a crease here and there, his cheeks streaked wet. He steps forward, slipping a CogKey into each of Titus's hands. It's an ancient Steampunk Ritual. Ritual portal keys to the next life. As Magnus leaves the room, he shakes his head and gives my shoulder a soft squeeze. Last year Magnus would never have spoken to me, let alone given me a comforting squeeze.

There's only Kato and me left, so I take a deep, unsteady breath and walk toward Titus's bed. His blond dreads are lank; tufts of hair unwound and loose. I scan his room looking for a pot of dreadlock oil to twist the strands back in. But I find nothing. Tears spring into my eyes.

"I don't want him going to Obex with his hair a mess," I mumble, more to myself than Kato. I march around the room lifting piles of papers, knocking clothes off chests of drawers, upturning books, searching until Kato touches my arm.

"Stop," he says. "It won't bring him back."

I knock his arm off, heat rushing into my fingers. "Don't you think I get that?" I say, breathing heavy. There's a flash of fire-yellow. I glance down. My fingers are flaming up.

Kato reaches out, clasps me around the back, and pulls me into an embrace. Where his hand touches my shoulder, a cool sensation that tastes like cream and snow slides down my neck and into my chest. I lean into his arms and rest my head on his shoulders. Tears fall in giant rolls and blobs and pool on his t-shirt. He takes away just enough of the sting of anger for the fire in my chest to extinguish. But it leaves a shadow in my ribs, the pressure of a hurt that will ache itself into another painful memory.

I squeeze my eyes shut, hating myself before I utter the words. But there's been too much. I've gone through too much. I just want the pain to stop.

"Take it away," I breathe into his neck. "Can't you just take it all away forever?"

He pulls back and gives me a hard look. A thousand things pass between us. We both see the path this is leading us down, but neither of us can say it.

"It's getting hard for me, too. It's not just you falling down this rabbit hole. I'm harboring pieces of you, like you said, all these dark thoughts about Victor. They're not mine. No matter how disconnected I am from the pain you're giving me, I still feel things. Using my magic like this. It's... It's..."

"Addictive?" The word hangs between us, almost as if I could reach out and touch it. Both of us are silent for a while. Then, before I lose courage, I plead.

"Please help me through this, Kato. It can be the last time, I swear. I just need the hurt to stop. I can't say goodbye while I'm in agony. I won't ask again, I promise."

He hesitates, his forehead furrowing. But it's the pained expression in his eyes that makes my chest crack open. I don't want Bo to be right.

"The last time?"

"The last time," I say, the words spilling from my mouth. They sound like a promise but taste like a lie. What I've got to do, what I *need* to do—I used to think pain grounded us. That it told us we were alive, and reminded us to keep living and breathing and fighting. I was wrong. Hurt and pain are distractions. If I want to end Cecilia for good, I need to stay focused.

Again, Kato touches his forehead to mine, our eyes close, hands clasp each other. When it's over, the veins in both our arms throb. Our eyes blaze with hunger; not for each other, but for the pull of power and pain and the strange pleasure it brings.

"Last. Time," he pants. But his words are so hard they're brittle—brittle little things break. Underneath, he's weaving himself the same lies I am. I'm spiraling down a dark tunnel and I've dragged him with me. I should feel guilty. But I guess he's taken that emotion too because I am swimming in the calming clarity of relief.

I turn to Titus. His body is still, save for the shallow rise and fall of his ribs. But even those movements are slowing with every haggard breath he draws. His pot belly has sunk as if his body is struggling to hold up the weight of it. He won't wake. He's too far gone now. I link my fingers through his, gripping his limp hand: an apology of sorts. This is one more in a long line of goodbyes I'll never get to have. One more in a longer line of deaths that are my fault.

I open my CogTracker, rereading the spell Arden sent. Images and memories from my parents' Dusting flash through my head. Arden said Titus's Dusting wouldn't be like theirs. Keepers don't have anywhere near the power of a Fallon. His Dust will create a dome over the flat we're in, cocooning us with his dissolving body for an hour at most. He will turn to Dust and his essence will move on to Obex —and I pray to Balance—for another life. Titus will leave, like everyone else I love. I'll be left here, with nothing but the frigid chill of loneliness and fading memories for comfort.

"It's time," Kato says, pulling me out of my thoughts.

My breath shudders out as I take a pinch of Dust. Then I whisper the spell Arden gave me.

O' the Balance, O' the Balance
It shall end as it began
Dust is to death as breath is to birth
From this life to the next
O' the Balance, O' the Balance

Kato stands beside me, and when my words stumble over my tears, he whispers them for me.

Arden was right, Titus's Dusting is slower than my parents'. But it happens the same way. First, his hair dissolves, like the sprinkling of sand through a timer. His dreadlocks rupture into a million tiny particles. They hover and swirl in the air. His Dust ball is green, my parents' was lilac. Before he was a Steampunk Transporter, he was a Sorcerer. A good one too, so my father told me.

Inch by inch, Titus dissolves into Dust and essence. It shimmers as it crawls down his face and neck, making him fade to atoms and air. The ball grows thicker and darker. Then, the swollen mass erupts and showers the flat in an arching dome of green.

Kato and I move to the living room, and for a while, we sit in silence as Titus's essence falls from the ceiling and evaporates into the next life. A wandering Dust particle touches my cheek. I tense—when this happened at my parents' Dusting, I had a surge of power course through my body, and I tried to suffocate Victor—I wish I'd succeeded.

I brace for the impact of power, but it doesn't come. Instead, a blanket of white envelops my vision and then a watery version of my parents' train appears.

I watch as a tiny, toddling me wobbles toward the engine cabin door. At a guess I'm two or three years old. I don't even remember this.

I push open the door and totter in. Titus is slimmer, his

dreads shorter, his face less wrinkled. He doesn't notice me at first. But as I reach for the coal furnace, he bends down and grabs me. "Ooh, you don't want to touch that poppet. You'll burn yourself."

He swings me around and I giggle, bouncing a tiny ember on my hand in protest.

"Look out at the view instead."

I babble for a while, pointing at things and saying, "What dat? What dat?" And each time he tells me the name of a button or lever or other train part. Eventually, my mother sticks her head in the cabin and says, "I hope she's not making trouble."

"Never. She was keeping me company."

The memory fades and is replaced with our home tower rooftop. It's nighttime, the desert is cold. My mother, father, Nyx and I are all huddled under a mountain of duvets and covers. We're stargazing. Tears prickle my lids because this memory I do remember. Titus and Nyx are teaching me about the stars, which ones we share with Earth and which ones we can only see in Trutinor. My seven-year-old self gets frustrated and throws a tiny ball of fire into the air. I smile to myself. I didn't understand how Titus just "knew" which one was the North Star.

"Patience, Eden," Titus says. He draws out his wand, waves it through the air, making a lasso in the sky. He pretends to reel in a star and at first, I think he's joking. But then I gasp and clamber out of the duvets as a giant star hovers above the rooftop. A light illusion, of course, but I didn't understand that then. He lassoed more than two dozen stars that night, making them twinkle and form different constellations. I ran around the rooftop, dancing and squealing under the sparkling night sky. And Titus laughed so hard his belly wriggled up and down.

The memories trickle in for another half an hour. Some make me laugh, others make me weep. All of them, despite the tears streaking my cheeks, are happy. I think that's what hurts the most. When the last memory is over and Titus's face fades from my vision, I'm left numb. Impenetrable. The only thing still inside me is a stony thirst for vengeance. Justice for Titus and Nyx, and cold, hard revenge for Trey.

My eyes meet Kato's; written between the silence of our gaze is a thirst for vengeance neither of us can seek. Cecilia needs to die. Victor needs to die. And we need to tear a hole in our world to do it.

TEN

'It is the cruelest twist of fate that the Balance doesn't allow a Keeper to search and find their Balancers in Obex once they pass. But life is nothing if not fleeting. This brief pain—to live a life alone—is the greatest sacrifice a Balancer can make to ensure they're reunited with their one true soul mate in all the many lifetimes to come.'

Excerpt—Balancer, Loss and Eternal Lifetimes, An Essay by Professor Cuthberg

---

TREY

Eve's face explodes into a grin. Her arms wrap around me. She squeezes so tight I swear it's going to split my neck wound open. Then, just as suddenly, she pulls back. Her face dark. I used to dread her fury; it still burns cold in her eyes.

She slaps me so hard across the cheek I stagger back as the sting penetrates right through to my teeth.

"You bastard. You removed her pain, and she tore my throat out."

I run my hand through my hair, trying to replay the battle she died in.

"Bo?"

"Yes, fucking Bo. If you hadn't stopped her leg from hurting, she wouldn't have been able to attack me."

"Eve, you tore Bo's leg off. She's my brother's Balancer. What was I supposed to do, let her bleed out?"

She's shouting and we're still in a street where the shadows crawl and creatures far worse than a bar full of demons linger. I glance around, my skin itching with the hunger and desire emanating from whatever creatures linger in the corners.

"Yes, and you are my Balancer," she snaps.

"Was."

Her face falls, her eyes skirt to her empty arm. Our Binding Scar vanished the moment Victor died, and I was Bound to Eden. Without a Balancer, she's trapped in Obex forever.

"We were never meant to be," I say, reaching out to her.

She steps back. "Fuck you. We made a great team."

"Team? Is that why you turned and fought for Victor? Come on, Eve. What did you really think would happen?"

She pouts at me. The cloying pull of starving creatures sticks in my throat. Their desire and impatience is sharp, ravenous and tangy.

"Can we move inside?" I say, scanning the street.

"You talk about betrayal like you're sweetness and

halos. You were Bound to me and trying to fuck that desert rat the whole time."

"Her name is E—"

"No. Don't come here pretending like there's no water under the bridge. I might've fucked up, but you weren't exactly good to me."

"And who started this?" I'm shouting now. This is a totally ridiculous argument. We're both to blame for what happened. "What did you do? Take a bribe from the First Fallon? Did she offer you a life of Balance and power and petty celebrity parties in exchange for ruining my life and my Binding?"

"FUCK YOU, TREY. She said I'd be with you forever. That our Binding would be permanent."

"Yeah, well, she fucking lied."

She looks away, her lips pursed, but she doesn't respond. She's gone past angry. Peels of ice are rolling off her and smack at my essence. It's like bitter snowflakes.

"God. Eve. I'm sorry, okay? I don't want to argue with you."

Her lips smoosh into a pout, so I reach out and pull her into my arms. She's rigid at first, then she softens and eventually she wraps her arms around me.

"Why are you here, anyway?" She mumbles into my shoulder.

"I died."

"You didn't die. I can smell the life on you." She pulls back to examine my face.

"Victor stabbed me in the neck when he opened the Door of Fates. Technically, I'm half dead." I point at my scar.

"How can anyone be half dead?"

"Accidental perk of a Siren ceremony. So I'm half dead,

half alive. Just enough life to heal wounds, not enough to get back to Trutinor." I tilt my neck and she prods my scar.

"Cute. We have matching scars. Almost like being..." her voice trails off.

"Being Bound again?"

She gives me a weak smile and then shifts on the spot. The air changes, fizzles, and relaxes. Her anger seeps out into the twilight sky, leaving sweetness and fluff tickling my senses.

"Just so we're clear," she starts. "You're an asshole of the highest order, and I haven't forgiven you. But... It's been a while since I saw a friendly face. Do you want to get a drink in your new pub?"

"My pub?" I say, staring at the keys in my hand.

"Well, you ashed the old landlord and were handed the keys. So yeah, I think that makes it yours. Unless you want to leave a bunch of anger-driven demons drinkless?"

I glance from the keys to her.

Something is off.

This is all too easy. First, I'm picked up by Rozalyn demanding an army. And just when I was giving up hope of finding a place to stay, I find the perfect location for me—a bar—and then my ex appears.

I hesitate, try to think through my options... I got nothing but silence. I want to get back to Eden more than anything, and the only way to return is to build Rozalyn a damn army. Perhaps the pub is Rozalyn's work—a helping hand? She did say she'd help. Whatever the reason, I figure I don't have any other options. Besides, staying out in the open overnight seems like a terrible idea.

We enter and a small inward smile flutters between my ribs. Owning a club is what I'm good at. The only question now is how I use it to create an army.

Eve walks to the bar and pulls out two stools.

"Seat?" she says, giving me one and sitting in the other.
"Two please."

A short demon with gray skin and cropped hair—that oddly reminds me of Felicia—comes out from a door behind the bar.

She hands us each a drink and grunts. Not like Felicia then.

"Er, thanks," I say and hold out my hand to shake hers. "I'm Trey." I hold up the bar keys. She raises a bald eyebrow and then bends down to lick my hand. Her drool is cold and tingles like pins and needles. Eyebrow still raised, she gives me a nod followed by another grunt and then turns back to serve the other demons. I wipe my salivary hand on my pants and give Eve a pinched look.

"You get used to it."

This is the first time I've been able to study her properly and I recoil at the state of her. Obex has not been kind.

"What in the name of Balance happened to you?"

Cuts and weeping wounds cover her arms. Around the edges of the wounds, her skin is turning the same gray as the other demons. Her face is bruised, lip cut, her arms are hard and sinewy and her once golden hair is lank.

I swear her eyes glisten, but before I can check, she turns away from me. "Survival first. Always. This place is rough on your looks. But I'm also turning into one of them."

"When you say them, you mean a demon?"

She nods, "That's what happens when you come here without a Balancer. Nowhere to go but to rot into demonism."

"I'm so—"

"Oh do shut up, Trey. You were right, we're both to blame. The First Fallon manipulated me and my family.

She promised me a life as a royal Fallon, gave my family riches beyond anything they could have earned."

"We were so young," I say, swilling the liquid in my glass before taking a gulp. It's bitter and not in a good way. I swallow it and hold back a gag.

Eve sniffs a laugh. "You get used to that too."

"I'd rather not." My face wrinkles as I suppress another overwhelming urge to wretch.

The giggle grows. "Do you remember that Fallon party we went to? It couldn't have been more than six months after we were Bound. We had that god-awful cheap mead at the dinner table and neither you nor I had ever drunk it."

Now I'm laughing. "Oh my god, I thought it was juice. I ended up puking in Cecilia's Yucca plant and you threw up over the balcony onto the server's head."

She belly laughs so hard it startles the demon next to her, which makes me laugh even harder.

She clinks her glass with mine. "Don't worry, no hangovers down here. No matter how rotten the beer is."

"Well, that's something to celebrate. Cheers," I say.

"Ha!" she says and clinks glasses with me. "What can I say? It's good to see you again, if only to have slapped you around the face."

"Charming as ever, Evelyn."

"I do try."

"Speaking of seeing. Where the hell is everyone? I walked around for hours before I stumbled across the pub."

"This is the demon quarter. If you want to find Keepers rather than demons, you need to go to the Soul Sanctuary."

"Soul Sanctuary. It scratches at the back of my mind. I've heard it before. Remind me?"

"It's a safe house for all the Balanced souls. All Balanced Keepers end up there to wait out the rest of their living Balancer's life. I guess you didn't go there because you're only half dead? Or maybe it's that piece of Imbalance you're harboring."

I take another sip of the vile, bitter liquid. "Another thing I can thank the First Fallon for."

"The First Fallon? I thought it happened because your parents passed away."

"So did I. But before I died, Eden said she thought my mom was still alive. I saw a message from Hermia confirming it."

"Well, shit," she says.

My mother might still be alive, but my father is definitely dead. His body was brought back from Earth for his Dusting ceremony so he would have come to Obex to wait for my mom.

A small breath escapes my lips. "Would... would my dad be in the Soul Sanctuary?"

"If your mom really is alive, then he won't have passed on to his next life yet, not till she joins him. So my guess is yes."

My heart thunders behind my ribs. The thought of seeing him again floods me with adrenaline.

"Will you take me?"

She looks away, her words barely audible. "I can't."

Then I realize, "Oh."

"Yeah."

"I'm sorry," I say again, but it sounds pathetic. A millennium of apologies won't make up for the eternity of misery she's going to have.

"I can show you where it is," she offers. "But it's highly unlikely you'll get inside. You're not dead-dead and you have to be to get inside the sanctuary. And you won't want to because once you get in..."

My face falls. "You don't get back out?"

"I can't imagine that's what you want?"

"I can't take the risk when there's a chance I can—"

"Find a way back to your desert rat?" Her words are cold, but she doesn't mean it because when I reach out with my senses, all I catch is a flurry of quivers that taste like fading memories and winter breezes.

"Rozalyn's asked me to build her an army in exchange for returning me—alive—back to Trutinor."

"Right," she says. "And you believe her?"

"Not sure I have another option. But yes, I do. She needs me to help her back so she can defeat her sister." I lean over and squeeze her hand. "What if there's a way to help you, too?"

She looks from our clasped hands to my eyes and gives me a limp smile. I want to tell how good it is to see her. That being around her makes me think I have a piece of home with me. But I don't. The words dry and clog in my mouth. I don't want to give her the wrong idea.

Instead, we talk about the time we escaped one of Arden's balls by stealing a train. About how the rice dishes were better in the South than the East, and how she would have continued studying sorcery long into old age. We talk and talk and talk. And reminisce about lost and forgotten things. Between us we patch full memories together and for a few hours, it's like I'm still in Trutinor.

Eventually, the demon drinkers dwindle and it's just me, her, and the short demon left.

"Bedroom," the Demon grunts and cocks her head to the door behind the bar.

"Great, thanks," I say, wondering what god-awful room the ex-landlord has left for me.

"Night," she says and throws a bottle in the bin and walks out of the bar, letting the door slam on her way out.

I shift in my seat, realizing Eve and I are alone.

"Where do you live now?" I ask.

"Here, actually."

"I see," I say, realizing that we're now going to be living in the same building. My stomach curls in on itself, and I wonder if it's a warning. This is way too convenient. A bar, a bed, and Eve? Something is definitely off. Alarm bells are screaming in some distant recess of my brain. But I decide to ignore them—for one night only.

Yeah. I'll just stay one night and then, I hope, find somewhere else to sleep while I figure out a better plan. It's not like I have anywhere else to go tonight and if I'm being honest, there's a part of me that's relieved to be in the company of someone I know.

"There's a few demons upstairs. The old landlord used to rent the rooms out to anyone who worked the odd shift for him."

"You work here too?"

"I've done the odd shift. It's all rather slack," she says.

"I'm exhausted. Will you show me upstairs?"

She walks behind the bar and pushes the door open to the back quarters. The stairs are on the left. There's a pile of ash about halfway up the stairs. It shivers and a slip of color drains into a patch.

I'm distracted by another door down the end.

"What's through there?"

"Not much."

I push the door open and it yawns open into an enormous barn or warehouse or...

"What the hell is this place?" I say.

Hanging from the ceiling are rusted iron chains, blades

and pokers. There's a mound of bones in the corner, a giant sea rope piled in a circle and the stench of sweat, decaying meat, and iron.

"It looks like a slaughterhouse," I say.

A slaughterhouse. My mind flashes back to the fight with the demon outside, the raw animalistic emotion flowing off the crowd. I smile, a huge grin. Maybe I'll stay a few more nights.

I turn to Eve. "I know how I'm going to build her an army."

ELEVEN

'The Dryads are the most mysterious of all beings in Trutinor. Some posit that they may even be Trutinor embodied. Living, breathing representations of the land. They, of course, come from the soil, earth and Ancient Forest. No one is sure whether they were here before the advent of the First and Last Fallon or whether they were a creation of the Fallons themselves, and of course, the First Fallon's memory has been notoriously bad in recent times.'

Excerpt—*Myths and Legends of Trutinor*

EDEN

After Titus dies, I decline. Not physically, so much as mentally. Loss after loss can have that effect, I suppose.

Titus was the last shred of family I had, so I spiral. *Hard.* The next three days are spent sleeping in Trey's mansion, in his bed, wishing the scent of him still lingered on the sheets. It doesn't. They smell of citrus and fresh linen. I dig through his washing bin and find a dirty jumper that still has traces of frankincense and summer lingering on it. I carry it everywhere—as if it still holds a part of him. It doesn't, of course. But I persist in dragging it around.

In the evenings, I hobble to Trey's bar. Dorian trailing behind me like a leech. I usually send Hermia a flurry of messages asking about progress updates on finding Trey. She sends a barrage back littered with swear words and demands to stop pressuring her.

The first night I turned up at Trey's bar, Felicia allowed me to drink. The second, she was reluctant. The third night, she refused. So I lit up the bar, sending plumes of fire billowing across the counter and her customers screaming from their stools. She changed her mind after that. I doused the flames with water, mumbled a halfhearted apology, my stomach laced with the guilt of being an asshole. That, though, hasn't stopped me from drinking. Quite the opposite. I continue to drink myself into a coma every night.

That first night, some regulars tried talking to me, a few even attempted to stop me from drinking. They learned the same way Felicia did not to bother me. Eventually, I became like the rest of them: another piece of the bar's furniture.

At the end of each evening, Felicia tells Dorian to take me home. I, though, am reluctant, so Dorian inevitably calls Kato for help because he draws the line at taking my pain away. Speaking of Kato, the two of them are developing some puke-inducing bromance—what even is that? Anyway, Kato continues taking pain and Dorian continues guarding me. Kato should take the lot. I want it all gone. I don't want to feel a goddamn thing anymore.

As Kato slides me into Trey's bed each night, he squeezes my shoulder, or sometimes my hand, and where his skin meets mine, a cool sensation slips into my limbs, coating everything in a thick, tarry numbness. Then I fall into an empty sleep, wishing for dreams of Trey but getting a fog of black. In the mornings, I stare at Trey's empty pillow.

I've repeated that cycle for... for... I don't even know how long now.

Tonight is different—worse. My essence is crackling, like there's static in the air that shouldn't be there. It tastes sour, sharp. Dangerous.

I should probably stop drinking. Oh, well. I swallow another shot of Mind Numb. It's my third, no, fifth shot already. The world is the best shade of blurred. Exactly how I want it given Kato—under Dorian's instruction—is being tight with his Siren abilities. Fucking bromance.

Felicia walks past, so I reach out to her.

"Feliciaaa, can I have another bottle of Minnndnuumb, please?"

"Don't you think you've had enough?"

"I've had enough when I say I have."

She rolls her eyes at me and thrusts her hand on her hip. "I used to like you. What happened?"

"I lost everything I love."

She looks away, shaking her head. When she turns back to me, her eyes are soft and round. An expression I loathe. If I were a Siren, I'd eradicate pity.

"Wake up," she snaps. "You didn't lose everything when Trey died. You lost everything when you gave up on yourself and those of us who were left."

Her words are as soft as her eyes and yet, laced through them, is a hardness that makes my body shudder. She waves a signal at a bartender who brings over a bottle of Mind Numb and a glass with smoking blue liquid and what looks like the remains of insect legs or shells in it. *Interesting.*

"I had so much respect for you," she breathes. She places the bottle on the table and vanishes.

I stare at the bottle, turning what she said over and over. Is she right? Is none of this really about losing Trey? If that's true, why does it hurt so much? I take a sip, then another and after the third, smoke billows from my mouth and I feel a powerful urge to lie down and throw up half a lung. The words on the bottle of Mind Numb skitter across the label. This is going to be one hell of a hangover in the morning. That's future me's problem.

The door to the bar opens and Dorian reappears after doing a security sweep, inside and out. He leans on his cane. Some days he walks just fine and then others, when the wind is cooler or there's a storm crackling above the atmosphere, he carries the hint of a limp and leans on the cane more. I don't know why I've noticed that, of all things. Despite the trace of pain lingering in his leg, he moves with absolute swagger. A confidence in the straightness of his back, the upward tilt of his chin, the smiling glint in his eyes. He's wearing a dark green suit tonight that shimmers under the dance floor lights. It's tailored and hugs his body as he saunters left and right to smile, nod, or chat to various people. He's not being nice though, not really. He's checking Keepers out, observing, analyzing, making sure they're not a threat.

He spots me, waggles his hand in a drinking motion, so I gesture no, and point to the bottle. I pour another glass of Mind Numb because that's precisely what I require.

He approaches and I gesture to the stairs. Once we've climbed into the only non-filmed and sound-proofed booth, Dorian rests his cane against the door and slides a fresh bottle of something green across the table. My lips flatten into a sly curve.

"Oh, this friendship is definitely going to work if you carry on like that."

He opens a bottle of water and glances at me, but it's not the grin I was expecting. His eyes are soft, wrinkled at the corners. Fuck that.

"I thought you were better than pity," I snap, and snatch the bottle of... wait, what is this? *Southern Rain Fire,* apparently, away from him.

"It's not pity, it's solidarity."

"Really?" I say, cocking an eyebrow at him.

He takes a sip, pauses and then shakes his head. His mop of loose brown curls spring around his head.

"My Balancer, Pax, died two years after we were Bound."

I stiffen. A lump appears in my throat. It's too hard to swallow. It's shaped like awful truth, and tastes like unwanted connection. Fuck this too. I am far too drunk for solidarity. And yet, Dorian knows what I'm going through. Kato might understand what it's like to lose Trey specifically—but Kato lost a brother. He hasn't had his soul torn in two, like Dorian.

He knows what it's like to be complete and then have a hole punched through your core. When I was with Trey, life was a series of smiles and warm summer days even when we visited midwinter States. Every time he touched me, his fingertips spread kisses over my skin. We could be silent and he still felt like home. He always felt like home.

Dorian's knee knocks into mine under the table, and I flinch.

"Everything okay?" he asks, his voice soft.

"Trey and I—just memories. It's nothing." This is where we met for one of the last times. I sit back, raise my glass. "Well, cheers to our lonely, broken souls and the next hundred years of solitude."

I lean forward to clink rims, but he pulls away.

"Never said I was lonely." His eyes curl up, a devilish grin on his lips.

"I'll drink for myself then." And I do.

"So, *Dooorian,* how long are you going to pretend to be my bodyguard when we both know you're really here to convince me to rip the world in half and fight to end fate?"

He laughs. It's short, sweet, rolling bubbles of laughter.

"I'm not. Well, okay, I am here to do that too, but I really am here to protect you. Castor needs you. We all need you, and not in this state, either."

I roll my eyes. He can fuck right off with that as well. "Anywaaaay, what can you tell me?"

"What do you want to know?"

"Are we going to play verbal ping-pong? Or are you actually going to answer my questions?"

"If you ask the right ones."

"Fine. How are you connected to the rebels?"

He leans back and tips his drink at me. "See, now that was the right question. They're family... of sorts."

"Literal or figurative."

"Both."

"I see. So the rebels, who are predominantly a bunch of Sirens I've never heard of, descending from Balance-knows who, led by an even more mysterious Siren, just happen to be trying to fight against the fate system? Doesn't sound like I'm missing any crucial pieces of information at all."

Another round of silence from him. I'm done with this bullshit. This is pointless. I put my drink down and stand up, my back hunched in the tiny booth. Dorian slaps his cane against the door.

"We're not done yet."

"Then you better start talking because my patience is running thin."

"We're not who you think."

"Then who, pray tell, the fuck are you?"

His teeth grit. "I can't..." His face slackens. "Listen, I want to tell you, I do. I just can't. Not yet. I'll show you. That I can promise. What I can tell you is that this is bigger than both of us."

"Yes, well, fate of Trutinor, Balance, Destiny, yada, yada... am I getting close?"

"You're drunk. I don't like your attitude."

"I don't like that my soul mate got stabbed in the carotid." Saying it knocks the wind out of me. I sit. Wipe my hand over my face. "I'm sorry, I am being an asshole. I just..."

"I get it. Unless you've lost your Balancer, no one really understands."

I stare out into the mezzanine floor, tables scattered at regular intervals, chairs stacked on top. Everywhere I look, everywhere I go, Trey is threaded into memories. "You were saying this is bigger than us both?"

Dorian breathes deeply before continuing. "Castor has an aggressive recruitment strategy. The bigger the rebel army, the better chance we stand of beating Cecilia."

"Makes sense. But that's not really new information." I shift in the booth, the chair beneath me swaying and moving. Oh dear, what the hell was that insect? Perhaps the Southern Rain Fire was one drink too far.

"One fucking prophecy and it's ruined everything."

He sips his bottle of water and then recites. "*The First Couple, two halves of one soul. Equal parts Balance to Imbalance, light to dark, and able to Inherit power. Together they will unite with the sister of darkness and wage war on the sister of light.*"

"Trey died, Dorian. It's all bollocks. How can there be a prophecy about us when he's dead?"

"It's not bollocks."

"How can you possibly know that?"

"Call it faith, call it belief. It doesn't matter, I know. Castor knows. And if you'd just accept it, you'd know too."

"Come on, Dorian, you really expect me to believe that Castor has a viable plan to end the entire Balance system?" I inch closer to him. "End fate itself just by bringing Rozalyn back?"

"Doesn't matter whether you accept it. He does have a plan, and I hope he's going to have you too."

I slug a load of drink down. Dorian reaches for my hand then hesitates. His fingers flex above mine, but he doesn't touch me.

"I understand this is hard, that the pain you're in is exquisite. But you need to believe me. The prophecy is real. And yes, Trey is gone and things aren't working out like we predicted, but that doesn't mean things aren't working at all. Rozalyn is coming. Castor has a plan and he'll need you to—"

He falls quiet. I yank my hand away. "Need me to what, rip a hole in the world? Yeah, I heard."

He rubs his chin. "I've said too much. It's not my place.

When the time is right, Castor will ask you to make a choice."

His words shake loose a memory. The last part of the prophecy said, "*But they will face a grave choice. Their decision will lead either to the defeat of the sister of light and restoration of Balance to all the realms or the end of the universe and all life within it.*"

I pick at a dent on the table. "Tell me something I don't know. Something true. Anything to make me believe I can trust you and Castor and the rebels."

He leans back, sips his water, his green eyes scanning my face. "The Keepers you saw at headquarters. What did you notice about them?"

"No Bindings."

"Oh, they have Bindings alright."

"They do?"

"Don't you find it odd that our Bindings are on our arms? They're the most intimate of connections. One that reaches our soul."

"Yes, that's why the Binding Scar is on our arm, connected to the radial and ul—"

"Ulnar arteries which connect to the Brachial artery and lead straight to the heart. Yes, I know. We've all heard the diatribe they spout in Keepers school. Use your brain, Eden. Where would it make more sense for the Binding Scar to be?"

I sit in silence, mulling everything he's said over. But I have most definitely drunk too much. My mind is fuzzy, but it claws its way through memories. Then my eyes bug out. "Oh."

"There she is. It's called a FreeBind. Most of the Keepers in the rebel camp chose their Balancer themselves. Their Binding Scars are over their hearts, a direct portal from the heart to the soul. Instead of the nonsense Cecilia has engrained in everyone."

"Well, shit."

"Exactly. By putting space between the heart and the Binding, she has an opportunity to interfere with them."

"Okay, Oswald, you have my attention. Where exactly do we go from here?"

"Well—"

My CogTracker pings. It's from anonymous. I scan it and groan.

"For fucksake. Are you ready to put your bodyguard skills to the test? I need to go exterminate a cockroach," I growl.

I get up; the floor tilts beneath me. Wow, how many drinks did I have? I stagger outside. Dorian is behind me, whining at me. Something about bad ideas. I stop listening.

A hand slides around my wrist. It's gentle and warm against my skin. A fleeting thought runs through my mind that the heat of him is nice. I pull my arm to free myself. But his grip is like iron. The thought vanishes.

"Get off me, Dorian."

"I am here to protect you. Please let me do my job. I really think this is a bad idea."

I reach inside myself, pouring low-level static and threads of electricity into my arm. "You can either let go and come with me. Or I can knock you out and go, anyway." I bring electricity to the surface of my skin. A warning. "But if you restrain me like that again, I will do more than knock you out."

His teeth grit, but he lets go and retreats to the shadows. He's never far from me, though. His presence is strange in the air. My senses can't help but assess and examine the ripples.

Victor and Karva stand in the alleyway, both their arms folded.

"What's this, a maaafia meeeet?" I slur.

Behind me, Dorian is rigid. I glance back, his knuckles are white mounds on his cane. That's odd.

"I want the blood, Eden."

"And I want my Balancer back."

Victor steps up to my face. He's so close his putrid stench mingles with the booze in my stomach. I lean forward and retch, vomiting right on his pretty toes. I stand up, stifling a snigger. He leans back, shaking his head.

"Wow, you deign to pity me? I must have sunk low." I wave my hands in mock shock.

"You're a disgrace," he spits.

"Says the rotten carcass? I'm just helping. Puke smells better than rot. It's not like anyone will notice."

He glances at Karva. She takes a step toward me. I hold my hand up. "That's close enough, bitch. None of your torture antics this evening. Think we can all agree I've tortured myself enough, don't you think?"

Karva notices Dorian. Her eyes widen, she staggers back and I kid you not, hisses. She hisses like a damn cat. Her silver hair frizzes out like hackles and the bronze tone drains from her face. What in the fresh hell? Not the reaction I expected. Maybe he's a better bodyguard than I gave him credit for. Karva takes a moment, brushes herself down, and then glares at me. But she continues to cast furtive glances at Dorian.

"It's a fair exchange," she says, more hesitant now. "Blood for blood. Cecilia for a vial."

My face wrinkles. "Oh yeah, because you can just drop a dead demigod in my lap with a click of your fingers. Give over, Karva."

Victor steps closer. Behind me I sense Dorian standing straighter, harder, stronger. The surrounding air is alive. It's driving my essence bananas. The pop and heat of adrenaline ripping off him. This could end badly.

"Karva is her daughter," Victor says.

"No way? Tell me something I didn't know. Being her daughter doesn't mean shit, Victor. How are you going to kill her?"

He shifts on the spot and swallows a few times.

"You have no idea, do you?" I say, and I can't help it. I start laughing. "You haven't got a fucking clue, have you? This is brilliant. Hey, Dorian? You hear these two jokers? Want the most precious resource in Trutinor and they haven't even got a plan for killing Cecilia. Think I should give it to them?"

No one speaks. Karva's lips press into a tight pout.

"That's what I thought. Pair of bullshitting bastards. You're never getting that blood."

"You're going to do this, Eden. Eventually, you're going to surrender and give me that vial of blood. Otherwise—" Victor sneers.

"Otherwise what, Victor? You'll waft a Siren in my face. When are you going to get it through your thick skulls? I will never help either of you."

Victor's lip curls over his darkened gums and decayed teeth. Karva snarls and raises her hand. My throat clamps shut immediately.

Dorian steps out from behind me. His cane rattles against the stone cobbles. Karva's eyes widen and she hisses at Dorian. She lets go of my neck and stumbles several paces back.

What. The. Hell is going on between them?

"Yes, well, I think we've established no one's getting

what they want this evening, are they?" Dorian says and moves in front of me.

Victor opens his wings, envelops the pair of them, and vanishes into nothingness.

"That, you're going to explain. What the hell kind of reaction did she have to you?"

"Are you going to explain what blood they want?"

"You first."

"I have absolutely no idea what you mean."

"Don't play dumb, Dorian. That was Karva Arigenza. You just unnerved a demigod."

"Did I?"

"That's cute. What did you do?"

Dorian smiles. "Must be the 'Ocean Breeze' perfume I'm wearing. You know Sirens hate the ocean."

I scan him up and down. "All I smell is bullshit. You said you'd answer anything."

"No." He smiles, that acre-wide grin disarming me. "I promised to answer anything about the rebels."

The cunning prick is right.

"Now, what blood do they want? Is it blood from the Heart of Trutinor, perchance?"

I smile. Two can play at that game.

"I'll take your silence as a yes."

"Take it as whatever you want. I guess you get to keep your secrets and I get to keep mine. I need another drink. Are you coming?"

He smiles at me, the bite of tension already gone. I'll get it out of him, eventually. One drink turns into half a dozen and instead of me grilling him, we talk about Trey and Pax and what our lives should have been. He makes me laugh and cry. I tell him what I thought my life was going to be, and he tells me about the life he would have led with Pax.

"I was addicted, after," he says. "It was the worst few months of my life."

I shift in my seat, warmth rising up my neck.

"And now?"

"Daily battle, but I survived, thanks to Castor."

"Castor, of course. Everything leads back to Castor."

"In more ways than you realize."

"What's that supposed to mean?"

He pours another drink, which I am one hundred percent sure I should not accept. My stomach is rolling so hard I am minutes away from being sick. But I take it because my body hurts and Kato is nowhere around and even if I ask Dorian to help, he won't.

"Castor helped me through withdrawal. He saved my life."

"Is that why you joined him?"

"In part, yes."

"And the other—" I gag. My stomach flips. I stumble out of the seating area holding my drink. The room drifts up, shakes, wobbles, veers down. I slam open the ladies' toilet door and puke in a basin.

Dorian appears behind me and helps me to the toilet. I grip the rim just as I projectile vomit the entire contents of my stomach, which is deep purple and ninety-eight percent Mind Numb. *Oh man, that was just becoming my favorite drink.* It burns like acid and tastes like gut rot as it comes up. The cubicle spins, time slides away from me. My eyes shut. There's darkness. There's puking and eventually, there are two faces. Dorian must have rung Kato because the pair of them find me in the toilet.

"Traitor," I say, still leaning on the toilet rim. I'm wrapped up around the toilet, puke crusting my chin, but still victorious in gripping my drink. "Just as I thought we were making friends."

Dorian shrugs. "You needed a lift home. I'm not exactly a fan of the city cobbles."

I glance at the cane and shut my eyes. The room is moving. I'm pretty sure it shouldn't be. "You're still a traitor."

"I'll take that," Dorian says.

Acid crawls up my throat, so I put the drink down. Time to stop, I think.

"Thanks again for calling me," Kato says and holds a hand out to Dorian, who places his palm up to meet Kato's. The air crackles around their fingers as they exchange a little piece of Siren power. I always thought the Siren greeting was weird, like dogs sniffing each other's butts. But whatever emotion Dorian shares with Kato must satisfy him as he gives him a soft smile and then they fist pump. Gross.

"Not a problem. And like I said last night, if you want to stop, I can help. I can get in touch with the program, and we can help both of you through withdrawal."

"I'm right here," I bark. But before I can finish my sentence, I hang over the bowl and hurl some more of my insides up. I wipe my mouth and suppress another gag.

"You look horrendous," Kato says, his arms folded as he glares at me.

I open one eye and peer at him. His blond hair appears to have been brushed. He's wearing a white t-shirt, maroon jeans and boots. Slung around his waist is a jumper.

"What the hell have you been drinking?" he asks, picking up my glass from the floor. It's one of the blue smoking ones again, and I'm fairly sure this one also contains some potent crushed insect. A poor attempt from

Felicia to stop me drinking, no doubt. She failed, the insect fermented in the drink and made it stronger.

I don't even think before I speak. "Can you take it away?"

Dorian bristles. Kato's skin flushes red. He glances from me to Dorian and back again. There's a stagnant pause. Kato's never taken my pain in public. All three of us are aware that what Kato and I are doing wouldn't exactly get us good headlines. While it's not illegal, it's completely shameful and Dorian disapproves on both his part and Castor's. If it ever got out, both Kato and my credibility would be shot.

Dorian raises his hands. "I'm here to keep you alive, not judge you."

"You're not getting any pain relief tonight. This was self-inflicted. Get up, you drunken heathen," Kato says.

"I'd rather not."

"Fine. I won't tell you how to kill Victor... I mean Cecilia."

I sit up, fast enough I crack my head on the toilet roll holder. Dorian's eyes are wide as he glances from me to Kato.

"You found a way?" I rub my head and check my fingers. No blood. Victorious again.

"No. But I found someone who knows."

"I thought you promised not to go after Victor. You swore you would drop it."

The toilet walls appear to be moving. I rub my eyes like that's going to stop the motion. It doesn't. *Fucking fermented insects. One nil to you Felicia.*

"It was just a bit of harmless investigation."

"I hate to interject, but isn't Victor your Balancer's brother?" Dorian asks.

Kato tuts. "Killjoy. Whose team are you on, bro?"

"Alright, Kato, I'm listening. But I swear to god, you even think about laying a finger on him... We are not doing that to Bo."

Dorian and Kato hold out hands. I notice there's a sheen of sweat on Dorian's brow. His eyes are skittish, like he's hiding something. *Interesting.*

"Not here. The library," Kato says.

"Now? It's nearly midnight."

"Do you want to hear what I've got to say or not?" Kato's tone is sharp, aggressive, almost. I frown, glance at Dorian, who shares my creased expression. Kato keeps doing that, being a little too angry, a little too forceful. It's so unlike him. I figure there's no point arguing with him. So I haul myself standing and lean on Dorian as we hurry after Kato.

***

Magnus—Kato's Steampunk Transporter—takes one look at me, raises a bushy eyebrow, and grunts as he holds the door open.

"Still polite, I see."

"Still drunk, I see," he says.

I smile. Aww, he likes me. My foot slips on the train stairs. Magnus grabs my arm and helps me up the final step. He eases me into a chair, wanders behind the bar and comes back.

He shoves a glass of water at me, hands me a pill, a bread roll and two pieces of fruit. "Drink it. Swallow it. Eat it."

Then he disappears into the train's engine cabin. *Still a shred of kindness in the grumpy bastard.* Kato eases himself into the chair opposite, looks me up and down, but says nothing. Dorian sits beside Kato.

"Don't give me those judgy eyes," I say to the pair of them. I swallow the pill and take a bite of apple before sliding it onto the coffee table and wrinkling my nose.

"You need to eat that," Kato says. "You're looking gaunt. When was the last time you ate a decent meal?"

"Don't know. Don't care."

"Dude, I thought you were looking after her," Kato says to Dorian.

"What would you have me do, force feed her?" Dorian raises an eyebrow. Kato opens his mouth to answer, but shuts it, and swipes open his CogTracker.

I coil into the armchair and pretend to sleep for the remainder of the brief journey.

We arrive at Stratera Academy's station and I spend the long, tedious walk up the hill throwing swear words and curses at Kato's back. Kato ignores me the entire time. Dorian stays quiet, matching my pace, pausing when I pause.

"You could have told me in the bar," I shout at Kato's back.

"You needed to sober up. Besides, you wouldn't have believed me."

"Believe *me*. You should have tried."

My head throbs, my mouth and throat are dry, and at this point, I'd rather be Bound to Victor than sober up.

"This had better be good, Kato."

"Trust me, it's better than good."

He leads us through the Main Street, into the library and down into the restricted section. When we enter, I inhale. There's something about the smell of stale old paper that reminds me of childhood. Perhaps it's because Keepers school library smells the same and we spent so many years there.

"Sit," he says and pulls out a chair.

I let my head rest in my arms while he wanders off to collect records and parchment. Dorian vanishes for a few minutes and returns with coffee and a bag of croissants. I suppress a snort. Clearly, I'm not the only one Kato can guilt-trip. Kato returns and pushes a scrap of musty scroll under my arm.

"You dragged me away from a brilliant night out for this?" I say and dangle the piece of paper at him.

"One: I'd hardly call a whiskey-driven night of vomit and self-pity 'brilliant' and two: yes, yes I did."

His plump lips stretch into a grin. I roll my eyes and pull the parchment closer.

"It's just a list of Soul Deaths."

Dorian stretches over my shoulder to get a look. Kato leans back in his chair, kicking his feet up and onto the table, and says, "Keep reading."

"Blah blah blah... limited numbers of Soul Deaths after it was outlawed..."

Kato, still reclined in the library chair, recites the next line. "There are three Soul Deaths that have caused catastrophic consequences to either Earth or Trutinor... Why don't you indulge me? Go right ahead and skip to the last one."

I scan down the list. When my eyes reach the last case, any alcohol still in my system evaporates. My blood stills, my eyes widen like orbs.

"It can't be her?"

"Can't it?" Kato says. Both Dorian and I snap to look at him.

"She'd have to be three thousand years old," I say.

"At least," Kato responds, a smug grin spreads across his entire face. His narrowed eyes twinkle at me.

I turn back to the record, but there, in black ink, is her name.

Victim: Broc (Human)
Perpetrator: Hermilda Endlesquire, Elf.
(1000BC)
Reason: paid assassination
Consequence: the creation of Obex

I blink at the page for a while, then turn to Kato. "You're telling me you think Hermia... Short, angry, Elf-shaped Hermia, committed a Soul Death?"

Kato says nothing. He stares at me. His blue eyes glitter as much as the smile on his lips.

"You expect me to believe she was an assassin and entirely responsible for the creation of Obex?"

"I am."

"But she's a drunk."

"And now we know why. Think about it... You told me she knows her way around Obex better than any Steampunk Transporter, and back then, Trutinor and Obex were still joined. She's able to track... nay, *hunt* anything that moves and does anyone really know her history? I'm not even sure Trey did..."

"Holy shit."

"Quite."

"Okay. You win, Kato. It's possible. Probable, even. Which reminds me, I asked Trey why she played double agent between him and Cecilia. He said it was because Cecilia took everything and everyone from her as punishment. But he didn't know what the punishment was for. This is it. This has to be it. She killed Cecilia's soul mate and in return, Cecilia killed Bellamy and her son and forced Hermia into servitude."

"I told you it was worth ruining your pity party."

I throw him a pointed stare. "Now what? What exactly do you want us to do with this information? I told you we're not doing anything that will hurt Bo."

Kato stands, resting both fists over the table. He leans toward Dorian and me. "Now we convince Hermia to help us kill Vic—"

My stare sharpens.

"Fine, Cecilia."

A long silent beat fills the room and then a slow grin spreads across my entire face.

TWELVE

*'It is said a magnificent palace stood in Truti-
nor, a shining white building with row upon row
of windows and acres of luscious fields. The
first family resided together, living in peace until
the world of Trutinor was torn in two. The
palace vanished, no photographs remain, only
pen and ink sketches that cannot be verified.'*

Excerpt—Myths and Legends of Trutinor

TREY

It took several days of hard graft to create the fight club.
When I told Eve, she was resistant.

"Are you sure this is a good idea? What makes you think
a demon is going to want to fight if it means joining an
army?"

"Because the prizes for winning will be spectacular."

She thrusts her hip out and shoves her hand on it. "And what, precisely, is a good enough prize to persuade a demon to fight for you?"

A nervous laugh tumbles out. I smile and pull her in for a hug. "Can't a guy have a secret?"

Except it isn't a secret. I can't tell her the prize because I don't have a clue. This whole thing is hinging on me being able to find something to tempt a thousand demons into fighting, and I haven't figured it out yet.

When Eve and I were a couple of days into clearing out the warehouse, Bellamy came to visit. Though he denied it, we both knew Rozalyn sent him to check up on me. The next day, Pest's skeletal frame arrived. Rozalyn was applying pressure. She wants results and so do I. Every day spent here is a day too long.

Eve tells me she can still smell the life on me, although this morning she hesitated before responding. She didn't say it, but there was an acerbic shiver coming from her. I have no idea how long this connection with the Heart of Trutinor will keep a part of me alive. But I pray it's long enough to get home.

Apart from a clean bar and a renovated warehouse, I have nothing to show Rozalyn, which means I'm no closer to Trutinor or Eden.

After their visits, I met Rozalyn and requested both Bellamy and Pestilence's help with the renovations. If they were going to hang around applying pressure, then they could get their hands dirty and speed up the process. After all, she wants the army and I want to get out of here. There was no way I could create the fight club any faster without more help. I needed tools and equipment and laborer hands to get the warehouse ready, let alone keep the bar running. She agreed, of course, this whole affair is a win-win.

"Careful, Luchelli," Eve says to me, wiping away a line of sweat from her brow. "You almost look like you're enjoying yourself tonight."

I smile at her, but as I reply, the warehouse door creaks open and Bellamy appears.

"Her majesty requires another progress report," Bellamy says, walking toward us. Bellamy's bad horn isn't oozing as much today, and his pants and shirt appear a little cleaner.

"Well, there's not much more to report. We've made progress in here. Thanks to Pest, we've sped up and I don't think it will take much longer before we're complete."

I scan the warehouse, it's unrecognizable. The chains, blades, and weapons hanging from the ceiling have gone. The bones cleared up and even the stench of stale blood has softened. We've cleaned the walls, cleared out the rubbish and built the frame of a fighting ring, reusing steel reinforcements and sea rope.

"Drink?" I ask Bellamy, who nods.

"I'll have one," Pest grumbles from across the warehouse.

"Me too," Eve says.

"I'll be right back."

The first thing Pest created was a walkway between the pub and the warehouse. He said I'd have to keep an eye on both areas because fueling demons with booze and aggression was asking for trouble. I cross the balcony walkway, joining the bar to the warehouse, and step down into the pub.

The pub is completely different to the night I arrived

here, too. It's clean for one. The floor isn't sticky or covered in glass and dust, and the whole place is lighter.

I grab several cold bottles of whatever god-awful shit they brew down here and return to the warehouse, handing one each to Pest, Eve, and Bellamy. Then I sit in the fighting ring and the others join me. We drink and chat, and for a short while I forget I'm in Obex. I forget Eden's not here and I live in the moment.

But Eve turns and smiles at me and it throws me back to the first time I ever met her. I remember sitting on Cecilia's white Chesterfield sofa. My insides in knotted pieces, wondering who the hell this girl was that I was meant to be with. Her hair held the sun in its strands, her eyes were cool green like tarnished copper. She seemed so bright, so happy. Instead of smiling back, my heart drops into my stomach. The light in the warehouse highlights her gaunt face, the dark shadows under her eyes and the gray shimmer of her skin. Everything rushes back, a squeezing pressure crushes my lungs so hard I gasp for breath. It's my fault she's here, it's my fault she doesn't have a Balancer.

"We should turn in for the night," I say, suddenly getting out of the ring and cutting the conversation.

Pest and Bellamy glance at each other, but to my relief, they leave without complaint. After they're gone, Eve walks over to me, a twinkle in her eye I recognize far too well.

"Eve... I've told you."

"I know, baby. But look at what we've built. Look at how far we've come..." She swings her arms around my neck, nestling into the crook under my chin. The same crook Eden used to nestle in. Mentally, I pretend it is Eden. But then the cloying smell of sweet warmth and prickled bubbles catches my senses. Desperation. Oh, Eve. I pull myself out of her arms.

"We should be celebrating," she says. "Why did you send them home?"

I disentangle myself from her grip. "Celebrating? What do we have to celebrate? I've been here too long already. I don't have an army and I'm no closer to finding my way back to Trutinor."

Her eyes darken, a pout plumping her lips.

"To Eden, you mean."

"That's not what I said."

"You didn't have to say it," she whines. "God, Trey. I'm the one that's been here. The one who helped you build the club. I'm the one that's always been there for you. You only had five minutes Bound to her. Despite that, she's the only thing you care about."

"You know I care about you, Eve."

"No." She wipes a tear away. "I'm here, loving you, dying for you and the only girl you've ever cared about is your precious princess who's shagging whoever she wants as a free woman."

The vault judders, a thin crack splintering its wall. I tense, my back and shoulders priming themselves as if they're my mind's armor.

Eve takes a step back, realization flitting through the furrow in her forehead. She's seen the vault snap open before. She spent long enough with me to know the consequences of it opening.

"I'm sorry," she says, her voice anemic, "but you don't get to open that vault just because you're hearing the truth. Figure it out, Trey, because you're never going back. You're going to spend a lifetime waiting for her right here. You can do it alone or you can pull it together and we—you and me—can build this army."

I'm silent, too busy trying to win the fight in my head to

argue. The full force of darkness seeps into my arm and fingers. I slam my fist into the wall beside her body. She doesn't even flinch. Eve never flinches. She likes the game of chance too much. She craves the violence like its sunshine and sweets. Something glints in her eye. Something warm: longing. It slips through my powers and tastes deep, like hot cherry pie and festive spice. She glides seamlessly from sadness to lust. It gives my essence whiplash.

I shake it away, cling instead to the slices of heat bursting through my knuckles. It feels good. I focus on the throb in my hand, the grazed skin, the ache in my finger joints, and I breathe. In and out, in and out, until the frustration wanes and the vault seals itself back together, patching up the crack with pain. I smile. Eden used to tell me to stop taking away my feelings because pain grounds us. I guess she was right.

"I take it back. I'm not sorry," Eve says and lays her hand on my cheek. Her tongue slides over her lips. "Not if it means I get you back. If I get to take that piece of your heart, that always should have been mine."

I place my hand over hers and she stills.

If I open my mouth, I'm not sure what I'll say.

So I don't say anything. Instead, I walk out of the fight club, grab the notebook and pencil I found when I first arrived from behind the bar and leave her shouting after me.

I step into the eternal twilight, hoping for fresh air, but swallow a gulp of Obex's stale atmosphere. I glance up, thankful that at least something down here is beautiful. Burned oranges and blush pinks dress the sky this evening. In the distance, there's hollow shrieking and the clattering of bodies against walls. Some kind of demon brawl, no doubt.

I keep walking until I hit crossroads and stamp mindlessly on the cobbles that move the streets. I don't know how long I walk for and I don't care. When I'm far enough away from the Fallen Fallon, my chest loosens. I sit on the edge of a park. I'm all too aware parks are hunting grounds for demons. While the demons in the pub are warming to me, the rest of Obex doesn't have the same familiarity. But if I stay near the edge, I'm usually safe. I write for a while. Always memories, always regrets. I have so many of them. When I'm done writing, I stroll for a while longer—aimless meandering, anything, so I don't have to go back to the bar. The scenery changes. I turn around, expecting to see streets of tall marble houses and cobbled paths. But I'm at the edge of a long road lined with decaying trees. At the end of it is an enormous house. No, not a house, more like a palace.

"What the?"

It takes a good ten minutes to walk up to the front of the building. Dozens of windows and square porches break up its square front. It's not until I reach the huge round driveway that I realize what this place is.

In the center of the circular driveway is a statue; two figures united with clasped hands raised in the air. The figures are a coppery bronze but mottled tarnish-green in patches.

I glance at each of the faces; faces I know far too well. The First and Last Fallon; Cecilia and Rozalyn. They stare down at me, their bronze features vacant and hollow.

Holy shit. This must be the First Family's palace. I've read about it, but none of the books could ever confirm it was real. I've only heard of it as a myth. It must have been pulled into Obex when Trutinor was torn in two.

I turn around, but there's no one behind me. There's no one anywhere. The place is desolate.

I hesitate, flutters writhe in my gut, but that's the

problem with curiosity. Its sweet redolence is far too appealing. I've always found it an addictive mix of sugary treacle and static. It dances, pulling adrenaline into my system and urging me on. My brain, however, is screaming for me not to go in. The palace is derelict for a reason. If Rozalyn wanted people in it, she'd be living here. But she isn't. She's chosen to live in central Obex.

Curiosity wins.

I inch toward the house, checking around me the entire time. But I'm alone. I push against the door in the main porch. It resists but after a hard shove, it cracks, and the lock snaps off the door and clatters to the ground. As I step into the doorway, my skin tingles sharp and hot, and I can't push any further. I frown, shunt my body forward into the stinging fizzles. The hinges groan in protest, but I stumble through the door.

"Weird," I breathe.

Fire lanterns flicker in arches. I wonder how lanterns can burn if the place is empty. I reach toward one, but no heat comes from it, it's just light; enchanted, I assume.

The foyer is vast. Six sets of wide staircases twist upward. While the paint is chipped and stained, I can tell from the faded colors that there's one staircase and one floor for each of the state powers, including the Mermaids.

I wander through halls and rooms for a while, staring openmouthed at the intricate artwork on ceilings and the ornate decoration. I can't believe I'm in the original palace. My mind meanders, thinking of all the memories the rooms hold, the secrets the walls might've heard.

Then I come to a room that's empty except for two giant glass tubes and two coffins next to them.

As I near them, I shudder. Who keeps coffins inside a house? I peer over the top of the first coffin. There's an enormous glass panel, and a preserved face peers back at me. I recoil, my heart beating in my ears instead of my chest. I stare at the occupant. It's like he chose to sleep rather than die. Beneath the glass viewing panel, is a brass plaque with the letters RA carved in it. I know the face. I've seen it in paintings and books. Rueben Arigenza. The first ever Shifter and the first-born child of Cecilia. Why is he in a coffin, though? I peer inside the other one, it's Clarissa. Cecilia's youngest child and the first Sorcerer.

I scratch my brain for my history lessons at Keepers school. Rozalyn Soul-Deathed Cecilia's soul mate: Broc. Cecilia responded by tearing Trutinor in two—creating Obex and banishing Rozalyn. Rueben and Clarissa vanished shortly after—presumed kidnapped and taken to Obex by Rozalyn as revenge for her banishment.

Supposedly it was easier to cross between Trutinor and Obex back then—the fabric and barrier were newly formed, still malleable. Not for Rozalyn, of course, Cecilia had banished her. But it was for everyone else. It's only over time the barrier has thickened, hardened, like a scar, I guess.

No one knew what happened to Rueben and Clarissa after they vanished, though history and logic assumed Rozalyn had a hand in it. I guess history was right.

I turn to the two giant tubes and realize they actually contain a set of smaller cylinders inside them. Swimming in the smaller, inner tubes are shreds of material that shimmer and appear almost phosphorescent. It reminds me a little of the Binding Chamber where the heads from our Binding Ceremonies live.

The glow from the fire lanterns makes the material inside the pipes sparkle. I lean forward, squinting. The hairs on my arm pimple up as if I'm being watched.

I snap around, but there's no one there. When I turn

back to the tubes, the shimmery material has formed a face, or a part of a face and is pressing against the glass closest to me.

I leap back and yelp. Its mouth opens wide, its translucent eyes drawn down, pleading.

"What the hell are you?" I breathe. I circle the cylinders, frowning as I examine the face. It follows me, it's female, that much I can work out. It twists inside its tiny pipe. A piece of material quivers and slams into the tube nearest me. It's a girl's hand.

I stagger back, my skin crawling. I glance from the face to the hand and then to Clarissa's body inside the glass coffin next to it. The faces are the same. My blood runs glacial cold, the chill of recognition splintering down my spine. The material inside the tubes is a person. A soul—Clarissa's. Rozalyn tore her soul into pieces.

"Holy shit," I whisper.

I skirt to the other glass cylinder, straining to recognize Rueben's face in the pieces of soul.

"If Rueben and Clarissa are here. Karva is back in Trutinor, and Aurora is banished to the oceans. That just leaves Darique. So where is he?"

"Dead," a voice behind me says.

My back snaps straight, tingly pins trickle down my back. I turn around expecting a legion of demons ready to devour me, but all I find is Bellamy.

"Sweet mother of Balance, Bellamy, you scared the life out of me."

"Rozalyn knows you're here. She's on her way."

"Okay...?"

"It's abandoned for a reason."

"I understand why now. She tore her nephew and

niece's souls to pieces and trapped them in jars. I doubt that would go down well at the next family dinner."

Bellamy raises an eyebrow at me, his green horn twitches, and a small globule of puss oozes out.

"Can't you treat that?" I say, wincing at the horn.

He ignores me and glances at the tubes. "It was Retribution."

"Because Cecilia trapped Rozalyn in Obex?"

He shakes his head. "That came after."

"What do you mean? I thought they were brought here after the world tore?"

"They were. But originally, Cecilia struck first."

"Why?"

He huffs, his horn oozes a little more gunk out.

There's movement behind him.

"Love, Mr. Luchelli. Isn't that what all the great wars are about?" Rozalyn says as she sweeps into the room. I stand a little straighter, shifting on my toes.

"You shouldn't be here. It's abandoned for a reason. In fact, it's a wonder you got in. That little piece of life of yours got through my barriers. No demons allowed."

I glance at Bellamy, who's wandering out of the room.

"He doesn't count. He serves me directly, has free rein down here. If you'd been a little more dead, you'd have been fried on the way in." She smiles at me, and I shudder. I wish she wouldn't. Her rows of spiked silver teeth send shivers down my back.

"Love is the reason you and your sister tore the world in half?"

She bristles. "If you must know, Broc was my lover. Cecilia never liked me having things she didn't. So she took him. Made him hers. I was, of course, devastated. We argued. She broke my heart twice over. We'd always fundamentally disagreed on what constituted fate, what constituted rightness and fairness. Her love of Balance and her greed far outweighed her love of me."

"So you killed him? Broc?"

She shrugs. "I was more impulsive back then. They both broke my heart. If I couldn't have him, she didn't deserve him. It was better that way."

"But you didn't stop. You took her children? They're your nephews and nieces."

She sighs. It's deep and fills the room with an exquisite bitter tobacco taste, edged with the sweetness of honey. Bellamy reappears with a cloth and rubs at the coffin plaques. This whole thing is bananas.

"After she banished me, Rueben"—she wafts a hand in the general direction of his coffin—"started a war with Darique. He said Darique's line—MY line—had been overthrown and thus he shouldn't rule Trutinor. Darique won the war, of course, cementing the Elementals' rule."

"But how did that lead to you ripping Rueben's soul apart?" I ask.

"Rueben might've lost the war, but he had his mother's lack of morals. And I'm sure Cecilia aided him. Darique vanished. To this day, no one knows what happened to him. Lost to history and fading memories." She pauses for a moment, her eyes fall on Rueben's coffin. "He's dead... Darique, I mean. I tortured that much out of Rueben before—" she stabs a nail at the glass tubes. "But I couldn't grieve. I couldn't lay my baby to rest. And so, neither shall they. And if that means their souls shall be torn in three for all eternity, so be it."

"Cecilia took one child, so you took two?"

She pouts. "Something like that."

I run a hand over my face. "How the hell did you even do it?"

"Sever the souls?" she asks.

"Yeah, I mean, what kind of weapon is capable of cutting a soul?"

Rozalyn raises a hand, pointing at a box on a fireplace. She nods to Bellamy who shuffles over and pulls it down. I hadn't even noticed there was a fireplace in here. I was so mesmerized by everything else.

He pads back to me and hands me the box. Something inside my mind tickles like the scratch of a new idea. I open the box. Inside is a knife. The hilt is silver, but the blade is an eerie ivory.

"What is it?" I ask.

"Bone," Bellamy says.

"What sort of bone?"

Rozalyn plucks the blade from my hand. "Mermaid. Aurora's knuckle, from memory. Mermaid blood is particularly potent. Their magic and marrow are in their fingers. So a Mermaid finger bone, if cultivated in the right way, can be extremely powerful."

"And I assume the purer the Mermaid, the stronger the blood?" I ask.

"You presume correct, Mr. Luchelli," Rozalyn says.

"I can't imagine Aurora was a willing donor."

"She wasn't." Her smile softens. "But she is a dutiful daughter and eventually gave willingly to help our cause. One finger is all I took. One finger made two blades."

"Two? Where's the other one?"

She shrugs and looks at Bellamy.

"I hid it for Hermia," he says.

"Hermia?" I ask, my head now swimming with information.

"She worked as an assassin for me for a time," Rozalyn says.

I laugh. It rumbles out, half snort, half gut-buster. Bellamy's expression is mute, unchanged.

"Oh wait, you're serious?"

Bellamy looks up at me, his eyes slow-blinking as if he's bored. "She killed Broc."

My mouth gapes open. I lean against the coffin. "As in... As in your Broc?"

"A mistake that created Obex, and banished me here for millennia," Rozalyn says.

She's silent, then. So we stand quiet, Rozalyn and Bellamy watching me as I try to process the fact that Hermia—very drunk, very angry Hermia—is some kind of assassin.

I change tactic because the itchy tickle has finally formed an idea. Something that will change the whole shape of the fight club.

"So, this blade." I hold it up carefully between my thumb and index finger.

"It can cut a soul in two?"

"It can," Rozalyn says.

I glance back at the glass tubes, a writhing, uncomfortable sensation in my gut. This is an awful, but brilliant idea.

"Could it... could it cut just a small piece of soul off?"

Bellamy's eyes narrow. Rozalyn tilts her head at me. "In theory, yes."

"And demons are demons because their souls are imbalanced? Incomplete, even. Incomplete enough, they're unable to pass on to the next life...?"

"Yes, Mr. Luchelli. What is your point?"

"Then I think I need to borrow it."

Her expression widens. "You're asking me to lend you the most powerful blade in all existence?"

"Yes, Your Majesty, I am. Because I know exactly how to get the demons to fight for you."

I put the blade in the box and close the lid.

"Oh, this should be good," she says.

And so I explain.

THIRTEEN

'While there are more modern forms of transport, the train has always maintained its popularity. There are hundreds of disused rail lines littered across Trutinor alongside many that have been repurposed, outfitted and used for private speed-efficient lines for the Fallons.'

Excerpt—The History of Trutinor's Transport

EDEN

Spurred on by the revelation about Hermia, Kato and I spend the rest of the night in the library searching for some additional proof. I sleep, wake, research and sleep again in patches, curled in a chair, trying to prevent a stinking hangover. At some point, I sent Hermia a message asking about Trey; she sent a stroppy one back demanding I leave off her and let her do her thing. She's trying to find him. But I just... I don't know why I'm asking her to hunt. What's it going to prove? That Trey is dead and never coming back? It's a foolish quest. Hermia knows it. I know it. Yet neither of us are stopping.

Although we continued researching, we found nothing new, just an additional scrap of evidence about the Soul Death Hermia committed. The short paragraph was in a tatty copy of *The History of the Balance: a Longitudinal Study*, which the original listing referenced. The paragraph, at least, confirmed that it really was talking about our Hermia.

Hermilda Endlesquire, Elf and assassin, committed the last known Soul Death. The victim, Broc, was known to—and of some importance to both—the First and Last Fallon. The reason for the assassination remains unknown, and despite being pressed under intensive torture, Endlesquire never confessed the reasoning. Her punishment is singular immortality. A curse greater than any. Endlesquire remains stuck in Trutinor, unable to meet her Balancer in the next life. Records show that she kept her Balancer, Bellamy Endlesquire, alive for an extended period, using forbidden magic to lengthen and protect his life, until the First Fallon eventually tracked him down and slaughtered him, separating the two permanently. Having exacted revenge, the First Fallon demanded a lengthy period of servitude from Endlesquire. Once completed, the two developed an uneasy truce.

"An entire night, and this is all we've got?" I shove the tome across the table, my stomach rolling in protest. It must be midmorning now. My head is throbbing and there's a waft of stale sick emanating from my body that I can't locate the source of.

"Darling, please, did you really think we were going to unearth a manual with point-by-point instructions on how to Soul Death a god on our first night?" Kato says.

Dorian's pale, his eyes flitting from me to Kato.

"Something you want to add?"

Dorian clears his throat, wipes his mouth and then gets up. He takes his CogTracker with him and stalks off without saying a word.

"What's his problem?"

Dorian plonks himself in the corner and glares at his CogTracker.

I turn to Kato. "Would you mind? It's been a really long night and everything hurts."

Kato's neck tightens.

"Don't glare at me like that. I'm aware we shouldn't."

"Then why are we?"

I return the glare. "Because it's fucking agony."

He tuts and shoves his chair back from the table and points to a secluded corner where there's a row of silent booths for students. We climb inside one—even though it's late and we're unlikely to get caught, it's not a risk either of us can afford. The minute we're sealed in, Kato relaxes, his eyes burn blue, his mouth drops open. He wants this as much as I do. I spy Dorian. He's moved from his corner seat to a chair in the same area we're in. I assume so he still has sight of me.

"Hand."

I give it to him willingly. The milky coolness threads

through my arm, saturating my throbbing muscles, pumping into my torso, dampening the flames, the hurt, the hole in my soul, and, conveniently, the hangover. The world quiets, stills. It's ecstasy. A moan slips out. Kato grips my hand harder. Taking more. More than he normally does, but I don't want to stop him. Violet and black pour into his veins, rippling across his face and into his other arm and the growing memory ball.

Both of us are panting, sweat slicks our brows. There's a thump on the door and we snap apart.

Fuck.

There's a girl, a Shifter, holding a pile of books. Another girl presses up against her. Their mouths locked on each other. The first girl moans, drops the books which land with a thunk. I bang on the door and they fly apart.

"Ladies..." I say, and wrench open the door, "perhaps you need the booth more than us?"

Dorian is behind the girls, his fists clenched. I roll my eyes. "It's fine. They're just making out."

Kato's hair is more disheveled than usual. He brushes it into place.

"That was dangerous. We need to be careful," I say under my breath.

"Yeah, we do," Kato mumbles.

There's a moment of silence. Neither of us says anything, but we both stand, locked in place. Frozen in the comfort and relief of our satiated addictions and the horrifying truth that actually, we shouldn't be careful, we should just stop. My stomach turns. My skin crawls. I hate doing this with Kato.

If I don't eat something, I'm going to be sick.

"I'm going to get coffee," I say.

"Black, no sugar. I'm clearly sweet enough." And just

like that, the tension is gone. What we've done erased like it never happened. Our filthy secret stowed away for another day.

He blows me a kiss.

I slap on a fake smile and stick my middle finger up. He laughs so hard I can still hear him as I leave the library and wander down the corridor toward the coffee hut.

There's a short queue of Stratera students holding folders and textbooks waiting for breakfast. The rumbling din of chatter makes my head pound. Whatever disgusting creature Felicia put in my drink last night has created a killer hangover. Thank Balance, Kato's taken the edge off.

A hand slips over my forearm and loops through my fingers and pulls me into an alcove sitting area off the corridor. I'm so shocked, I stumble and end up sitting on their lap. It's only then I realize who it is.

Bloody Dorian.

Heat rushes everywhere, my cheeks, my neck, my legs. I'm suddenly aware of how our bodies are pressed together. This is the closest we've ever been to each other. I'm pressed against his thigh—which is hard under my legs. His bulging arms are wrapped around me where he stopped me from falling. I take a breath, try to push the sudden rising heat back down and scramble off his lap. I hesitate. Decide to stand. But that makes it awkward. God, I'm awkward. There's silence. Why is it silent? SAY SOMETHING.

"Great. Umm. Body... guarding. Yeah," I mumble.

He laughs. "How's the head?"

"You're lucky I didn't electrocute you." I flap my arms in the general direction of his ample thighs.

"I do apologize. In my humblest of defenses, I called your name twice, but you were in your own world."

"I... oh."

"I take it Kato removed your pain this morning in that booth?"

My face grows hotter. I'm not answering that. "Do you want a coffee? I'm just headed to pick some up."

"Well?"

I shift myself so I'm not pressed against him.

"I'm taking your silence as a yes."

"Take it as whatever you want."

"Don't be like that with me. I'm here to help."

"No, you're not. You're here to keep an eye on me and make sure I do exactly what Castor wants."

He reaches for my hand. "Yes, I have a job to do, but I also want to help you. I appreciate that you don't want to talk about this, but it's getting out of control. Do you want to stop the addiction?"

"Obviously."

"I can help. I can take you to the rebel camp and help you through the same procedure I went through. It's not like you can fight Cecilia in your current state and you certainly can't join us with an addiction."

I yank my hand out, stepping out of the alcove and back into the sunlight striping the hall.

"I'm not ready."

"You never will be." He lowers his voice to a whisper. "That's the addiction talking."

I ignore him. Fuck him and Castor. I will stop. Can stop... if I want to. I just don't want to. It's helping, right?

"Eden?" a familiar voice calls. *Thank Balance.*

I spot Sheridan walking over to me. She's wearing multi-colored bohemian pants that flap and waft around her as she walks. Her wrists jangle from the number of bracelets she's wearing and her chocolatey brown-colored hair is scooped into a loose knot.

I wave her over.

"Coffee?" I say to Dorian.

He nods, his eyes turned down, shoulders slumped. "I'll see you back in the library."

I don't need the guilt trip, so I hug Sheridan and we join the queue.

"I've got a bone to pick with your girlfriend," I say.

Sheridan snorts. "How's the head?"

"Terrible, thanks to Felicia."

"Mmm, perhaps a little less indulgence is required?"

"Oh, not you too."

She raises her hands. "I'll stop. How are things since…? It's been weeks since I saw you. I mean that both real and dream world."

"I'm still not dreaming. Other than when I was in a coma, I don't think I've dreamed since…"

"Since Trey died?"

I nod and realize it's the first time someone said that he's dead and I haven't had to instantly suppress a lump in my throat.

"I… umm…" Her green eyes skirt away from me, and she fidgets with her top.

"Just say it."

"Well"—she lowers her voice to a whisper—"is anyone taking your pain away?"

I grimace. "Why?"

"I don't mean to pry, but having your pain removed can stop you from dreaming."

"It can?"

"Of course, your brain assimilates information in your sleep, including your feelings. If you remove them, it can shock the system into dream failure."

"Oh." I bite my bottom lip, my chest tightening with

realization. I used to see Trey in my dreams. They were prophetic of sorts, each dream showing me a different version of his death.

"I assumed I wasn't seeing the dreams anymore because he was dead."

"That's possible."

"But unlikely?"

She nods. I stare at my feet, nudging a cracked tile on the floor. If I want a chance of seeing Trey in my dreams, I need to give up Kato's pain relief.

"It's actually why I'm here," Sheridan says. "I've come to the library to do some more research on your dreams from... from before. One of these days, I'd love to put you in an enforced dream state so I can study them further, see if we can make them happen again. But I can't if you're..."

"Having pain removed?"

She attempts a smile, but it ends up pinched.

My lips press shut and face the queue. I can't give up the pain relief. But I'd do anything for a moment with Trey, even if it was just a dream.

We grab coffee and sausage rolls and make our way back to the library. Bo has arrived. She's talking to Angus Hathaway. He's a hulk of a man, looks more like a bear than anything, always wearing mud brown clothes and is hairy enough it's hard to see his squinty features. He's also one of The Six, the elite Shifter squad Bo is now in charge of. They had a rocky start, but she proved herself in battle and now they're an amazing team. She gestures, points to her CogTracker, and he nods and leaves her in the library. She bounces over, waving at me, and then sits on top of Kato in a big library armchair. Kato's arms wrap around her. Her hands twine through his bird's nest blond hair. Their lips lock.

"I think I just regurgitated my coffee," I say as Sheridan and I reach the table.

"You haven't had to sit here trying to ignore it for the last ten minutes, before her visitor. That was my view," Dorian moans.

Sheridan laughs quietly. "Come on, it's cute. I love a bit of romance."

"Dorian Oswald," he says, holding out a hand to Sheridan.

"Sheridan. Pleased to meet you."

Bo and Kato part, their cheeks flushed, Bo's lipstick smeared over Kato's face.

"Red's a good color for you," I say to Kato. He smiles at me before wiping his mouth.

"What happened to your no-smear enchanted gloss?" I ask.

"I'm out." Bo winks and then glances at Kato. In that moment, their eyes hold each other, captured in a web of love. The air fissures around them as if a single gaze can still time and evaporate the world. As much as I'm happy for them, watching the world dissolve for them makes another piece of me splinter. I miss Trey so much it makes my chest smart, my muscles ache, and my soul throb in places I can't reach. I tear my eyes away. They remind me of what I can't have. I'll never have the intimacy of someone so utterly connected to me that they're a part of my very being.

"I'm going to search through some records," I say. "Here's your coffee."

Neither Bo nor Kato respond. I doubt they even heard me.

"I'll be back soon. I'm going for dream books," Sheridan says.

"Good job I have work to do," Dorian says, opening his CogTracker and plugging headphones in.

I wave to them as I leave. It takes me a while to find the right section. This library is so much bigger than Keepers school.

I search the Siren section for a while, scanning history books, records, hunting for anything about Soul Deaths. There's nothing useful, so I change tact. Instead, I hunt for information about the Heart of Trutinor or ancient Siren ceremonies. I swear the scar on my arm throbbed, or I heard the heart beating or... something. Is this all a waste of time? I suppose I could ask Amori and Bertram. They were the two senior Sirens who conducted the Heart ceremony Trey and I did before he...

I decide I'm being ridiculous and try something altogether different. Maybe I can find something to help Hermia's tracking of him. Parchment scroll after parchment scroll litter an entire set of racking. There's a musty stench in the air: the decay of paper and knowledge rotting in forgotten book racks. I scan the shelves and find what I've come for. A chunk of ancient records.

I pull an armful out when the air cools. My Elemental senses scream to life.

Son of a bitch.

"You've made a habit of creeping in libraries," I sneer.

"I'm only here to say one thing," Victor says.

I don't even bother to turn around. I'm not poisoning my day by looking at his face.

"Well, get on with it." I might've promised Bo I wouldn't kill him, but I said nothing about maiming or harming him. I bite down the urge to punch him. I'm more likely to puke on him in my current state, anyway.

"I want to prove I'm trustworthy, that there's a reason to

save me. I'm not saying anything can be done, but if you look in the Binding Chamber you might find hope."

"Hope? Hope for what? Teddy bears and candy?"

"Just do it, Eden."

"Get fu—"

I hear the air crackle. No doubt his usual trick of wings spread and dissolving into nothingness. Hopefully, he's gone to crawl back to whatever stinking cesspit he just came from. There's about as much chance of me doing anything he says as there is of Trey spontaneously coming back to life. And yet, my traitorous heart wonders for a minute what kind of hope he might be offering.

I'll give Victor one thing. He's bloody persistent. I collate a huge armful of records about Obex; I notice an Obex map, so I stuff it under my arm and carry as much as I can—without spilling my coffee—back to the table. Sheridan is already back, head buried in a huge leather book. Kato is doing the same and Bo has an array of ocean maps sprawled open, searching for Aurora, I suspect. After discovering Israel wasn't her birth father, she told me she wanted to find him a few weeks ago. I said I'd help her in any way I can.

I roll the Obex map-scroll out across the table and sip my coffee. Sheridan leans back in her chair and twirls a thread of her rich brown hair around her finger.

"The Balance won't let you find him," she says, eyeing the map. "You sure that's a good idea?"

"No. Of course not." I put my coffee back on the table and continue studying the map.

"You're aware of what the Book of Balance says...?"

I don't glance up. "The separation of life and death is a thin veil covering the soul. Blah, blah, blah, yearning guides the soul to find its Balancer something, something in the next life. The fabric must prevent the living from finding the dead for the longevity of their Binding."

I dismiss the words and Sheridan grins.

"Aren't you the textbook geek."

"Shall I name the page and paragraph, too?" I mumble.

"No, but I'd rather appreciate it if you didn't die before I at least get some academic research and journal publications out of you."

She winks and pulls the map toward her. "So this is Obex?"

"Yes, and no. This is the original map from before the world split. In reality, we've got no idea what it looks like today. The streets move and shift constantly. Hermia once told me it was one of the Last Fallon's jokes, a game to confuse and torture her residents."

"I'll remember to avoid her after I die," Sheridan says and then frowns. "If you already know the streets will have a different makeup, why bother studying the original map?"

"Because Hermia knew her way around when we went, which means there must be a way to navigate."

"You've been to Obex?" Sheridan says, her eyes widening to orbs.

"Last summer, shortly before Victor died."

Sheridan opens her mouth as if to speak, but I frown at the map.

"Bo, Kato, does this map seem familiar to you?"

"It's Obex, of course not," Kato says.

"I mean the shape. The bend of the River of Souls, the enormous green area up there. The location of the buildings. Don't you recognize it?"

Bo looks at me with a blank expression. "Umm, no?"

I reach for my CogTracker tapping out some keywords in the search function.

"Here." I point, making the map that's appeared project up from the Tracker.

All three of them lean forward, their eyes skipping between the map projecting up from my CogTracker and the scroll map of Obex.

"Okay," Kato says, "you have my attention."

"That," I say, pointing to my CogTracker, is a map of London today. And while it's not identical, the map of Obex is similar enough. I'm convinced the current iteration of Obex is based on the structure of London."

"Or more likely, London is based on Obex. In any case, so what?" Kato says.

I slump. "So nothing, I suppose. I just thought if we had a head start, we might be able to search for him."

Bo, Sheridan, Dorian, and Kato glance at each other and then back to me. All of them are wearing identical expressions: eyes soft, foreheads lined.

Fire bubbles and spits in my chest. I don't need their pity. I know you can't bring someone back from the dead. Do they think I'm an idiot? No one saw Trey's body. What if he didn't die? It's stupid and childish. He had his throat cut, for Balancesake. Nevertheless, I need to see him. I need to know he's dead because, without knowing, there's always going to be a tiny piece of hope fluttering around my body.

One by one, they return to their work. Kato rubs my hand under the table, then buries himself in records of Soul Deaths.

I glance down at my pile of record scrolls and back to the Obex map. The shapes of the roads, the twist of the river. All of it is so familiar, and yet the pity on their faces makes my insides twist. Is it all futile? The tiny shred of hope buried inside me like a golden anchor holds on to the belief I will get him back. Hope is sly. It seeps into your veins, masked under the pretense of medicine. They say it's the cure for everything. I think they're wrong. Hope is poison. It will drive me to madness. I know the Balance laws. There's no way the fabric of Obex will let me find Trey.

I scream.

Loud, shrill, it reverberates through my ribs as I swipe the map off the table and onto the floor.

All four pairs of eyes snap up. As too, do all of the other eyes in the library. My skin is instantly hot.

There's that expression again. I want to claw it off their faces. Kato reaches out to me, but before he can remove the frustration, I'm in Dorian's arms. He did it to stop Kato from removing my pain. But he's so warm, and big and his arms wrap all the way around me and before I can stop myself, I'm crying great heaving sobs that wrack my chest and leave tear-streak trails on his shirt.

"It's okay," he's says. "It's okay."

But it's not. Nothing is okay. Nothing is ever going to be okay again. He strokes my hair and slowly the sobs dissipate.

I pull myself away, and he caresses his thumb over my cheek, smearing the last of the tears away.

"Better?" he says, his voice soft and rich.

I nod because I don't trust myself to respond. Kato is standing, his neck flushed, something flashes across his eyes, but it's too fast for me to register it. Before I can work out what he's feeling, all of our CogTrackers buzz simultaneously. Like trilling birds, CogTrackers ring out in echoes around the library.

I glance around the table. Sheridan, Bo, Kato and Dorian all wear the same lined expression.

"Public announcements are usually bad news," I say.

"Nothing like a spot of optimism," Kato says, pulling his Tracker toward him and opening it.

Sheridan, Bo, and I all do the same. Hovering above each of our screens is a projection. Regular CogNews reporter Tarkin Tavas appears. His hair is parted in a neat line at the side of his head, his teeth are a fraction too large for his mouth, and when he's not speaking, they press into his lips.

I glance at Kato. "Care to change your wager?"

"Hush now, Elemental. Even when I'm wrong, I'm right."

I open my mouth to argue, but Tarkin speaks.

"We apologize for the interruption to your regular morning CogNews. I'm Tarkin Tavas, and this is a breaking news item. I'm broadcasting live in the center of The Ancient Forest with a special report. After the Disturbances at Stratera Academy a few weeks ago, The First Fallon's sudden seclusion and retreat into her personal quarters in the Forest rocked Trutinor. Rumors were rife. There were reports of a battle in the school that destroyed the Door of Fates and, more suspiciously, eyewitness accounts of the sky tearing in two and even the death of our beloved Siren Fallon Trey Luchelli. What is more, there have been increasing pockets of skirmishes, outbreaks of Alteritus and border wars."

My hands ball at the sound of Trey's name. Hearing that phrase, those words, doesn't hurt the way it used to, but I'll never get used to it.

Kato reaches across the table and places his index finger on my fist. Dorian fires him a violent stare. Kato glares back just as violently. What happened to bromance central?

"Stop. It," I growl.

Kato rolls his shoulders, cricks his neck, but he doesn't

let go. "There's a lot of rather expensive books in here. Fancy taking a deep breath? Aside from puke, you reek of coal and ash and all things explosion."

Steam is hissing from the gaps between my fingers.

"Should I...?"

"I, umm..." I glance at Bo. She looks up, her eyes narrowing. Sheridan's brow is covered in worry lines. "No. I'm fine."

Kato leans in and whispers, "You recall that I'm a Siren? I know when you're lying."

Maybe I do need him to take away the anger. But we're in the library, and Bo, Dorian and Sheridan are all staring at me. More to the point, Kato isn't being himself and no doubt that's because of what he took from me this morning.

Where his finger touches my fist, the hiss intensifies. He catches my gaze and I give him a weak nod. The hiss instantly falls silent as a thread lifts from my palm and floats through the air and withdraws into his other hand.

My lids flutter shut, the smooth coolness of his compulsion settles over my chest like a silky sheet. I sigh, long and deep. The prickly sensation of everyone's collective frown punctuates the numbness.

Tarkin's voice shatters the relief and I refocus on my Tracker, ignoring them all. I said no. Kato chose to take it this time.

"I'm excited to bring you an exclusive interview with the First Fallon herself. It's only her second interview since the events... Your Majesty. Last time we spoke, we didn't have a chance to discuss the disturbances. Would you like to tell us about them in your own words?"

The First Fallon's face appears, hovering above our Trackers like glowing ghosts. Liquid rage pools in my chest.

Heat slides between my ribs and over my heart. Kato inches his seat closer to me.

"You need to get control."

"I know," I snap. Does he really think I *want* to burn down a priceless library? I inhale, slow and steady, trying to still my thumping heart.

"Thank you, Mr. Tavas. First, let me assure the citizens of Trutinor, I continue to be perfectly well."

Her eyes bore into the camera, almost as if she's staring at me, addressing me personally.

"I'm aware there are rumors of my being severely injured, but you need only look at me to see that I've never been in better health." The last word is drawn out, exaggerated. I know then she's talking directly to me. A message buried within her words. *You might've injured me, Eden. But you'll never kill me.*

Well, I've got news for you, bitch. Even gods have weaknesses, and I'm coming for yours.

"We're all pleased to see it," Tarkin says, his face appearing next to hers. "Can you confirm the rumors that the Door of Fates was, in fact, opened inside Stratera Academy during the academic term time?"

The First Fallon laughs, gentle, polite. Totally fake.

I hate her.

"Of course not, Mr. Tavas. The Door of Fates has been inanimate for centuries. Why, in my entire life span, I don't recall a time it was opened. It's practically mythical."

Tarkin nods, licking up every word she says. I bet she's using compulsion to make him say what she wants.

"But then, why was the door moved?"

"That's an excellent question. It was moved simply for an in-depth study the Guild of Sorcerers are undertaking."

"I see. And would you like to address the rumors that

the sky was torn in two? There are more than a dozen eyewitness accounts of a great cleave in the sky?"

"Mr. Tavas, let me ask you. Do *you* see a tear in the sky? Do you see monsters from Obex? Do you see anything but beautiful sky and puffy clouds?"

"I..." Tarkin falters.

"Of course he doesn't," Kato says, rolling his eyes. "Could this be any more of a cliché? How do people believe this bullshit?"

"Global compulsion, societal norming, expectation, habituation, brai—" Dorian starts.

"Dude, it was a rhetorical question," Kato says.

When Arden visited me, he'd explained that the Guild of Sorcerers were all over the tear in minutes. Masking it behind a floating quarantine dome until they could seal it up. But it was there for a while. Hidden. Like everything in this world. He told me it took three quarters of the Guild's Sorcerers, funneling all of their magic to seal it. But the Imbalances, the fights on the borders are becoming more frequent.

When we were hunting Victor, Trey found dying plants between the North and Ancient Forest. Those aren't isolated cases. Arden sent me a string of emails and it's always in CogNews. We don't need a reporter to tell us it won't be long before the sky cleaves in two again—or worse. Like Castor said, war is brewing, a big and terrible war that will carve a new world for us all and everyone can feel it whether consciously or not.

"I mean, no, Your Majesty. But the eyewitness accounts?"

"Clearly, they were mistaken."

Tarkin gives a nervous laugh then clears his throat.

"And what can you tell us about the sudden death of Mr. Luchelli?"

Her lips pull into a thin smile. Her eyes narrow, glinting at the camera.

I'll fucking kill her.

Dorian stands. Kato's hand is on my shoulder. I glance at it. Realizing I'm suddenly standing too. My fists are flaming, embers are flaking off and drifting toward the ground. Is everyone right? Am I losing my mind? He draws more and more out of me. Pulling, yanking. Kato is as angry as I am.

Deep lines etch into Dorian's face. He's twitching like he wants to intervene. He must be able to sense what Kato's doing. Bo's face has darkened. Kato tugs at my emotions again and a little gasp escapes. I'm no longer sure if it's me pushing my emotions on him, or him stealing them from me.

"A tragic loss, mourned by all of us. In fact, that is the real reason for this broadcast. The loss of any Fallon is heartbreaking, but this death is more so because we cannot commemorate his life in the proper fashion. Without a Dusting, our nation cannot grieve. We cannot get closure..." Cecilia pauses.

Kato holds my arm tight. Under his palm, a flood of ice splinters into my body. Instead of relief, it hurts. He drags the rage through my veins, but instead of relief, he freezes me out until I feel nothing. But he doesn't stop there. He keeps taking and taking.

My body stiffens. He's hurting me. He needs to stop. It's too much. Dorian snaps. He steps between us. His hand drops on top of Kato's and my connection.

"Enough," he says, and it's so cold, so cutting that Kato snaps back to reality. I tear myself away, severing the connection. He stumbles back. Both of us are panting.

"Are you okay?" Dorian says to Kato. His voice is warm, worried. Kato shakes himself off.

"Yeah. I... Thanks. I don't..."

"It's okay," Dorian says and taps Kato softly on the shoulder. "I got you."

Bo must have stood up at some point too, because there's fire in her eyes, her arms folded. Kato's shaking. I'm shaking. What the hell just happened?

"Therefore, I am honored to announce that we will have a national holiday and festival in honor of Kato Luchelli celebrating his inauguration. Three days from today," the First Fallon says, capturing everyone's attention.

"Were you aware of this?" Bo says to Kato.

His expression is wide, his brow crumpled. "Not a clue."

"There will be celebrations and festivities in each of the State capitals. The largest of which will be in the Ancient Forest. And of course, attendance is mandatory," she smiles sweetly. It doesn't reach her cheeks, let alone her eyes.

She turns to the camera, her lips tight, eyes cold, empty.

I might not be able to kill Victor. But she has to die and if I have to work with the rebels to do it, then so be it.

FOURTEEN

***Lost Soul Demons** - Over time, if a soul without a Balancer remains in Obex, it will become a Lost Soul Demon. These are flesh-hungry demons. Hairless with vein-speckled skin, long distended jowls and extensive teeth. Caution advised.*

***The Fear Demon** - a rather erratic demon who's become the embodiment of its own fear. It feeds off fear and pieces of soul and typically inhabits the Soulless regions of Obex. Extreme caution advised.*

The Dictionary of Imbalance

TREY

Fight night is finally here.

It took all of us, me, Eve, Pest, Bellamy and Rozalyn to recruit enough demons for the launch of fight night.

Rozalyn was reluctant at first. This was my problem, so she said. But after highlighting the faster we built the army, the faster she could tear down the barrier, she helped by applying pressure to a few of the larger demon gangs who had done some work for her in the past. It worked. Once a few of the popular demons got involved, the rest fell in line.

Eve found me a suit jacket for the opening fight night. Its dark maroon fabric is smooth and thick, a long tail in the back splits and extends down my legs.

I glance at Eve. "This isn't a circus, it's a fight club."

"I'm aware of that." She tuts and pulls the jacket out of my hands. "I liked it because it's the color of blood. Besides, you need to look the part. It's better than those rags you insist on wearing. I never liked your vest tops. But you wear whatever you want, my love."

I sigh. "Fine. But I'm keeping the vest underneath."

"Okay," she says, her mouth thinning into a smile. She's practically giddy with excitement. She helps me back into the jacket and flattens the lapels. Her hands linger on my chest. I place mine over hers. She smiles. I smile. For the longest time, I hated the way she touched me. So soft and tender, full of the feelings I couldn't summon for her. But she needed the comfort of connection, so that was how we worked. United against a common enemy. Cecilia took Eve away from her family and took my family away from me. It might not have been the life either of us asked for, but for a while we made it work. And eventually, I too, found comfort in our mutual solidarity. Eve became a home of sorts. Us against the world. We were friends, family, comfort. No matter what happened, we had each other.

She breaks away, and the moment is gone.

"Always lost in your memories," she says. "I hope they were good ones."

I don't want to have a hard conversation, so I change the subject. "Are you sure you want to fight?"

"Are you kidding me? If the blade really can cut pieces of soul off. If I can win even a few fights... a few pieces of soul..." She looks at me. "Don't you get it? This is my chance. If I can get enough pieces to fill the hole in my soul... I get out of here."

"I can't promise you it will work though... This is an experiment. What if it doesn't do what we hope?"

She rounds on me and pulls my chin to face her.

"It will work. I won't end up like them..." Her voice fades, her shoulders droop and a pang of guilt loops around my stomach.

"I'm sorry, E—"

"Don't. Not tonight. We both know it's not your fault I'm stuck here. This is on Cecilia. She orchestrated it." She runs her hand through her golden hair and then turns to the rusty mirror and starts plaiting it into a braid. "I'm not willing to lie down and fade into demonic oblivion. If there's a chance I can make it to my next life and find a new Balancer, then I'm going to do everything I can to get there."

"Even if that means risking pieces of your soul? It works both ways... If you lose..."

"What choice do I have?"

"You could make it worse. What if this is the worst idea known to Keepers and instead of healing your soul, it creates some rabid hybrid demon beast?" I pace up and down. "We've had our issues, but I still care about you, Eve. Don't speed up the process, not if we can find a way to help you."

She stops working her hair. "You're right, there's a real chance it could make things worse. But I could also heal my soul and get the hell out of here. I mean, wouldn't you?"

"Wouldn't I?"

"If you were trapped here, knowing Eden was never coming, and you were going to become one of them. Wouldn't you fight for another chance at life and love and a Balancer?"

I fall silent. Would I? Isn't that what I'm doing? Isn't the point of me creating the club to fight to go home to all of those things?

She ties a band around the end of her plait. "Wouldn't you do everything? Risk everything? Even those you love to get back to Eden?" She rubs her hands and looks back at the mirror.

There's a soft wave emanating from her, but it's peppered hot and spiky like cotton candy and chili. I can't work out what it... She won't look at me. Oh. She's done something she shouldn't have. I just hope it's nothing stupid because tonight is not the night to question her. Tonight I have to focus on getting this army built and making my way back to Trutinor.

"I guess I would," I say.

She finishes pushing a stray lock of hair behind her ear and comes over. My notebook journal catches her eye, she fingers the pages. My gut twists. I don't want her reading it.

I take her hands and pull her close, her eyes drawn, tired almost.

"Are you sure you're okay?" I say.

"I just... No matter what happens. No matter how many pieces of soul I lose, I'm not giving up. Not ever. Not until I either complete myself or a demon rips the last piece from my screaming hands."

I knead my temples; we might not be Bound but I don't want that for her. "What then...? What if you lose the last piece of your soul?"

She smiles, but it doesn't reach her eyes, and no matter how much she tries to push down the fear, it crackles under her skin like the popping of a newly stoked fire.

"I won't lose," she says, each word pointed.

"And if you do?"

She shoves a hand on her hip. "Then I guess I'll vanish into oblivion. But at least I'll have done everything I could. I'd rather be a warrior than a sacrifice."

She pulls the blade box across the bed. Ornate, black filigree patterns adorn the glass box. Black claws grip the corners and sticking out from the lock is a spike. She pushes my finger onto the point. Her nose wrinkles and a faint shiver passes over her. She glances up at me. "It's... your..."

"It's fading, isn't it?"

She bites her lip and nods. I pull my finger away and suck the tip until it stops bleeding. Bellamy suggested we make the soul scythe box safer. Given the place will be swarmed with demons, it made sense that the only people that should be able to open it are Breathers, like me and Rozalyn. That way, if they want the blade and piece of soul that comes from winning, they can't touch me. The drop of my blood rolls down the spike and the box clicks open. Eve picks up the soul scythe blade and twirls it between her fingers.

"How can something so delicate be so powerful?"

The light glints on the blade's hilt. After some intensive questioning back at the palace, Rozalyn highly approved of my idea, so she reinforced the blade hilt with demon steel to make it extra extravagant.

"The blade is made of bone," I say.

"Whose?"

"Aurora's apparently. One of the joints in her finger."

"That's not creepy at all." She places the blade in the

box and closes the lid, her fingers pausing on the top. "Listen," she says, her face tightening, the edges of her eyes are strained and she's emanating a strange billowing coolness.

"What's wrong?"

"I've been thinking."

"Okay?"

"You need the demons to follow you, right?"

I nod.

"They're not going to do that unless you prove yourself. It's not like being a Fallon anymore. This is a whole different ball game. It's survive or die here. There are no laws, no order. Obex is the living embodiment of chaos."

I pull my hand through my hair, chewing over her words. She's right. There is no hierarchy down here. None except the Last Fallon and her only rule is that chaos is king.

"I mean, you had to prove yourself to even get inside the bar in the first place," she says.

"I've been thinking about that. It was harder than I expected to recruit demons, even with the prize at stake."

"Yeah, well, one pathetic bar brawl does not a leader make. Not down here."

In my heart, I've always known it would come to this. I can't create a fight club and not expect to be a part of it. "I need to fight to earn their respect in the ring, just like I did in the bar."

Her shoulders slump. "I've been trying to think of a way around it. But I don't think there is one, not if you truly want them to buy in to being in Roz's army."

"In that case, I'll challenge the first fighter every night."

Eve reaches out and touches my arm. "When you get in that ring, don't underestimate them. This is dangerous. The old landlord was exactly that. Old, lazy, and a shit fighter.

These guys won't be. You've heard what they call you. You're a Breather, which means you have far more to lose than they do."

"It does. But it also means I have more to fight for."

She sits up straight, pushes a lock that refuses to sit behind her ear back again. "I'm just saying they will gun for you. Pieces of your soul will be more valuable than pieces of mine or any of the other demons. Part of you is still alive. They'll want that. I suspect they'll fight harder and dirtier for a piece of your soul than they will for anyone else's."

She kneads her forehead, lines etching into the pale skin. I shut down my essence; I don't want to take in her worry. It's sour and sticks to my insides. It's always been one of the hardest emotions to process. I adjust the maroon coat, ready to walk out and pick the fight of my life. I slip my hand into hers, pulling her to the door.

"Then I guess we'll both have to fight hard tonight."

FIFTEEN

'Scrying—a rare form of sorcery. Also known as "seeing" scryers have predicted visions of the future.

N.B. Scryers are a dying art in Trutinor. Over the last two centuries, fewer and fewer scryers have been born. The Guild of Sorcerers has an open investigation but is yet to find a reason.'

The Dictionary of Balance

EDEN

The days that pass between the First Fallon's announcement of Kato's inauguration ball and the actual day drift like a meandering river. When I'm not sleeping and recovering, I spend most of my time researching "how to kill a god" in the library.

Today, there are festival celebrations all over Trutinor, but the main event is in the center of the Ancient Forest, along with Kato's inauguration. And of course, the First Fallon will be there too, which is why Kato, Dorian, Bo and I are headed there instead of our respective State celebrations. I'm going to use it to scope Cecilia out, check her security, study her for weak points. Dorian helps. I have to say his company is so easy. We've slipped into a comfortable friendship. He gives me information from the rebels to help with the research. Supposedly, they're hunting for a weapon strong enough to kill Cecilia. Though there are the occasional moments when I feel like it's all just a pretense and he's only there to stop me tipping over the edge or doing something stupid. He's being patient with me, but I can tell Castor is putting pressure on him. They want me off Siren pain relief and clean.

Most nights when Bo and Kato finish classes, they join me for the evenings. Last night, Bo said she thought Dorian was dishy like a sailor—and I had to agree. But that upset Kato and they had a fight about respecting Trey. Like always, their argument lasted all of a few minutes. I get it. Kato's in a difficult spot. It's not like I'm dating Dorian, god no. He's here for protection. But Kato's made friends with him and he's still reconciling the death of his brother. No one can take Trey away from him. But I get the turmoil.

Yesterday, Sheridan came to see me. She brought snippets of information about the dreams I had. She still wants me to spend some time in an enforced dream state so she can study them. But that has to wait until I'm fully recovered—or, more realistically, when I stop using Kato's pain relief.

Bo, thankfully, has stopped mentioning it. But her gaze twitches whenever Kato helps me. My CogMail stays relatively low thanks to the East State Council. I have to sign a few papers, and have a few state calls, but mostly, they leave me to heal, and to Felicia's relief, I'm now spending more time in the library than the bar and as a result she's stopped shoving insects in my drinks. It's the little things.

The agony of moving around day to day has lessened. To the point where a week ago, Kato moved back to Stratera and into the penthouse academy flat the four of us were sharing. He asked me to go with him so he could monitor me. But I'm not ready to leave Trey's mansion yet. Instead, I wander the long marble corridors hoping for whispers of Trey; I always receive silent responses. Everything is quiet, except the pad, pad, pad of Dorian's feet against the marble.

Kato, along with Dorian, takes me home after the library every evening. Kato stays to remove pieces of pain, but I think he just feels guilty for leaving me in the mansion. He doesn't need to. I'm so empty now I'm not sure if I'm healed or just numb.

The morning of the inauguration ball, I open my eyes to streaming sunlight pouring into Trey's room and roll over, throwing the pillow over my head. When I eventually sit up, I find a black and purple ballgown on the end of the bed. Nyx used to arrange things like that—there's a note:

Love Bo xx

Bo? That was sweet. She really must have forgiven me for everything that's happened. My chest pinches at the thought of Nyx. I miss her. I miss Titus. I miss my parents.

Trey... How many more names will I have to add to my list of people to miss?

The dress is beautiful; the bodice is a black corset. From the right hip, up and across the breast and spiking over the shoulder to hover above my ear, is a flash of violet. The flash wraps around the back of the dress and down the skirt, carving a violet line all the way to the ground. The shoes match, black patent leather with a stroke of violet sweeping horizontally from toe to heel, and the soles match.

My chest has throbbed since the ball announcement a week ago. A subtle warning sign I should have paid more attention to. I take my time showering, shaving my legs, lathering on soaps, moisturizers and oils, and get dressed before I do my makeup. There's food on a tray on the table in the corner, so it must be lunch already. I grab a sandwich and nibble at it while picking through makeup options.

Eventually, I move to the mirror to at least attempt to cover the dark bags under my eyes. I swipe a line of black over my lids and dab concealer. But then I catch sight of my arm and the tainted patch of skin that's really a lock.

Images of the First Fallon gripping me, breaking my arm and turning me into the lock, smash into my vision. She's in the mirror, her white skin, white hair and lilac eyes boring into mine. She laughs at me because she won.

I drop the eyeliner and stumble back, hitting the bed and sliding to the floor. I can't breathe, my fingers are tingling, the dress is suffocating me. Someone is screaming. My heart thuds like thunder in my ears, static speckles my vision.

Then I'm in a pair of arms. Watery coolness swallows me whole. I'm drowning. No, not drowning. Floating in calm water, in serenity.

I blink.

"Kato?"

"I can't leave you for five minutes, can I?" he says. He's

dressed in a maroon suit, tailored and fitted to his body. If it weren't for the mess of his blond hair, he'd look far too grown up.

"Don't know what you're talking about. I'm fine." Of course, it's a lie. I'm feigning a confidence I do not feel. I scramble out of his arms and brush myself down.

Kato raises an eyebrow. I can't lie to him. My anxiety will be flowing off me and into him like a giant tsunami.

"Kato, today... This ball... Cecilia..."

He nods. "That's why I'm here."

"I want to be in control tonight."

He runs his hand through his shaggy blond hair—which does nothing to soothe the scarecrow appearance—and looks at everything but me.

"I understand, that's why I came."

"I wish it wasn't like this, but... But, I think you should take as much as you can. Given my reaction to her on our CogTrackers and I need to last all evening."

His arms fold.

"Don't be angry with me."

"I'm not angry," he snaps, his eyes are fiery blue. "I'm struggling. There's a difference," he says.

He's using his Siren power, but not on me, on himself. I frown, my insides gnarl up like broken old trees. As twisted and warped as the things I want from him.

"What do you mean?"

"I want to do it. I want to help you heal. There's this carnal need to protect you. You... you make me feel like he's still alive." His eyes drop to the floor. "But it's like I'm losing control. Every time I compel you, I... It's getting harder to fight the addiction. It's getting harder to *want* to fight it. All I want is to take it all. I should've known better. This is why Sirens aren't supposed to compel anyone healing from

Balancer loss. I'm not like Trey. He was so much more powerful than me. He has control in a way I'll never have. I've been trying to compel myself to stop the addiction. But it's not working. Can you imagine what the press would do? What the Council would say?"

I take his hand and squeeze, and he trails off. He's babbling. This is hurting him, and it makes bile claw at my throat.

"You're helping me. We can fight the addiction together. I'm struggling too. It won't be much longer. I'm so much better than I was."

Kato looks at his feet, shaking his head. I'm disgusting. I shouldn't push him to help me when I can see what it's doing to him. My mouth is sour. Even as the words flow, I hate myself a little more.

"Please? Just take a bit... Just for today. Anything is better than nothing. We can find another way for me to cope. But I can't see the First Fallon without you. I don't know how I'll react."

His head snaps up, his eyes blaze with blue fire. But that's not what makes me stumble back. Under the flames, something more terrifying burns. A lust for emotion, for compulsion, for control of another. Control of me. His face is tight, hard like granite. I step back until my back hits the wall. My lips part.

This is wrong.

I was wrong.

"Maybe we shouldn't," I stammer.

"I want to," he says, his voice a growl. "It's simple. You need to stay in control. And I need to take all those broken emotions."

"I..."

"Do you want to be in control today?"

"Of course."

"Then give me your pain, Eden. Let me take. It. Away..."

His hand tiptoes toward me. The seduction of numbness flickers like static between our fingertips. He wants what I want to give.

I relent.

He steps into me. I lace my fingers through his and between the crack of our palms, a molten thread connects us. Bitter regret, the hot slice of anger and smokey pang of longing slither through and out of my veins like liquid gold. Everywhere his compulsion travels, through every cell, and scrap of tissue, it grasps at pain and hurt and ache and siphons it until my insides feel like glass. More and more he takes. Just like last time, I reach the threshold of numbness, the point he should stop. But he doesn't, his face wrinkles, his eyes a strange contortion of desperation and desire. I'm too breathless to stop him. A slow, sharp twist grabs my insides, relief mutating into something darker, sinister. I gasp for breath, reach for my strength and rip my hand from his.

"KATO," I yelp.

A furrow nestles in my brow as I mentally check myself over. "What the hell? You took way too much."

There's a rustle by the door. I crane over Kato's shoulder, but there's no one there. Just someone walking past.

When I turn back to him, something inside me cracks. Kato's face is stony. His jaw is strained, his bright eyes so fierce I want to turn away, but I can't. This is when I know it has to stop. I just have no idea how to.

Kato might be a diva, but he's soft, and loving and sweet. He's the definition of puppy dogs and sunshine. But the Kato standing before me is full of anger and hatred, *my anger and hatred.* As my emotion passes through him and he stores it away, his eyes soften. But not enough. There's something there. A shield. No, worse than a shield, a scar, and I made it.

"I'm so sorry. This... All of this." I cup his face. "It's my fault. I shouldn't be doing this to you."

"You're not the only one to blame. I have a choice too. I don't have to do this."

"Then why are you?"

He leans his head down so that both our foreheads touch. "Because I can't lose you, too. I just can't. Everyone has gone... If you go... I know I make jokes and put a brave face on, but I'm not okay. Mum, Dad, Trey. They've all left."

I pull away. I can't look at him. My belly riles roils and froths, a bitter acrid taste swimming around my tonsils. His mother is alive and I still haven't told him. How can I tell him after all this time? Tears stain his cheeks as his body relaxes against mine and the puppy dog I love reappears.

"I will do whatever it takes to keep you alive. To keep you here. I'm not letting you go. Even if it means fighting an addiction. Even if it means walking to the ends of Trutinor and killing a pair of errant gods. You're not dying, Eden. Not while I'm still breathing. You're the only family I have left."

There's another shuffle by the door. I crane over his shoulder, wondering if it's a Keeper who doesn't want to intrude. But there's no one there. Before I can check, he kisses me on the forehead and pulls me into an embrace. His arms wrap tight around my back and all I want to do is dissolve into tears because it doesn't matter what he says. I will ruin him. How separate can he really keep my emotions? Wherever he's storing them, the rage is seeping out. It's spreading under his skin. There are trails of darkness and emotions left in its wake—and none of it belongs to him.

But if I take back my emotions, I'll break. I realize I'm helpless. I don't know how to fix this. Two tears roll down my cheeks and plop onto his suit jacket. I could talk to Dorian about how he can help and what the rebels can do about addiction. But I dismiss the idea. We don't need anyone else. We can figure this out on our own.

"I'm so sorry," I breathe into his shoulder.

"There's nothing to be sorry about."

But there is. I want him to keep me emotionless. But asking that of him means I have to watch the Kato I love vanish. I'm not strong enough to stop it.

Worse, I'm not even sure I want to.

As the midafternoon sun draws over the sky and warms the air, Magnus bundles us into the train and drives us to the Ancient Forest. I want to use the ball to see how Cecilia really is. How healthy she claims to be in CogNews. I need to understand the level of security she has. There has to be a way to get to her.

By the time Bo, Kato and I reach the Ancient Forest station, it's dusk. The sun is yawning into darkness and the station bustles with Keepers ready to party. We walk through the forest, evening insects chirp and click as the air settles into a late afternoon daze.

Someone bumps into Kato. He stumbles a few steps, spins around and shoves them hard. "Watch where you're going, moron."

"Kato," Bo and I bark.

I catch her attention, and I know she's thinking the same thing: this isn't like Kato at all.

"What in the name of Balance was that? It was uncalled for," I say.

His breathing is elevated, a vein in the side of his neck throbs and I swear I see a flash of violet and black ripple through it.

Shit.

"Well, he needs to watch where he's going. Fucking idiot." He snarls like there's acid on his tongue, glares at the pair of us, then marches off. I stare after him in stunned silence.

"He's behaving like that more and more recently," Bo says. I chew on her words. Knots cluster in my gut. They're as lumpy, hard, and uncomfortable as the truth I don't want to acknowledge. We continue through the forest, but after a while, Bo holds me back.

"We'll catch up, babe," she shouts to Kato. When he's out of sight, she rounds on me. She's wearing a fitted leather bodice and pants embellished with Kato's maroon colors. Over her shoulders is a floor-length cloak. How she's not sweating in the forest's humidity, I don't know. Her hair is plaited and her lips plump with her signature red lipstick. Her expression is stiff and twitchy, as if she can't quite decide what to feel.

"Thank you for the dress," I say.

"You're welcome," Bo says and gives me a hug. "I just figured with Nyx..."

"It meant a lot. It made me smile, and a little nostalgic. I hadn't even considered what to wear. I'd probably have ended up in combat pants."

She tuts at me like there was no way I'd have rocked up wearing combat pants, but what else would I have worn? I decide not to correct her. She kindly saved me from that awkwardness. She fidgets with her cape. "I had something made for you," she says.

"You did?" A rush of heat climbs over my cheeks. I didn't get her anything.

She digs into her pocket and pulls out a small box. I open it and tears spring to my eyes. I pull the necklace out and clutch it in the palm of my hand.

"It's made from pieces of Trey's CogTracker," she says.

I rub the tears out of my eyes so I can see it better. The necklace has the East and South symbols entwined side by side. It's made of a mash of silver and coppery bronze cogs and metal.

"I found his Tracker in the mansion and I just figured whatever happens in the future, you'll carry a part of him with you always. A screw you to Cecilia, I guess."

"It's beautiful," I breathe and pull her into my arms. When I let go, she gives me a limp smile.

"You should be looking far more smug than that. You get total BFF points."

"Thanks," she says, her smile barely wider than it was.

"Okay, come on, tell me what's wrong."

"Nothing." This time she grins, but the smile doesn't reach her eyes.

"Liar."

"Not today, okay? Let's get through this farce of an inauguration and talk tomorrow."

She turns to walk, but I grab her wrist.

"Bo? Come on. You can't tell me something's wrong and then not tell me what's actually wrong. Spit it out. It's me."

"Yeah, it is." She glances down, her voice quiet. "That's the point."

"What do you mean?"

She pulls her hand away from me and mumbles, "You need to stop."

"Huh?"

Her voice is so soft I can barely hear it. But there's no mistaking the tremor in her words. "You're pushing Kato too far. He's spiraling."

"I—"

"No, you asked. So I'm telling." She's so quiet, but her words are ice sharp and it stings. "I saw you."

"Saw me what?"

"In the mansion, before we left. I saw you with Kato in Trey's room."

I bite my tongue, trying to feel something, anything. The tingle of panic and guilt must be bubbling somewhere under the numbness. But all that's left inside is a vacuous cavern.

"It's one thing you falling into a pit of grief and pain, but how can you drag him with you?" Her eyes well up, she's shaking, and I'm not sure if it's anger or sadness.

"I didn't mean to."

"You didn't mean it? Is that a joke? Come on, Eden. You think he'd ever say no to you? You heard what he said. He'll do anything to keep you alive. No matter the consequence. You're the only family he has left." Her lips tremble, she dabs a tear from her lid.

"That's not... He didn't mean it like that."

"That's exactly what he meant."

I wish she'd shout at me or slap me or something. How can such velvet words needle so much? Tears spill down her cheeks. "Can't you see what you're doing?" she says.

I shift my footing and stare up the path. In the distance, through the meshy tangle of leaves and forest canopy, lights twinkle.

"Well, can't you?" she says, taking my hand and squeezing it.

I take a deep, thick breath that's hard to gulp down. "Stopping is harder than you think."

"If you care about him at all, if you care about me, stop. You might want to self-destruct, but please don't take him with you."

Her porcelain skin looks as though it will crack, her brows are nipped together, her eyes pinched. What am I doing? I'm hurting the only ones left around me. And for what? Cheap booze and emotional apathy?

"Please?" she says, her voice a whisper.

My mouth drops open. I want to say something, but no words come. When I don't answer, she shakes her head at me. "I thought you were better than this."

Her cloak swishes as she vanishes up the path and toward the clearing. I pull my hands over my face. How the hell am I going to stop?

My memories are blurred. My head is a haze of nights in the bar or library and oceans of numbness. My chest grips the truth: the darkness inside him is because of me, but it's pain I never want to take back.

As I scramble back onto the path, I run straight into someone.

"Shit, sorry," I say, wiping my dress down—which is now sporting one or two too many creases.

"Fallon East," a voice says, with a smile that radiates through his entire face.

"Dorian. I figured you'd catch us up."

His eyes scan me up and down, his mouth drops open and it makes heat flush straight to my cheeks. Thankfully, I can't feel the embarrassment as it's hidden under the numbness.

He clears his throat. "We must stop running into each other like this." His grin is so perfect and wide, I find myself smiling back.

"Hah, I'm wondering if I'll ever get rid of you." I nudge him in the ribs. "I thought I'd lost you on the platform."

He scoffs out a snuffled sort of laugh. It makes my lips stretch into a smile.

"Oh please, like I'd let you out of my sight. That seemed... private, though. Thought I'd give you space. Besides, I'm delightful company."

I roll my eyes. "You mean to tell me you don't have a big date for the big inauguration?" I say, changing the subject.

"But Fallon East. Didn't you realize? You are *my date*."

A stuttered, nervous laugh tumbles out. I brush down the front of my dress to avoid staring at the exquisitely shaped suit he's wearing, which nips and tucks in all the right places. He tilts my chin up so my gaze meets his and then holds his arm out. His dark green suit makes his eyes pop, his arms bulge under the fabric and his cane is the perfect complement—dark green with shimmers of emerald. He looks... God, I'm not doing this. Thank Balance I can't feel the adrenaline I am certain is flooding my body right now.

"So, umm. Shall we?"

"It would be my honor. You look stunning."

I swallow. Drag my eyes away from his and take his arm.

"I need a drink. Care to drown your miseries with me before the inauguration?" I say.

"You mean stand there ready to call a Kato-shaped cab for you while I hold your hair up and you puke in the toilets again?"

"Too soon, way too soon."

He smiles and his eyes smolder. *Stop it, Eden.* Together

we hobble up the path using his cane for support. I can move so much easier now, but I'm still weak and walking for any amount of time exhausts me. He doesn't seem to lean on his cane as much as he was, though, so at least one of us is healing.

As we enter the clearing, my breath escapes in one long whoosh. It's beautiful. Floating above the field are thousands of tiny fire embers, each flickering like orange stars. On the far side are the five wooden root towers that spear the sky and form the entrances to the Council Chambers. Three of the root towers are dressed in maroon Siren colors. I squash the urge to roll my eyes. This is all a charade. The First Fallon doesn't give a shit about Kato or Trey. She wanted Trey dead, and she got her way. Sure, she didn't push the knife into his throat herself, but she might as well have. She might've conspired with Victor to bring Karva—her daughter—back, but Karva's harboring thousands of years of bitterness. Cecilia left her to rot in Obex after all.

I strain at the naked roots. They seem... lighter? This unsettles something in my chest, but I can't place why it bothers me.

There's a stage to my left opposite the Council entrances. A band plays, the beat thumps out across the clearing. In front of the stage is a tiled dance floor. It's huge, large enough for at least a couple hundred people to dance on. There are market stands and stalls for food and trinkets. The smell of warm garlic and roasted chestnuts fills the air. Everything is peaceful. Keepers are smiling and laughing and dancing with each other. Maybe I'm wrong and the First Fallon really is celebrating Trey's life. But I doubt it. It's *too* peaceful.

Kato only compelled me a couple of hours ago, but there's already a growing tightness in my chest and the cold slick of sweat pooling at the base of my back that always appears as my pain and emotions flood back.

I glance around as we make our way into the middle of the crowd. I've no clue where Kato and Bo are, though I spot the private Fallon dining area: an enormous circus-style marquee. Around its pointed roof are decorations— tributes to each state's power. Shimmering wolves and bears prance around the tent, sand, water, fire and electric clouds float beside the animals. In between them are wisps of green and smokey plants in among other tributes. As they circle the teepee, it almost looks like a child's merry-go-round. It doesn't take long for the clearing to heave with Keepers. Dorian and I grab drinks—Mind Numb for me, soft juice for him and we sit at the bar at the back of the clearing.

He spots someone he knows in close enough proximity he can stand and talk to them and keep his eyes on me.

"Will you stay put? I need to know you're within reaching distance."

I glance at my full glass and shrug. "Sure, I don't need to go anywhere for a while."

He moves a few paces away and positions himself so he can see me while leaning in for a conversation with whoever the random Keeper is.

I quietly sip my drink and watch as he glides through the crowd, sliding circular coins into pockets, and whispering promises of rebellion in ears. Everyone he leaves is smiling, their eyes bright and round and full of hope, like he's seducing them one by one. I didn't think Sirens could do that. More control emotions. I shrug it off. Must be the charm.

An hour later and I've consumed my body weight in Mind Numb. I'm sat at the bar, Dorian my constant shadow, except for when he's a grand total of two feet away talking to someone—Kato and Bo are still missing and I'm feeling more and more sorry for myself, so I get up and wander around. It's almost like I'm alone—if it weren't for the constant fizz my essence senses whenever Dorian is around.

A girl with long dark hair catches my eye. She seems familiar, though I can't place where I know her from. I follow her, twisting in and out of bodies, moving through the dance floor like a ghost. She approaches a man in a dark suit. I strain to see between the crowd. It's Trat Riplock. Trat's father is second in command in the North. He was also Bound to Rita. The girl flicks her hair back, her head kicking back as she laughs.

"No way." I strain to see who it was or who she might be. While her hair and figure are identical to Rita's, her face is different. Instead of dark eyes, they're blue. Her nose is pert instead of finely set and her skin is lighter. They talk for a while, her laughing, him offering her drinks and his arm, which she takes. The last time I saw Rita in the rebel camp, she promised Trat would get what he deserved. She suffered a misbind—something that happens when you're not Bound to your Potential. Hers was Tiron, but she ended up with Trat, who is an abusive piece of shit instead. Trat beat her for not falling in love with him. The longer I stare, the more convinced I am. It's Rita. I just don't understand how she's changed her appearance. I move through the crowd, following Rita's movements. The whole time I stay parallel to her until I reach the exit into the Forest where I lose her. There's a sudden movement, a scuffle, and she vanishes. I scan the Keepers, searching for where she went. A hand grabs me from behind. My spine tingles and I let out a yelp.

Dorian appears out of nowhere and has the girl in a headlock before I can even open my mouth.

"Would you calm down? It's Rita, get off her."

Dorian, wide-eyed, releases her, holding his arms up. "It is my job." He tuts and retreats a few spaces, merging into the threshold of the Forest, never far, eyes always on me.

"Serves me right for stalking you, I suppose," she giggles.

"Rita? Is that really you?" I ask, scanning her features.

"The one and only." She peels something off her lips and her face shudders, her features realigning.

"How did you do that?"

She holds up a lip-shaped piece of material. It's rouge and floppy. She flings it into the woods and grins at me. I glance back to Trat. "What did you do to him?"

He staggers across the dance floor, his skin a glorious shade of yellow.

"Nothing he didn't deserve," she says, a smile curling the corner of her mouth.

"Is he going to die?"

She turns to me, her dark eyebrow raised. "Death is a punishment the weak and cowardly dish out. I let him make me weak once. I promised myself I'd never be weak again."

"You're terrifying, you know that?"

"I try to be."

Trat stumbles a few paces on the dance floor.

"What is wrong with him?"

"Let me put it this way. The line of Riplocks ends with Trat. No more abusive assholes will be born into that family."

My eyes widen like orbs. "Like I said. Terrifying."

"It's good to see you, Eden. I hope you'll join the rebellion for real."

I smile. Deep down, I think my heart's already joined. I'm just waiting for my head to catch up. I glance over at Trat, who looks at the liquid in his cup and slides it onto the bar. Then he glances at his crotch, a halo of red forming around his zipper. His face pales and he bolts from the clearing.

With that, she nods. "Job done."

"Did Tiron ever find his way to you?"

She gives me a curt head shake. "Not yet. Maybe he really was meant to be with Eloise."

"No way. You two are fated."

As she leaves, her face is hard. "Perhaps fate's the problem."

Dorian—the charming schmuck—has taken himself on a tour of Council members, trying to woo his way into their affections. First it was Arden, whose handlebar mustache wriggled and wobbled as his mouth split wide with laughter. Dorian's next victim was Israel, who—much to my disgust—cracked a smile. A fucking smile? From Israel? What is Dorian selling? He must exude some kind of Siren charm on steroids. This must be the real reason he's here. Connecting with Libra members ready to recruit them to Castor's team.

I shake my tumbler at the barman who I'm fairly sure tuts under his breath and then fills my glass with the cheap whiskey from under the counter instead of the Mind Numb I was drinking. *Asshole.* Half of me wants to burn his fingers as he hands the glass back, the other half doesn't care enough. Alcohol is alcohol.

Twice Dorian clocks me watching him. He smiles, a

bright white, perfect grin with an accompanying nod for me to join him on the dance floor. His eyes glitter under the blanket of fire embers.

I hate him. I hate him because he's not Trey. Because he's handsome enough, I enjoy looking at him. Kind enough, I like hanging around with him, and charming enough I could totally fall for him.

But more than any of that, I hate him because he's clean and free of addiction—he represents everything I know I should be doing, and can't. So I don't join him because that feels like a betrayal to Trey and too much like a reality I'm ignoring.

Instead, I sit and invisible tears slide down my cheeks. Tears I should be feeling but can't because I'm numb. I wipe my face anyway.

As evening draws in, I've lost count of how much I've drunk. The music's beat kicks up a notch; the crowd is consumed by the music and the Mind Numb has well and truly kicked in, thank Balance. It's masking the fact Kato's pain relief has worn off. Instead of the nasty tinge my reality has, the world is hazy; the edges blurred and sparkling. My belly is warm and for one brief moment, I forget about Trey. I live in the moment, the numbness, the music and the thumping bass beat.

Although I'm sitting, my body sways beneath me on the stall, it moves on its own, at one with the rhythm. Dorian smiles at me, returning from yet another round of Council charming. He holds his hand out. "Would you care to dance?" His voice is smooth and melodic, like the cellos and drums playing in the background. I look up at him. The hum of his voice sings one persistent lyric: he's the kind of trouble I want right now.

He bows, one hand extended, the other leaning on his cane.

I glance from his hand to the cane and then to the crowd of Keepers. Their bodies jump and twirl and part of me wants in. But I hate dancing—I can't dance. My feet fall over each other. Trey was the only one I could dance with. He had these magical feet that dragged me through the right steps. I'm not sure whether it's the booze or the fact I've got nothing else to do, but the word spills out.

"Sure." I take his hand. He leans his cane against the bar and pulls me in, spinning me into his arms and onto the dance floor.

"Oh," I gasp. He flings me around and slides me into a leaning position near the floor. His face is inches from mine.

"You don't impress me," I say as he pulls me upright. We stand, face to face, motionless in a circle of Keepers who have stopped to watch us. He pushes a stray strand of hair behind my ear. Where his fingers brush over my skin, heat glitters in trails and bubbles.

"Really?" he says, his eyes twinkle under the flames and candles, the green bright against the ring of black around his pupils. "Then you should probably stop smiling."

My fingers reach up to my traitorous mouth. I *am* smiling. My face falls. Which only makes him grin harder. He pulls me upright, places a hand around my waist. I take it, reluctantly. We step together; he leads. He doesn't cover his limp, instead he embraces it, guiding me in a rhythm, step, slide, step, slide, step.

"What do you want?" I ask.

Dorian's eyes skim over my face. "I want what you want."

"I highly doubt that, Mr. Oswald," I say into his neck and catch a whiff of his scent. He smells fresh, like an ocean breeze, salty cheeks and pine trees. He smells like freedom. I like it.

"Why?" I say.

"Why am I part of the rebels?"

"Yes. Why do any of this? Why join Castor? Why fight this fight?"

"Justice."

I've been thinking about this ever since the night I eavesdropped. Being part of the rebels, being so determined to eradicate fate. There has to be something more, something deeper. His Binding peaks out from under his suit sleeve, and that's when I realize.

"Cecilia killed Pax, didn't she?"

Dorian looks away. I guess that's my answer.

"Then what you just said is bullshit. You were right the first time. We do both want the same thing. But it's not justice. We want vengeance."

He pulls me around to face him. My words hang between us as we're motionless in a swaying crowd. He stays silent, but there's something between us, a knowing, an acceptance. I see him and he sees me.

"Who are you?" I whisper as he moves again and spins me out.

"You know who I am, Dorian Oswald."

"I didn't ask for your name. I asked who you were. There's something you're not telling me."

He pulls us to a stop. His green eyes stare into mine. He blinks, scans my face and says, "I'm a rebel, a bodyguard. I suppose I'm something of a recruiter, too. I was Pax's Balancer."

And he is all of those things. But he's something else. There's more, but I can't quite reach it.

He scans around us, swinging us into the center of the

dance floor. He pulls me in tight. I lean into his ear and whisper.

"What aren't you telling me?"

"Slide your hand into my back pocket."

"You want me to touch your ass? In public?"

He looks at me, his eyes glint. "It's pert, and I don't have Altiritus. You'll live."

I glare at him because that was entirely not my point. Kato's eye catches me on the far side of the dance floor, and I straighten up. His expression is dark, his jaw hard. He doesn't look in the best of moods and—as harmless as the dance is—I'm in the arms of another man. Even though they're friends, I'm not sure how he'd react if he sees me grope Dorian, especially given his previous outbursts.

"Umm. Turn me around first."

He does. He pulls me in so tight my chest touches his. Then he leans into me. Our cheeks press against each other. My breath catches. This is closer than I've been to anyone since... Our breath mingles, his long eyelashes flutter, and I swear my stomach furls into a knot. His lips slip closer to mine. We're millimeters apart. My heart rate climbs. I shake myself clear and slide my hand around and into the bottom of his pocket. There's something small. It's smooth on one side and rough on the other. I pull it out. It's a shell.

"Huh? A shell?"

Dorian brushes his lips against my cheek and leans in. "It is a shell."

My heart stills. He leans in. Closer. Closer. God. Don't kiss me, don't do it.

He holds my gaze. "I can't tell you. But if you ask, I won't lie to you..."

What does he me—I glance up and my blood, my heart, my breath... Everything stills. Kato must have made his way around the dance floor. He's facing me at the edge of the crowd, his back stiff, his face harder than steel.

Shit. Shit. Shit.

Before I can go to him, he spins on his heel and vanishes into the crowd.

SIXTEEN

Soul Sanctuary—*The safe haven Balanced Keeper souls wait in until their living Balancers join them.*

The Dictionary of Balance

TREY

The fight club is rammed. Bodies pressed against each other crammed into the warehouse. The room stinks of stale sweat and the cool tingle of anticipation. It's the freshest emotion I've sensed since I've been here. Cut with aromatic mint and crisp fall mornings, it's almost like being back in Trutinor. Rozalyn peers over the balcony into the fight club. Her lips curl into a smile. She turns to me, arms folded over her white dress. "Well done, boy. I'm almost impressed. There are an awful lot of recruits here this evening."

"I had a reason to get it done," I say.

"And go home, we shall. But first, are they all signed up?"

I nod. "We have three hundred sign-ups already. We've got the fitter demons running recruits through training, drills and military maneuvers. A couple of them used to be part of the Trutinor army, so that's helped. We have another twelve hundred waiting to join, but we can't get through the Blood Oaths quick enough."

"I'll send bodies from the castle to help swear them in. And the specifics of the oath?"

"In exchange for joining the army for one war, they receive the opportunity to fight at the club. Each fight winner receives one piece of soul. The better the fighter, the higher the chance of completing their soul."

"Any resistance?" she asks, leaning over the balcony railing and peering into the crowd below.

"A little. Nothing that was unmanageable, though."

"Excellent. Well, I have one further sweetener to add. I've been studying the Book of Imbalance. I believe, even if your Scythe trickery doesn't work, the Heart, once whole, may just be able to help."

"I'll tell them."

"Excellent. And you'll lead my army?"

I sniff. "That wasn't part of the deal, Rozalyn."

"It wasn't," she says, turning to me and stepping closer. "But I do hope you'll take up the offer."

"Can I do it from Trutinor?"

She smiles, takes me in. Then shrugs. "Such a shame."

"What is the plan, anyway?" I ask. "Once we get enough demons, how do we defeat her?"

Rozalyn sighs, picks at the fabric on her dress sleeve. "There's time to discuss the details, but, the rebels are planning to create a doorway for us. We, with the army, will march on Trutinor and march on Cecilia. Once we have reunited the Heart, we will destroy my sister and all live happily ever after."

I raise an eyebrow.

"What, did you think I was going to pour out thousands of years of plans in a pithy sentence? Dear boy, honestly. Shall we?" She gestures to the waiting crowd below.

As we descend into the fight club, three hundred sets of demons' eyes crane up to watch us. There's a lot of muscle, pincers, claws and teeth. My stomach drops. I'm not sure I can win a fight against this lot.

Eve appears at the bottom of the stairs. She exchanges a tight glance with Rozalyn and then parks herself next to me as I step down.

"Pick the biggest one," Eve whispers.

"Excuse me, Mr. Luchelli, I believe a drink is in order before the fun begins," Rozalyn says and disappears into the bar.

"Why the biggest?" I say to Eve.

"Because you're a Breather and they're stupid. The biggest one will be slow and lumbering, but to the other demons, they'll see a tiny breathing human trying to take on a giant beast. When you win, it will make you look twice as impressive."

"The bigger the demon is, the stronger he'll be, though."

She nods. "See this scar?" She points to a scar on her arm that looks like it was a nasty gash. "That came from an enormous fear demon. Easily a foot or two taller than me. But he was a lumbering idiot. He might have been strong, but I was much faster than he was. I dodged most of his attacks and managed to get behind him. Swift knife to the spine ashed him."

I stare at her, wondering when she became such a

fighter. Was she always like this? I remember her wearing silk dresses and having golden skin and flowing hair. Much as Eden hated her and told me how spiky she was, Eve was always soft to me.

She puts a hand on her hip. "Whoever you choose needs to be as strong as a tank. As long as you're faster than him, you'll be able to win."

"Most of the larger demons are fear demons—they're the most dangerous demons down here."

"Exactly."

"What if I lose control? What—"

"I believe in you. You never lost control with me, no matter how hard I pushed you." She sticks her tongue out, and I can't help but laugh.

"Yeah and you tried."

She elbows me in the ribs, but it's gentle. "Look, everyone here is dead. What's the worst you can do? It won't be like before. You won't hurt anyone."

I stay silent and pray to Balance she's right. A rumbling roar breaks out, punctuated by the occasional demonic screech that makes my teeth chill and my ears shudder.

The fighting ring itself is a simple platform with old sea rope as a barrier. There's no boxing pads or foam to prevent injury. This is survive or die.

Demons have spread around the ring and through the warehouse. There's so many bodies crowded in they've spilled out through the doors and into the streets. There are a few faces I recognize from the bar, but most of them are new to me. The demons range from freshly dead to barely recognizable as conscious.

There are several rows of spotlights hanging from the ceiling. Pest fixed them because he wanted to see every pound of flesh torn off in the fights. I raised an eyebrow, but let him get on with it. As I circle the fighting ring, there's a waft of stagnant decay mixed with the warm bubble of hunger peeling off the demons. My skin ripples with the waves of energy and excitement. Pest stands at least two heads higher than the majority of demons. He's in the corner, arms folded, ready to referee.

Rozalyn appears back on the balcony. Eve catches my eye.

It's time.

I step into the ring and raise my hands, signaling silence. There are two demons next to Pest, one is glaring in my general direction. His head is cocked toward Pest as if he's sharing a secret. The other demon is shortish, with sickly green hair covering his body. He appears to be grunting at Pest. I swear Pest rolls his eyes even though his sockets are eyeless and then he punches the green demon clean in the temple. The demon slithers to the floor, silent. The other demon inches away from Pest and a few seconds of jostling later, the mumbles quiet.

"Demons, monsters... Your Majesty... Eve..." I grin. "Welcome, welcome to The Fallen Fallon's first ever fight night." I open my arms and bow. A cheer booms around the room.

"There are only two rules this evening." I raise a finger. "Number one, no weapons inside the ring other than your natural power."

There's a grumble and some fidgeting and the clank of metal as several blades, swords, and maces fall to the floor. There's a shuffling and I spot Bellamy scurrying through the crowd, picking up the dropped weapons. Pest, Eve and I decided it would be easier to referee and keep the scales balanced if we didn't allow weapons.

"Rule two, inside the ring, you fight. Outside the ring

you don't…" I let the crowd swallow the information. "Pestilence is referee both inside and outside the ring. If you're found fighting outside the ring, you're barred from the club for eternity. No second chances."

I pace a full circle, eyeing as many of the demons as I can. Enforcing the rules, measuring up the power plays and competitors. I slide to a stop.

"In exchange for getting to fight this evening, you will swear a blood oath to join Rozalyn's army. The prize for winning each fight is a piece of soul… ONE PIECE. Not an entire soul. One piece for one win. The more pieces you win, the more chances of healing your soul."

There's a rumbly cheer clanging around the warehouse, jumps and shouts and hoots all full of grit and gravel.

"But there's more. Her Majesty has unearthed some research that promises if we win the war, and reunite both halves of the Heart, there may be another way to heal yourselves. But if you don't join, if you don't fight, there will be no such prize. Got it?"

The roars and shouts are muted this time, more pensive and curious. God, I hope Roz was telling the truth. Whatever happens, I do not want to have broken promises to an army of pissed-off demons.

"Training will happen before and after fights. And as for the details of the war, I will defer to our Majesty." I give the Last Fallon a bow.

The demons holler and a few of them beat their chests, spittle sprays the edges of the ring. One gray, skinny demon with sticklike arms raises a hand.

"Yes?"

"How do we claim the pieces of soul?"

My eyes and lips narrow into a dark grin. "I'm glad you asked. Pest?"

Pest walks around the ring and reaches a shelf set high above the crowd. He pulls down the box containing the blade Rozalyn gave me.

Pest brings the box to the ring entrance. He holds the box out to me. I push my finger onto the spike. A drop of blood runs down the spear and touches the lock.

There's a hiss in the crowd as the smell of "living" blood permeates the room. The air prickles as the demons fight to control themselves. Lust and hunger pummel me from all sides. It smells like raw meat and smoke. A few of the demons shake their heads like dogs, slather spinning off and hitting me and Pest.

I breathe deep, raise my defenses, and block out their emotions.

"Silence," I demand. After some grunting, the demons abide.

As a few more drops of my blood spill into the lock, it clicks open. There's an audible rush of air and the lid pops open. Lying in a bed of blood-red velvet is the blade.

I pick it up and thrust my hand in the air. There's an explosion of howling and bellowed roars.

"DEMONS!" I shout. "I hold before you Rozalyn's Soul Scythe. The only weapon capable of cutting a soul."

There's more cheering. I glance up at Rozalyn. Her expression is severe; watching, assessing. Above the roars, I hear Eve's screams of delight. Her eyes are alight and focused solely on the blade. In that moment, I finally see how much she wants this. How much this tiny piece of bone has filled her with hope. Her cheeks flush with rouge, but hope has always been a dangerous emotion. I've told her many times I have no proof this will work. Who can say whether a mosaic of soul pieces will complete her enough she can move on. I can't promise her anything and yet still she clings to the possibility it will.

My chest tightens. Have I made a mistake? *No. Pull it together.* This is how I get back to Eden.

"The winner will wield the blade while they take a piece of soul, and then the blade will be returned to the box. Anyone tries to take the blade, mess with the blade or otherwise, they'll be banned from fight nights and handed to the Last Fallon, and I hear roasted demon is her favorite delicacy."

Right on cue, she raises her hand and waves at the crowd. Several of the demons suck in air and drop to their knees. My point is made.

I place the blade back in the box and shut the lid, handing it to Pest, who places it on the shelf.

"I, Trey Luchelli, challenge the first fighter." I shake off my jacket and tank top and throw them to Eve. It leaves my torso bare, but that also keeps my arms unrestricted. Eve's lips part, her eyes locked on my abs. I've lost weight since being in Obex and my skin is taut against my muscle. The heavy labor of renovating the club didn't help and I guess part of me—the living part—isn't getting the sustenance it needs. My abs protrude more than usual, muscles and lines carve through my torso and hips like canyons.

Eve throws me a roll of stained bandage, which I wrap around my knuckles. I doubt it will help, but anything is better than nothing.

I scan the crowd, looking for the biggest demon I can. There's three, one bald giant who must be twice the size of the rest of the demons and, thankfully, isn't a fear demon. His shoulders must be ten times the width of mine. How he got through the barn door, I have no idea. He's a suitable candidate, but too obvious. He'd be a lumbering oaf and it wouldn't look like a good fight.

I glance at the other two, both fear demons. *Shit.*

Before I can look for another opponent, the crowd makes the choice for me. There's shouting and cheering as they part and let one of the giant fear demons through.

I glance over at Eve. Her eyes are wide, she's blinking fast. But as much as I can see the chill of fear emanating from her, there's something else under it, a bubbling smokey heat: hunger. She wants to smell blood as much as the other demons.

As the fear demon makes his way to the ring, I swallow hard, trying to compose myself.

I can do this.

The demon jumps into the ring, slather drips over his lips and teeth. I don't wait for him to attack. I run at him, slide between his legs, and punch straight up into his balls. There's a garbled cry as he spins around and grabs my throat and staggers into the sea rope and steel mesh. He smashes me across the face and slams his fist into my ribs for good measure. Then drops me on the floor so he can lean over the rope and catch his breath.

Blood splatters across the floor, drips down my lips, and sprays my pants. I'm fairly sure he broke my nose and possibly a rib, too. It's impossible to catch my breath and even lying on the floor hurts. But there's no time to worry about the pain. I reach out to my essence, pulling on my Siren powers, drawing out the pain and pushing it away. I'll be a mess afterward, but the demon can't take his pain away, so I have an advantage.

As the beast draws himself off the rope, I realize I can heighten his pain. I focus on everything I pulled out of my nose and rib and instead of letting it go; I push it into my fists. Curling it around my knuckles. He can have my pain as well as his.

He darts forward, his arm flying out in a giant swing. I duck, step into his body and launch an upper cut straight to his chin. It crunches into his jaw and splinters the bone. The crack echoes around the ring and a cheer erupts. The demon drops to his knees and for a split second; I take my eye off him, playing to the crowd's cheers.

The demon snatches out, grabbing my leg, and I crash to the floor. He pins my body and climbs on top of me. His lips curl up, his yellow and black teeth grinding.

"Do you surrender?" He breathes over me, and I nearly gag from the stench of matted decay and stagnant blood.

"Never."

He sneers and takes hold of my throat, squeezing until my vision darkens and his powers fling into my most painful memories.

Eden appears in my mind. We dance in the Keepers school hall. It's the first time I'd seen her in years. Then we're kissing by The Pink Lake. The memory whooshes away and is replaced by the Obex ruins. Victor's hand on my throat.

A knife in my neck.

Eden's screaming.

There's a familiar thundering heartbeat. The same one I felt in the torture house Pest found me in. My grip on my memories slips, the vision graying and speckling. I'm losing. The fear demon is going to win and I'm going to lose a piece of my soul.

In that instant, I swear I can feel her. I can *feel* Eden.

"Wake up, Trey. WAKE UP," she says.

My eyes fly open. I clench my fist around the demon's arm and flood him with every ounce of agony I can summon. I draw from my memories: the guilt and anguish of killing a child after I Inherited, the torture of my Binding being torn, the searing pain of a knife in my neck and I push it all into him.

The demon yelps, his figure shakes and shrinks away. I shunt him back, lifting myself off the floor. My arms shove and push until he lands on his back and this time; I straddle him. I wipe my hand over my face, smearing sweat, blood, and grime out of my eyes.

Then I place my hands over his temples and pour emotions, pain, terror, anything and everything I have into him. My vault cracks, Imbalance seeps into my veins, the red veil drops over my vision as my power intensifies. That strange, disembodied heartbeat flares to life, hammering in my head. I blink, my hold on the demon falters.

I swear I hear Eden's voice screaming my name.

Get a grip, Trey. I shake her voice away.

I continue flooding the demon until he shrieks, blood pouring from his eyes, ears and indented nose.

"YIELD," I bellow.

He roars, his ribs vibrating between my legs. Waves of hot frustration and anger spill from his body. But I've wrapped him in a straightjacket of his own pain and fear.

"Yield. Yield," he shrieks.

Pest steps forward, his toes on the mouth of the ring. "WINNER," he cries and raises my hand. The demons jump and shout and jeer.

Pest drags the fear demon out of the ring and into a small space the crowd's made. Then he pulls the box off the shelf and, just as before, I push my finger onto the spike. The box clicks and the lid pops open and I take the blade.

The demon whimpers at my feet.

"Please," he begs, "please don't take any more of my soul."

My heart lurches. My stomach rolls and froths, bile rising in my throat. I knew this would happen. The whole point of fight night is to have a prize worth fighting for. But the consequences of losing are high. No demon wants to lose any more of their soul. I have to go through with it. If I don't, I'll lose everything I just fought for. I can't be immune to the rules or show mercy. I must command the respect I need.

"Did you willingly enter the ring?" I say, standing over him.

"I..." he grumbles. "I did."

"Did you know the consequences before you entered?"

He drops his head, unable to look at me.

"I did."

I swing the blade down and plunge it into his chest.

<hr>

"Are you sure you want to do this, Eve?" I ask. We're standing by the fight club ring. Eve's fight is the last one of the evening.

Her eyes skirt to my hand—it's gripping her arm. I didn't realize I'd grabbed hold of her. She peels my fingers off and holds my hand.

"With every fiber of my being."

"Okay," I nod. "Promise me you won't lose."

Her eyes drop, soften, her expression distant. "I appreciate the sentiment, but there's so much water under this bridge. I can't handle you caring about me now. It hurts too much. Not after everything we've been through."

"That's not fair. You know damn well I will always care about you."

Her shoulders sag. "I can't do this. Not again."

She steps away, but I pull her back into a hug. "We have an unfathomable amount of history. While we can never go back, you were, are and always will be family to me."

She rubs my back. "I have no intention of losing, anyway." Then she wriggles out of my grasp and steps inside the ring.

My muscles tighten. No matter how much has passed between us, I will always worry about her. She may not have been my soul mate, but she was in my life a long time, for a while she was all I had, when I was trying to brother and father and parent Kato, keep him away from Cecilia, run the South. She was everything, even if she never had my heart. The urge to protect doesn't just vanish.

"WHO WILL CHALLENGE ME?" Eve bellows.

There's a hesitance in the crowd. Then a stocky demon with dark red scaly skin steps forward. Its head is covered in horned spikes, its hands are clawed and sharp. Pest appears beside me, his skeletal fingers grip my arm, shoulder me back. "It's not your fight," he breathes.

Eve waves for him to enter the ring. He steps over the ropes, his eyes fixed on her.

"Fight," Pest cries over the crowd.

I glance at him. He gives me an encouraging nod. "She'll be fine."

But I don't believe him. When I turn back to the ring, there's blood on Eve's face, her arm is sliced open and dripping congealed blackish-red. But she's pinned the demon to the ground. Her knees are pressing his demon arms into the ring floor and her fists are pummeling his face. Blood bursts from his head and her knuckles and splatters the audience. Three drops hit my boot.

"Delightful." I wipe the blood off against my calf.

The demon slaps the floor. It's over. I can't help but laugh. The whole thing can't have lasted more than eight seconds.

The demon lies in a crumpled pile. Pest glances down at me. "Told you." He leaves my side, enters the ring and raises Eve's hand, pronouncing her the winner. The crowd erupts; Eve is their champion. Champions are loved and adored, for today anyway. This crowd is fickle, their adoration given to the winners for one reason only. The prize.

Pest hands the Soul Scythe to Eve. He picks up the demon by the throat as if he's nothing more than a rag. The demon struggles against his grip. His skull is already healing, pieces of bone and sinew matting back together. I'd be kicking and swinging my arms too. If you're going to have a piece of your soul cut off, it's best to do it unconscious.

A shrill roar bursts from the demon's throat. Eve takes the Soul Scythe from Pest and steps up to the writhing demon. She drops her head, whispering something in the demon's ear.

Then her head snaps up, and she swipes the blade through his chest. The scream that emanates from the demon rips through the crowd. Everyone's hands clasp their ears. It's the same sound every time. When I took the first piece earlier this evening, I thought it was the demon screaming. Now I've heard it over two dozen times. I'm not sure if it's the blade's war cry shrieking as it slices through skin and sinew, or the weeping cries of the soul itself.

My skin prickles, not from the scream, but from the emotion flowing off the demon. A shiver of hopelessness crawls over my skin. It's icy cold. So cold it tastes of infinite loneliness. It jars and undulates through my taste-buds and into my whole body. Hopelessness is the emotion I hate the most. The demon's eyes widen as he stares at a shimmering transparent strip of material floating on the tip of Eve's blade: a part of his soul. Around the blade, the air hums and reverberates with power. Then he falls limp in Pest's hands. The crowd can sense the tingle of dark, Imbalanced magic. The spectators inch back, the room is laced with the sickly stench of awe.

Eve holds the slice of soul up to the crowd, who shout and cheer in response. Then she takes the blade and draws it down her arm. The demon soul slips from the blade onto her arm like floating silk, then it vanishes into the open wound. Her body judders, then stills. Her face is calm, smoothed soft with a moment of peace—in that split second, the hope and faith that she can return to Trutinor is restored. Color flushes her skin as if she were alive again. But then it fades and so too does the look of relief.

It wasn't enough.

My chest clamps—I'm not sure it will ever be enough. What if I've cursed her for an eternity, stuck in Obex regardless of how many segments of soul she collects?

A dark look descends over Eve's face. Pest shifts his footing like he's ready to strike.

Eve pounces at the limp demon, blade extended, screams pouring from her mouth. In a single second, Pest swings the demon around, dropping him behind his towering figure and extends his forearm out like a shield. Eve halts less than a millimeter from Pest's arm. There's a single beat, the crowd hushes. No one breathes. The entire room is poised. The crowd's eyes dart between Eve and Pest, who are locked in a silent battle.

Pest snaps first and grabs Eve by the throat. She slides her hand, blade point extended out, under his skull-chin.

"Try it," she growls, "no skin and tissue to cut through. All it would take to knock your thick skull off your spine is a flick of my wrist."

Pest's lipless mouth contorts into a thin smile. "Kinda hard if I crush your spine." His white fingers tighten around her throat. Her blade slips under his skull, inching toward his spine. The pair of them are rigid. One false move and they both die.

"Enough," I shout, clambering onto the outside edge of the ring. I extend my arms, sweeping a sweet-honeyed calm across the room. The crowd visibly relaxes and half of them rush for the exit. The demon on the floor twitches and pushes himself up. He gives Eve a sideways glance before running for the exit. When there's only Eve and Pest left, I lower my arms.

"If you could refrain from killing each other, that would be lovely."

"We're already dead," they both say simultaneously. But Pest drops Eve and although she's scowling, she hands him the blade which he locks in the box.

After everyone else leaves, Eve and I are alone.

She's smiling, a light burns in her eyes. But my heart is shrinking and my stomach so tight I can barely breathe.

"We're going to do this, baby. I'm going to complete my soul and I will move on to the next life," she says and slides her hand up my chest.

I don't understand why she's so positive. The first piece of soul didn't work, and part of me thinks no matter how many bits she wins, it never will. The brighter her hope burns, the worse I feel.

Her fingers tiptoe up my chest and onto my neck. She used to do this. Used to tiptoe her way to wherever she wanted my attention. This is all so familiar.

She brushes the scar on my throat, and it sends a shiver out. She weaves her fingers through my hair. It's even longer than normal, tangled loose curls as wild and glowing as Eve's eyes. She almost looks alive. Almost. Her cheeks are spattered with crusty black blood, her shoulders are strained, the skin pulled tight over her body.

"Eve," I say, closing my eyes and giving her a single shake of my head. "Stop. Neither of us wants this."

When I open them, her lips are millimeters from mine. And while it's partly true, it's also partly a lie. I don't want this, not entirely. I want Eden. Need her. But Eve... she's... she's so entangled in my history, I can't just erase her. We were together just a few short months ago. When she's here, like this, it all feels right in a way I know it shouldn't.

Get it together, Trey. You don't want this.

And yet she gives me a comfort I can't let go of. She gives me hope I can go back. She was with me during the worst times of my life; we see each other in a way no one else can because it was just us against the world. Eve died once with no chance of moving on to the next life. I owe it to her to help her move on.

"You gave me a chance to save my soul..." She looks up at me, her green eyes boring into mine. "It's a good day. Let's celebrate."

She pushes her lips on mine. And for a brief second, I lose myself in her kiss. Her lips are just like I remembered, hard and taste of a deep moreish longing that radiates from her core and washes over me. Longing always was an addictive emotion. She nudges her body up against mine, pushing me into the fight club's wall. Her hands sliding down my back and around the front of my stomach. Like spider legs, her fingers dance over my belt buckle. When she slips her thumb under the leather strap to unhook it, I jolt back to reality and grab her wrist.

"Don't."

"What's the problem, baby?"

The problem is, I'm not sure if I can stop myself. But I won't tell her that.

"Eve..."

She hardens, her eyes blazing, with anger or the new piece of soul fueling her.

"Eden's not here, Trey. You're dead. She's alive."

"You think I don't know that?"

"You're never going back. Breather or not. Rozalyn will never let you go. You're too useful."

"What the hell is that supposed to mean?"

She looks away. "Nothing. Sorry. I just... Can't we celebrate? I'm one step closer to another life. It's a good day. I just want to have a little fun."

She leans in, kisses my neck, but this time I have control. I reach out to my essence and push a wave of fear out.

She backs off. "Really?" She shoves a hand on her hip. "You're going to play that game? I don't get it. I've done everything I can for you. Been there for you, died for you and I still have your back. What does Eden have that I don't?"

I raise my arm, brandishing my Binding Scar. She blinks at me, her eyes welling. It's a low blow. But I needed her to stop. Down here with barely a shred of hope, she's the kind of temptation I don't need.

"Lest you forget so quickly, *Trey*. We had one of those too."

"Our Binding was never complete," I say. But the words are weak. I don't want to hurt her.

"Well, it's the only Binding I ever had." A tear spills down her cheek.

"Eve, wait," I say, reaching out.

But it's too late. She spins on her heels and marches out of the club.

SEVENTEEN

'CogNews is pleased to report a number of prestigious awards, including the Lifelong Transporter award, which is being awarded posthumously to Titus Kilburn, Transporter to the East State. May he rest in Balance.'

CogNews Report, January 2018.

EDEN

I have to find Kato and explain it wasn't what he thought. It wasn't. Right? We didn't do anything. We didn't kiss. The fact it kind of almost sort of felt like we might isn't the point. We didn't. There was nothing to see. I have to explain before the rage of mine he's harboring goes off and he does something he'll regret.

But I can't find Kato. The crowd is enormous. There are bodies everywhere. My chest is growing tight. There's a prickly sensation in my gut, like pins and needles. And just like the blood returning to limbs, my emotions are coming back, too.

I kick at the ground just as the stage lights burst to life and Tarkin Tavas appears on stage. Well, that's just fucking perfect. Inauguration time.

I fight my way to the middle of the crowd and a few moments later, Dorian appears at my side.

"You okay?" he says, his face scrunched.

"Pain relief has worn off."

His expression scrunches as he takes in my face. "I can tell."

A CogCamera hovers a couple of feet in front of Tarkin. In his hand he grasps a CogMic. He clears his throat, and the band stops playing. There are a few seconds of muffled chatter, then it dies and thousands of eyes are all focused on him.

"Welcome, Keepers, Fallons and, momentarily, our Gracious Majesty, the First Fallon." He pauses.

"I need to get closer. I should be there when Kato gets crowned." If for no other reason than to prove I didn't do anything. My mind is fuzzy. A fog of confused emotions coat my skull like thick curls of butter.

"I'll come with you," Dorian says.

We push and shove our way closer. Kato and Bo must be out back behind the curtain because I can't see either of them anywhere. Tarkin swaggers toward the front of the stage and the CogCamera zips along, following his movements.

"You might be wondering what a lowly news reporter is doing as compere of an inauguration." He gestures wildly while talking. He's so dramatic, but it ensnares the watching Keepers, anyway.

"But due to the exceptional circumstances surrounding the inauguration, CogNews has been given special permission from the First Fallon herself to exclusively live stream the day's events. So, without further ado, it gives me great pleasure to welcome to the stage, our Majesty, our God incarnate, supreme Keeper of the Balance, the First Fallon."

Cheering erupts across the clearing.

Dorian touches my arm. "You okay?"

I nod because I can't speak. If I speak, I may actually breathe fire and burn the clearing to the ground. She's destroyed everything. She orchestrated Victor, killing Trey. It's her fault is Nyx and Titus are dead. She turned me into the lock. The only thing going through my mind is how much I want to end her.

Bo materializes and takes my other arm, though the way her fingers are stiff against my skin, I know she's still upset with me. She has every right to be.

I lean into her. She puts her arm around me. "I'm sorry," I breathe into her ear.

"Okay," she says. And pulls me tight.

"Thank you, guys," I say. They both inch closer. "I thought you'd be backstage."

She nods to the stage. "Kato has to go up alone, and I figured you might need the support."

She gives me a warm smile, and then it drops. "Kato's furious. He was stomping around backstage moaning about the fact it shouldn't be him up there and how the whole thing's a charade. And what the hell did you two do? He was frothing over Dorian. I thought you two were bezzie mates."

I give Dorian a side glance.

"I just took something out of his back pocket, and Kato was across the dance floor and it looked dodgy. But honestly. It was nothing."

She pouts her lips in and out, her eyes narrowing. But she can't stay serious and a giggle bursts out.

"I mean, honestly, I wouldn't blame you. Look at him, Eden. The man is runway stunning."

I laugh, uneasy. "Oh, stop it."

Dorian blushes, clears his throat and focuses on the stage.

"Anyway. How did you calm him down?" I ask.

She raises an eyebrow, her lips giving me a sly grin.

Right. Of course. "And now I must bleach my mind of the images."

She giggles. "What? It worked."

The music flares to life, drum rolls and entrance music beat through the air as The First Fallon pushes open the drapes and floats across the stage. The fabric of her white dress drifts in the air around her like satin smoke. Her skin and hair are the color of ivory bone. She moves across the platform like an ethereal being, as if she was sent to save us. But it's all a lie. Under the faux white purity, are clever tricks and games all so she can squeeze tighter and control every living thing. My body moves forward, pressing toward the stage stairs.

My senses shut down.

My emotions flare. My mind kicks into overdrive.

The vault—the darkest, most Imbalanced part of me—splits wide open. It shatters, my vision funnels, my hands pulse with electricity. I lose any concept of control. The sharp smell of electricity crackles around me. A charged power begging for release. Somewhere behind me, my name is being called. But I don't care. I see my target and I want to destroy it. Cecilia has to die. She's taken everything from me and now I'm going to take everything from her.

I shove through the crowd, bodies pushed out of the way, until hands grab me from behind. We're standing a few rows from the stage. So close. Yet an eon away from where I want to be. I whisper promises to myself. Promises of death and vengeance. Promises of a war the rebels are starting and I intend to finish.

"Do something," Bo growls under her breath at Dorian. "You're a fucking Siren. Do something before she does something."

Dorian glances from Bo to me, holding my fiery eyes in his gaze. My vision is red, which means my eyes must be too. "Just don't slap me," he says.

"Wh—?"

He spins me around and pulls me back in, dropping me over his arm and leaning me back. The music playing for Cecilia's entrance crescendos up and then drops. It beats once, twice, three times and stops. As it does, his face drops to mine, and he kisses me.

Son of a bitch.

He actually kissed me.

My stomach erupts with bubbles and flutters. I'm not sure if it's adrenaline, or shock, or rapidly dissipating rage. Probably all three. I'm so shocked, my lips move automatically.

Son of a bitch.

I actually kissed him back.

He pulls his lips off mine, a flicker of doubt wrinkles through his forehead and I swear for an instant his skin flashes silver. But the silver sheen vanishes just as quick as it appeared. By the time he pulls me standing, he's beaming, and the crowd are entirely unaware, cheering and shooting magic in the air for the First Fallon.

I glance at Bo. Her eyebrows are raised, her lips squeezed shut as if suppressing a laugh.

"Not quite what I meant," she says.

"It worked," Dorian shrugs.

"That it did," she laughs. "But for the love of Balance, never let Kato see you do that."

"He won't be doing it again," I bark.

I glare at the pair of them—my traitorous lips tingle like they enjoyed it.

"Feeling better?" Dorian asks.

"You kiss me again, Oswald, and I swear to Balance I will burn your lips off and punch your perfect teeth out of your perfect face."

He chuckles, a muffled laugh, and leans in to whisper. "You think my face is perfect?"

"Unbelievable. That's what you take from that sentence?" I mumble. But his mouth is twitching as if he's trying to quell an even bigger laugh and it's infectious and I don't want to give the cheeky bastard the satisfaction of a smile. So I turn toward the stage and file away the flash of silver I saw for the next time I have him alone.

The First Fallon is center stage. Her lilac eyes are the only speck of color in her pure white appearance. She takes the CogMic from Tarkin, her voice smooth, warm, full of compulsion. I smile to myself. The people can't revolt if they're constantly compelled into submission. She thinks she's clever, unbeatable. But what God needs to enforce devotion? *We're coming for you Cecilia.*

As if she reads my mind, her eyes skirt the crowd and find mine. Around us, the crowd of Keepers cheer praise and adoration for her. Orbs of electricity, fire and water leap above the crowd, exploding like mini fireworks. Shifters jump or fly into the air, flitting between Keeper and animal, and wisps of magic fill the spaces left. But all of it drowns into silence.

Our eyes lock together, a thousand silent threats passing between us. The air simmers, thorny and violent like boiling poison. I don't know if she's doing it or if I am. A gap forms around me, Keepers unconsciously edging away from the rage as they prance around, shouting their affection to our "great" leader. Bo, Dorian and I are motionless, three anchors in an ocean of gyrating bodies.

"Eden," Bo growls.

"I'm in control," I breathe. *Just.*

The First Fallon's lips form a thin white smile, curling up at the corner, her eyes radiate beams of hate. She blows a kiss at me.

I smile as sweetly as I can back at her and silently think about all the ways I could tear her apart cell by cell.

I will destroy you.

Her lips stretch into a glittering smile as she turns to the crowd, blowing a dozen other kisses at them. This time, her face is smooth, serene, loving even. She only loves things she can control. Her hands spread out and gesture for quiet. It arrives. Of course it does. She's probably compelling them to listen.

"Keepers, Fallons, guests. Thank you for your kind welcome. Today is both a day of reflection for the loss of our beloved Siren Fallon, Trey Luchelli. But it is also a time for celebration. For rejoicing in the knowledge that life must go on. That we must continue to live, to Keep and serve the Balance."

She pauses, the crowd bursts into cheers.

"Today we crown a new Siren Fallon, Kato Morello

Luchelli." She turns to the back of the stage, opening her arms to signal him in.

The curtains part, Kato walks in, the vein in his temple is throbbing. His arms spread open wide to greet the adoring crowd. I glance at Bo. Her jaw is iron hard. It makes my stomach fold in on itself. She's right. Kato isn't just sliding down this hole, he's jumped in feet first with me.

When the cheering quiets, the First Fallon raises the CogMic.

"It gives me great pleasure to crown you, Kato Morello Luchelli, Siren Fallon of the South." The First Fallon picks up her wand and makes a stirring motion over a mortar on a plinth. She adds herbs and wisps of magic float from the bowl. Then she dips her finger into the bowl and smears the reddened liquid down Kato's forehead. She mumbles an incantation and the red patch glitters and sparkles and dissolves into a hissing smoke. Cecilia picks up the Siren crown, it's maroon, encrusted with diamonds and rubies. In the center of the peak is a two-tone heart. Half opal white and half the deepest ruby I've ever seen. It glistens and twinkles. It's beautiful and looks just like the Heart of Trutinor hidden in Trey's basement, or at least the white half does.

She lowers the crown on Kato's head. Her lips move, but she's at the wrong angle for me to read what she's saying. Kato goes rigid. Bo straightens next to me.

But there's no time to question it. The First Fallon guides Kato to the front of the stage.

"Ladies, gentlemen, Keepers and Fallons. Please welcome your new Siren Fallon, Kato Morello Luchelli."

The crowd whoops and shouts, and clapping explodes around the clearing. The First Fallon raises her hands, and the crowd mutes its cheers.

"Under normal circumstances we would have had a Dusting, for our fallen leader. But without a body—Well, my gift to you today is something special. I've created an artificial Dust to allow us to commemorate our lost Siren Fallon and celebrate."

"I really dislike the sound of that," I say.

Lines creep into Dorian's forehead.

"Neither Kato nor I need any extra power right now. We're teetering on the edge as it is."

The First Fallon opens her arms spraying maroon-colored Dust over the crowd. She waves her hand beneath the Dust. There's a swoosh and it flies into the air. It dances and swirls and then explodes, raining down on the crowd to excited screams and jumps.

The music blasts to life and Kato walks down the stage steps and into the middle of the crowd. Hands brushing him, bodies pressing against him, filled with cheers and praise. He cocks his head back as the first particles of Dust land on his face and the faces of the Keepers surrounding him.

Then a piece of Dust lands on me. I catch the shared glance between Bo and Dorian. It pulses down through my skin, temptation vibrating through my veins, the throb, throb, throb of the vault pushing and nudging at me to let go.

"This isn't going to end well," Dorian says over the cheers. "Let's get you off the dance floor. That's where most of the Dust is."

Bodies rub against each other, gyrating, skin rippling from the injection of false power. Kato's arms fly up as he moves and wiggles in amongst his Sirens and Keepers.

I release a breath. "We're holding it together," I say to Bo over the crescendoing music.

"For now," she says and pushes her way into the crowd after him.

Dorian pulls me behind a tent. I'm vaguely aware that it's the Fallon tent. A safe space. It's quieter here. There's only a few Keepers working for the bars and food stalls. The embers lighting up the dance floor flicker in the distance. Above us, the sky is sparkling with white-hot diamonds. The air is full of music, warm foods and Keepers high on Dust.

Dorian faces me. We're both quiet. I'm suddenly aware that we're on our own.

"So, umm. I guess we should talk about the rebel's plan or something."

Dorian smiles, gleaming teeth, full lips. We're very alone. I shift on the spot. Rub my hands.

"You look mesmerizing." He looks at the floor. "Just thought I should tell you."

My cheeks heat.

"I... umm. Thank you?"

There's another silence. This time thick with things we're avoiding. That kiss. The way we've been sitting closer, spending more time alone. The fact I like the way he smells of oceans and freedom and the way Dorian seems to find any excuse to brush his hand against mine. Like right now. He inches closer to me, slides his fingers through mine.

Shit.

Actually fucking shit. Because I am wildly confused. I shouldn't be doing this. Trey is... I can't think about that. But this is... Christ, I don't want to think about that either.

"We shouldn't," he whispers. "But I want to." One of

his hands tips my chin up toward him. The music drums out a rhythmic beat, as if it's goading me, encouraging me.

Beat. Beat. Beat.

Kiss. Kiss. Kiss.

Shit. Shit. Shit.

"You're right," I say. My breath is short. "We shouldn't..."

"But I think we're going to..."

"I..." I can't breathe, let alone speak.

"I want to kiss you... for real this time."

He leans so close our lips skim each other's. My heart thuds loud and fast in my ears. His mouth is so smooth, soft, warm.

I want to. But I shouldn't.

Except I'm leaning in. My eyes close. Our lips brush.

"What. The. Fuck."

My eyes snap open. Kato is standing there. His face is dark, hard lines carve the cut of his jaw. He's shaking. Bo is behind him, gripping his hand.

Her face pulls into an apologetic scrunch. "I'm sorry," she mouths.

"How could you?" Kato whispers. And then he stalks away.

I turn to Dorian. "This is bad. I have to go to him."

"Let me help."

"Is that really a good idea?" I say, shrugging him off. I run after Kato and dive into the Fallon tent door after him. The thumping bass beat vanishes. The tent must be enchanted. My shoulders sag, relieved there's privacy in here.

Bo and Kato are the only ones inside, save for a couple of Keepers attending the bar in the corner and a young Shifter girl dressing the long bench tables for a late dinner.

"You're overreacting," Bo says, trying to take Kato's hand.

"How dare he! Fucking imposter. It should be Trey dancing with her, kissing her. He was supposed to be my friend," Kato shouts.

Bo looks at me, fidgeting. Kato spots me, his glare darkens.

"I understand, baby," Bo says, "but it was... Well, it wasn't... They didn't... Look, he's been really helpful to Eden." She can't look at him. She knows as well as I do. I might not have kissed him just now, but I definitely did earlier when he snapped me out of a complete vault-bursting breakdown. I silently thank the Balance Kato didn't see that because if this is how he reacts when we *almost* kiss... God forbid...

My eyes widen. Oh my god, we *almost* kissed. We ALMOST kissed. What the hell was I thinking? We can't kiss. I can't even process that right now. Of course Kato is cross.

"Trey hasn't even been dead for two months and you're wheeling in some slime ball already?" Kato snaps at me. His face is flushed, his cheeks deep red. Next to us the Shifter dressing the long bench—a girl with coal-colored hair—screams and keels over on the floor. Her form flickers in and out of Keeper and panther.

"KATO," Bo shouts, grabbing him by the shoulders and shaking him. "Stop. Look what you're doing."

He shakes his head, as if clearing something—clearing a part of me. A tangled thread of rage leaking out from wherever he's storing my emotions.

"Eden?" Bo snaps. "Do something."

There's a rustling behind us, movement, shadows, people entering the tent.

I slip my hand into Kato's. "Kato, take what I feel now. I'm calm. It will calm you, too."

His eyes widen. "I can't. I need to stop taking your emotions."

The Keeper whines and falls limp. The other three Keepers run over, their eyes wide and orblike.

"Kato, TAKE IT. TAKE IT NOW."

He flinches, but an icy tingle bursts through my palm. The thread tugs at my insides, a cold chord splintering through my ribs and into my muscle and sinew. It yanks everything out. My eyes roll back, not with pleasure this time, but with the hot rush of shame. He takes the curiosity, the intrigue and the flutter of adrenaline, the murmurs of lust Dorian made me feel. My cheeks burn as I realize how exposed I am. Kato sees everything. There's no shadow to hide secrets in. I'm on show. Cut in two. Every shred of privacy I have left on display. Kato knows I find Dorian attractive. He absorbs the adrenaline and flutters he creates in me.

My insides writhe in the sharp light of observation. I want to crawl into a hole. But that disappears into the chord joining us and out of my body, too. Feathers of black and lilac thread down the vein in Kato's neck and vanish under his suit shirt collar. His hand opens, a giant ball of black and violet in his hand.

But instead of calm washing into his features, his face darkens further. Shit. This was a mistake. I thought it was going to help.

"You whore."

"You don't mean that, I didn't—"

"I meant it. How dare you sully Trey's name!" Spittle flies from his lips. His eyes bulge, contorting his face.

He raises his hand out flat. A giant black and violet ball

swarms, its threads and ropes of emotion and hurt inch toward me. My blood runs cold. The veins in his forearm pulse violet and black and bulge like swollen worms. It's all pouring out of him.

All of it. Every piece of pain and anger and hurt I've given him.

"Kato, don't," Bo says, pulling at his arm. But he can't hear her. He's not in his right mind. It's months of my emotion controlling him.

"Not like this, you could kill me," I scream.

A flash of violet passes over his eyes. The ball sparks, black smoke and violet threads roped around his arms come loose, pouring into the ball, making it grow and swell. It pulsates. He pauses, violent shakes attacking his body. He's holding back.

"Please," I whisper, tears streaking my cheeks. "This isn't you. I'm sorry. I didn't. There's nothing going on."

But Kato's face is cold, void of anything but iron rage. This isn't him. He wouldn't do this. It's all my fault. I didn't think my heart could break any further, but as I stare at him, my chest shrinks and crumbles, cracks appear in my soul. My legs buckle and I fall to my knees. My arms wrap around my chest. I swear my ribs are going to splinter. I can't lose another person I love.

Dorian steps close to me, reaching for my arm.

"Get up," he breathes. "You need to get up." He hauls me standing and places one foot in front of me.

"Get the fuck away from her. You've done enough damage," Kato spits.

But Dorian doesn't move.

"I said..." Kato pulls his arm back. The ball shudders and drifts backward.

I won't move. I stay exactly where I am and close my

eyes because I deserve this. It's all my own pain and if it kills me, at least it saved Kato.

I brace for impact. There's a scream; it's raw, hollowed out by too many things that shouldn't have happened.

There's a beat.

Another.

The impact doesn't come.

My eyes snap open.

Dorian's standing, swaying on the spot. I scan around. The ball has gone. The blood drains out of my face and into my feet. I'm faint, nauseous.

Oh shit, oh fuck, what the hell did he do?

I look at Kato, he's pale, tremors rock his body. His eyes are wide as they skitter from me to Dorian. He clasps his hands to his mouth, his head shakes.

All my pain slammed into Dorian. He falters and I scramble to slide my arms under his before he collapses. A glaze of silver passes over his face and hair. But as his head lolls onto my shoulder, it vanishes. *What the hell is that?*

The silence in the tent is charged, potent, resolute. Then one sharp intake of breath shatters everything. Our heads snap to the tent door where Tarkin Tavas and his TV crew stand. A single red blinking light on a CogCamera tells me everything.

A thousand unbalanced fucks.

Tarkin's eyes narrow as a venomous smile spreads across his lips. "Well," he says, and turns to the CogCamera. "As you can see, Keepers of Trutinor, the inauguration is full of more than just celebrations. It's complete with Fallon-shaped revelations. Of 'addictive secrets.'" He wags his fingers. "And secret relationships. This is Tarkin Tavas reporting for CogNews." He winks. The cameraman flicks a button, and the red blinking light vanishes. Then he lowers the camera.

"I'll be winning awards for this." Tarkin snorts, and vanishes, taking his crew with him.

Kato mouths the air, frozen to the spot. I glance down at Dorian and check for a pulse. I get one, thank Balance.

"He's alive," I say. And Kato visibly sags. Before I can say any more, his shoulders rock and he bolts outside.

I turn to Bo, who gives me a stare that's dangerous enough I have to look away.

"This is on you," she spits.

I swallow down a lump in my throat, but it doesn't stop the tears.

"You should have listened to me. All you're doing is hurting everyone around you. God. This is exactly why I made you promise not to hurt Victor and precisely why I've been begging you to stop taking Kato's pain relief. This is an absolute mess, and it's your fault. I can't do this anymore. I love you, Eden. But I am done with you hurting everyone around you. Sort yourself out or don't come back."

Then she, too, is gone.

BREAKING NEWS

"Good evening, Trutinor. This is Tarkin Tavas reporting for CogNews TV. I'm deep in the Ancient Forest, at Kato Luchelli's inauguration ceremony. The Dust for Luchelli senior has been released and celebrations commemorating his life are underway. However, this evening it seems is full of revelations as well as celebrations. As you will have seen from the live footage moments ago, Fallon East and Fallon Luchelli have been engaged in post Balancer-loss pain removal. Something we all know is deeply frowned upon. We tried to speak to Fallon Luchelli. This is what happened. Studio, roll the footage."

The screen flickers and moves to a different image. Tarkin Tavas is running after Fallon Kato Luchelli.

"Fallon Luchelli, Fallon Luchelli, can

you spare a few moments to discuss what just happened with Fallon East?"

Fallon Luchelli continues walking. Tarkin speeds up, shoves a Keeper aside and grabs Fallon Luchelli by the arm. He stops immediately, turns to Tarkin, his eyes a blaze of furious blue.

"Get your hand off me," Fallon Luchelli says.

Tarkin hesitates, glances back at the camera, his mouth dropped open, but releases Fallon Luchelli's arm.

"I do apologize, Fallon Luchelli. If you could spare a few moments for your Sirens and the Keepers of Trutinor, we would be most grateful."

Fallon Luchelli's eyes dull. He shakes out his shoulders.

"What can you tell us about the incident a few moments ago in the Fallon tent?"

"Well, Tarkin, I'm sure you've already covered that in your broadcast."

"Do you refute the fact you were assisting Fallon East with pain removal?"

Fallon Luchelli hesitates, glances at the cameraman, and then sags on the spot.

"I do not refute it. She is dear to me, and I just wanted to help her."

"When you say dear to you. We all know the closeness and proximity this kind of addiction can lead to. Were you sleeping with your brother's Balancer?"

Fallon Luchelli's jaw flexes.

"Who the hell—"

There's a scuffle. The camera drops. There's a hollow thumping sound followed by groaning. The camera continues rolling briefly. Fallon Luchelli's feet can be seen walking off.

EIGHTEEN

Excerpt—Trey Luchelli's Journal, written in Obex

TREY

I lean against the balcony railing, clutching my notebook. It's become a habit to spill memories and thoughts. Helping me cope, helping me cling to the memories of what was. It makes me feel closer to Trutinor, like for the brief moments I reminisce, I'm still connected to Eden.

From the balcony, demons still conscious and not recovering from having a piece of their soul torn off are making their way inside for a drink. I've never seen the Fallen Fallon so packed. Sign-ups to the fight club, and therefore Rozalyn's army, have exploded so quickly we've had the club, oaths, fights and training running twenty-four hours a day to cope. Rozalyn devoted three-quarters of her staff from the castle to helping us. I'm grateful. Every day that passes makes panic crawl up my spine. How long will the life inside me last? Every day here is another day I risk it running out.

I step down the balcony stairs, into the pub and behind the bar.

Eve is talking to someone at a table. She catches sight of me and gives me a short wave. She smiles, but her face doesn't light up. Things were tense between us for a couple of days after that disagreement. They've eased now, but she's definitely holding back from me and she's been conveniently busy enough we've not spent much time together.

"Drink?" I mouth.

Eve's lips purse in a line as sharp as the angles of her body, but eventually she nods once.

I pour her a drink that was probably vodka once, but is now far too bitter and poisonous. I add a cube of brown ice, and a dash of lime. The same drink she used to have in my bar, kinda. I have no idea why she drinks this. I down a double shot of something that's a bit like tequila and sour baileys and take her the vodka.

She swallows it in one. Wipes her lips and says, "Another please?"

I pour both of us another one. When I'm finished, she's made her way to the bar, so I slide her drink across and take her hands in mine.

"I am sorry. I get that you don't want to hear it. But I am sorry. I was tough to live with. But I'll always care about you. Please don't be mad at me."

She swallows her drink in one. I follow suit. And then she sighs.

"Okay." She pauses a while, then she sits up, her eyes glitter dark. "Let's get pissed. Like old times?"

I laugh, raise an eyebrow, but what the hell? I have nothing else to do; the army is growing, my fight is done for the day, Pest has control of the ring and blade, Bellamy and the ex-Trutinor army demons are dealing with training. I might as well.

So we do. A couple of hours and five...? Seven...? Several shots later, my stomach is warmed through, my vision soft.

Eve leans back laughing, "Oh my god," she breathes through the laughter-tears. "Kato was as furious as Cecilia. Neither of them could work it out and the longer it went on, the funnier it was."

I'm bent over laughing, too. I have to wipe the tears away and gasp for breath just to respond. "She... She... Her face. It was her face."

Eve nods and bursts into laughter all over again. Then, just as suddenly, she stops. Something flashes across her eyes, a fleeting moment, an emotion residing deep enough I didn't catch it before it vanished. Her eyes burn hard, but not with the heat of anger or sadness or resentment, but with something else.

She's created a void so I can't sense her emotion. Either she's playing games or trying to block me out. Maybe both. She takes my hand and pulls me behind the bar, tugging until she gets me through the door to the rooms upstairs. We climb, she's in the lead, I follow.

"Eve. This is... What are you doing?" I ask.

She stops halfway up the stairs and pushes me against the wall. Then she leans so close her lips brush mine. It makes my chest hum. The booze has well and truly kicked in because, in one giant wave; she loses control. The void crumples under the weight of a throbbing heat. It cloys fiery and sweet and so sticky her emotions fog my mind. And then it hits me, wave after wave of loneliness, and it breaks pieces of me.

"Oh, Eve..." I start, but she pushes her lips on mine and pulls me down onto the stairs, her hands knotting through my hair.

My body tenses hard against hers. My lips aren't hers to kiss anymore. As if she can read my mind, she pulls away, cupping her hand against my cheek.

"The life is fading from you. There isn't long before you have to leave..." Tears streak her cheeks. It's too much. It's cutting me up inside. I hate seeing her so broken.

"I know you're going to leave," she says, her voice cracks. "Just give me this? One last time."

Her words wrap around me, all guilt and claws. I ruined her life, all her lives. The only Binding she ever had was a few short years with me. Her words are thorns and flowers. Beautiful on the outside, but grown from hurt and lies.

I understand this, and yet, she is still comfort; she is still a reminder of home, of what I yearn for. Eve was there in my darkest hours, my loneliest years. She knows all the things I keep secret because for a long time, she was my home. A home I want to leave behind and yet it still feels safe. I lean into her lips, knowing I shouldn't but wanting the comfort all the same. She arches her back against the stairs and moans.

Jesus, Eve.

Blood floods my groin, and she knows it because she pushes against me. Her arms lock around my neck and she nudges me to pick her up.

I do.

So she wraps her legs around my waist and locks them behind me. As I carry us up the stairs, her lips roam my neck, my collarbone, her tongue sliding over my skin, leaving a cool shudder in its wake. What I'm doing is wrong and yet my body reacts automatically. As if it's sentient. My body knows Eve. It—I—loved her. I was never in love with her, but I don't think she was ever really in love with me either. We clung to each other, two lost beings trying to survive broken lives. We were in love with the idea of us. The idea was always better than the reality.

We reach my bedroom. She jumps down, her hand slides to the door handle and twists it open.

"We shouldn't..." I say, but the words are feeble.

"There are lots of things we shouldn't do, Trey," she breathes, all the while sliding her hand down to my trouser buckle. "But who's going to stop us?"

The door clicks shut behind us. She grabs my belt and pulls me deeper inside my room, shoving me against the back wall. She bounces on her tiptoes and jumps up into my arms, wrapping her legs around me. I turn and lean her against the wall. She moans as her back hits the wall. A darkness in her eyes. She knows she's winning. It was always like this.

Cat and mouse; a line we used to tread between lust and anger. I think, deep down, we both knew we weren't meant to be together, so we danced around our emotions, trying to work out how to fit. It was always a game to her. It still is. Her mouth inches toward mine, her head tilted, her lips pulled back, showing a strip of white teeth.

"Are you angry?" she says, her expression glittering in the dim light.

Oh, I'm angry. I'm furious with myself for ending up here, with Eve for tempting me, with Rozalyn for not sending me home right away, with Cecilia, Victor. The list is endless. My face pinches.

"Good," she says and kisses me once, twice, the last time sucking my lip between hers.

"Show me how angry you are." She nudges into my neck, drawing her teeth down my throat until I shudder. "For old times' sake?"

I spin around, holding Eve's arms, and throw her on the bed. She squeals in delight and then tuts.

"We can play better than that," she purrs, her words like liquid silk. She bounces up and into my arms. "Harder," she breathes into my ear.

I grip her arms tighter until she gasps and the grin spreads from her mouth to her eyes. I want to tell her to stop, that we shouldn't. But the words don't seem to materialize. She kneels on the end of the bed, all the glitter and sparkle gone.

"This is goodbye, baby. We both know it." She's gentler this time. Another set of tears fall. My eyes sting. It is goodbye and I'm surprised how much that hurts. A cocktail of emotions clog the air. Wrapping us in what was, what is, and what should never have been.

Her fingers tiptoe across my jaw, she kisses, soft, once, twice, three times until she meets my lips.

"Trey," she says, making me look at her. More tears bubble and roll down her lids.

"Did you hear me, baby? No more games. This time it's forever." A breath catches in her chest.

She leans in, hovers millimeters from my mouth. Then

her lips are on mine, pushing, coaxing, pulling me into her goodbye. I push her back and throw her on the bed. Hard. She giggles and pulls off her top, watching me while she dangles it at me, then drops it on the floor.

I climb on the bed, on her, my hands moving over her skin. Eve yanks her pants down and unhooks my buckle. Her arms wrap around my back, her nails dig into my skin hard enough it stings. She pulls her nails out as I groan.

"Mmm hmm. Will you miss me?"

I push myself down on top of her, my mouth moving over hers. She strokes my back, gently this time. I pull her underwear off and slide myself inside her. Her back arches, and a gasp rips from her throat: it's vulnerable and tentative. I lose myself in the rhythm of her body. Our bodies pressed together, hot and sweating. I close my eyes, surrendering to the moment and motion. A wave of sweetened honey and deep warming spice washes over me. It's peppered with a tainted softness that aches. She's crying. I'm crying.

"Goodbye," she whispers. Over and over. "Good bye, baby."

She pants and gasps and bites my neck. My eyes roll shut as I collapse next to her. When I open them again, she's grinning at me, sucking in half her lip. "One more for the road...?"

The green of her eyes is cool, metallic. All I can think is that Eden's eyes are violet. My face flushes and my chest hollows and one repeating phrase screams in my mind.

This was a terrible mistake.

BREAKING NEWS

Tarkin Tavas's face appears. His usual orange hue is ashen.

"This is Tarkin Tavas reporting for CogNews TV."

He pauses, looks offscreen, and swallows. His expression graver by the second. Behind him the inauguration ball cleanup crew are flurrying around, tidying up and dismantling the structures.

"It's three AM here in the Ancient Forest and I have some deeply troubling news to bring you. There are reports of multiple bombings across multiple locations. The sites are said to be defector sites. A…"

He looks at a piece of paper.

"Libra Legion."

He clears his throat.

"Bombs are reported inside the Keepers school grounds, the South State, a further bombing in the West and one in the North. A number of Keepers have been killed and injured. Initial figures reported are upward of thirty dead and one hundred and twenty injured."

He pauses, looks at his notes.

"As yet, no one has claimed responsibility for the bombings. Early reports indicate the loss of several Council members. No names have been announced. This is a deeply sad end to what was a delightful celebration today. We will, of course, be reporting throughout the night to bring you updates on this tragic occasion. Pray to Balance, Trutinor, stay in your homes. No more lives need to be lost this evening. This is Tarkin Tavas reporting for CogNews TV."

NINETEEN

'The First Fallon has indicated that if the skir-mishes do not cease immediately, a curfew will be placed upon all those residing in main cities across Trutinor. Civil war will not be tolerated, the cost to the Balance is too great.'

CogNews Report Post Inauguration

EDEN

I stroke the hair away from Dorian's face, partly to wipe the sheen of sweat off and check he's okay, but also because I'm desperate to find the silver I saw. *Did I make it up?* His green eyes flutter open.

"You could have died," I snap.

"Maybe," he mumbles, pulling himself upright, "but

you *would* have died if I hadn't stepped in the way and caught it."

My mouth clamps shut, trying to prevent the rising sob in my chest. I lean into his shoulder and grip him, surprised at how much I care that he's okay. "Thank Balance you're alright."

It could have killed me, but I'd rather that than live with the knowledge Kato was angry enough with me to do that, or with the knowledge that Dorian died trying to protect me from my own stupid inadequacy.

"He still loves you," Dorian says. I pull back. He reaches for his cane and I help him up.

"I doubt that," I say, blinking rapidly.

"Trust me. He threw it at you because he was angry, but underneath the rage and hurt and frustration, there's still love."

I can't comprehend what he's saying. How could Kato possibly still love me after what I did to him?

"I need a drink or something to eat," he says, his body visibly shaking. I give him my arm. We stumble to the bar and I pull a stool out for each of us. But my hands tingle. Something swirls around my stomach and licks up my throat. It's acrid and bitter, like I'm going to vomit. But I haven't had a drink in a couple of hours.

"Are you okay?" he says.

"N—Not even slightly..." I look from him to the CogTV that's blaring and replaying Kato throwing my pain and emotions at Dorian. The screen flashes. Fucking Tarkin chases after Kato. Oh... Oh fuck. I think Kato punched him. We're so screwed, the whole of fucking Trutinor has seen our dirty secret.

The words tumble out, "I'm sorry, I can't... Can you help him eat something?" I say to the barman. "I need to..." I point outside. Bile fills my throat and I clasp my hand to my mouth.

The last thing I see is the barman slipping Dorian some meat-filled roll before I slip out of the bar tent. As soon as the air hits me, I know I'm going to puke. I stumble around the back of the tent, desperate for privacy. Thankfully, there's only one other Keeper lugging a barrel back here.

"You alright, Fallon East?" he says.

I nod and wave him off. As soon as he disappears, I fall onto all fours and throw my insides up. I'm shivering so much I can't stay upright, so I collapse on my back and curl into a ball.

The hem of a shimmering white dress appears and my heart sinks.

"Oh dear, you are in a pickle," The First Fallon says.

"Why don't you fall in a vat of Imbalance," I sneer. The vault cracks. I don't stop it. I don't care.

She laughs. "Petty insults all you have left?"

The maroon veil descends, my vision fading to red, red, red. "Is control by force the only thing you have left?"

She grabs me by the throat and hauls me to my feet. "I'm doing this for your own good. For everyone's benefit. You don't know what you're talking about."

"Don't I?" I choke out. My body floods with electricity, it pulses around my limbs, growing, building, pluming until I pump it all into her. She yelps, releases her grip, and shoves me back.

I point a finger at her. "You're pathetic. You want to be loved and adored, but this isn't Balance, not really. Not if you're brainwashing us all and forcing compliance."

"You're a fool. This is about saving you all. You don't understand."

She screams, launches a fireball at me. I bat it away and

it crashes into a tent, setting it alight. Wisps of sorcery and magic fly at me. I launch electricity loops to knock them off, firing rapidly. I draw off the fury in my chest. She needs to pay. She needs to die for what she's done, is still doing. My hands are alight. I'm pumping fire at her over and over. But then something inside me switches and I'm no longer in control, the vault is. Fire crawls up my arms. My heart pumps faster. Prickles nestle in my spine and between my ribs as I struggle to gain control. The tent is on fire. Flames lick up into the night sky. She's still attacking, throwing fire, water, electricity, sorcery, anything she can at me. I advance on her.

But she's laughing, laughing, laughing. I'll kill her. Then suddenly she's quiet. I glance up. Tarkin fucking Tavas is there with his camera rolling.

Fuck.

She evaporates, leaving a trail of billowing navy smoke.

"Go," I scream at Tarkin. "It's not safe."

He hesitates but nods and shoves the cameraman behind the tent. Dorian appears, lunges for me but I stumble back, the fire past my elbows. My feet are smoking too now. Shit.

"Look at me," he says.

"I'm losing control."

"Close your eyes."

"I can't, I'm going to flame up and burn the whole fucking area down."

"Eden. Close. Your. Eyes." There's an edge to his voice, like when Trey compels someone, only this is different, more melodic, rhythmic, almost like a song. His words sing and trill into my head and then... then... nothing.

I wake on the floor. My head spins, and I swear there's

the echo of a harmony I can't quite replicate still floating around my head.

"I feel horrendous," I mumble.

I look up at him from the floor, my stomach folding in on itself. What the hell is wrong with me? Dorian kneels next to me, placing his cane on the grass.

"You attacked the First Fallon and then you collapsed as I got here."

Everything is hazy. I can't remember what happened. My teeth are chattering.

"You're going through withdrawal."

"What do you mean, withdrawal? I'm not an alcoholic, I'm not even drunk... Well, not much anyway."

"Not the alcohol," he says, checking my wrist and pulse.

Ice tiptoes down my back. Inch by inch, the cold leaves a harsh realization in its wake.

"Kato's compulsion?" I whisper.

Dorian nods.

"But he only compelled me a few hours ago."

"He did, but when you're addicted, the rate at which you need compulsion increases just to keep the side effects at bay. And what Kato did. Releasing it all, he cut you off cold. He's severed any connection you had to him and his Siren abilities. He's making you go cold turkey."

"Fuck," I say and slide back to the floor, putting my hands over my face. My eyes tingle with the prick of tears. I knew the whole time, but I didn't want to accept it. But there's something about hearing the truth in someone else's mouth that makes the blunt reality of it so much more acute.

"I'm holding your pain, but there's no connection between us."

I mumble through my arms, "N—Now what?" I chatter.

"You have to get help. There's a center in the Ancient Forest, but…"

I peer out between my hands. "But?"

"I think it's time you go back to the rebels. They can help you faster. You can detox there like… Like I did. Then we can talk about what's next."

Dorian's face is stiff, but he holds my gaze.

"I can take you to the Forest if you'd prefer?" he says.

"I just want to fix things with Kato."

"I understand, but you're in no fit state right now. The withdrawal is going to get worse, and if you don't get treatment, it will kill you."

"How long does it… it…?" My teeth chatter and I can't get the words out.

"The forest is a few months. They're set up primarily as a Keeper treatment center. But I don't think—"

"No. Unacceptable. The rebels?"

"A few days, maybe a week. Perhaps a little longer. I doubt more than two."

My eyes narrow. "Why such a difference?"

"It's a more intense detox, and because of that, not every Keeper can handle it. As a Fallon, you shouldn't have any issues…"

"But there's a chance?"

He nods. But I've already made my mind up. The risk is worth it. I have to fix things with Kato, no matter what.

"Don't let me quit, no matter the cost," I say. "I have to make it right with Kato and Bo."

"It won't be easy," he says.

"No matter the cost, Dorian. I mean it. This can't go on. I have to fix it." I take his hand.

"Well, okay then."

I grip his hand tighter and he pulls me up. "I'm ready. Take me back to the rebels."

It's dark. The air has that stagnant water smell—it's stale and wet. We must be in a cave. Where the hell has he taken me?

"I can see how much pain you're in, but truly you're doing amazing," Dorian says, leading me over craggy rocks. My footing slips every few feet and I grip his arm tighter.

"Oh, bugger off with your charm and pearly whites, which..." I halt, and look up at him. "I didn't need to see to know you were showing me."

He laughs and I smile a genuine smile despite the overwhelming urge to vomit my insides up. He's still grinning as he tilts his head, those piercing green eyes bright despite the darkness; almost as if they're glowing. I scan the cave. It's so dark, I can't see more than a few feet ahead. Why doesn't he have a flame?

I flick my wrist and launch fireballs both ways down the cave tunnel.

"If you weren't in the early stages of withdrawal, I might be offended."

I glare at him, somewhere deep in the sludge of my unconscious the vault rattles. The embers in my hand fritz and spit, begging to erupt. All I want to do is destroy things and dance in the ruins. I take a deep breath. There's something about Dorian—a pull I can't place. I don't think it's compulsion. The whole point of this stupid intervention is to stop me using Siren compulsion. So I doubt he's compelling me. It's something else. There's something about him I haven't figured out yet and I'm convinced it's connected to whatever the hell that silver thing is that passes over him.

"How much further? I'm sweating and thirsty and probably going to vomit."

"Five minutes at most."

"Fine."

He waves me off and continues walking. I stumble after him and, after less than a minute, I have to grab his arm for stability.

"How are you not slipping?"

"I recognize these caves."

"We should have gone to the Ancient Forest."

"And waste the next four months not making up with Kato or fighting this war? The Forest isn't safe, anyway. I was never taking you there."

"How isn't it safe? It's full of Dryad's who, might I add, are the living embodiment of trees. They're literally the definition of peaceful."

"Ponder for a moment, who else lives in the Ancient Forest?"

Oh. "The First Fallon?"

"Precisely. I tried to explain, but you kept interrupting. The forest isn't safe for you for extended periods of time. I would have dragged you here kicking and screaming if I had to."

I fall quiet. The embers in my palms burn a little harder, but I swallow the rising pressure and extinguish them.

We walk in silence. Although I cuss Cecilia in my head every time I slip or stumble or lose my footing and have to squeeze his arm or hand.

Light appears as a speck at first, then as a blade of light. It's blinding after so long in the dark. I squint against the brightness, but hurry, curious to see where we end up. When we're a few yards from the exit, I stop dead. A shiver rolls down my spine. We're in the North. We're going to come out of the cave mouths I saw in the central square. But that's impossible. We've only been walking for two hours.

"How are we in the Nnn...?"

I can't form coherent sentences. A thousand questions spin through my head, making my brain swim. A roll of nausea punches into my stomach and I buckle, dropping to my knees and heaving the contents of my stomach up.

"The withdrawal is getting worse," Dorian says, placing a hand on my back. "I hate to bear bad news, but this is only the start. It's going to get really bad before I can help you get better. Be strong, Eden. We need to get you to a room, fast."

He helps me up, but gray and black speckles smatter across my vision. My legs give way. Dorian catches me and swings me into his arms as the shivering spreads from my spine to my entire body.

There are gaps.

Time skitters.

I'm moving, shivering, sweating. It's bright. The light bores into my eyes even when they're shut. Then I'm on my hands and knees. The carpet under my limbs is itchy. I vomit into a bucket someone must have placed in the room.

I'm made to drink something.

I vomit harder. The light dims into night.

The next time I rouse, Dorian is in an armchair watching me. He stands, scoops me up into his arms. He strokes my face. I lean into him and he whispers things. Promises. Secrets. He tells me I'm going to be okay. He's there for me. Daylight mutes. It's night. Sometimes it feels like afternoon.

I'm in a bed.

Time fractures.

Light becomes dark; night becomes day. Days slip away from me, I lose track of how long I've been here.

Dorian is there.

Dorian is always there. Sometimes he's mopping my brow. Sometimes he's pushing my hair back as I throw up. And sometimes he's cradling me in his arms as I cry into his shirt. He is warm. Safe. He is everything as I dissolve into nothing.

Spasms grip my muscles, making them coil and cramp as months of Siren compulsion seeps out.

Then one morning I wake, and the pain has receded. Light streams through the tarpaulin window, striping the patterned rugs. Burgundy colors flare into reds. Dust and sand dance through the air in sunbeams. Dorian's sitting in the same armchair he's always in. Several tufts of curl are out of place, and even though he's snoring softly, there are bags under his eyes. I wonder how many days he's been in here with me. A breeze ruffles the tarp, the buckle keeping the window open rattles and Dorian stirs.

"You're awake," he says, rubbing his face and pulling his hands through his brown locks. "How are you doing?"

I roll onto my side to face him. "Like a Soul Demon's been gnawing on me for several weeks."

He smiles. "A rather excellent analogy. But the bright side is you're halfway through."

"Halfway?" I say, sitting bolt upright. "I can't go through that again."

"What you just went through was the withdrawal of Kato's Siren magic. You're in a temporary reprieve. What you've just done in a few days takes most Keepers weeks. You still need to complete the cycle and take back your pain so you can fully heal. If you don't, you could easily slip back into..." His words fade.

I pull my knees up under my chest. "Into addiction."

He doesn't answer; he doesn't need to. My eyes squeeze shut as my thoughts drift to Bo and Kato. Even though I feel like I've been hit by a train physically, my brain is clearer, like a fog has lifted. Though I'm not sure it's a good thing. I'm left with the reality of what I've done. I knew I was dragging Kato down the rabbit hole with me, but it was all so distant. Like another me was doing it. Now I realize how much damage I've caused.

"Whatever it takes," I say, and my head slumps against my knees.

Dorian slides onto the bed and wraps an arm around me. "Don't. Don't do it to yourself. The guilt, the shame, none of it is worth it."

"How did you...?"

"You know how." He stares at me, his expression firm. Under it is a softness, a knowing. No, underneath his expression is understanding. We're both addicts. We share a flaw. We're connected by the same shame and darkness. A uniquely shaped parasite that only a fellow sufferer understands. I wrap my arms tighter around my legs, as if that can somehow hide the dirty I feel.

"Just tell me who you are. Enough mystery."

"Are you strong enough to walk?"

I nod and stand, but my legs wobble. He offers me an arm. I dither because I want to stabilize myself. But despite trying, I continue to be unstable, so I take his arm.

"I have a million questions and no answers," I say.

"I know."

I pull him forward, suddenly desperate to leave the room I've been trapped in for days. As he guides me out of my fabric cell, I glance over my shoulder at the scene of the crime. Sweat-stained sheets, rags, bottles of water, a lone pillow on an armchair and a crusted bucket with the remains of my dignity. In that moment, I feel closer to Dorian than I have to anyone in a long time. What he's done for me. What he's seen, the worst and lowest sides of me and he didn't run away. He didn't die, didn't abandon me.

He guides me through the mainstay of the rebel camp. The central corridor with its dozens of offshoots is so familiar this time. It's the third time I've been here. Twice sick. All the rebels have ever done for me is look out for me. Red carpets similar to the ones in my room cover the floor. It must be early because all the tent doors are pulled shut, and it's quiet. There's only the occasional muffling of children nudging at their parents to wake. He guides me outside. The air is cold and refreshing and edged with the scent of brewing snow.

"How do they stay warm when it freezes? There's no heating dome."

"The fabric is imbued with magic. If we used a dome, we'd be visible for miles."

"Oh," I say, and, "It reminds me just how advanced the rebels are compared to the Libra Legion." Arden's never going to win this war through political talks and safe bets. Dorian pulls short and turns to me, a grave expression marked on his face.

"What's wrong?" I say.

"There, umm... the night of the ball, there were a series of explosions targeting the Libra Legion."

I clasp a hand to my mouth. "Are... were there any injuries?"

Dorian looks away. "There were. Arden's okay, Hermia too. But... he... Ren and Cassian... They didn't make it."

"Fuck." Poor Israel and Maddison, and Arden, shit, Ren was the last family he had. "Arden..."

"I know," Dorian says. "He's actually reached out to the rebels. Understandably, says he's done playing politics and wants to join forces. No one's claimed responsibility for the bombs, but our sources say it was Cecilia. Not that it will ever go public."

I sit with the knowledge that Ren and Cassian are gone and the resolve inside me hardens. I need to know about the rebel's plan. Cecilia cannot and will not continue destroying Trutinor and its people.

We climb the rocks above the plateau the camp is nestled in. Each step I take is tentative, my footing unsure as we clamber over rock and ice. After half an hour, the ground evens out. There's very little shrubbery or foliage at this altitude, just barren rocks and gravel. We pass around an enormous boulder, carving the path in two, and my breath slips away.

"It's beautiful," I say as we pull to a stop.

We're standing above a deep mountainous ravine.

"It's a glacier," he says.

Like a capillary, the glacier wiggles its way out of sight and up between the dips of two gray mountain peaks. As I follow the path of the glacier down, it billows and tumbles over rocks, tiny waterfalls and chunks of ice rushing down the mountainside. The water is a mosaic of pale green and turquoise against the white ice blocks. Giant boulders slicked in ice and covered with dark mineral-rich veins scarring the pure white are perched on the shore of the fledgling river. I close my eyes, listening to the bubbling rush of water crashing against boulders as it slides its way south. After a moment, I perch on a rock. I hold my hand out and reach out to the glacier, calling and coaxing the icy water up. It's cool and fresh and smells like clean air and crisp winters. My hands move automatically and the water responds, forming a shape, shimmering faces peppered by icicles: Ren, Cassian... Trey. I stare at his watery expression, tears welling in my eyes. Every part of me aches for him. I throw my hands down, sending the water crashing back into the stream.

"Who are you, Dorian?"

He sits next to me, zipping his black jacket tight over his dark green top. "I love this place. It reminds me of home."

"Are you going to avoid all my questions?"

"That was an answer of sorts."

"Are you actually a rebel?"

"Yes. Well, I'm an independent."

"This won't work if you don't give me straight answers."

He takes a deep breath and sighs. "There's only so much I physically can say. I'm bou—" He grunts as if grappling with something. Picks up a pebble and launches it into the glacial river. "Look, I can answer questions, but you have to ask the right ones."

"Are you a rebel?"

"Yes, but my boss isn't Castor." His fingers hover above the surface of the water, tracing the waves and eddies. Then he turns to me. "Can I trust you?"

My forehead wrinkles. "I think the real question is, can I trust you?"

"That depends on what you want," he says.

"I want a free world," I say, realizing for the first time that truly is what I want. The end of control, the end of chaos. Maybe even the end of fate. But more than anything, I want freedom. And yet, after all the research I've done, I've come up with nothing. The rebels are no further forward with this supposed weapon that can kill Cecilia. I don't see how we can beat her.

I sigh. "I don't care what the prophecy says, we have no way of killing a god. And I want to help you, I do. But this freedom you're all chasing is a myth."

Dorian's skin is smooth. I swear in some lights it shimmers, but as soon as I glimpse it, it's gone.

"But if you could... If you could remake our world, would you remove fate and get rid of destiny?" he asks.

I turn to him. "Of course I would. After everything that's happened? That's not even in question. I think Keepers and humans should be free from control. The only thing that should stand between them and their dreams is choice. But that kind of world is a fairy tale. And I don't believe in fairy tales. Mine died."

"There's more than one fairy tale," he says, slipping his hand over mine. "I think it sounds like a plan."

I snort, indignant. "You really think we can take down a system that's thousands of years old? Eradicate the First and Last Fallons maybe. But you can't possibly think we can destroy fate."

"I do, actually."

My voice is quiet. I don't mean to hurt him, but this is all fantasy. "That's some seriously misplaced idealism you've got there. Trey is dead, therefore the prophecy is dead."

I pick up a rock of my own to skim out on the glacier. "Us? And what army is going to take on two bitch-gods from hell, exactly?"

"One bitch-god. If you united the rebels with the Libra Legion, you'd have almost enough Keepers. You'd have an army at least. You can't be a god without worshippers. Take them away from the First Fallon, and what's she left with?"

"I'll tell you what she's left with, more power in her little finger than the entire rebel army. That's what. Like you said. We've got an army that's almost big enough. But who else is there to recruit?"

He huffs and looks away.

We fall silent. The sound of rushing water and cracking ice filling the surrounding air. I shiver, not realizing how cold I've gotten since we sat down. I cup my hands together and draw three embers from my palm, coaxing the orange sparks into flames and then a roaring fire. It hovers between us, so I look up at Dorian.

"Tell me about your addiction."

His body sags. "I knew it was happening and I let it."

"What happened to Pax?"

He wipes his face before turning to me. "Pax was my everything. We always thought we'd be together. But she died at sea two years after we were Bound."

"She was an ocean worker?"

"Of sorts."

There are very few Keepers who risk working at sea, not for centuries. But there are always Keepers needing to travel between realms or anglers and the odd trading route.

"How did Cecilia...?" I trail off, wondering whether it's right for me to ask.

He shakes his head, wrinkles forming in the corner of his eyes. "Cecilia happened. Like she always happens. She ripped the boat in half, drowned the crew and sea beasts took the rest."

Cecilia is death's blade. Everywhere she goes, misery follows. I wonder if I'll ever be able to talk about Trey's death, or are there some wounds that never heal?

"I survived her death and the initial tearing of my soul. But instead of rebuilding my life, I slid into depression. I drank. I blamed myself. I should have been able to save her. So I drank some more. And then I found myself in Siren City." He doesn't look at me. At first I think it's pain, but then I wonder if he's leaving parts of the story out.

"I wanted everything to stop. While I don't condone what I did, if I hadn't used a Siren, I don't think I'd be here. I paid for them to take it away just for the night. But I liked it too much. The relief consumed me. I wanted it to consume me. So I partied, and I drank and I slept around. But the pain came back because relief is only ever temporary."

I nod, knowing the ache that creeps into your muscles, the gnawing that eats away at you, whispering, calling, begging you for one more moment of relief.

"So I went back, again, and again, and again."

"How did you stop?"

"I didn't. Not by choice. Castor found me. Hauled me here and forced me through detox. Of course, I didn't have a Kato. None of the Siren's I'd paid kept my pain to give it back."

"So, how did you heal?"

"With difficulty."

When it's clear he's not going to give me any more, I fall silent. After a while, I ask, "Now what?"

"Now we return to base, we eat, and then you take your pain back."

I'm laid on the carpets in the main communal area of the rebel camp. Dorian is in my room, prepping to give me my pain back. The tarpaulin roof and walls ruffle in the wind.

Smoke from the huge fire in the center drifts toward the only hole in the sea of fabric roofing.

People mill in the main area, all of them smiling, happy. Some play music, children run around throwing element orbs and essence apparitions at each other, screaming and laughing.

The rebel camp, despite being in Eris mountains is warm in a way the South never is. It's not the heat from the fire, or the number of bodies crammed under one roof. It's something more. A warmth that wraps your insides in comfort, a warmth your hands can't touch because it's entwined in your heart. It's not the mountains, or the food or the enchanted fabric, it's the people. An ancient community all driving toward a unified goal. The comfort that tells you this is home. But that knowledge tears at my heart. I always thought the East no longer felt like home because my parents weren't there. This might feel like the home I've always wanted, but it will never be mine. As an Elemental, a Fallon, a queen, I made an oath to my people. I belong in the East and all I've done since my parents died is run away. It's time to change that. It's time to go back and take up the slack the East State Council has picked up. But as I think about it, the hot prickle of longing stings my eyes. I already yearn for this place and I haven't even left.

I pull out my CogTracker and message Hermia.

Hey, I've only just heard what happened. Are you okay? How is Arden holding up?

He's... been better, he blames himself. He's taken to the bottle. They didn't have a great relationship and I think he has a lot of regrets.

Tell him I'll come and see him as soon as I can. I wish I could be there for him.

He understands. He'd rather you lay low after the inauguration drama.

Just give him a hug from me.

I will.

I pause... Knowing what I want to ask her and knowing the response I'll get.

Don't shoot me, but please... is there an update on Trey?

For the love of fucking whiskey, East. Give me a break.

Cherry on top pwretty please?

Fine. Nothing yet. All my previous trips to Obex have been futile. But I think I caught a whiff of a trail last time I was there. A demon who owes me a favor said there's some ruckus being caused at a bar. Sounds like Trey to me. How is treatment going?

Holy shit. I sit up, suddenly alert, all my senses kicking in at once. I type as fast as I can.

OH MY GOD, HERMIA. Forget rehab. Why the hell didn't you tell me? This is amazing. This is… why are you still here? When are you going to investigate?

Balance give me strength. Later, okay. I'm going in a couple of hours. I'll report back anything I find. But listen, this doesn't mean anything yet. Hell, it doesn't even mean I'll find him. Don't go getting your hopes up. Now. I tracked you; I see you're with the rebels. Are you finally in rehab?

I am. I'm better. Good even and halfway done already. I'm so much clearer. It's the first time I've believed I can do this. Like I can survive. I *want* to survive.

That's my girl.

I'm up and pacing and fidgeting and practically vibrating with excitement when Castor appears on the other side of the communal area, his white hair tied back in a loose braid, his rouge lips seem brighter than normal today. His silvery green eyes spot me, so he readjusts his course. There's something about Castor, something familiar, like the comfort of an uncle. We walk toward the food stalls and he buys me a drink. It's honeyed and sweet and has a hint of gingery lemon. It's delicious.

"How's the treatment?" he asks.

"Do I really need to answer that?"

He laughs. "You look better, at least."

"Thanks, better. Clearer maybe." I sip my drink for a while and then say what I've needed to say for a long time. "Look, I want to work with you. I do. But I need to understand what the actual plan is. It's one thing building a rebellion, but you don't do it unless you have a solid plan. If you truly believe you can take Cecilia down, take this whole system down, then I want in. But I also want to know what's going on?"

He takes a sip of his drink and scans the communal area. "Are you really ready? You're only partway through your healing."

"I'm ready. I'm done with all the mystery and secrets. Just tell me how the hell we're going to defeat her."

"Come with me."

He leads me to his office. The same one we were in before and offers me tea. I refuse this time, given the last cup was dosed with sleeping drugs.

"It's clean," he says. "No sleepy time for you. You have healing to do."

I laugh. "I'm still going to pass." And then I sit against one of the giant floor cushions.

"What makes you so sure you can kill her?" I ask.

"Well," he says, sitting against the cushion opposite. "There is a weapon stronger than any other. It can cut souls, tear holes in the universe's fabric. Commit Soul Deaths."

My eyebrows knit together. Hermia Soul Deathed Broc, but I hadn't even thought about how. "What kind of weapon?"

He sips his drink. "It's called a Soul Scythe. There are two blades, one in Obex and one here. Well, not Trutinor. We've finally tracked it down, and it's in London."

He pauses to drink more tea. Takes in my expression. His movements are slow, precise, gauging. My stomach drops. I'm not sure why. But suddenly I'm cold and ice is seeping into my fingers and toes. I don't like where this is going.

"What do you... What are you going to do with it? Will it kill Cecilia?"

"To kill Cecilia, one needs to merge both blades together. One is a start, but it won't do it. For that, it has to be brought from Obex."

"When you say 'one' needs to merge it. Who or what do you mean?"

He smiles into his tea. It's a soft, knowing kind of expression and it makes me uncomfortable.

"Aurora is the only one who can merge the blades. They are, of course, her own bones."

I snuffle out a laugh. "You can't be serious. She's been banished for centuries. How would you even get the blades to her?"

"We don't. We bring her to the blades."

I stop laughing. "You're going to break her banishment?"

He doesn't answer. Instead, he changes tact. "I thought you'd like to know. We've found Victor."

"Victor? God. I'd like that tea now," I say, my hand shaking as I reach for the cup he pours.

"What are you going to do about him?" I ask, the shakes seeping into my voice. Because this is the moment I've been dreading. This is why I've been uncomfortable. Somewhere deep down, I've always known he was the problem.

Castor smiles. "The questions is, what are you going to do about it, Fallon East?"

A tear rolls down my cheek. "What I want isn't relevant. I made a promise to his sister."

"So don't get caught."

I look up at him. "Oh, come on, Castor. Someone Soul Deaths Victor and it's only going to be one of two people and we all know it won't be Kato. She will realize it's me." I knead my forehead. "I can't, Castor. You can't ask that of me."

"This is what we're asking of you, Ms. East. We need you to Soul Death Victor."

"Actual fucking fuck," I breathe. I pick up a pillow and throw it across the room. Then I turn on Castor.

"Do you realize what you're asking? How cruel this is? You banked on me wanting vengeance for Trey, and now you're saying you have a weapon capable of doing it to me? Jesus, Castor, I want him dead. I want to take Cecilia down, but at what cost?" The hiss of fire simmers under my voice. "How many more people have to die for this crusade? When will you have enough blood?"

"When the people are free and the First Fallon burns. Freedom is priceless, Eden. There is no cost too high. No price I'm not willing to pay."

"Then how are you any different to Cecilia?"

"Perhaps I'm not. Maybe it takes a monster to beat a monster. But what I can promise you is that I'm fighting for a better future."

I cover my face with my hands. My insides knot and mash together. There's an acrid bitterness on my tongue.

"If it helps, vengeance is not the only reason to end Victor."

"Then what, Castor?" I say, throwing my hands up. "What's the grand plan because I can assure you? Now is the time to tell me because I'm not sure I can do what you're asking."

He refills his tea.

"Victor is an anomaly. He is the reason Beatrice's blood is poisoned. He is the reason she hasn't changed."

"She hasn't changed? What the hell are you talking about?"

"Beatrice... She's..." He stands, turns his back on me and leans his fists on his desk. He takes two deep breaths and then he turns to me.

"She's my daughter."

TWENTY

'There are reports of a break-in at the Steam-punk center in the Guild of Sorcerer's building today. The Six, who were first on scene, have suggested a number of thefts took place, including an extensive supply of Obex pills.'

CogNews Report, May 22nd, 1950.

TREY

The door clicks shut and I sag against it, sliding down the wooden frame until I can lean my forehead in my hands. A vile, bitter churn claws at my throat. I swear my chest contracts, tightening like it's going to suffocate me. Is this the Balance's way of punishing me? Maybe I deserve it.

"You. Stupid. Son. Of. A. Goat whore," a voice says.

Impossible. There is only one person who sounds like that, who would speak to me like that.

"Of all the moronic shit you've done over the years, this tops it all," she growls.

Oh, yeah. It's definitely Hermia. No one scolds quite like her. I glance up.

"What are you doing, idiot? Hug me. It's been too long," she barks.

So I do. I wrap my arms around her and pull her so tight I worry for half a second that I'll crush her. But she squeezes me so hard it makes me cough. Then she strokes the back of my head. "I've missed you. How are you?"

"As well as can be expected."

We stand like that for a while, neither of us wanting to let go. Her stroking my head, me rubbing her back. Then I break away, remembering the door I've just come out of, the shame of it spreading heat prickles up my neck.

"Look at me, idiot"— she kicks me in the shin, which makes me wince and rub my leg—"And tell me you didn't just sleep with Eve?"

"I—"

She fires a fierce glare at me. "Don't answer that. What the hell were you thinking?"

"I—"

"Don't answer that either. You clearly weren't thinking. Your dick was. Jesus, fuck, son of a tit, Luchelli. Get me a drink. I haven't been here three milliseconds and I already have a headache."

"How is she? How's Eden?"

Hermia huffs. "As well as can be expected." She doesn't look at me and the blank emotional void in the air tells me she's suppressing her emotions or at least locking them up so I can't read her.

"How about that drink?" she says.

We walk down to the bar, and I pour her a drink. Eve doesn't appear, thank Balance, though I continue to scan the bar for signs of her. Hermia swallows the whiskey-like drink in one and pushes the glass back to me.

"That is the most putrid shit I've ever drunk. Bring me the bottle."

So I do, along with a glass for me.

We sit in the corner of the bar. It's about the only free spot in there. The pub is packed full of demons. Some waiting for their fights, some on breaks from army training. The noise is loud enough in here that we have privacy by default. I pass Hermia the bottle and she pours us both a drink, which I swallow gratefully.

"If it's not Eden, it's you. I swear if it weren't for the Balance, I'd euthanize the pair of you."

"What do you mean if it's not Eden?"

She looks at me, her orange eyes sharp.

"Nothing."

"Hermia... You don't get to come here and not tell me everything about Eden. How the hell did you find me? We're close enough that I didn't think Obex would allow it."

Hermia shrugs. "I really am the best tracker that ever lived."

I nod. "You are..." I'm silent for a while, but the urge to drill her for information, is overpowering. "I need to know. How has she been? Did she cope with the soul separation?"

Hermia hesitates. "She's getting better. She was in a bad way... Kato... She..."

"Oh god, no. Addiction?" My gut rolls up on itself. Bile licks at my throat. I've seen it happen so often. Balancer loss is poisonous, but Eden's so strong. She's a Fallon. I never imagined she'd suffer like that. Hermia avoids looking at me.

"Is... Is she okay now?"

"She's in rehab, getting the help she needs. She's doing a lot better than she was."

I wipe my mouth, fidget in my seat, suddenly uncomfortable. "It barely scathed me, I think because I was dead. But I realize it can affect the survivor terribly. What about Kato? Is he okay?"

"Doing better than Eden. But it's been wobbly for them both."

I thought hearing about how they were doing would fill me with joy and relief. But I drop my head into my hands. My insides cremate themselves into tar and concrete. The air around me chills and cools. That familiar gnaw of loneliness that stretches into infinity. Bitter, acrid, an ice that can never thaw. Only this time, the hopelessness isn't coming off the demons, but from me. Everyone I love is suffering and there's nothing I can do about it. I push it down, hide it away. Lock it in the vault, just like Eden used to say I did. But thinking about her just makes everything hurt more. So I lock that thought away too.

"Did they instate Kato?"

She nods.

"Hates the work, loves the attention?" I say, and it's the first thought that truly brings a smile to my face. He always thought I was the perfect Siren Fallon. But he was wrong. Kato is far more of an extrovert than me. All I ever wanted was me, Eden, and a little life together somewhere. Kato would love the attention being Siren Fallon gave him. He was born for the role.

Hermia grins. "Absolutely laps it up. A born leader, that one. But, things are tense, civil war is brewing. God, those idiots, they got caught. That orange imbecile managed to film Kato and Eden in a pain relief compulsion. It's all over CogTV."

My hands ball into fists. I want to lash out, break something. I need to get back. Pest appears on the balcony bridge between the bar and the fight warehouse. I sit up. A hollow sensation balloons in my chest.

"I have to tell you something," I start.

She stiffens. Even her orange curls go rigid. Two slow blinks, her face frozen—as empty of emotion as my chest.

"Bellamy?" she whispers. "Sweet fucking merciless Balance, you found him?"

"He's... I've been working with him." I brush my neck, a shadow-tingle flickers through my fingers. "He helped me. Saved me, actually. Stitched me up, stopped the infection."

She snaps. Her eyes are watery and hard. She drinks the rest of her tumbler of whiskey and this time, fills it to the brim.

"Is he well?" she says. Her voice is so cold it trembles, just like her eyes. She's radiating a concoction of emotions. It's giddy and intoxicating. I'm just grateful she's attempting to hold it in, or I'd be woozy.

"He's okay. I know he misses you."

"Did she get to him?"

"Rozalyn?

Hermia gives me a curt nod.

"She did. But she treats him well, for the most part."

She looks away, her hand brushes her face, and when she turns back to me, she's as stoic as ever. "I knew it. There had to be a reason I couldn't find him. I don't care what the laws of Obex are. Don't care if they say you can't find your Balancer until you die. I can find anyone. Fucking found you, didn't I?"

She's babbling. I shift in my seat, unsure how I should comfort her.

"Do you need me to give him a message?"

She pauses. Scratches her face. Slurps whiskey and then nods.

"Actually, I do. Tell him not to give up. That I'll find my way to him no matter what it takes."

"I'll make sure he knows."

She scans my face, my body, my neck. Each place she examines makes her forehead furrow deeper. "For a dead guy, you still look pretty fresh, especially compared to this lot." She lifts the tumbler.

"Well, that's the thing. I'm not. Dead, that is."

She wavers. A splash of whiskey hits the table.

"I beg your pardon."

"I'm not dead-dead."

She shakes her head. "WHAT?"

"I... It's complicated."

"Well, you better un-fucking-complicate it, and fast." She leans forward, drops her volume. "Because if you're not dead, then why the fuck aren't you back in Trutinor already?"

"I'm half-dead. Victor killed part of me, so I'm not alive enough to return. I did an ancient Siren ceremony with Eden shortly before Victor stabbed me, and it connected me to the Heart of Trutinor. That connection is sustaining me and keeping a part of me alive."

"Holy assbadgers. So... So you can come back? Because if you can come back, what the fuck are we doing sitting here drinking like old-timers? Let's get you home, son."

"It's not that simple. Rozalyn can send me back using some kind of magic she's refusing to tell me about. But there was a price for my return."

"And? What does she want?"

"She wants me to militarize the demons."

She swigs a hefty gulp of whiskey and then shudders. My lips quirk, but the vicious glare she gives me suppresses the rest of the brewing laugh. Hermia prides herself on being able to handle all forms of booze.

"We're almost done. The vast majority of demons have taken Blood Oaths, but we're still doing some training and fights with them. She said I could return as soon as it's done."

"Trey, Eden needs to know. You can't hide this. It's huge. I have to go. I have to tell her. She's going to lose her shit. This is exactly the kind of hope she needs." Hermia stands. But I grab her wrist and pull her back down.

"No."

"No?" she says, her orange eyebrows inching together. "The fuck you mean, no?"

"What if Rozalyn doesn't let me return? She said she will. But you've worked for Cecilia. How often did she go back on her word?"

"Roz isn't like that. I worked for her for a while too."

"You did?"

She kneads her forehead, then gives a sniffly sort of laugh. "That's what got Bellamy killed." Hermia stops, her shoulders stiff. When she doesn't say anything else, I reach over and rub her hand.

"I'm sorry."

She waves me off, then checks her watch. "Millenia old. Forget it. Are you sure I can't tell Eden you've found a way home?"

I stare out across the bar. Hermia thinks Rozalyn will follow through, but experience tells me these sisters are devious, unrelenting gods. There is nothing I want more than to get home. But if Eden is in recovery, I don't want to give her hope, only to rip it away if Rozalyn reneges on our deal. A lump lodges in my throat.

"I um..." This is harder than I expected. "The piece of life inside me has a time limit. It's fading and if I don't make it back for whatever reason, then I'll die for real this time."

"I see," Hermia says and shifts positions in her seat. She can't bring her eyes to meet mine. "What am I supposed to tell Eden?"

"I don't know. Of course, every single piece of me is fighting to get home. There's nothing I want more than to hold her, kiss her, have her connected to me again. But, you said she's going through addiction. What if you tell her I'm coming back and then... and then I..." I choke on the last words. They fizzle out. I wipe my face, pushing everything into the vault once again. I have to keep it together. There's no way I'm letting myself crumble this close to getting home.

"Don't make it back?" she says.

"Then Eden needs to live her life. Much as that makes me feel sick because I want to live that life with her. It's not fair. She might have a century without me. I can't expect her to live that alone." I have to pause again. My throat is so tight it aches like granite and sandpaper.

"You can't tell her. It's too much of a risk. Even if the worst happens and the connection I have to the Heart of Trutinor fades, I'll never stop trying to get back to her. But until my feet are on Trutinor soil, there's no guarantee. I don't want to give her false hope."

I rub my face again. It's wet and streaked. Hermia reaches over the table and takes my hand. "You're going to make it. You will, dammit."

"I hope so. I really do... Hermia?"

"Yeah?" Her voice is crackly. She understands because she's been separated from Bellamy for so long, she knows the pain I'm in.

"Promise me you won't tell her."

She shoves the glass across the table and shunts back into the chair. Wrinkles draw into her brow and around the corners of her eyes. Hermia looks around the bar. Her gaze is pointed, hard. Her jaw flexing.

"Hermia...? Please, I need to hear you say it," I beg.

She turns to me, her mouth scrunched and puckered. "Fine, goddammit. I promise."

TWENTY-ONE

'Mind Numb—a potent alcoholic spirit made from the petals of the Pink Lake mixed with tequila and sorcery.'

Trey's Bar Drinks Menu

EDEN

"I'm sorry, what?" I say as I get up and pace around Castor's office. "Bo... As in my Bo? As in the Beatrice Dark, is your what?"

Castor's gaze follows me as I pace up and down his office.

"My daughter."

"No."

"Actually, yes."

"But I thought she was Aurora's grandchild," I say, stopping in front of my cushion. Bo's mother made an oath with Aurora in order to save Cassian. Bo found out a few months ago and she's wanted to find Aurora ever since.

"That's correct."

"But that means... Aurora's your... Then you're a..." Slow and steady, my ocean-wide eyes fall on Castor. "You're a Mermaid."

I sit very rapidly on the cushion.

"Fuck."

I take a breath.

And then another.

This is insane.

Mermaids have been banished for eons. I have a thousand questions spiraling through my head. Castor gets up and collects some mugs and herbs. When he returns, I haven't moved. He hands a mug to me.

"Drink, it will help."

So I do. And he's right. My chest loosens after the third sip and my brain slows enough I can order some coherent questions. Castor pulls two giant bean pillows and encourages me to sit on one.

"So. So? To be clear, you're a Mermaid?"

"I am." A muscle in his jaw flexes, his eye flinches. It's so subtle I almost miss it.

My eyes scan down his body to his legs.

"It appears in water. We're sort of like Shifters and sort of like Sirens in terms of our abilities."

I shake my head, trying to clear my thoughts. "Right. Yes. Of course." *Of course? Jesus Eden, of course, nothing. You're staring at a fucking Mermaid. A MERMAID. They're real. And here. And in front of you.*

"You're the father Bo's been looking for? But she's been

here. OH MY GOD, SHE'S BEEN HERE. If you knew, why didn't you talk to her?"

"It's complicated. What do you know of the blood oath Maddison made with Aurora?"

"Only that she made it to protect Cassian."

Castor stares into his mug, swirling the tea. "Maddison always loved Israel, and I always loved... It doesn't matter now. The point is neither I nor Maddison wanted to have a child together. But we both had our reasons. She took the oath to save Cassian."

"And you?"

He looks up at me. "To save my mother. To save Trutinor. Without Aurora's legions of Mermaids we don't have enough Keepers to defeat Cecilia. We'd already sacrificed so much that I didn't want to intervene in their family unit."

"But I still don't understand what this has got to do with Bo. Why does having Bo mean you're saving your mother?"

"After the Mermaid-Siren war, Aurora slaughtered Karva. Cecilia was not pleased. But as cruel as Cecilia was, Aurora was cleverer. My mother knew Cecilia would prefer to torture her for eternity than to exact a swift death and send her to Obex, where Karva would be. So she made a bargain. In exchange for her life, Aurora would be banished from the land and her bloodline ended."

I narrow my eyes. "And yet here you are."

His lip curls, a dark glimmer burns in his eyes. "And yet here I am."

"But how?"

Castor leans back on the giant cushion behind him. "Cecilia placed a curse on Aurora. With any curse, wording is always crucial. From that point forward, Aurora could keep her life in exchange for banishment and infertility.

The curse said nothing of current pregnancies. And what Cecilia didn't know is that Aurora was already pregnant."

"Shit. But why didn't that? Why didn't you break the banishment? Why wasn't your birth enough?"

"If I'd been female, it would have. Mermaidism is a matriarchal gene carried on the female chromosome. And that's why she needed a female heir."

"But then, why hasn't the ban already been broken? Bo is a girl."

"That she is. But Maddison didn't want to have a child with me, so when she had Victor before Beatrice, it poisoned the Blood Oath Maddison made with Aurora. Victor existing stops Beatrice fulfilling her destiny."

"But Victor is already dead."

He shakes his head. "I'm sorry, but Victor needs to be eradicated from existence. Dying isn't enough. We have to reverse the effect Victor created when he was born. When his soul is destroyed, it will remove the anomalous poison from Bo's system. Leaving her with Shifter genes and pure Mermaid blood." He winces.

"But that's... That's impossible. You can't be a Mermaid and a Shifter. It must be against a thousand Balance laws."

He sips his tea. "It is impossible, unless you made a Blood Oath mixed with magic. The moment Beatrice can shift into her Mer-self, it will break the banishment. Aurora and all of her Mermaids will be free to walk the land..."

I run my hand over my hair. "That's the missing piece. When I was talking to Dorian, I was saying if you united the Libra legion with the rebels, you'd almost have enough. Almost because there was no one else. Except there is. But no one ever considered Mermaids, not even me. You need an army big enough to take Cecilia down and Dorian couldn't tell me because you were bound by the curse."

"There were some of us left. We thought of ourselves as land-based when the banishment kicked in. They could never return to the ocean. Over the years we found magics and methods to break elements of the curse on a select few individuals like myself and Dorian. I can say the word, identify what we are, but it causes pain. Dorian is unable to speak of what we are. But this is an aside. The point is that to win this war, we need Aurora and her legion. They are the fiercest fighters Trutinor has ever known."

Dorian? DORIAN. Oh my god, Dorian. Images of his face with a silver sheen flash through my mind.

He's not a Siren.

He never was.

Oh. My. God. I've been with a Mermaid this entire time. I rub my face, and pull a tie off my wrist and draw my hair out of my eyes. My father's bedtime stories come to mind. How he'd tell me the most beautiful things were usually the most deadly. I guess he was right on a lot of levels.

Fuck. My heart bangs against my ribcage. My mind fights against the calming tea, a swirl of thoughts and questions and panic. Dorian? This whole fucking time. And then my mind turns to Bo and my heart sinks.

"What if she doesn't want to become a hybrid? She certainly doesn't want Victor dead. She's hardly going to be compliant."

"This is the way it has to be, Eden. The prophecy said 'they will face a grave choice. Their decision will lead either to the defeat of the sister of light and restoration of Balance to all the realms or the end of the universe and all life within it.' This is your choice. It has always been your choice. Can you break a promise to your best friend? Can you risk that friendship in order to save the fate of all of us?"

It's too much. My head is pounding. I've done so much damage I can't do this. I made a promise, or a half promise or... What the hell will she do if I cause both Victor's permanent death and change her life forever? She will never forgive me. All I can think about is the look she gave me, the desperation in her eyes when she made me promise. Nausea rolls around my tummy. This would end things between us forever. And if I don't? Do I doom us all to a fate controlled by Cecilia for the rest of eternity?

"I can't..." I turn on him. "Is it really that simple for you? Another life, another person's blood? Kill your daughter's brother to get what you want?"

His eyes darken, his stare hard. "If it furthers our cause, yes. There is no faith and belief in a cause without sacrifice. And, Eden, we have all made grave sacrifices. This is serious. One way or another, this has to happen. Victor must die in order to start this chain reaction. We have to open the worlds and let Rozalyn in if any of us stand a chance of living free. I understand this is hard to process. But it's also bigger than all of us. We need you. I need you. Beatrice, whether she knows it or not, needs you."

"And all I have to do is break a promise, destroy my greatest friendship, Soul Death my Balancer's murderer, help you merge some ancient blades and kill a living god?"

"Exactly," he says.

There's a rustle and Dorian's head pokes through the door. His gaze dances between us, furtive, strained.

"Is everything okay?" he says.

"But first, you need to heal," Castor says and helps me to my feet. "We'll talk again Ms. East. One thing at a time."

Easy for him to say.

Dorian smiles as I leave Castor's office. "That looked intense."

I hesitate, if I open my mouth, I'm going to ask him. I give him furtive glances. My eyes grazing over his body as if scales might pop out and appear.

Like Castor, he's a Mermaid. I want to see him, the real him.

"I... I know what you are," I say.

Dorian halts. His body stiff, taught. He's not looking at me.

"It's okay. We're okay." At this, Dorian turns to me. His expression crinkles.

"You're sure?"

I nod.

"Part of the magic allowing us to be here prevents us from saying it. How did Castor tell you?"

I think back to the conversation and let out a sharp laugh. "Would you look at that? He didn't. I figured it out because he said Bo was his daughter."

Dorian's shoulders slacken, his body relaxing. "I wish I could have told you."

"I understand. Can I see? The real you I mean?"

Dorian steps closer, his fingers inch toward mine. Then his hand is laced through mine. His other pushes a curl that's fallen from my bun behind my ear. Where his fingers touch my skin, they leave a trail of featherlight sensations. I shouldn't want this. I shouldn't want him. But Trey is gone. It's the first time I've really been able to say that and accept it as true.

"I'll show you everything once you're healed."

"Okay," I say, the word barely a whisper.

We stay there a moment, both of us looking at each other in a new way, a true way, a complete way.

"I see you, Dorian Oswald. For the first time, I really see you."

He smiles, leans in, hovers so close to my lips for a fleeting second that I think he's going to kiss me. I stop breathing. Do I want this? I'm not moving away. But before I have to answer it, he tilts and kisses my cheek; tender, full of static.

"Thank you," he says.

My stomach falls, disappointed. *Shit. I wanted it. Oh god. I actually wanted it? What does that even mean?*

"Come on, Ms. East. We have a date with destiny."

I snort. "Yeah, for destroying it."

Dorian leads me back to my room, my muscles tense. He places his cane against the chair. He shuts his eyes and raises his hands, palms out. Above one hand, an enormous spinning ball appears. His free hand coaxes the ball until it stabilizes and floats between his palms. I take a step back. There's no way I can survive this. It's huge, the size of a small deer, at least.

"Are you sure that's all mine?" I say.

"Every particle."

"That's a lot of pain."

"It's a lot of loss."

Even though his words are meant to be comforting, they sting.

"Can it kill me?"

He takes a deep breath and his face pinches. "If you let it, yes."

A jittery laugh spills out. Dorian pulls one palm away from the ball and gestures for me to take his hand. My smile fades. The blood drains from my face and my fingers tingle.

"What if I can't take it all back?"

"You can, and I'm going to be here the whole time."

"What if I don't want to?"

"The choice is yours. If you believe your fate is sealed,

I'll let this fade into the atmosphere. You can leave and we'll be done. But if you want more. If you want revenge, if you want to end Cecilia, you have to do this."

I toe the carpet under my feet, my toes kneading the rugs.

"What do you want?" Dorian says, his fingers twitching over the spinning ball. "Do you want to wallow for the rest of your life? Or do you want to take your life back?"

I close my eyes, breathe deep, and step forward. "This won't be pretty," I say.

"I've seen worse. Ready?"

"No. But do it anyway."

He flicks his wrist; the ball explodes into a thousand threads. They hover, poised in midair. Dorian catches my eyes. Then, the threads lunge for me, and my world turns black.

I expected physical pain; searing spasms and the echo of my soul tearing. I was taking my pain back. Surely it would hurt? But that's not what happened.

Instead, everything I've suppressed comes rushing back in a tsunami. The moment Trey died appears in my mind. Glints of silver shine from the blade as it punctures his neck, and scarlet rivers spurt down his torso. The scene flickers over and over, the knife moving in and out. My scream, a desperate hollow sound, claws at my insides. My hand stretches for Trey. But I can't reach him and he dies again and again. I'm stuck in an endless looping failure. The knowledge that I couldn't save the person I loved more than anything is suffocating.

When the visions change, they show me the life I

wanted; the life I've lost. Trey and I dance in the desert under moonlit skies and twinkling stars, with sand between our toes and laughter on our lips. Our hands locked in each other's, we pirouette and the scene shifts to the Pink Lake. Blossoms and petals rain from the trees like confetti as he tells me he loves me in this lifetime and all the lifetimes to come. Our children run around the lake, picking up the leaves and throwing them up in the air.

But as I push my mouth against his, he fades. The soft pink of his lips grows lighter against my mouth and his cheeks soften until he's mist and memories. Our children disintegrate until they're nothing but a faded "what if" and I'm left standing alone.

I collapse on the floor, sobbing. Great cleaving cries tear through my chest. This time, I let them come. This time, no one will take the pain away. No one will let me deny the truth that Trey is dead and I have to carry on living.

The dream dissolves into a muted twilight—Obex.

Trey?

My heart thuds between my ribs. I'm propelled into a warehouse. There's a giant cage. It's mesh of metal harboring two creatures. One enormous demon towers above the other person. I catch a flash of the man. He's thin, tiny compared to—

A hollow shriek cuts through the air—disjointed, shrieking.

"TREY?" It—no, I scream.

My hands are out. I claw at the air, desperate to reach the cage. To pull him out.

The demon grabs Trey's leg, and pins him to the spot. Its teeth are yellow and black, its face is so close to Trey's. It's going to bite him or eat him.

I glance around for Sheridan, but she's not in my dream.

She's nowhere. She can't help me or pull me out of this nightmare.

The demon grabs Trey's throat, and I scream. I scream and scream and scream his name until my throat is hoarse and cracked.

The dream disintegrates and I drift in and out of lucidity. The Pink Lake reappears. I'm lying by the shore. Night turns to day and back to night again. And I wonder if the same is happening outside of my mind. How many days have I been trapped? Night crawls over the sky, dawn peeks its head above the horizon. I swear I've been asleep for an eternity. But release never comes.

I give up trying to track the dusks and dawns. I don't know how long I lie curled in on myself with memories of death, love and what-ifs swirling around my head. But it's long enough for the cold to leach into my bones and a layer of flowers to cover my body.

Under the visions, there's a heartbeat, a slow rhythmic thumping that doesn't match my racing chest. I frown, remembering this heartbeat. I sit up, brushing the blanket of pink off.

My fingers move to my wrist and the heart-shaped scar, straining to hear the thumping. The Pink Lake vanishes and I'm thrown into the warehouse full of demons. I scramble back, blood pounding in my ears. But they all ignore me. They're chanting and jeering at the ring.

I still. My ears fill with the hollow rattle of my breath.

Trey.

At last, his face appears again. He's in the ring. His face is smeared with blood, his skin gray, and he's thinner than I've ever seen him.

I don't call his name this time. It's not real. He can't hear me.

Trey swings a silver blade down and plunges it through the demon's chest. Then everything fades.

When I finally wake, it's dark in my room. Dorian snores softly at the end of my bed. He's fallen asleep, one arm lying over my leg, his curls flopped over his face.

Castor has given me an impossible decision to make. I don't want to betray Bo any more than I want to doom Trutinor. Both choices suck. I've never liked either side of this war. So maybe there's a different way. I know what I have to do, the risk I'm going to take. If this doesn't work, I don't want to think about the consequences.

I pull out my CogTracker and notice the date. It's been days since I was awake. It felt so much longer, like an eon. I'm just grateful it's over. I type out a message with shaking fingers.

We need to talk. Can you come to camp?

All I can do now is wait and hope.

TWENTY-TWO

*'**The Heart of Trutinor is said to be the most
powerful weapon in existence, capable of giving
and restoring life, destroying souls and
harnessing all forms of magic at once. Its
whereabouts have been unknown to the public
for as long as records have been kept.**'*

*Excerpt—The Manual of Dangerous and Forbidden
Weapons*

TREY

I wake early the following morning—early enough. What
masquerades as sunrise here is only just painting the sky a
lighter shade of twilight. I'm sweating, the shadow of nightmares replaying through my mind. Guilt is an awful thing.

If I get back to Trutinor, I will tell Eden what I've done. I don't want secrets between us. I'm busy spilling memories, stories and confessions in my journal when Rozalyn appears in the warehouse doorway.

"Good morning, boy."

"Your Majesty."

"You've done well. Pest reports the army is ready?"

I stand and welcome her into the warehouse. "There are very few demons left who need to take the oath. We should be ready tomorrow."

She nods, satisfied. "Then tomorrow you shall return home."

A jolt fires through my gut. These are the words I've been praying I'd hear. "You're... You're actually going to send me back?" It's not until that very moment that I realize how much fear and doubt I'd be harboring. My childhood taught me Cecilia was fickle. I'd assumed her sister would be the same.

She cocks her head at me. "We had a deal, did we not?"

I pull my hands through my hair. My body is lighter than it has been in days. I have to take a deep breath to stop myself from floating away. For the first time, I truly believe I can go home.

"Thank you," I say, the words barely a whisper.

"When the job is done, see to it you come to my castle. I'll arrange your return."

She leaves and I sag against the warehouse wall. I've been so skeptical, so afraid to let myself believe I can get back. But she said she'll fulfill our bargain. I want to shout and let the joy burst from me. But this hope... it's so fragile, like promises made of glass. I've tasted Cecilia's betrayal. I want to believe Rozalyn, but I can't stand the thought of being so close to seeing Eden and having it ripped away.

Is this really my last day in Obex? I take a long breath and exhale, allowing myself one fleeting moment of belief, of hope, and joy before slamming it all into the vault. I won't celebrate until Eden's in my arms.

After sleeping with Eve, I avoided the bar for the whole day. I took a walk, journaled, walked some more, spilled a few more memories onto ink and paper. Every time I write a memory down, it's like a little bit of pressure lifts. Memory is my essence, so I always assumed the weight they placed on me was normal. But holding them, harboring them the way I did, makes my whole being heavy.

I arrive back at the Fallen Fallon as the evening fight club shift is gearing up. There are twice as many demons in the club as last night. This, though, is the final group. At last. I can almost sense home. The proximity of Trutinor trickles through my emotions, tasting like candy and treacle, like warm rain and the scent of fresh snow. I'm so close to getting back to Eden.

Tonight, unlike the other nights, I'll be closing proceedings. I think it's fitting—I started this whole affair. It's only right I close it too. One last fight and the army will be full. One fight between me and Eden. One fight between me and home.

I dress, or more accurately, undress, leaving my usual bloodstained vest on ready for my fight. There are three of us undefeated: me, Eve and one of the older fear demons, Markuz, I think they called him. No doubt they'll have pitted me against him this evening.

When I enter the club, the air is different. Instead of the hot stick of rage, it crackles quietly with the sweet-sour of lemony pops. Anticipation? What the hell are they antici-pating? The fight club is heaving already, the warehouse doors are spread wide, the demon crowd rowdy and noisy. I open the cage door and freeze.

Now I realize why the club stinks like citrus-lightning. Standing next to Pest is Eve. Her fists wrapped in filthy bandages, her hair plaited behind her. She's standing in a fighting stance. I glance from her to Pest—he shrugs at me, as if he doesn't have some say in this.

"No," I shout as I close the cage door. "Absolutely fucking not."

Pest pokes me in the chest. "Inside the cage you fight. Outside you don't. Your rules, not mine. You're in the cage. She's in the cage. You fight now."

Before I can protest, he raises his arm and drops it, signaling the fight to start. A roar bursts from the demons.

"Are you out of your fucking mind?" I bark at Eve over the clamoring crowd.

She smiles and swings at me. Which I block, but it makes me stumble back.

"What are you doing? Stop it, we can't fight." I say, my voice ratcheting higher.

"We're going to fight, and we're going to enjoy it. Give the crowd what they want. Make a show of it."

She swings her leg out and down with an axe kick, which I swat away.

"For Balancesake. This isn't a game. Someone has to win."

"Exactly," she says and runs at me. She lunges, but feints left and punches me square in the jaw.

I stagger back, spitting blood on the ring floor. The crowd jeers.

"Either you fight, or you forfeit and give me a piece of your soul. Which is it, honey?" She puts her hands on her hips and saunters around the ring. She turns to the crowd, putting her hand behind her ear.

They respond, "FIGHT. FIGHT. FIGHT."

Goddammit, Eve.

She rounds on me, pacing closer. "Well?"

"I don't want to hurt you."

"Too bad. Guess I'll have to kick your ass." She launches at me, swinging an upper cut at my chin. I block and shove her back.

She staggers a few steps, collects herself, and lunges. I duck and move out of her grasp. She kicks. I block and block and block again. The crowd's shouts drop into boos and grunts.

"You gotta play the game. HIT ME, you fucking pussy."

"I'm not going to hit you," I say through gritted teeth. The vault rumbles, feather cracks splintering the walls.

She smiles, cocking her head as if she can smell the Imbalance leaking out.

"Too busy imagining Eden fucking someone else?" She leans forward, whispers, "Just like you." She snaps up, paces around the ring, snarling. "Imagining her pregnant? Happy? Living, loving, fucking someone else for the next century?"

"DON'T, EVE..."

"Fine, you don't wanna play?" she barks. "Then I will." She smashes her fist into my nose. It ruptures, blood sprays over her chest and I step back, dropping to the ground. She looks down, smears the blood over her chest and then pops her finger in her mouth.

A roar rips around the warehouse. She climbs on top of me. I cover my face, blocking a flurry of punches.

The vault bursts. My head snaps to face her. A veil of maroon descending over my vision.

Her smile deepens. "Do your worst."

I reach out, not to her body, but to her core, to her emotions. Her heart. I grip and squeeze, flooding her with loneliness. With the ache of loss. Everything she fears. Her eyes widen like caverns. She scrambles back.

I push memories into her, memories of me and Eden. Of perfect kisses, and whispered I love yous. I let her see me slide myself inside Eden, as the barrier of my emotions drops and Eden's flooded with love.

Tears streak Eve's cheeks as her head shakes from side to side.

"Do you get it now?" I snarl. My voice is detached, spiked with hate. I can't control the Imbalance. Everything is pouring from me. I don't want to hurt her, but all my darkness, my scars, the pain I should never let out streams in one giant flow.

"I will never love you like I love her."

"Stop," she breathes. But I don't stop. I can't. She opened the vault. This is the consequence. I force one more memory into her mind. Me, standing over her burial stone, feeling nothing but pity.

Eve raises her hand, signaling a forfeit, her shoulders heave as great sobs rip through her chest. The vault instantly vanishes, every trace of anger and hatred for her evaporates. Instead, I'm left hollowed out, a shell aching and empty. I want to be sick. To scour the Imbalance out of my brain.

"I'm sorry," I say and reach out. But she scrambles back. My chest caves in. I never wanted this. I never wanted to hurt her. Everything moves too quickly.

Pest raises my arm, signaling I'm the winner. There's a

box shoved in my hands. Then there's blood running down my finger and a blade placed in my hand.

"No," I breathe. "I can't."

Pest grips my elbow, shoves me forward, his voice a low growl. "You must. Do you want to lose everything?"

I waver. Pest holds the still-crying Eve up. I can't bear to look at her. She's wriggling in his arms.

"Please," she begs, her voice high, whiny. "This was all a stupid mistake. It was just a game."

I shake my head. I didn't want any of this but if I fold now and let her go, everything I've worked for vanishes. The demons lose respect, Rozalyn loses her army and I lose my way home.

"I'm sorry, Eve. I'm sorry." My voice is as hollow as my chest, disjointed. Like I'm watching myself.

I sink the blade in and tear the smallest piece of her soul I can. Her scream pierces the crowd's roars. It vibrates and scorches my ears. I will never forget the sound. I want this over quickly, so I plunge the piece of her soul into my torso and then everything falls silent.

Pest carries her out of the cage and upstairs into her bedroom. I walk in behind him. "I'll take it from here," I say.

He grunts and leaves. I reach down to comfort her. She's rocking on the bed, but as I sit, I realize it's not tears making her rock.

She's laughing. She grabs my vest, pulling me close to her face. "I win."

I frown. "No, baby girl. I won the fight. It's going to be okay now. You can rest."

Her head rolls back as her laugh reaches a fever.

"I always win, Trey. I've been winning this whole time. You're just too fucking stupid-obsessed with Eden to realize it."

"I... What do you mean?" I say, shuffling back.

She pushes herself upright. "Oh, you silly fool. Eden might get to have you. But now there's always going to be a part of me inside you. You'll always have me and I will always have you."

Her laugh claws its way inside me, fracturing, fragmenting. Something's shifted. She's hard in a way I don't recognize. The coldness in her eyes reaches deep into her soul. I get off the bed, suddenly needing to be as far away from her as possible. My fists clench and unclench. Memories flood through my head. The ease of finding the bar, of finding Eve, and then it hits me. A flash of blonde in Rozalyn's throne room when I arrived.

Oh god.

This whole time. This whole time she was playing me. Not just today. Not just the fight.

"What have you done?" I ask, the words shiver out.

She stays silent, her eyes cold.

"EVE?" I snap.

Her face is stony. Her whole body is a void of nothingness. She's purposefully suppressing her emotions. "Nothing, baby. I haven't done anything."

I know now, without a doubt, she's hiding something. Still, she's looking right at me. I reach out, my essence roaming toward her. I push. Shove. And then I punch right through. She gasps a tiny little thing. But it's enough. She's smothered in a bitter, awful stench.

Lies and betrayal.

"Goddammit." There's only one thing she'd lie to me about.

Her lips twitch as if she's trying not to smile, but they curl into a thin grin, anyway. She gets off the bed, steps up to me and places a hand on my cheek. "Are you really going? Are you really leaving me after everything we've achieved down here? After everything that came before? After you fucked me the other night?"

I wipe her hand away from my cheek, and she steps back, examining me. Her gaze makes my skin writhe. I want a shower. I want to clean this place—and her—off me for good.

"That was a mistake, and you know it. It—us—will never happen again."

She rolls her eyes. "That's what they always say." She throws her hands up. "If you leave, Trey, that's it. There's no coming back. I won't be waiting for you next time." Her eyes are feverish and bright.

"Don't you get it? I was never leaving Obex with you. Even if I wanted to—which I don't—I can't leave with you. I'm Bound to Eden. This whole fucking club"—I gesture at the floor—"was about her. About getting back to her."

She slides her hand on her hip and rolls her eyes. Bored.

That one action shatters my whole world. I step back, clattering into the dresser. This was the lie. The moments of hesitation I sensed in her. The strange, conflicting emotions. This whole time I knew there was something, and I was too fixated on getting back to see it.

"You... Fuck, Eve. You know how I can get back, don't you?" I say through gritted teeth.

Her jaw flexes.

"How long?"

She's silent. Her lips bunching up. The vault crackles and judders. I flick my hand out. One punch of power and she catches her breath.

Her eyes gleam. "You can't play the pain game with me anymore. I like it too much," she says.

I drop my hand. "How long have you known, Eve?"

"A while."

"Before or after I got here?"

She nudges the floor with her toes. "Before." She looks up at me. "When I arrived and realized I couldn't get into the Soul Sanctuary, I was desperate. I didn't want to turn into one of those lost Soul Demons. So I dug around. I did some favors for some demons and found out some stuff." She fingers an old scar on her arm.

My fists ball, my jaw flexing hard and fast. "You found out 'stuff'?"

She glares at me. "What do you want me to say? I was alone. I had nowhere to go or stay and was constantly on the move trying not to get eaten by a fucking rabid demon. So I went to the only place I knew I'd find weapons and maybe someone to protect me."

"Rozalyn?"

She nods.

I run my hand through my hair. "For Balancesake, Eve."

"Oh, come on, don't tell me you didn't have fun, baby."

"Fuck you. Fuck you for not telling me. For knowing this whole time there was a faster way back. For fucking seducing me."

"Oh please, you wanted me as much as I wanted you. You're a big boy, Trey. You could have said no."

My eyes snap to hers. I grab her by the shoulders. "Tell me what you know right fucking now or I swear I will go back to the club, get the blade and sever your soul in two."

"Alright, alright," she says, shrugging me off. "You don't need Rozalyn to get home. You need blood."

"Blood?"

"A vial of blood from the Heart of Obex will give you the ability to roam between worlds. But to regenerate back to life, you need blood from the Heart of Trutinor as well."

"How the hell do you know that?"

"Because Rozalyn promised me a vial of both."

/ # TWENTY-THREE

'Where there is love, there is life.'

Mahatma Gandhi—Activist

EDEN

"Eden?" Bo's voice, delicate and feathery, filters through the fabric door. I sit bolt upright in bed, bright morning light streaming into the room. Dust motes dance in the beams. I rub my face, my eyes protesting against the morning.

"You came," I say and throw the covers off me and clamber out of bed. Bo's in leathers, her cloak trailing the floor and she's clasping a mug of coffee. Dorian's stirring in the armchair in the corner. But he's suited. This time his suit is a rich green and flecked with silver, so he must have gotten up already.

"You're here?" I say, my voice a whisper. She must have

traveled through the night to get here. No wonder she's holding coffee.

"I am." Her words aren't cold exactly. But they're not warm either. They crackle in the air. I stop midway across the room, look at the floor, rub my wrists, glance at Dorian, do anything but stare at her.

"I'm so sorry," I say and pause. She says nothing, just stands there rigid. "I really am sorry, Bo. Was I... Was I truly awful? On a scale of one to apocalypse, how bad was it?"

"I'd say biblical flood, combined with plagues of locusts. Oh, I'm still pissed with you, Eden. You might've gone through rehab, but that does not repair the colossal fuckups you've made."

I open my mouth to respond, but she holds her hand up, and I fall silent.

"You dragged Kato into addiction with you. You've been flagrantly disregarding any responsibility to the East, you've not even attempted to return to academic studies. But more than any of that, you've been selfish and a truly shit friend." Her nostrils flare as she huffs. "Just so we're clear, if you ever use Kato like that again, I will kill you myself."

I lower my eyes. "I pleaded with myself to stop."

Her shoulders sag and her face softens as she shakes her head at me, her blonde hair loose for once. "No more talk. I love you..." She draws a long breath. "And I say this from a place of love. But I don't know how many more times we can forgive you."

My lips part, my eyes wide. "You have to believe me. I'm so sorry."

"I know." She steps in close, then opens her arms. I fly into them, almost knocking her over.

We stand there crunching and squashing each other as tight as we can.

"Right now, I care about you getting better so we can sort this absolute cluster fuck you and Kato created," she says into my shoulder. She runs a hand over my back, then she pulls back and takes my shoulders, her face straight, serious. "Listen to me. I am so sorry Trey's gone, but you have to keep living. Kato and I... We both need you."

"Okay..." I say. If there were any more tears left inside me, they'd spill out. But there's nothing but bruises and exhaustion in my chest. Ironic that I craved numbness all along and if I'd just let myself grieve, I'd have found it anyway.

"You shouldn't relapse now," Dorian says, sitting up and stretching. He gets up, potters in the corner, and passes me a mug of something green and unnecessarily healthy looking.

"Thank Balance," Bo says. "Now you can get your shit together and fix the mess."

"How is Kato? Is he okay?"

"He's doing better than you, but it was a rough couple of weeks. How do you feel?" she says, taking my hand.

"Mostly numb."

"Mostly?"

I shrug. "Under it there's so many emotions, sadness, shame, guilt, maybe even a little ray of hope."

Bo rubs my arm. "Sounds like you're finally healing."

"I hope so. I... umm... I asked you here because I have something to tell you. Or maybe show you."

Her CogTracker rings. "Wait one moment, it's Kato. I'll be right back." She steps outside, so I sip the vile green shit Dorian handed me and shudder as it goes down. A memory pops into my head: Nyx used to give me the same putrid green stuff. I smile to myself, my belly warm with memories. It aches as much as it fills me with warmth, but there's a strange comfort in just *feeling*. I'd forgotten what it was like. What anything felt like. It's been so long since I allowed myself to embrace my emotions.

"How could I be so stupid?" I shake my head and swill the green liquid.

Dorian reaches out and pulls me in. His arms are strong and safe. He strokes my hair and lets me just be still in his embrace. I like being here—safe in his arms, knowing he won't leave me because I fucked up.

"I did everything I swore I never would. I vowed never to let anyone take my emotions away," I say into his chest. He pulls me tighter, his hand runs up my back into the back of my hair, stroking. His hands are warm, the heat from his body melts into mine like a protective layer. I don't know what this is between us. What I want. I close my eyes and lean in because right now, this is enough.

"It's over now," he says.

"I always told Trey it was wrong—an abomination. Pain grounds us. Tells us we're alive. I nearly lost myself in nothingness."

"But you didn't. You chose to save yourself."

"You may have only come into my life to protect me, but I'm grateful for everything else. The comfort, the friendship. If it wasn't for you, I'd never have clawed my way out. I'd never have let myself feel again."

He shifts position, pulling me in front of him, his eyes glimmer.

"And now? Can you feel this?" he says and places his hands on my cheeks. I nod. His fingers are soft and comforting. He glances at me, hesitation written in his eyes.

"Can you feel this?" he says and leans down to kiss my forehead. My stomach skitters, adrenaline pumping through my chest. My heart beating in my ears.

"I can," I whisper.

His face is so close, his lips almost touch mine. His breath trickles over my smile. He stills, his brow furrowed, unsure. As unsure as I am. We really shouldn't.

I could lose myself in this moment.

In him.

In his ocean breeze and green eyes and fucking intoxicating smile. I could. I really could. Hell, part of me wants to. But the image of Trey beneath a demon, so thin his face is gaunt, haunts me. Maybe it will haunt me for the rest of my life. But he could also become an addiction and I don't want to go back there. Not now, not ever. Something inside me hardens.

Dorian bites his lip, releases it, inches closer. It brings my attention back to the moment.

"Can you fe—"

I pull away and place my finger over his lips.

"I can," I tell him. "And I would because when you touch me, every cell of my body lights up. My body wants this. It wants you..." I step away. "But I can't. I can't do this, or you, or what my body wants. Not now. Maybe not ever."

Dorian straightens up. His face is soft, understanding. He takes my hand and squeezes. "Okay," he says, and he means it.

"Okay."

"Umm... Sorry to interrupt," Bo says, a wash of pink on her cheeks. She can't quite look at us.

"You weren't interrupting. Right. Dorian, if you can give me a minute, I'm going to get dressed and then I need to talk to Bo."

"Of course," he says and leaves.

I get dressed, taking my time with each item of clothing

because I'm not sure how to have this conversation with Bo. By the time I'm fully dressed, Bo is scowling.

"What on Earth's wrong? You're shaking," she says.

I wobble on one foot, trying to pull my boot on and then pace back and forth, running my hands through my knotty hair.

"God. I don't... I'm not sure where to start. There's something I have to tell you, and I don't know how you're going to react. I found out last night. I just. It's... And the prophecy. Oh Balance. How do I do this?"

Bo's neck is stiff. She rubs her brow. "You're scaring me."

I reach out. "No. This isn't. Let's... I need coffee. Okay? Let's start there."

So we leave the room and make our way to the main food court area, grabbing breakfast and coffee. Then we find a seating area around a fire. The embers are fading, so I wave my hand over it, drawing my essence out along with the fire until it's roaring and warming the air.

"What I have you tell you, you won't like."

She furrows her brow, but nods for me to continue.

"Do you remember the prophecy?"

"I do, that you'd join with the Last Fallon?"

"Yeah, but that's not the bit that's important right now. The prophecy says, 'they will face a grave choice.' I think you are my choice. The rebels, they want me to do something and I can't. Not unless. Well, look. God, this is so difficult. What I brought you here to tell you is that... I... I know who your father is."

Her bottom lip drops, her eyes widen, she sucks in a breath. "What? What do you mean?"

"I found out last night, he told me himself. And honestly, it makes sense, he... he looks like you. I can't believe I didn't put it together before. There was something familiar about him, now I realize what."

Bo's mouth is still dropped, her eyes well.

"Who... who is it?" she says eventually.

I can't bring myself to say the words. They're on my tongue, rolling around, ready to ruin everything.

"He's here. Isn't he?"

I nod. It's weak. This isn't my secret to tell and yet, I have to. I have to try. "Should I take you to him?"

Her mouth gulps at the air, but after a while she nods, closing her mouth. So I hold out my hand and together we walk the corridors of the rebel camp. Silently, I am a mess. My stomach licks with adrenaline, my mind races, wondering if I'm about to make a huge mistake. I am risking everything. If this goes badly, Bo will never forgive me.

We reach Castor's office and I pull open the curtain. He's sitting at his desk.

"Fallon East, what brings—" I step aside and Bo slides into the space. He stops talking, the pen he was holding falls from his hand.

There is one vacuous pause. The space between Bo and Castor unravels, a lifetime of questions and memories not made, resentment, regrets. All of them fill the air and I thank Balance. I'm not a Siren and I can't sense what they're feeling.

After an age, Castor stands. "What have you do—"

I hold up my hand to silence him. "You gave me a choice. I made it. I choose Bo."

He drops his head, rubs his forehead.

"I should leave you two to introduce yourselves." I turn to leave, but Bo grabs my arm.

"No. Don't leave me."

So I sit quietly in the corner, my stomach in knots, and I

try not to listen. There's shouting. There's crying. There are apologies and then there's silence. Neither of them speaks, so I stand and their eyes snap to me.

"You have to tell her, Castor."

Bo glances from me to Castor. "Tell me what?"

"Give me strength," Castor says, kneading his temples. "This is not how it was meant to go, Fallon East."

So he explains everything he said to me last night. That Victor has to die and what Bo will become and I watch as the father-shaped gift I just gave my best friend turns sour. Poisoned. Ruined. Another thing I messed up.

She turns to me. "This is what you wanted to tell me?" She's sobbing, so I pull her into my arms.

"I made a promise to you. If Victor has to die, I wasn't going to be a part of that unless you knew."

"You can't," she cries into my shoulder. "Neither of you. You can't do it. Please don't hurt him. There has to be another way. With all the magic in Trutinor, there has to be." She's shrieking, desperate.

Castor sighs. "Beatrice, this is about more than Victor, or you or me. This is about everyone. We need Aurora's banishment lifted for so many reasons. Not least because we need the Mermaids to help us defeat Cecilia. But also because Aurora is the only one who can merge the soul scythes. And without that blade, we cannot bring Rozalyn back to Trutinor. I have spent hundreds of years searching for ways to realize this plan. There is an ancient saying, some say it's as old as the sisters themselves: Rozalyn taught it to me: the blade, the blood and the bodies. It's how we kill her."

Bo weeps all over again. "There has to be another way. There has to be."

Castor squeezes Bo's shoulder. "I'm so sorry. I wish there was..."

But there isn't, and deep down, all three of us know it. So I sit there and I rock her, and I hug her tight and I apologize over and over because I'm not sure what else to do. And when the time comes, and Victor is before me and I'm holding the blade, I have no idea what I'll do then, either.

Dorian, Bo, and I leave the rebel camp. The entire journey back is silent. Dorian surreptitiously glances at me enough times I relent and message him privately on his CogTracker to explain what happened.

You did WHAT?

Don't look at me like that. I did what I had to do to protect my friendship.

Yeah, and you've risked the entirety of Trutinor because of it.

She's worth it.

Dorian looks out the window. "We're approaching Siren City. It won't be long before we're in Siren station."

"I'll get Magnus to call ahead and clear the area of paparazzi," Bo says, and vanishes.

Dorian and I are left alone. I'm silent until he comes to sit next to me.

"I owe you a thank you. I'm not sure I can repay," I say.

"You don't need to thank me."

"I do. You saved me."

He holds my gaze. The air is suddenly tight. "There's only one thing I want from you, but I'm not sure you're ready to give it."

I pull my gaze away, force a smile down. He's right. Even though he's deeply attractive. I'm still healing on so many levels. Now is not the time to go racing into the arms of an unacceptably handsome Siren... Mermaid. Dammit, I still cannot get my head around the fact he and Castor are really, truly, Mermaids.

The station is dead thanks to Magnus, The Six, and a few favors. In the distance, paparazzi holler. I can just make out their clicks and snaps from outside the platform. Such a shame to disappoint the likes of Tarkin Tavas. I grin at the thought. The sun beats down warm, sticky, filled with the humidity of a brewing storm.

Kato's hair is—as always—a fucking mess, but I've never been so relieved to see him. His hair might be in a state, but he looks a darn sight fresher than me. There's a hesitant moment as Kato walks across the station and greets Bo. Dorian is a few feet behind. Close enough, he can reach me, far enough this conversation will be mostly private. I glance over my shoulder and he's at least pretending not to be watching and listening to my every move.

There's a stagnant pause. One horrible second where I question everything. Where Bo and Kato vanish from my life. Where I spend endless nights alone, signing Council documents, streams of meetings and applauding crowds in the East, but through all of it, I'm alone. I can't breathe. My chest is tight. I've lost him. I've lost everything.

Kato opens his arms.

I suck in oxygen and fly into his embrace. Everything I was holding. The tension, the fear, explodes in one long exhalation. *It's going to be okay.*

"There are no words to explain how sorry I am," I say into his neck. He squeezes me.

"It's at least twenty-seven percent my fault."

I laugh. He's such an idiot. "I love you."

"I love you too. Now." He pulls me around to face him, holding me by the shoulders. "Let's never do that again."

"Agreed. God, I am so agreed I'd take a Blood Oath on it."

"No need to be extreme, darling." He shuffles on the spot, looks at the floor, then back at me. "That was a bold move, telling Bo. She messaged me while you were on the way here."

I nod. "It was. But I think I've done enough lying and hiding for two lifetimes."

"I have class," Bo says. Kato turns to Bo and kisses her. "Okay, I will see your fine ass this evening."

Bo turns to me, holds my gaze. I swallow hard, wondering if this is the moment I lose her, if this was just another in a long line of fuckups. Instead, she grabs my hands and pulls me in. "Thank you," she says. Then she kisses me on the cheek and says those words that mean everything.

"Friends always..."

"And forever Balanced," I say, pulling her back in for another hug. "Thank Balance, I thought I might have lost you for good." The anchor that's been weighing my chest down lessens for the first time in a long time.

"I'll never resent you for telling the truth," she says. "Okay, I have to go. I have piles of coursework, and I need about eighty coffees to get through the day."

She kisses Kato. "Have a good day." She kisses him again and takes a step, then halts.

"It's good to have you back, Eden." She saunters off the platform and out of the station to a roar of clicks and paparazzi calls.

It's just Kato and me left on the station platform. Dorian appears in the doorway, his eyes gleaming, a wide grin on his lips.

"It's go time, East," he says.

"Go time? What's—"

"The Soul Scythe, we've finally located it."

Kato glances from me to Dorian. Oh shit.

"Castor wants us to collect it for him," Dorian says.

I raise an eyebrow. After spending all night telling Bo her brother needs to die, I'm not sure I'm ready to gallivant off to pick up the weapon that will do it.

I give Dorian a grimace.

"Well, what are we waiting for?" Kato says. "Let's go."

I glare at him. "You can't possibly be coming with us."

"To pick up a weapon that will end the son of a bitch that killed my brother? You had better believe I'm coming. Get on the train." He shoves me playfully toward the door.

"But I thought you wanting to end Victor was all fueled by the compulsion and my emotions. You still want to..." I glance around the station. "... to end him?"

Kato looks at me, his eyes fierce. "Absolutely. Yes, I was partly fueled by you. But you have to understand, Trey was more than just a brother to me. He was my best friend, a father figure. He looked after me when both our parents were gone. That piece of shit might be Bo's brother. But he took someone who meant everything to me. For fucksake, he almost took you too. He's hurt enough people. I'd lost hope we could do anything about it. But after what Bo told me... She might not be on board, but I'll be damned if Victor gets to live while the rest of us suffer under Cecilia's reign for the rest of time. Fuck that, and fuck Victor too."

"She'll never agree to any of this. Not if it means ending Victor."

"What choice do we have?" Kato asks. He touches my shoulder. "Whatever you choose, whether we end Victor and go through with this, or if you choose Bo, and protect him, I will support you."

"And what about Bo? If we get this blade and we go through with it? What then? How the hell do we explain it to her?"

His shoulders droop. "I..." He wipes his face. Tension pulling at his forehead. "I don't know."

"One step at a time," Dorian says. "Unless we secure the blade, none of it will be possible."

I knead my temples. "If we do this, there are going to be consequences. Bo said this was the last time she would forgive me. What if... What if she never forgives me?"

"She will," Kato says.

"How do you know?"

"Because she loves you more than anything."

He steps onto the train, but I'm paralyzed. I can't lose Bo and she still thinks I made her a promise.

"Are you coming or not?" Kato says.

This is one of those crossroad moments people talk about. Where everything freezes and time is infinite. One of those moments we wish there was a third way, a different option. A path that doesn't lead to mutual destruction. But every option I think of leads to the same conclusion.

The same choice. Hurt my best friend to save our kind. A memory flashes through my mind.

"I think some part of her knows this is coming."

He looks up at me. "Really?"

"When I went to the Binding chamber all those months ago, I saw my mother's last moments through her own eyes. When Bo gave my mother and father the vials of her blood, she knew then. Maddison had told her she could help bring the Mermaids back, though I don't think either of them understood how. They can't have. Maddison would never have gone through with it. But Bo was aware she had a choice: hurt me or risk the fate of us all."

Kato's expression pinches. "She chose to hurt you, for the greater good."

I nod. "I guess we're facing the same choice. Only none of us know how this is going to end."

He holds out a hand. "Now or never, East."

I swallow hard, then take his hand and climb onto the train.

A couple of hours later, we arrive in the East. The desert air is so dry my lips stick to my gums. My skin is slick with sweat. Even the meager shade the train is providing from the blistering heat isn't enough to stop me sweating. We're meeting on an old disused track in the ass of the Eastern desert. Or we were meant to be. We've been waiting for forever. Dorian's taken his suit jacket off, his sleeves are rolled up, his forearms on show. He had to leave his cane on the train. It would just sink into the sand.

Finally, Castor appears around the peak of a dune. Where the hell did he come from? We're literally in the middle of a barren desert. There's nothing for miles. And yet, a few short hours after we left the South, here he is.

Kato stands straight, cocks his head to the side, narrowing his eyes. "Holy shit, he looks like her, doesn't he?"

"I can't believe I didn't figure it out. Those lips. Their face shape, it's uncanny."

Kato stops dead in his tracks. His eyes are wide. "Shit and balls. I've just realized. That means he's... He's a..." He pales, drops his voice. "Mermaids kill our kind."

I grab his hand. "We're on the same team. He wants what you want."

"Eden, Fallon Luchelli," Castor says, holding his hand out to each of us. "It's good to have you join the rebellion officially."

Kato swallows a few times. He looks like he's going to puke. But eventually he holds out a hand and Castor shakes it, nonplussed.

"You're... You're Bo's father?" Kato says.

Castor's brows narrow as he glares at me. "You told him too?"

I shrug. "He's her Balancer. It's not like Bo was going to keep it from him."

He grits his teeth and sighs. Then he turns to Kato. "When this is all over, it would be lovely to meet you under more informal circumstances. A dinner perhaps. Beatrice still has many questions for me. And, if she permits it, I should like to get to know her too."

Kato nods, slow, steady, his eyes never leaving Castor's face.

"Our teams have located the Soul Scythe that's this side of the barrier. We can't track the other one down yet. It's in Obex. We will deal with that once the fabric is open. For now, we want you three to steal it and bring it back. It's hidden on Earth. In a London museum. I've sent you the schematics and planned entry and exit routes."

"Okay," I say. "And after?"

"One thing at a time. Get the blade and let's regroup. I've forwarded the information to your CogTrackers."

He turns and pauses.

"And, Eden. Be careful. It's the most dangerous blade in existence. If the First Fallon or anyone in the council discovers you've secured it..."

He doesn't need to finish that sentence. I understand the consequences. We part, Castor disappears back into the yellow oasis, and we board the train. Kato takes my CogTracker and places it next to his. Tapping and clicking until a giant schematic appears above his tracker like a ghost-building.

He leans back, a devilish grin on his lips. "Oh, this should be fun."

Kato is lying on one of the train's comfy booth seats, his head buried so deep in his CogTracker he doesn't respond when I ask if he wants a drink. He clacks and clicks as he types furiously on his keyboard.

"So my bodyguarding charm paid off then? Finally coming to the rebel dark side." Dorian grins as he pours us both a drink. The train rattles, making the liquid slop up the side. I look at the glass, wondering whether I should steer clear. I think I've drunk enough booze.

"Don't worry, it's alcohol free," he says.

I pick up the glass, grateful for the liquid and grateful he always seems to know what I want. The hot desert air is unrelenting. Even inside the train with air con, it's uncomfortably warm.

Kato slams his CogTracker down and swallows his rather more alcoholic beverage in one. "God. I needed that after meeting Castor. No more revelations. Okay? I mean, I knew my Balancer was hereditarily like half Mermaid. But there's a difference between knowing it and fucking seeing it. Sirens and Mermaids... we don't exactly have a great history. Hey, buddy," Kato says and slaps Dorian's shoulder.

"Umm, Kato..." I start, giving Dorian a sideways glance. We haven't exactly talked much about the fact Dorian is a Mermaid, but Kato should probably know his new BFF is, in fact, a Mermaid.

Kato looks from me to Dorian, his face falls. "Oh, fuck me. Not you too."

"We're not actually as bad as we seem," Dorian shrugs.

Kato raises a hand to cut the conversation dead, grabs a bottle from behind the bar, and says, "I'm going for a shower. I don't get how you deal with all the desert sand and grime, East. It's not doing my royal complexion any good. The blade is in The Natural History museum in London in one of their collection rooms, labeled under a deeply original title of 'unidentified.'"

He wanders off upstairs doing an excellent impression of Hermia, muttering to himself and swigging from the bottle he just poached.

"Approaching the barrier," Magnus's gruff tone says through the train speakers. We jolt forward, my hands reach out to stop me falling. Only I don't fall because we slam into the barrier and everything slows. My hands land on Dorian's shoulders. He, thankfully, grabbed hold of the booth table, so we won't crash to the carriage floor when we break through.

Our faces are so close to each other's I'm certain I'll face plant his cheek when we come out the other side. His lips pull into a slow grin. His green eyes sparkle like the sun glittering on ocean waves. Cheeky bastard. Though it doesn't stop me from smiling back.

Time stretches inside the barrier, it warps and stills. Loose locks of my hair and his floppy mop dance and twirl like ribbons. A shimmer of silver passes over his face and penetrates his eyes. His hair washes out, fading into gray and then silver-white. His smile sharpens. Teeth warp, the flat edges dissolve into sharp peaks. I blink, but his face is normal. My eyes widen. So many emotions run through my body. It's like static and lightning and horror rolled into one. I want to see him in his full Mermaid form. But the shadows of what I just saw were terrifying.

His face flickers, his expression tightens. In slow motion, my eyebrows knit. Our eyes lock. Recognition passes between us. He knows I saw the real him. He saw the fear and now, his head is lowered, his mouth a tight grimace.

We slam through the other side of the barrier and into Earth as I crash into his cheek and neck. His arms pull me in to prevent me falling. My brain screams at me to back away, but I don't.

"I know what you saw," I say, "but I'm not afraid."

His eyes are round, but before I have a chance to grill him, Kato calls us from the cabin upstairs.

Dammit Kato.

The three of us are dressed in dark clothes, combat pants, boots and t-shirts. Kato insisted.

"If we're going to steal a priceless artifact that shouldn't exist—and if caught with will probably get us sent to Datch, or worse, I might add—then we're at least going to prison looking the part."

He has a point. Not about looking the part, but the clothing makes us blend into the shadows.

Dorian brushes past me. Our eyes catch each other as he glances over his shoulder.

"Dorian," Kato barks.

Dorian's so blasé it's infuriating Kato. Especially because Kato drank a bit too much on the way here and instead of the happy drunk he usually is, he's unnerved. I think one too many revelations, one too many secrets are getting to him. He might be resolute in wanting to off Victor, but he knows as well as I do. The Bo-consequences will be severe, even if she's had advanced warning.

I smile, first to Dorian, then to myself. Dorian doesn't even attempt to stay in the shadows. His walking cane clacks against the cobbles as he sidles up to Kato. I watch the way he moves: his left foot—always a fraction out of time—gives him the faint limp.

Dorian's waving at me to hurry. He's almost at the side door of London's Natural History Museum. He signals the coast is clear. I sprint up the pavement under the cover of the museum shop awnings. When I reach the cove of the museum door, Dorian pulls me close, giving me a look that radiates through my entire body.

"We have to talk," he says.

"I told you, I'm not afraid."

Our breath mingles in the icy air, puffs of wispy-white billow between us. He holds my gaze a moment longer than necessary. Then Kato pushes me out of the way, breaking the tension.

"Less of the Balance fixing, East. We haven't got time tonight. Or would you prefer the skeletal troglodyte to run around Trutinor for the rest of time?" Kato says.

He holds his CogTracker over the museum's door lock, then tries the handle, but it doesn't budge.

"What's wrong?" I whisper.

"Nothing, give me some space."

There's tapping and clicking, and then the smack of a boot against a door. But it doesn't budge.

"Did that make you feel better?" I breathe, uncurling my fingers and shooting a bolt of electricity into the door lock.

It swings open. He turns to me. "Much."

I jab him in the ribs, then cock my head at Dorian to follow him in.

"Oi. What the hell?" A rather plump security guard stands up from behind his desk, picks up a baton and runs— no, waddles—toward us.

"Really?" I moan. I throw my arm out and shoot a bolt of electricity straight at his head. He drops like a stone to the floor.

Dorian pulls a set of handcuffs off the security guard's waistband and cinches his hands together.

"He's out cold," Dorian says, dragging the guard by his arms.

"According to my CogTracker, that," Kato says, pointing to an innocuous door, "is a closet. Dump him in there."

"How many guards are there?" I ask.

"Not that many. But it's not the guards you need to worry about. It's the digital security systems that will give us issues. Lucky for you, I'm a genius, and I could disable these things before Keepers School," Kato says, slipping behind the security guard's desk and connecting his CogTracker to the computer. He taps a few buttons and disconnects his Tracker.

"You're done?" I say as Dorian and I are still struggling to shove the guard in the closet.

"Please. Of course I'm done. These things are antiques. Even Dorian could hack them." Kato's eyes flick to Dorian and he gives him a wink.

"Savage," Dorian snorts. I roll my eyes at them back to bromancing each other already.

We enter a huge, cavernous foyer. The flooring is ornate, with tiled patterns arcing out in swirls. At the other end of the room is a huge sweeping staircase made of gray stone. It leads to the floor above which has an open hallway the entire way around the landing. I look behind us and spot another staircase and floor above that. This place is vast.

In the middle of the foyer is a gigantic skeleton that reaches almost to the roof, its huge skull leers down at the three of us.

We enter a long, thin hall. It's cool and dark and on either side of us are wooden cabinets. Their rich brown frames hang from the hall walls, large panes of glass display their contents as if a surgeon had spliced open the museum and put its innards on display. Inside each cabinet are an array of animals, insects and collections of strange-shaped creatures. Each animal is fixed to the cabinet with hooks, pins and clips. My gaze darts between them, squinting to make out their forms in the shadows. I can't see properly, but my skin crawls like they're watching me.

We move out of the hall and toward the cafe area.

"Stop," Kato says, coming to a halt and shoving his arm out to stop me. "Don't move." His eyes scan the walls, up and down and around the edges like he's undressing the cafe.

"What's wrong?" Dorian asks.

"Infrared movement sensor. Top corner. Must have been added recently because it's not in the schematics."

"Do we have a problem?" I ask.

"Not if you quit asking questions and let me think."

Kato closes his eyes. His breathing slows as he concentrates. "How accurate can you be with those weapons?" He points at my hands.

"Which element?"

"Electricity. I could try to hack the system wirelessly, but we're sitting ducks in the middle of this room. It would be faster and easier to attach the CogTracker to the mainline cabling running along the skirting boards. But to do that, I have to move. Best option is you fry the camera. So, I ask again, how accurate are—"

I raise my hand and fire a bolt straight at the camera. It crackles and screams as sparks halo the camera like a crown. Then it sags and droops down the wall.

"—Accurate then."

We move through the cafe area; the floor is made of checked tiles and it reminds me of the West State and Keepers school.

"Here," Kato whispers and points to a door that says:

STAFF ONLY

Dorian moves out of the way so Kato can take his place by the door. He slides open the first cog on his tracker. After tapping a few things into the keyboard, he holds it against a square patch on the door. The door clicks and swings open.

We walk through and onto a set of stairs and the door

clicks shut, sealing us in, drawing darkness around us. Kato stares at blueprints of the museum which are now projected above his CogTracker. They hang suspended above the screen like a phantom.

"We're here," he says, pointing at the translucent projection. Spinning it around, he points at a separate section of the building. "But we need to get to there."

"What floor?" I ask.

"Five and a half."

I fire a glare at him. "We don't have time for jokes."

"Do I look like I'm joking?"

He doesn't.

"Fine, floor five and a half, after you."

He presses a button, and the projection vanishes, reappearing on his CogTracker screen with a flashing blue dot marking our position. We make our way through the museum bowels. Even with white walls and the occasional security light, it's dim down here. Dark enough, it feels like a warning. We're seeing this through and I'm getting what we came for, no matter what. Each area we pass through smells different from the previous one. Some are earthy, like fresh rain on granite boulders, others reek of clinical plastic and chemicals.

We reach a huge arched door. There are no cameras here, just metal chains. I place my hands over the chains and light up. Underneath my fists, there's a small glow. Orange first, then yellow, then a bluey white as they burn hot enough to melt metal. A line of sweat coats my forehead as I concentrate on restricting the flames to the palm of my hand. The last thing we need is a fire down here. Kato and Dorian step back as heat billows out around me. Drip by drip, the chain dissolves, pooling on the floor. Steam hisses and rises as the drips splash against the tiles and I spray them with water to cool them down. Eventually, the chain slackens and I release the door, flooding us with crisp night air.

"Down there," Kato says, pointing left down the delivery road to another part of the same building.

"I thought Trutinor had strange architecture," I say, glancing up as we walk under a cover and into the next building. The buildings are joined by a faux ceiling, and there's no door. It's just open.

"This is the lift we need," Kato says.

Dorian and Kato push their fingers in the slim gap and heave the doors open. Once inside, I glance at the panel. Sure enough, there's a button marked five point five.

"Humans are weird."

"You're telling me," Kato says. "I'm the one that compels them. You wouldn't believe the shit they think about."

Kato pulls the metal panel open and tugs at the wiring. He clips his CogTracker in and the lift jolts, flaring to life. In seconds, the doors ping open on floor five point five.

The corridor we step into is white. Kato leads us to a door at the end where Dorian kneels and fiddles with the lock. This deep in the museum, there's no need for digitized locks or at least, not for what we're hunting. The door opens and Kato waltzes past both of us into the collection room.

There are row upon row of gray cabinets lined up along the walls. The walkway is so narrow it's suffocating. At the end of each row of cabinets is a wheel.

"This one." Kato stops at a cabinet a few feet ahead and the blue dot on his CogTracker turns green. "Pull it open."

Dorian takes the wheel and spins, the cabinets judder and grind in protest but separate.

Kato steps between them, and I step behind him. Dorian, however, keeps his distance.

"You do the honors," Kato says, pointing at the middle cabinet. "Fifth tray down."

I open the door and count the trays. Then slide the fifth one open. There, nestled in the tray, is what we came for.

"How imaginative. They've labeled it 'unidentified weapon.' You'd think they'd at least come up with some fancy scientific name," Kato says.

"What, for a sculpted bone from a mythical creature they think only exists in fairy tales? Budge up. I want a closer look." I pull the tray out and reach in.

"STOP," Dorian says, making me jump.

"Jesus, Dorian. There are still security guards on duty."

"Sorry, I just... Don't touch the blade. That's all."

I turn back, Kato's reaching for the finger bone. I grab his wrist.

"He's right. All the texts say Aurora's finger is poisonous even without the magic imbued. Do as Dorian says and only touch the hilt."

"Fine," Kato says, pulling his hand away.

I reach for the blade and take it out. I frown. "Doesn't look like much."

"I wouldn't underestimate it," Dorian says.

"We don't have time to worry about aesthetics," Kato says, grabbing the blade from me and dropping it into a hip holster. He hands it to me and I attach it to my belt and around my thigh.

We close the cabinet door, sealing everything back as we found it.

"There," Kato says, grinning at us. "Told you it would be easy."

An explosion of shrieking rips through the collections

room. Red strobe light flashes on and off as the Museum alarms scream to life.

"What happened to 'I'm a genius and you're lucky to have me'? Mr. I've disabled the fucking security alarms?" I bark.

From behind us, the thunder of footfall, clinking metal and shouting guards punctuates the sirens.

"Shit," Dorian says.

"RUN," I bellow.

BREAKING NEWS

"Good evening, Trutinor, this is Tarkin Tavas reporting for CogNews TV. This evening there are reports of Fallon East's reappearance. You'll remember a couple of weeks ago, after the salacious events at the end of Fallon Luchelli's inaugural ball, Fallon Luchelli was caught conducting Siren pain removal on Fallon East. After capturing on film Fallon Luchelli throwing all of Ms. East's sizable ball of pain back at her, an unknown male caught it, preventing Fallon East's untimely death. Following on from that event, Fallon East hasn't been seen since. Until this evening.

There are multiple reports from Keepers at various train stations having seen Fallon East on a train. Indeed, there are reports from our Earth-based stationed Keepers reporting having seen an unscheduled train arriving in London. It's unclear

where Fallon East has been or why she was
in London, but we will, of course, bring
you all updates as soon as we have them.
This is Tarkin Tavas reporting for CogNews
TV."

TWENTY-FOUR

'While smaller in stature than Keepers, the Elfin race is notoriously fit, flexible and deceptively strong. Many Elves find their trade in physical labors, armies, combat training and, it is rumored, assassination.'

Excerpt—The History of Trutinor Vol. 4

TREY

"What the hell do you mean, she told you?" I snap. The vault rattles, tempts, coaxes me toward darkness. Inhale, Trey: one, two, three. I need answers. I can't afford to go off until she's told me what I want.

What little color Eve has left in her has returned to her face and she seems stronger, recovered from losing a piece of soul. Not that I give a shit.

"I'll tell you. I just... Can we get a drink? For old times' sake? I'll explain everything." Her whole body has sagged, as if keeping this secret was holding her upright. Her voice is weak, flimsy, pathetic. I don't want to drink with her, I don't want to be near to her, but if she has information I can use, then I'll pry it out of her any way I can.

I kick the bedroom door open and march downstairs. She can make her own fucking way down.

She rests on a bar stool as I serve a couple of demons. The distraction helps to calm me down, keep me centered and rational. I want to know exactly what she knows. When the queue has lessened, I take the stool next to her.

"I was in her castle the day you arrived here."

"I saw you. I just didn't realize it was you."

She reaches across the bar to touch my hand, hesitates, and then pulls back. "I'd gone there for help and answers. I was desperate. But she was distracted with you. I had no idea you were there until I was about to sneak back out. I caught sight of you in her throne room, which is when Bellamy found me."

My mind flies back to the first day I was here. Pest had dragged me into her castle, the flash of blonde. I can't believe it was her.

"What happened when he found you?" I ask.

"After you were gone, he brought me to her chambers."

A tear spills over her cheek. She looks at the bar, and then the floor.

"What did you agree to do for her?"

"Rozalyn said she would help me if... She wanted me to... To make sure you concentrated. She wanted me to help you build her army. And make sure you didn't do anything stupid, like get eaten or fall into the Soul Sanctuary."

"And in return for guarding me, you what? Got two vials of blood?"

"It was meant to restore my soul. The blood has magical properties that enable the dead to do things, to pass between worlds or something. It's what she used on Victor. But she said she had just enough Trutinor blood left she could restore my soul and help me move on to my next life. What was I supposed to do?"

"Fucksake, Eve. Why drag up all those old memories of who we were? Why try to get me into bed?"

"Because you never chose ME. I deserve to be chosen, Trey. And not once did you ever choose me."

She looks down. The silence between us is stagnant, full. My insides bubble and froth. What can I say? She's right. I didn't choose her and I never will.

She continues, "I followed you back from Rozalyn's the day you arrived. Coaxing you toward the bar she'd told me to use. It was the perfect place for you. So I hid in the shadows while you fought the landlord. I'd have jumped in if you were going to lose that fight, but you had it covered."

"You played me." I can't look at her.

She touches my knee. I flinch. She keeps her hand there. "Trey, truly, I am so, so sorry. It was never about hurting you. I just... I needed a second chance. Isn't that what you've been doing this whole time? Looking for a way to have a second chance with Eden? You must have known... deep down? You know me too well... how we work. Didn't you think it all happened a bit too easy?"

Did I? I knew something was off, but I didn't want to accept that Eve was betraying me. I was too relieved to have the comfort of a friendly face. Finally, our eyes meet. Tears smear her cheeks. There's a heavy dullness emanating from her, stained with a stale sourness. It's bitter and acrid and tinged with ash, and none of it is aimed at me. It's directed inward. God dammit, Eve.

"Don't," I say, shaking my head. "Don't feel like that. I can't bear it."

"I'm so sorry," she says, her lips wobbling as if she might cry. Her expression evaporates all the heat of my rage and in an instant we're young again. She's that girl with hair like sunshine and feverish green eyes staring at me, asking me to make her safe and even though I'm cross, she's still Eve. I pull her in, stroking her hair.

"Where are the vials of blood? Where is the Heart of Obex?" I ask.

Her shoulders sag. "I don't know. I never saw it, but she has it somewhere in the castle."

"I'm leaving in the morning," I say. "Rozalyn came to see me earlier. She said she's sending me home."

Eve's lips pinch, two silent tears roll down her skin. She takes a shuddering breath. "But I need you."

"I..." I need to be away from her. She's fucked up, and I need to reconcile the deluge of emotions swirling around my head. There's a queue again at the bar, so I get up and start serving.

When she doesn't get a response, her bottom lip wobbles. "Fuck you, Luchelli." And she storms off.

Pest strolls into the bar and gestures for a drink. I pour him a pint of the dark stuff just as a brawl breaks out. He marches over, but the demons break it up before he reaches them. Good job too, because they'd be out, barred from the club. The shorter demon raises his arms in surrender. I leave Pest's pint on the bar when the air tingles. A flood of emotions flies through the room. They're rich and thick and so sweet. I haven't sensed emotions that powerful in forever. I glance around the bar, but there's nothing unusual. Eve makes her way behind the serving counter and walks up to me.

"Okay," she says.

"Okay what?"

"Okay, goodbye. I give up. You'll never be mine. So I'm letting go. My job is done. Rozalyn only ever asked me to keep you here until she had her army. If you're done, then I guess we're done, too."

I bite my lip. Is she really giving up? After all this time? She places her hand on my cheek. I still. She doesn't get to be close to me anymore. A putrid guilt and rage and a thousand other things gnaw at my mind.

"I mean it, Trey. Go to her. Go to Rozalyn and get your ticket out of here so you can be with your soul mate."

The air sharpens and cools. I can taste something sour, dark, laced with betrayal. Before I can search for the source, Eve says. "I'm sorry."

I frown. She laces her fingers through mine and I wonder, is she really sorry? I don't trust her. I need to know what she's hiding. So I push my senses out until they prickle with sour berries, a strange liqueur of regret and tenderness. Perhaps she is sorry.

"What are you sorry for?" I ask.

"For everything. For this... Goodbye, baby."

Then she spins me around so I'm facing out into the bar and she kisses me. My eyes shut. At first I'm rigid, but there's something so tender, so real in her kiss that it catches my chest. I'm not sure whether it's the slice of her inside me, but she kisses me so deeply I feel it inside, like a thousand memories, like all the moments we shared rolled into one press of the lips. She really is saying goodbye. I don't understand. Where her hand rests on my cheek, I lace my fingers through hers and kiss her goodbye. One last time.

I open my eyes.

Everything freezes. My blood. The air in my lungs. I pull away. Standing in the bar is Eden. Not a mirage, or a vision.

Not a memory.

But Eden.

Real, fleshy, full of color, gorgeous curves and lilac eyes.

Her mouth drops, horror spreads through her body. Wave after wave of sour, icy emotion hits me.

She saw me kiss Eve. I want to scream out, tell her it was a goodbye kiss. It meant nothing, but I'm suspended in place. I catch a breath. Enough to utter a single word.

"Eden," her name rushes out. But as soon as I've said it, she vanishes.

"EDEN," I bellow, but she's gone. I run around the bar and wave my hands through the air, but there's nothing left. Not even a strand of hair. She's gone.

My chest burns hot as Eve's words ring through my mind *"For everything. For this... Goodbye, baby."*

I march back to the bar and grab her by the scruff of her top.

"Did you know she was there?"

My ribs are heaving as I struggle to catch my breath from the caustic rage bubbling in my lungs. The vault is trembling, splintering. Cracks ripping through the cage.

"TELL ME YOU DIDN'T KNOW, EVE!" My voice breaks on her name. She refuses to look at me, so I pull her chin up until her eyes meet mine.

"Say it. Say the words..."

Her bottom lip is wobbling, tears falling down her gray

cheeks, her green eyes bright with tears. Her nose flares as she draws in a breath.

"I..." she says. "I have always loved you faithfully, and it was never enough."

I drop her chin and shake my head at her.

"Every part of me, Trey. Everything I did, it was always for you."

"Answer the fucking question. Did. You. Know?"

A giant sob rolls out. As she takes a juddering breath, she looks me square in the eye.

"I knew."

I don't wait for her response. I leave her. Leave them all. I pick up my journal, stalk through the warehouse and pick up the Soul Scythe box and walk out of the bar for the last time. Even as I march up the street, I can hear Eve screaming my name. Screaming apologies. Screaming anything to make me turn back. But I don't. I don't look. I don't say goodbye, I just walk and walk and walk. Away from this place, from her, from everything. No matter what happens this evening, I'm walking back into Trutinor.

TWENTY-FIVE

'Entrance to The Binding Chamber is forbidden. Centuries ago, the Chamber was open to all to visit. But Keepers whose Balancers died would often lose themselves in the chambers, searching for glimpses of loved ones, forgetting to live themselves and so the Chamber was sealed off from everyone except those with training.'

Excerpt—The History of Forbidden and Lost Magic

EDEN

Kato drops Dorian and me in the East. He's returning to the South for the night. We'll regroup tomorrow when we will probably have to confront Bo about what the hell we're going to do about Victor. She might not want us to kill him, but I don't see what other choice we have.

Dorian pushes the door to my home tower roof open. I was here fleetingly for Titus, but it's been a long time since I spent the night or any amount of real time here. Too long, really. I thought I'd be uncomfortable, I've spent so long disconnected from my home. But for the first time, I actually feel relief. My body relaxes into a state of knowing, of comfort and safety. I know the corridors; the shadows are filled with laughter and memories, the walls with photos and portraits that make me smile instead of cry. Everything has a sense of familiarity that's warm, like winter nights and roaring fires and family hugs.

I stare up at the sky as I walk across the roof thinking of Titus and his magic star lasso. I ache for him, for my parents, for Trey. But instead of hurting me, the memories and surroundings bring me comfort.

We walk over a bridge onto a side roof. I don't want to think about Trey. Not tonight.

I walk toward our rooftop pool. It's secluded, surrounded by palm trees and greenery, hidden. Exactly how I need it to be.

It's late. The sky has the inky darkness of midnight, the kind of darkness that makes the stars sparkle like mirrors and glass. I stop, take a deep breath and let my essence roam, stretching, stretching until I can sense the lightning charge high in the atmosphere.

It's been so long since this place *felt* like home. I reach inside myself, drawing power into my arms, letting the desert air slide like silk over my skin. Feeling the crust of sand drifting in the ebbs and flows of wind currents. This is where I belong. The sizzle of electricity connects with my essence, firing down from the cloudless sky and sparking bolts of electricity and static from my hands.

I smile to myself.

This is home.

When I open my eyes, I know I'm going to be okay. Everything will be fine. Tomorrow, we meet Castor and plan how we will take Cecilia down, how and when we open the worlds and how we might finally free ourselves from her tyranny. Trey might be dead, but I can seek vengeance for his death, and Victor will die for good. That last thought brings a slew of worry and elation, relief and fear—Bo in the middle of it all.

But finally, what being here has made me realize is that after the war, when it's all over, I am ready to return home to the East—to lead.

"Are you okay?" Dorian asks.

"For once, I am. But are you?" I point in the direction of the pool. "Are you sure you're ready to show me?"

I asked him to come here to my home tower because it's private. There's a pool and we can swim in privacy and I can see who he truly is. He steps off and onto the rooftop, his expression is tense, his eyes tight. He slides his hand out, catching mine, and pulls me forward.

"Yes, and no. I've spent so long hiding who I am, avoiding water, avoiding connecting with others, avoiding anything that could get me caught. I almost forgot this part of myself."

I rub my thumb over the back of his hand. "I understand that in more ways than I can explain." Because isn't that exactly what I've been doing? Avoiding the East, this part of me?

Dorian pushes a lock of my hair behind my ear, then he turns and walks through the green hedge protecting the pool. I follow him. The pool stretches out in front of us, glistening under the starlit sky. It dawns on me. This could be one of my last nights alive. This war, ripping the fabric open. Cecilia won't go down without a fight. She's protected herself for thousands of years.

"We could die," I say, the words slip out. I meant to keep them to myself.

Dorian cocks his head toward me. "We could," he says. "There are going to be casualties, a lot of them. But we all die. Why not die for something bigger than ourselves? For something that will change the course of fate and history. To protect the millions of Keepers that come after us."

"There's no guarantee we'll win. What if Cecilia wins?" I say.

"She won't."

"But if she does..."

"She won't, but if she does, and tonight is one of our last nights, then maybe we should make the most of it." His eyes twinkle like the stars above us, a devious grin spreads across his lips. And my stomach, the traitor, flip-flops like a roller coaster.

My hand reaches up to his cheek, my fingers hovering over his skin. I want to see what he's like under the mask he's been wearing. My fingers tingle. I'm not sure whether I'm mesmerized or terrified.

"I still can't believe this is possible. That you're... That Castor is."

Dorian sniffs out a laugh. "You realize half the rebels are Mers? We've been around for far longer than anyone knows. What do you think happened to the land-based Mermaids who refused to go back to the sea? They were banished from society, but they weren't driven off the land. Cecilia was arrogant. There were so few of us left, we couldn't do any harm. But that was then. Our numbers grew. We played the long game, stayed hidden away. Let her think we'd fallen into extinction. We've been planning this war and making alliances for centuries. There are ways and means of doing anything if you look hard enough."

I wipe my hand over my face, trying to process everything he's saying.

"So your boss... your real boss is...?"

"Aurora." He nods.

I shake my head, awed. "Enough talk. I want to see you," I say.

He leans down, the black rings around his green pupils make his eyes pop. He's so close to me, our breath melds in the shrinking space between us.

His lips inch toward mine. "I want to show you," he says. His grin deepens. "But you have to take your clothes off."

"I beg your pardon?"

He laughs. It's soft and watery, like the lapping of waves against the shore. My heart beats a storm in my chest. His hand slips around my waist, pulling me closer. He places his cane against the pool stairs and says, "If you want to see, get in the water with me."

His expression glitters with temptation under the moonlight. I glance at the infinity pool, at the fire embers hanging above the surface shimmer, making it look like a kaleidoscope. It's kind of romantic. *Stop it, Eden.* I swallow hard and nod because I'm not sure what I'll say if I open my mouth.

Dorian slips off his shoes and socks. He doesn't have any flippers or fins, just normal feet—for now. He unbuckles his belt, and peels off his suit pants and slides his jacket to the floor. There's a huge scar running from toes to knee. It wraps its way over his foot and up the back of his leg. It must be the injury causing him to need the cane.

Button by button, he peels off his shirt. Holy Balance. He's getting naked. But of course he is. How is he supposed to wear underwear with a tail?

I swallow again. My insides writhing. I've not seen anyone naked since Trey. His shirt falls to the floor and, of course, his abs are insane. I look down; look at the water; look basically anywhere that isn't at him.

"You're going to need to look at me if you want to believe it," he says.

"Right. Yes. Of course."

I breathe, shake the heat from my cheeks away, and then steady my gaze firmly on his eyes. To my relief, he's left his underwear on, for now.

I peel my clothes off. First my pants, shoes, then I'm standing in my underwear, desperately trying to suppress the rush of heat in my cheeks.

Dorian smiles at me and pulls his underpants off, dropping them onto the pile of his poolside clothes. And oh boy, does he have something to smile about.

He stands there. Utterly naked. Long body, long—sweet Balance—I force my eyes up his abs and lock them onto his face.

"This better not be some Mermaid seduction kill-method because I'll cut your tail off."

He smirks and walks along the pool edge until he's parallel with me. I shiver, tingles run down my body. The desert is deceptively cold in the thick of night—it's definitely not the sight of his very naked body. Probably. I slip into the warm water and swim closer to his side.

"Are you ready?" Dorian says.

"To see a real life Mermaid? The savages my father

warned me about? The ones that eat you if you dare set foot in the Blood Ocean?"

He flashes his pearly white teeth at me and says, "Lies, rumors, half-truths and only if you deserve it." He pauses, his gaze intensifies. "Savage? Certainly not. Ravage you... well, that I can't make any promises about. Now take a deep breath and try not to panic."

He points down.

"Underwater?"

"Insurance policy. I don't want you screaming."

"Okay," I say, unease creeping into my gut. The only thing I know about Mermaids are the dark fairy tales and horror stories my father used to tell me.

"I won't hurt you. But I will look different," he says and dives into the water.

"Right," I say and this time my stomach folds in on itself, as every bedtime story and warning my father ever told me runs through my mind. "The most beautiful things are usually the deadliest," he'd say. And as Dorian's head pops up, I recognize my father was right about one thing. Dorian is certainly beautiful.

"Just so we're clear," I say, bringing my hand out of the water and letting the tiniest of sparks of static off my balled fist. "If you go all Mermaid-psycho on me, electricity and water aren't a brilliant mix."

He laughs, ignores me, takes a breath, and dives under the surface. I take as deep a breath as I can and descend.

He slips his fingers through mine. As they interlock, his skin pales from olive to white to silver. The color ripples from his fingertips up to his shoulder, down his neck, and inches down his chest. The shimmering silver crawls up over his jaw. He gives my fingers a gentle squeeze and then his eyes close. The silver climbs over his lips and nose and past his eyes. When it reaches his forehead, the color from his thick brown hair drains away until it's as pale and silver as his skin. When he opens his eyes, the green is even more vibrant. The sides of his neck burst open and gape in the water. I recoil in horror until I realize what they are: gills.

Mother of Balance. He has gills. Of course he has gills, you idiot. He's a freaking Mermaid... Wait... Merman? Merperson?

Whatever. Dorian has GILLS.

When he smiles, I snap back to reality, and my blood runs cold. Everything my father told me screams into focus. Dorian's pearly white teeth have vanished. In their place are sharpened spikes, like the razor tips that fill a shark's mouth. I yank my hand away, reminding myself Mermaids are killers.

His smile falls.

I surface for air. He might not need to surface, but I do. I take three huge gulps before descending underwater once the tingles leave my spine. I swim closer. As close as I dare. The closer I get, the more his body softens, the tension leaves his shoulders and the smile returns, although this time, he keeps his lips shut.

My brain is screaming for me to run, to get out of the water and away from the predator, but there's another part of me that knows him, is fascinated by him. I've never seen anyone's body change like this. It's nothing like a Shifter. When they change, the light around their body blurs. Their skin gets all fuzzy and ripples like tuning one of those antique human TVs. Then for a split second a Shifter vanishes and when they reappear it's as whatever animal their essence is. But this is different. I've watched every moment of Dorian changing. I didn't realize Mermaids could shift, I assumed they lived in their Mermaid form.

I swim up for air and catch a flash of color just as I break the surface. I take another huge gulp of oxygen and drop under the water. My eyes bug wide as scale by scale, his legs disappear in a haze of deep emerald. The same color as his suits. His tail looks so smooth. We surface at the same time. He holds himself just out of my reach, his brow wrinkled.

"I'm okay," I say.

"Sure?"

I nod. "It's... You're beautiful. Can I touch you?" I ask, my fingers hesitating.

"If by 'you' you mean my tail, then sure. I don't bite... At least not cute Fallons, anyway."

My eyes meet his. He swims to the shallow end in about half a second and perches on the steps, half in and half out of the water. Where his face and torso hit the air, the golden olive tones melt back into his skin, and the rich brown I'm used to floods his hair. I hesitate, but he nods approval. I can't quite bring myself to touch him, so my fingers stay hovering over his scales, tracing the curves and lines where they meet and layer over each other. The colors in his tail glisten and reflect the flickering embers above us. The scar that was on his foot wraps around the bottom of his tail and fin, buckling a few scales.

"It's beautiful," I say to myself, "like a waterfall of color."

"Thank you," he says.

I look up at him, my cheeks blushing pink. He reaches for my hand and presses it to his tail. I gasp.

"It's not slimy?"

"You thought I'd be slimy?" He laughs, and pushes his mop of wet curls out of his face.

"I didn't mean it like that, I just. I figured it would be

fishy. Wait. No. I meant. Never mind, it's more like a snake, warm and soft."

Oh god. Shut up, Eden, what are you even saying?

My whole body is tingling. I want to kiss him. I automatically lean in. I don't know if it's the intoxication of seeing a real Mermaid, the knowledge that we might die, or if I have feelings for him. But there are no flashes of Trey. My heart still aches for Trey. It always will. But it's also strong for me now.

Right now, as the water laps against my body and night air caresses my skin, I want the kiss. I want Dorian.

"Can I kiss you?" I say, it tumbles out of my mouth before I can stop it. I bite down before I say anything else. Dorian grins, pure white. Infectious. He leans forward, his breath trickling over my lips.

"I want to kiss you so bad..." I inch closer, threading my fingers through his wet, brown curls. He drops his head and places his mouth on mine.

As Dorian kisses me, I want to feel the ecstasy Trey's lips used to pour over my skin as our essences melded together. But I don't. His kiss is gentle, warm. He is, as he has always been, comforting. The soft push of his lips makes my tummy tingle, and I like it, but he doesn't make me feel the way Trey did. Dorian's hands slide down my back, unhooking my bra. A tear rolls down my cheek. He pulls away, wiping my cheek clean with his fingers.

"Do you want me to stop?" he says.

I stare into his green eyes, wishing my heart would throb to life, beat with love. Anything is better than this frothy confusion. I like Dorian, a lot. We understand each other in ways no one else can, the addiction we've both beaten. I love that he knows my darkness, my weaknesses. He's handsome, kind, charming to a fault. But I'm not in love with him and maybe I never will be. That part of my heart will always be Trey's. Dorian is safe, and alluring, and seductive.

"No. No, I don't want you to stop," I say.

And I don't. Because at this moment, I know I'll never feel for him the way I did for Trey. But that's okay. Dorian isn't Trey, and he doesn't need to be. He's something else entirely. He's sanctuary and relief from addiction and a support mechanism. The fact he is extremely attractive is a bonus. And tonight, he can take my pain away in a different way altogether. He can make me forget. Distract me long enough. My heart stops beating its ragged rhythm. I can indulge in him and it's okay.

He smiles and cradles me, laying me on my back on the pool tiles. Then he slides on top of me, his legs flicker from scale to skin, skin to scale and back again.

He glides his lips over mine, pulling me through the glistening shallows. We dive under the water, him still kissing me. His skin changes instantly. I try not to stiffen as he holds on to me and cuts through the water. We move so fast the water rushes over my skin and the pressure almost makes me gasp. We surface at the other end, the shallowest area of the pool with smooth tiles. He lays me flat just out of the water. Then he reaches under me and helps slip my underwear off my legs. He kisses down my chest, leaving a trail of watery impressions. His lips caress my nipples and I let a moan out.

I stretch down. He's hard against my legs. His thighs ripple from skin to scale where splashes of water touch him. I pull him closer. His hands caress my body, roaming, moving between my legs until I sigh into his neck and beg him for more. The water laps at our feet, embers flicker above us, the cool desert air wrapping us in serenity, distraction, pleasure. I pull him inside me.

And for a while, everything else disappears. No more pain, no more hurt, no worry about war or what's coming. Just silk waters and the tingling pleasure of Dorian moving inside me.

Several hours later, Dorian and I huddle together and doze on the rooftop sofa, blankets thrown over our legs. After, we ate, and talked and laughed until I fell asleep in his arms. I rouse as the desert sunrise pierces the horizon. There is no sunrise like the desert. Orange splinters the sky, pinks and burned yellows spidering across in a webbed mosaic.

An explosion of blue smoke erupts in front of me. Hermia bursts through it, waving her arms to clear the smog.

"Where exactly have you been?" she demands.

"Hermia." I sit bolt upright. A hundred emotions curdling. "You're back. Oh my god, HERMIA, YOU'RE BACK, YOU'RE HERE. Did you...?" I hesitate, glance back at Dorian. Drop my voice lower. "Did you find him?"

Hermia scowls. "I'd have come sooner, but you blipped out. Couldn't find you."

I hesitate, unsure how Hermia would react if she realized we'd found the blade she used to kill Broc with.

"Odd. I've no idea... Anyway, you, Mrs. Endlesquire, have been somewhere far more interesting. What happened in Obex? Did you find...?" My voice trails off, my chest twists. I just slept with Dorian. What if she found Trey?

In my periphery, Dorian sits up, rubs the sleep out of his eyes. I can't look at him. Hermia plonks herself in one of the rooftop's large armchairs, reaches for my discarded glass from earlier, and swallows the whiskey in one.

"More." She thrusts the glass at me.

I raise an eyebrow and take the tumbler from her and dutifully fill it up again, though the bottle I took from the bar is almost empty.

"Why are you being cagey? Did you find him or not?" I ask.

She sighs. A full-blown shoulder-sagging, heavy-breathed sigh. I don't think I've ever seen her sigh like that. And now she's the one not looking at me. Her fire-orange eyes are focused firmly on the surrounding city, the sky, the rooftop.

Finally, she looks at me. "Get up, we're leaving."

I laugh. "It's like four in the morning."

"I'm not asking."

I lean forward, a hitch in my breathing. "Hermia, what's going on? Did you find him?"

She hesitates, lines and frowns and waves of something pass across her expression.

"I found him."

Three little words, and my world falls apart.

I don't move. I blink at her. Time passes. I'm not sure how long, because there's only the rushing thud in my ears, the haze of reality blurring. I can't breathe. She... she found him?

I'm shaking.

No.

I'm being shaken.

"Eden, get it together. Fucksake," Hermia is shouting in my face. "Get your ass up. It's time to go."

The daze fades, but I'm left uneasy. I sent her on a hopeless chase. I didn't think she'd ever actually find him.

"Is he... You found him?" I breathe, my words fragile whispers.

Hermia softens. "Yes, I found him. But I need you to come with me."

"What? Why?"

"Because I made a promise to him. But despite what I promised, you need hope."

"Hope?" I sit up. Adrenaline floods my body, firing tingles into my fingers and spine. "What do you mean, hope? What promise? Oh my god, is Trey...?"

She doesn't answer.

"Hermia? In the name of Balance, tell me what is going on." I grab her arms, forcing her to look at me. "Is he alive?"

She shakes her head. "I can't."

"Can't what? What the fuck?"

My chest is hammering so hard my pulse is in my mouth. Pins and needles tingle their way down my spine. Dorian touches my arm, startling me. It pulls me back to reality, to a level of calm.

"You need to go to the Binding Chamber. You'll find what you need there. I can't say any more."

She puts a familiar cog device on the table, swallows the rest of my whiskey and vanishes in a violent puff of navy smoke.

"HERMIA?" I shout, waving through the smoke. "For fucksake, tell me if he's alive." But it's too late, her chair is empty, she's gone.

"Hermia," I whine and punch the back of the seat until my eyes burn so much tears roll down my cheeks and I've got no energy left to hit. A soft hand settles on my shoulder. I turn and Dorian pulls me into an embrace. I mumble into his shoulder. "Why won't she tell me what's going on?"

He rubs my back. It's soothing, but it doesn't reduce the anxiety.

"Will you come with me?" I ask.

"To the Binding Chamber?"

"Yes. He's... our Essence Heads are in there. I haven't seen them since... I haven't seen any of him since. When I was there before, I saw Arden and Tilly Winkworth's heads. Hers was all gray and limp and yet looked exactly like her. I don't want to see Trey like that."

"I'll come," he says, but his voice is flat. It makes my chest tight. This is why we shouldn't have... It's too soon. This is a mess.

"I... We..." I rub my forehead, unease swirling between my ribs.

"You need time?" Dorian says.

I nod. "To process. If there's a chance... If Trey is..."

"It's okay. I understand."

"I'm sorry."

Dorian brushes my cheek. My stomach flip-flops in response. But I push it down. I can't do this with him, not now. Not if there's hope. So I disentangle myself and change the subject.

"How do you feel about breaking and entering this evening? The chamber is always locked up tight."

"Apparently, I'm a dab hand at breaking into museums. What's a chamber?" He dusts his shoulder and I smirk. "There are several guards and a few traps, but seeing as we just broke into one of London's most famous museums, I reckon the Binding Chamber will be a piece of piss."

TWENTY-SIX

'Aurora's Cove—An island created from an extinct volcano fifteen miles offshore. Said to house the banished Mermaid queen Aurora. Although no official reports have been accepted, shipping routes no longer veer near the island after a series of shipwrecks lost several hundred Siren lives.'

Excerpt—The Geographical History of Trutinor

TREY

I don't stop until I reach Rozalyn's mansion. I march through the darkened street and bang her door until it opens. Darkness spills into the alley, and a figure appears in the doorway: Bellamy.

"Oh," I say.

"You okay?" he asks.

Some of the heat dissipates from my chest. "I... yes, is she here?"

"In the back. Come in. You can wait inside." I enter the dimly lit room, shapes curl in the corners, the wall-creatures licking out, tempting me to slide into their shadowy arms.

"I'm glad I caught you. Umm. I saw Hermia."

Bellamy stands straighter, his eyes a little wider.

"Here?"

"She's spent centuries looking for you down here, but never been able to find you."

He shakes his head. A globule of ooze rolls down his horn. "Obex would never let her."

I reach for his shoulder. "She found me instead."

He rubs his throat, his gaze drifting to the floor. He sniffs, wipes his face and nudges the floor. "That's... that's..." His eyes are watery.

"I'm sorry she couldn't come to you. Obex can be cruel." I kneel, take his hand, and rub it, hoping it provides some comfort. "Hermia gave me a message for you. She said to tell you not to give up. That she'll find her way to you no matter what it takes."

He gives me a weak smile. The faintest hue of red rushes up his neck and cheeks. He gives me a curt nod. "Thank you."

I'm not sure how to help him. It doesn't seem right to influence his emotions. I can't imagine being separated for as long as they have been. He doesn't ask me anything else and I have nothing to offer. So we fall into silence. His eyes roam the room, distant, glossy. Then he startles himself out of his reverie and says, "I'll get Rozalyn."

He disappears. The room lightens. Razor sensations creep down my spine. Suddenly, Rozalyn is sitting on her throne. A goblet in one hand, with red drops dripping down the side. In her other hand is a chunk of liver... I think. She takes a bite, chews slowly. All the while, her eyes rake up and down my figure. And although she isn't touching me, everywhere her eyes grace, she leaves a coldness behind. I raise the Soul Scythe blade box and pop it down on her table.

After an age, she says, "You're not due till the evening." The gravel in her voice cuts shivers through my soul. She licks her fingers, savoring the raw meat remnants on each one. "Why are you here?"

I open my mouth, ready to hurl obscenities and rage, and then I stop. Rozalyn hasn't broken her word. Not yet. She asked me to create an army and in return I can go home. She might have used underhanded tactics, but the only person who lied is Eve. I rub the back of my neck. I was so sure I was ready for a fight, but now I'm here, I realize it's not Rozalyn I'm angry with. It's Eve.

"The army is complete," I say.

"It is? Excellent." She slips off the throne, picks up her goblet and makes her way toward the shadows where she clinks glass and metal and then there's the tinkle of pouring liquid. The smoke behind her clears, and rolls of parchment, maps with pins and squadrons of demons represented by little angry figures fill the walls. Preparations. War. It's all building and the only thing I want to do is get home to Eden.

A quiver lodges in my throat. I try to bite it down, but it betrays me. "I—I want the blood. I want to—to go back today. Now."

She stops pouring, tilts her head to focus on me. "I see our mutual friend has told you how to get home."

"You didn't have to use her against me. I would have

done anything to get back to Eden. All you've done is drive a wedge between us."

She waves a dismissive hand at me. "But wasn't it a fun few weeks? Chaos is always better than Balance." She sniffs her goblet and then takes a drink. "Besides," she says and points a sharp fingernail at me, "how do you propose I manipulate you without her? I needed you under my control, focused."

I'm not playing her games. I'm done. With Rozalyn, with Eve, with all of them.

"I've done what you asked. I want the blood so I can go home."

"Not so fast, boy. Let's have a drink first." She offers the goblet full of blood—the wrong blood. My nose wrinkles.

"No, thank you."

"We could achieve big things, you and I. All you'd have to do is stay a little longer. I'd make you my general. You could lead the army."

"Pest will make a far better general."

"Perhaps. But the rebels are about to start the greatest war in history and we're going to finish it. Don't you want to be on the winning side?"

"I'm on your side. I've done everything you asked. Besides, prophecy or not, winning doesn't always look the way you want it to."

She huffs, a quiet sort of sound. "Wiser words than you could understand. But I'm not sure returning to Trutinor is the win you think it will be either."

"What do you mean?"

Her lips stretch into a narrow smile, separating into a silvery sheen of teeth. She's always had an ugly smile, one filled with poison and malice. "Would you care to look upon Eden as she did you?"

I balk, my eyes narrowing. "How did you kn—"

"I know everything that happens in my realm."

"So you could have let me see her this whole time, and you chose not to?"

"You didn't ask."

My fists ball. "If I'd known it was possible, I would have."

She walks me to the back wall in her chamber. "After you, boy." She vanishes.

I eye the wall. Its rhythmic waves of dark mist shiver and undulate. I can't think of anything worse than walking through it, but I'd do anything to see Eden. I steady myself and step into the wall. The darkness is so absolute it crushes the air out of my lungs. Light flickers. Rozalyn's hands are out in front of her body. Moving, sweeping. Static images flash, rewind, stop, fast forward. It reminds me of the Earth Simulators from Keepers School. The images slow. Eden's face shimmers into focus. She's in a pool. Her rooftop pool in the East. My muscles tighten.

"Is this now?" I ask.

"It was last night. Time is strange here. Sometimes we're ahead, sometimes we're behind. Obex does as Obex will."

I'm surprised Eden's in the East, let alone her home tower. She didn't want to go home after her parents died. It was too painful. Her hand clasps the back of a guy. Someone I don't recognize. My jaw clenches, my teeth biting hard against each other.

She's lying in her underwear in the shallow water next to him. His hair is brown, his green eyes glisten against the flame embers lighting the pool area. I'll kill him. And then an image of me, of Eve, of last night flickers through my mind. The guy shifts in the water, and a flash of deep emerald green swooshes through the water.

"What the fuck?" He's a Mermaid? "How the hell is there a Mermaid in Trutinor?" I say.

The image shudders like waning CogTV signal.

"Can I kiss you?" Eden says.

He grins, one of those pure, straight smiles you can't help but return. I hate him. I'll rip his fucking tail from his torso and feed him to the Blood Ocean.

"You have no idea how much I want to kiss you..." he says, so he does. My chest hollows, my gut folds in half and all I can taste is bile and the acrid, stale wrench of regret.

"Do you want me to stop?" he says.

I can't watch this anymore. Sick rolls around my gut. I want to tear him apart. Rip the fabric of the world apart and march into Trutinor. But underlying all of that is the knowledge that I did this too. I slept with Eve and it's so much worse knowing how it feels. If this was last night, it was before she saw Eve kiss me and I don't know if that's better or worse. The pull, the yearning ache to get home, is even stronger. I have to see her, to talk to her, to understand. And then I'm going to have to explain myself.

She bites her lip and says, "No. No, I don't want you to stop."

The image blurs, shifts. They're at the other end of the pool. He lays her down then reaches under her, slipping her underwear off.

"Make it stop," I say, my jaw flexing in and out as I bite down hard.

"I think I'd rather you watched," Rozalyn says.

Eden pulls him closer. His hands caress her body, moving everywhere, touching all of her. Sliding between her legs. She moans.

"Please?" I snap. "Turn it off."

Her lips brush against his and the bile lingering in my throat burns hot like lava. She doesn't need me anymore. I've ruined everything.

Rozalyn's blood-red eyes burn bright. "And I said no. You're going to watch so you know exactly what you're going back to and everything you're giving up. You could be a great leader, Trey. You could be revered, leader of the dead."

I drag my eyes back to the vision. My mouth sours, dries. I can't look anymore. I'll never be able to stop seeing their bodies pressed together, moving, pulsing, rhythmic. Just like last night. Just like Eve.

Finally, Rozalyn says, "Well, I think we've seen enough now, don't you?"

"Fuck you."

She spits out a laugh, icy hatred in her eyes. "You can use pain like that to good effect here."

I harden.

"If you think seeing my soul mate fuck someone else was enough to stop me from leaving, I'm going to disappoint you. I'm going back. Now more than ever. We've both made mistakes. That doesn't mean we don't love each other."

"So be it." She clasps my elbow and pulls me back through the darkness. Then she floats back to her throne, collecting a jug, pouring more blood into her goblet. "Unfortunately for you, the price has increased."

"Is that a joke?"

Her eyes flash to mine, her face concrete hard. "Do I look like I'm joking?" She sips her drink and takes a seat on her throne. "Trutinor's rebel army has done well. The rebel runners have informed me that my grandson, Castor, has swollen their ranks and is almost ready for attack. But their army exists to defend against hers and make a way for us to return. This is their job. They will defend against Cecilia so that we, the demons, can return. We will help you and Eden get through Cecilia's personal guard and close enough to kill her. I will ensure word is sent back that we are ready for war. But, even having a dozen armies isn't enough."

"It isn't?" I say, my face scrunching.

"Not if you want to kill my sister."

"Then how?"

That makes her laugh. It's a soft chuckle of a thing. It's then I realize how rare it is for her face to express anything other than perpetual dissatisfaction. Her eyes drop. She gives me a smile that's too quick. Her hand presses against her stomach. "I'm afraid *you* don't. There is only one way to kill my sister. You need the blade, the blood and the bodies."

"I don't... What does that mean?"

"The blade." Her eyes fall on the box I returned to her. "This is only half of the blade. There is another half. They need to be joined. The blood means the blood of the Hearts of Trutinor and Obex, but once they've been healed and rejoined."

"And the bodies...?"

"Well," her voice is distant, "that would be hers and mine."

I let out a deep sigh.

Her eyes snap up to mine. "Indeed. Much to do. Your task, once I've sent you back, is to ensure the blades are united..."

"How do I find the other one?"

"The rebels have it. Go to them. They will bring Aurora back, give her both blades. It's only then, once she's merged them, that you and the girl can cut a hole in the fabric. This is how we"—she gestures around the room—"myself and the demons return."

"Okay," I say through gritted teeth. Heat and prickling rage simmer under the surface. Rozalyn has tricked me, manipulated me and kept me away from Eden all for her own cause. Eden has... I can't think about it. All I want is to rage and burn and break. But I have to stay focused. Just get home. Deal with what's happened when I'm home.

"Once the door is open, we will bring the Heart of Obex with us. A demon guard will protect it, but it is vital. Essential." She grabs my shirt, bringing me close. "I cannot overstate this enough. We must unite the pieces of Heart. Without it, we can't die."

"We?"

She falters. "I mean my sister, Cecilia, cannot die unless the Heart is joined. Blood from the joined Heart must be on the blade to defeat her. We will bring the Obex Heart, ensure that wherever the door is cut, the Trutinor Heart is near. Once joined, she will fall."

She moves to the shadows and disappears. When she reappears, she's holding a single red vial and a hip holster.

I stand straighter, suck in a breath.

This is it.

She's actually going to let me go back. I'm finally going to get to Eden.

She returns to her throne of bones, crosses one leg over the other, holding the vial between her fingers, and hands me the holster. I attach it to my thigh and then she gives me the blade.

"I mean it, boy. Make sure that hole is cut, and the doorway created or I will hunt you to the ends of Trutinor for the rest of time."

"If you truly send me back to Eden, if you give me back

my life," I vow, "I swear to you, I will make Trutinor bleed at your feet."

That earns me a smile that lights her face with darkness and demons and a glitter that is terrifying. She holds out the vial. I hesitate, step closer, and reach out. When my fingers close around the vial, she places a hand over mine.

"Swear to me," she says. Her essence creeps over mine, probing, nudging. She's testing me.

"I swear to you." And I do. If she gives me Eden, I'll give her anything.

"Very well then." She releases the vial. "Drink up, boy."

I do as she says, gagging as the cold iron liquid coats my throat. She slices through the palm of my hand, allowing drops to fall to the floor. She takes the vial and tips a single drop on the floor. Closes her eyes and holds her hand over it. The ground shudders, quakes. The stone cobbles rumble. A flash of light rips through the dim room, so bright I'm blinded.

"Home time, Mr. Luchelli," Rozalyn's voice calls. But I can no longer see her. "When you reach Trutinor, you must make your way to the Heart of Trutinor. Drink its blood. You don't have long. Minutes at most. I only had the tiniest of blood rations left, but I've given you all of it. Really, you need the hearts together to resurrect someone. But if you can get there fast enough and drink the blood with the Obex blood still in your system, it should complete the restoration."

She grabs my arms, her nails digging in, her eyes flitting across my face. "Be fast."

For an instant, my mind clenches. If she's given me all the blood, that leaves none for Eve. And then I remember what she did and grit my teeth, a froth of confusion coating my insides.

"And if I don't make it?" I say.

"Then you'll end up back here, and this time, I won't be able to help you return."

I'm shoved, yanked and pulled and then everything goes dark.

TWENTY-SEVEN

'Datch prison's longest-serving inmate was Hermilda Endlesquire. Said to have committed the last known Soul Death, she was subjected to sixty-six years of torture. Only released to pay a debt of servitude for a further six hundred years to The First Fallon. At which point her life was intentionally extended in order to keep her from her Balancer and serve further penance.'

Excerpt—Myths and Legends of Trutinor

EDEN

We arrive in the West a couple of hours later. We used the disused service lines and got there faster than normal. The device Hermia gave us was the same gadget Trey and I used to trick the door scanners a few months ago.

Kato and Bo agreed to meet us there. I figured I couldn't see the heads without them, not if there was information about Kato's brother. We leave the station, and together the four of us walk through the school grounds. All four of our mouths drop. There used to be a Libra Legion base here. Now, there's a hole in the ground, shrapnel, splinters of wood, piles of bricks and burned bungalow straw litter the area. I glance up, the school buildings behind the old Libra base are scorched black. Blast marks carving black streaks into the brickwork.

"Shit," I say. "Is this where Cassian and Ren...?"

"No," Bo says. "It was a different base."

We stop at the foot of the crater. All of us taking a moment to pay our respects for the fallen Libra members.

"She's responsible for so much. Trey's death, the civil unrest, for brainwashing half of Trutinor, for Cassian, Ren... Too many lives. Too much pain," Kato says, piercing the silence. "Cecilia has to die."

Dorian nods. "She really does."

We leave the ruins and make our way toward the Binding Chamber.

"So do I get to hear what this is about?" Kato says.

"If I knew, I'd tell you. Hermia appeared, demanded I go to the Binding Chamber, and vanished again. I figured you'd want to be here."

There's a storm brewing out at sea. The air bristles with charged particles, electricity hums over the bay, waiting like a soldier to ambush us with thunder. A cool breeze peels off the Blood Ocean and rushes through the school grounds, making me shiver. As we walk through the grounds of Keepers school, I realize how small it seems now. We were here studying less than a year ago, but already it seems tiny.

"Down there," I say, pointing down the side of the

school. A set of gates with a huge "no trespassing" sign looms in front of the building's sandstone walls. We move along the hedge and pause to scan for guards. When it's clear, we push through the bushes and stand by the same solitary dark green door Trey and I did all those months ago.

"It's locked," I whisper. "Let me."

I grip the handle, and reach for my essence, pulling slivers of icy water through my body until it chills forming ice in my palm. Just like before, I freeze the handle until it's so brittle I can snap it off.

Kato takes out the small bronze double cog Hermia gave me. He twists the base and slides it in the door. It clicks and then shoots out a translucent field that fills the doorway.

The four of us pass through the same trickery as last time, making the door scanners think we're guards instead of trespassers.

"You need to make the guards sleep. And don't forget the memory wipe. They're stationed every few meters, so pay attention."

Kato nods and disappears down the spiral staircase to the corridor below. A few minutes later he reappears, a grin spreads to the corner of his mouth.

"Ladies..." he says, giving us a deep bow and swinging an arm out toward the staircase.

Bo giggles. "You moron, I love you."

We reach the chamber doors and I slide my fingers over the handle. The metal melts, flowing over my hand and forming a cuff.

A disembodied voice reverberates from the door. "State your intention in the chamber."

I glance at Kato and Dorian, my cheeks color and my eyes drop to the floor. "I want to know if my Balancer is dead."

The handle melts, the door clicks open, and a rush of cool musty air washes over us. Their mouths drop. Mine did the first time I came here too. But tonight, the beauty and vastness of the chamber passes me by. I just want to find my Essence Head. The stone chamber is huge, stretching further than any of us can see in all directions. Hundreds of enchanted flame torches hang from the walls, creating a blanket of flickering phosphorescent light. And in the air float thousands of ghostly heads matched in pairs and all Bound at the neck.

I meander through the phosphorescent heads, dodging tendrils and head straight for the second chamber on the opposite side of the room. We reach the Fallon chamber, and I leave Dorian to stand guard. Kato and I split up, looking for Trey's and my Essence Heads. It takes me a while, but I spot my face and race over to where we're floating. I reach up and tug my face around, bringing Trey's with it. As his head spins around, everything disappears. Sound, sensation, the room. It all vanishes as the oxygen slips from my lungs. I can't breathe. I'm frozen to the spot. My eyelids are the only thing moving, blinking in confusion.

When someone dies, their head grays out. I remember seeing Arden and Tilly's heads. Hers was wilted and gray. His was vibrant, ghostly, a mirror image of whatever expression he was pulling at that moment.

My face is like Arden's. Bright, glowing with life. Trey's should be gray.

My heart hammers in my chest. I stumble back, a swelling tide of emotions engulfing my chest, pressing, pushing, suffocating. This can't be real. It's impossible.

When I'm steady enough to look up, I stare at Trey's head.

It should be gray.

It should be fucking gray.

It's not.

Not completely anyway.

The exterior part of his face is gray, like Tilly's was. But inside his head there's a strange soft light shaped like a half oval. The light brightens and weakens, over and over it throbs rhythmically, almost like a... "Oh my god," I breathe. My fingers tremble as they press my scar. It's not an oval but half a heart. It's THE heart. I glance at my head, examining it in more detail now. Behind the glow of my face's exterior, the same heart beats inside my head, although much brighter than Trey's. This is what I could hear.

I stagger back, words bubble out of my mouth, a jittery garbled mess growing in volume until I'm screaming. My mind tangles, adrenaline pounds through my ears. I grip my chest, my heart squeezing and clamping. Squeezing and clamping.

It's not possible. I watched him die. I watched Victor slide a knife into his throat and his blood spill down his chest.

Gray smatters my vision. The floor tilts. My stomach rolls, bile licks at my tonsils.

"He's alive. He's alive." I'm screaming, "KATO, HE'S ALIVE. TREY'S ALIVE."

Footsteps clatter in a thunderous echo as they sprint through the forest of heads and appear panting at my side. My knees buckle just as Bo and Dorian appear. Dorian sweeps in and grabs me under the arms. I grip hold of him, mumbling as I wipe the tears from my eyes.

Kato holds an arm out, and I take it, steadying myself. "What the hell do you mean, he's alive?"

"I mean," I say, grabbing Kato's jaw and turning him to face Trey's head. "Trey Luchelli is alive. Or maybe alive. Or partially alive? Or, god, I don't know. Look at his face. Look at what's beating inside."

Tears well in Kato's eyes. His head shakes as if he doesn't believe me.

"Look at it. Look at my scar, it's the same shape. Whatever we did in that Siren ceremony must be keeping him alive."

"But for how long?" Kato's voice slices through my hope like a sword severing arteries. "It's been weeks," he says.

I frown at him.

"I didn't mean..." he says, his words fading. "But if you compare the hearts, yours is like sunlight compared to his."

My jaw flexes. "I can see that. But his still has color. Which means we have time. Right? It means he must be alive? Surely?" My voice is whiny, pleading.

"I don't know," Kato says.

"You can find out," Dorian says, drawing both of our attention. "The heads, they're part of you. If you touch it, it will show you him."

"Of course," I say. "I did the same thing with my mom."

I roll my sleeves up and positioning myself under our necks, take a deep breath and push my hand inside the Essence Head. The moment my fingers touch the silvery heart, my vision blurs and the chamber vanishes.

My arm swishes through the smoke and a stream of moving images hovers in the air like a floating film. The film shows some kind of pub. Wooden tables and chairs fill the floor. There is a bar with optics hanging on the back wall, and alcohol pumps along the front. It's busy. But not with dead Keepers. With demons. They're everywhere, filling every seat, standing in the gaps and chattering, talking and cheering. There's a faint bitter stench, stale beer and drunk logic. A fight breaks out to the right. An enormous skeletal demon appears, and the fight stops immediately without him having to say a thing. The demon mutters something, retreating away from him. Their hands up in defense.

The film thickens, solidifying. I reach out, I can almost touch the place. It smells and feels so real.

"What is this?" I whisper.

I stumble further into the pub. A demon walks straight through me. I shudder, my body cooling with the sudden violation.

Then, behind the bar, I see him.

My heart thuds so violently in my throat, I can't call to him. I can barely breathe. He's leaned over a beer pump, pouring dark liquid into a glass. His hair has fallen over his face. It's so much longer than normal. I can't see his eyes, but it's him. My whole body urges me forward.

His skin is pale, he's achingly thin. He looks... Fuck. My heart drops to my feet. He looks dead. *Oh, Trey.*

A girl with long golden hair wearing the shortest denim shorts I've ever seen wiggles her way through the tables toward him. A strip of her buttocks pokes out from under her shorts. Her skin is gray, her arms covered in scars. A demon pushes out of his chair, making the girl stumble. He grabs her ass. She spins around, snapping his elbow at an awful angle that makes me want to throw up. The demon roars. She drops his arm and looks up.

I freeze, my blood curdling in my veins. A scream contorts the pit of my stomach.

Evelyn.

She looks right at me. Or through me. I'm not sure. But her lip curls. She turns her back, slaps the punter upside the head, snarls "Watch it," and carries on, sliding behind the bar and right up to Trey. He steps back, shaking his head.

Good. Fuck you, Evelyn.

But she steps closer, takes his hand.

This time, he doesn't pull away.

What. The. Fuck? And then images of Dorian and me flash through my mind. Our bodies moving and sliding. Hot, syrupy shame washes through me.

The chatter, the cheering and clinking of beer glasses are swallowed by the roar of my breath filling my ears. I want to close my eyes. But I can't. I need to see what happens. I have to see if he walked right back into the arms of *her*.

They're exchanging words. I try to step closer to hear, but I'm stuck. The Essence heads won't allow me any further. She places her hand on his cheek. He stiffens. Good. He doesn't want her touching him. But he also doesn't push her off.

My heart shrivels.

Her eyes dart to mine. The bitch definitely knows I'm here. She looks back at Trey and this time I can lip read what she's saying.

"I'm sorry," she mouths.

Trey frowns.

"Goodbye, baby."

Then she spins him around, so he's facing me, and kisses him. His eyes shut. At first he's rigid, then he relaxes, his fingers lace through hers.

Hot, serrated pain digs into my chest like boiling irons. I want to cry, or scream, or burn her. But I can't. Because I'm frozen to the spot, watching my soul mate slide his hands over his ex's shoulders and kiss her the way he used to. What has he done? What have I done? This is a mess. We are a mess.

I take a sharp breath. It hurts like burns and toxin and

venom. It slashes through my throat, halting my ability to speak.

Trey pulls back. As if through the clamor of the pub, he heard my drawing of breath. For one brief second, our eyes lock. His expression widens, horror pouring through his slackened face. Mine close.

He breathes my name, "Eden."

A tear falls down my cheek. I let go of the heart inside Trey's Essence Head. I'm yanked backward and the vision vanishes.

"Did you see him?" Kato says.

I did.

I really did.

"Well? What the hell happened?" Kato says as we leave the Binding Chamber. We hit the fresh night air, and it stops me in my tracks. The cold leaches into my skin and hardens my insides.

"I saw him kissing Eve."

Dorian and Bo appear at my side. Kato's mouth forms a little "O" shape as he glances from me to Dorian. He shifts on the spot, uncomfortable. What I don't tell Kato is that I am just as guilty as Trey. Even though every ounce of my mind is screaming and sobbing, what am I supposed to say? I slept with Dorian. How can I judge Trey?

"I... I'm sorry," he says, still fidgeting. "But... umm..."

"Just say it, Kato," I say, my voice quiet, resigned.

"Is he alive? Can he come back?"

I shake my head, tears roll down my cheeks. "I... I wish I had something useful to say, but he looked..."

"What? Just tell me." His eyes are wide, bright, and jittery.

My stomach coils. "Dead, Kato. He looked dead. I don't think... Honestly? I think he really is dead."

"But the heart? The light beating inside?"

Bo slips her hand in Kato's, rubs his arm.

I fling my arms up. "We need answers. But I don't have them. Where the fuck is Hermia? She's the one who told me to come here. You should ask her."

"So you're just going to give up?" Kato snaps.

"I didn't say that. But I don't know what to tell you, Kato. He looked dead. What if that is nothing?" I gesture to our Essence Heads.

"Wait." Kato holds out his hand. "You did the Siren ceremony."

I shrug a nod out and pull my sleeve up to brandish my heart scar.

"Then what about Bertrum and Amori? They conducted the ceremony, right? They're our most experienced Siren elders. They might know something specific about the intricacies of the ceremony?" Kato says, his voice high and strained.

"They might," I say, standing a little straighter, a vein of hope weaving its way through my chest. "We could ask them to meet us at the Heart. We'd need to rearrange where we meet Castor, ask him to come to the South."

Fire passes through Bo's expression, but she stays silent. None of us are talking about the Victor-shaped problem. I am desperately hoping there's another way to initiate the change in her.

"To the South then? I'll liaise with Castor," Dorian says.

His voice is curt, and it loops a rope of guilt through my ribs.

"I'll contact Bertrum and Amori," Kato says. "I should probably get a faster train so I can meet them before we regroup with Castor."

"But... Just... Please don't get your hopes up. This could be nothing."

"Yes, or it could be everything." And the feverish light in his eyes breaks something inside me. Hope... insidious, dangerous. It terrifies me and I have to laugh because I always used to berate Trey for compartmentalizing. But that's exactly what I do. I store this tiny shred of hope somewhere deep inside my mental vault. I lock it tight and pray to Balance it doesn't tip me back into addiction or worse.

Dorian and Kato march off ahead. Dorian doesn't even glance back. I get it. This is awful timing, after we... But what am I meant to do? Not look for Trey? If I'd known there was a chance...

"Hey," Bo says, interrupting my thoughts.

"Hey, yourself. I guess that means we're tagging along for the ride." And then, under my breath, I whisper, "I did a bad thing."

Her eyes pop, she leans in, takes my arm in hers. "Get out. You did not sleep with him?"

I give her a look, because sometimes a look is all a best friend needs.

"It's not... What if Bertrum and Amori can help bring Trey back? God, Bo. What have I done?"

"Tell me everything, right this second. Start at the beginning. We can fix this together."

So I do because right here, we're just two best friends talking about boys. No dead parents, no murderous brothers, no prophecies and definitely no promises, just boy problems.

TWENTY-EIGHT

'London's School for Wayward Keepers—A school created for the more rebellious and difficult to train Keepers. Located in London, England, where students can gain hands-on experience of Keeping the fate of humans.'

The Dictionary of Balance

TREY

When the darkness clears, the air is hot and sticky against my skin. My head swims—there must be Keepers everywhere. I'm on my knees in front of my mansion, but as I squint at my surroundings, I realize there's no one in the courtyard.

A breath hitches. I'm home. At last.

My vision blurs, my senses attacked by all the emotions

from Keepers in the surrounding area. The emotions in Obex must have been so muted. I don't know how the hell I coped when I was alive. I want to stop and inhale the viscous monsoon air, lie on the cold tiles in the foyer, and laugh as I run through the halls, soaking up the vibrant feelings of everyone in the mansion. But I can't, I have to get to the Heart first. Finish what the Last Fallon started.

I stagger toward the mansion porch. My legs are unstable, the air chaffs my throat as if it's wrong, alien. I try to breathe deep to fill my muscles with oxygen, but it only slows me down and makes me stumble. I haul open the mansion doors and move as fast as I can across the foyer. It's messy in here. What the hell? There's broken vases and tables knocked over. It looks like a disaster zone. So much for keeping the place tidy, Kato.

There's a sharp intake of breath. A clattering of tin and glass and then a scream. Someone is shouting my name, but there's no time. I can't stop.

I head down the marble staircase and use the walls to steady myself. My body is so unsteady. I guess it's not alive, but not dead either. But what my body does know is it's not supposed to be here. Not yet. It makes moving that much harder.

I have to get to the Heart.

I stumble along the basement corridor. One moment I'm standing. Then my knees hit the marble floor and I collapse on my back. My breath is labored, my body heavy, reluctant, like it wants to sink through the earth. Like Obex is demanding me back, a blood debt it doesn't want to pay to Trutinor.

"Get. Up. Trey," I breathe. "You get one shot at this."

I haul my body onto my front and crawl to the first gate. I grip the iron railing and raise myself enough I can place my palm on a set of interlinked locks. But they're already open. The gate clicks and grinds, and the wrought-iron gate shunts open. The distance between the first set of gates and the second is only a few meters, but it feels like a desert marathon.

My movement is cumbersome, the air thins, like I shouldn't be breathing, like Trutinor doesn't want me breathing. I grip the second set of gates. These, though, are shut. Over the lock is an iron spike. I push my index finger onto it. At first, no blood flows. A prickle of cold shivers down my spine. Can I not bleed anymore? If I can't bleed, I can't get into the room and to the Heart.

I push my finger down on the spike harder and in a slow protest, a single drop of blood oozes down the spike. The gates groan open and I want to cry out with joy, but there's no time. The pull of Obex grows stronger with every step.

I reach the final door. It's large and black and engraved on the outside are two words:

DEFENSOR CORDIS
"Keepers of the Heart."

I push through the door, my vision spots with gray. I clutch my throat. It's dry, every breath is sandpaper rough.

I'm not going to make it.

I launch myself into the middle of the room toward the fountain. I can see it. The Heart is here. As I lurch toward the rim, I'm vaguely aware of people in the room, laughing or crying. I'm not sure which. I grab the ledge, but instead of pulling myself over and into the blood, my body hits the floor. My fingers stretch toward the fountain. I desperately inhale, but nothing fills my lungs.

One last attempt.

I gasp. But the atmosphere has no air. No. My lungs can't breathe it.

I reach up. My muscles burn. Spasm. Fail.

I'm done.

It's over.

Gray speckles my vision.

The last thing that runs through my head before I black out is: I failed.

TWENTY-NINE

*'**Soul Scythes were outlawed when Soul Deaths were made illegal. There was an amnesty for blades for six months. After the amnesty ended, anyone caught with a Soul Scythe was prosecuted and sentenced to life imprisonment in Datch.**'*

Excerpt—The Manual of Dangerous and Forbidden Weapons

EDEN

The blade presses against my thigh; it weighs nothing—bone-light, yet held to my leg, it's an anchor. It's a constant reminder of what I have to do. The life I have to end forever. The promise I'm going to have to break.

We take a train straight to the South. Castor is meeting there, along with the majority of his senior rebels.

"The rebel army has dismantled their Eris base and they're making their way here using the underground tunnels. Those trained and ready for war will be with us by evening," Dorian says and puts his CogTracker down, leaning back into the train booth seating.

Bo is twitchy, fidgeting in her seat. "Eden," she says, the tone accusatory.

"I know you've asked me not to hurt him. But... But how else can we solve this?"

She nods, but her eyes flit rapidly between me and Dorian. Under the booth table, she rubs her hands. She knows. Deep down, we all know. None of us say it, though. It hovers around us, a filthy, unsaid truth connecting us all, keeping us all apart. One of us is going to try to protect Victor. One of us has to kill him.

My fingers skitter over the holster attached to my thigh. Such a delicate thing and yet it's going to tear all our worlds apart.

The train pulls into Siren city just as we're eating dinner on the train.

Kato took a faster train, so we're meeting him at the mansion. He's already messaged to say Bertrum and Amori had nothing of use, other than to remind us that the Heart has healing properties. There are, however, rooms for Castor and his team when they arrive.

The three of us finish dinner. Bo moves to the next carriage to make a call to her parents. Neither Maddison nor Israel are coping well after losing Cassian.

Then we're alone. Dorian is finishing up dealing with some messages, and I sit and stare out the window at the city beyond the station. Trey's city. And before I know what I'm doing, I've let that tiny bit of hope I locked away crawl back in. It fills my chest and head and it spreads like a virus. What if? What if?

Dorian's voice breaks me out of my thoughts. "Should we talk about what happened?"

I look down. I've been thinking about what happened ever since. Everything is so complicated and it shouldn't be.

"I like you," I say and pull my eyes up to meet him. "But what I saw in the chamber... Dorian, if there's any chance, no matter how remote... I can't be with you. Trey... he's my Balancer. He's..."

"Everything?" Dorian says, and his voice is as strained as his expression.

"I'm so sorry. I don't want to make things any worse or messier, I just think until I know for sure, it's not fair to you or to me."

"I understand, if I could bring Pax back... Well... I get it, is all I'm saying." He leans down and kisses my cheek. When he pulls back we share a look. It's sweet and rich and filled with all the futures we'll never have, and it makes my chest ache.

"Sorry, am I interrupting?" Bo says, closing her CogTracker and appearing at our sides.

And just like that, it's over. All our potential futures dissolve as I break eye contact.

"No, not at all. Are we ready to go?" I ask.

"I am if you are."

So together the three of us leave Siren City station and make our way toward the mansion.

We enter the mansion courtyard and stop dead. I put my arm out in front of Bo. It's deathly quiet. There are no Keepers, no house staff, no rebels.

"Wait," I say. "Something's wrong. The air is... off." Those prickle patches, dead spots. Voids that have signaled trouble.

Dorian steps out and runs to the side of the house, turns back and gestures that there's nothing. Bo and I inch forward one tentative step at a time. When we're about twenty feet from the mansion door, Dorian appears behind us, and then the front door clicks open.

Kato's foot inches out. Then an arm. And then...

"Oh, shit," I say.

Bo inhales.

Kato struggles out the door, Karva's hand around his throat. His eye is swollen, his lip bloody. One of his fingers is bent at a strange angle and there's a laceration across his cheek.

"Don't you do a fucking thing she wa—" Kato says, the last words cut off by the squeeze of Karva's hand.

"I think doing what I want is exactly what they should be doing, sweets," she says. "Shall we, ladies?"

Karva kicks the mansion door open and indicates for us to follow. Bo is shaking beside me. She slides her hand into her pocket, then pulls it back out. My fingers instinctively drift to the holster attached to my thigh. "It's okay," I say to Bo. "We'll fix this."

Dorian, Bo, and I step inside the foyer and it looks like someone blew it up. There's shattered glass and ceramic pieces. Broken furniture shards splinter the foyer. A window in the corner has been smashed and there are flowers scattered everywhere.

Karva stands by the sweeping staircases. To her right,

Kato stands separate, immobile, bleeding. Her right hand is in a fist shape, her power keeping him locked in place. Victor appears from behind the stairs. He's hobbling. Skeletal. He wraps his arm around Karva's for support and the pair stagger across Trey's mansion foyer toward us. Victor's skin is a mosaic of necrotic black and withered white. The stench of decay peels off him, polluting the air. It cloys in my throat, a putrid mix of rotting flesh and musty sulfur. I gag, Dorian's nose wrinkles. I try not to breathe.

Bo drops to her knees, her hands over her mouth. "Victor, what have you done? How could you hurt Kato?"

"What I needed to, Beatrice. I asked Eden for help. Begged even. Karva offered to assist in taking Cecilia down and, at every opportunity, she refused to help. So, dear sister, we are where we are."

It takes every ounce of restraint I have not to rip open my holster and stab Victor in the neck. All it would take is one swift movement. Karva's too busy keeping control of Kato. But if I ended Victor, would I lose Bo forever?

A shiver trickles down my back as I stare at Karva.

"We're going to be okay," Dorian says under his breath.

I remember reading about her legend in Keepers school. The myth says Rozalyn ripped out Karva's heart—which, as a Siren, is her essence and source of power. So when Rozalyn dug her nails in and crushed Karva's heart, she didn't just slice through muscle and sinew; she tore into her essence and powers. Her nails fed poison into Karva's soul as she whispered stories of the dead, broken, and vengeful like they were fairy tales. It made Karva stronger, stranger, more dangerous.

I can't focus on Karva. Her appearance is always unfocused, and in a way that makes sense—even the air is afraid to get too close to her. My stomach twists and yawns.

There's a dissonance my mind and body can't reconcile. Her beauty; perfect pointed lips, luscious dark skin and violet eyes, married with the unease and veiled violence she projects. It's a subtle thing, featherlight recognition that the only things filling her soul are horror and darkness.

Karva's white curls are in a messy bun. She's wearing maroon hot pants and a cropped top showing her defined abs. Despite being several thousand years old, her skin is smoother than mine, even without makeup on.

"I can't believe you stored it here in the Siren mansion. Stupid fools. So easy for someone to just pluck it away."

"Where better to hide than in plain sight?" I reply.

Her head cocks at me, her lips pinch into a pout.

"We don't have much time," Victor says. His voice is low and crackles with every syllable. His voice box must be decaying with the rest of him. He opens his mouth to speak, but the end of one of his fingers drops off and plops on the floor.

Bo draws in a sharp breath. Sour bile rises in my throat, and I have to swallow hard to force it back down. Karva's eyes skirt to the floor and she picks up the finger and pops it in her pocket.

"We can fix that. Don't worry, baby."

He looks pitiful. Despite his necrotic skin and skeletal limbs, in this moment, I see Victor as the skinny blonde child I remember. From before all the arguments and fights, from before the killing and hatred. When we were innocent and young and the most important thing in life was who won the Chase the Element game or snow fights in the Eris Mountains.

"What the hell happened to us?" I breathe.

Victor looks up and snorts, his gaze full of acid and any ounce of pity I had vanishes.

"We might not have been fated as Balancers, but we were fated to hate each other."

Yeah, well, all good things have to end.

I smile. "Let's get this over with. I take it you're here for blood?"

"Eden," Kato growls from the stairs. "Don't you da—" He's cut off with a sharp look from Karva. Kato's eyes wince, his body spasms in place, and he lets out a garbled cry.

Bo whimpers at my feet.

Kato coughs, blood sprays down his shirt. My nostrils flare, the vault trembles deep in my mind. If I let the Imbalance out, I could lose control of the situation.

"Come," Karva snarls. Kato shuffles across the foyer toward us. I help Bo up and Dorian follows behind. The descent under the mansion and into the basement corridors takes a painful amount of time. Victor is a bona fide Hansel and Gretel. Except instead of breadcrumbs and cookies, he leaves a trail of rotten flesh.

Karva shoves Kato to the front, his finger pressed on the spike until a droplet of blood rolls down it. It displays his essence—a small group of faces smile and hug each other. We move through the corridor to the next set. My heart pounds harder with each step closer.

We reach the last door.

"Why are you helping them?" Kato says under his breath.

"Because I'm not losing you too."

Karva kicks the door open, pushing both me, Dorian and Bo out of the way. She stalks around the room as Victor limps inside. Her eyes narrow, her face darkens, the fuzziness around her edges sharpens along with the air in the room.

"Where is the heart?" She spits.

"You're not getting it. Victor doesn't get to come back to life after what he's done," I say.

Karva marches around, her nose in the air sniffing like a dog. She turns to Victor. "She's lying. It's here. I can smell it." Her voice is a growl. It crackles and spits.

I glance at Dorian; he retreated to a corner. He scans the room, assesses, plots. Bo is behind me, her eyes frantic, skirting between all of us. Her outline shivers and vibrates like she's trying to stay in one shape. As if her mind is fracturing, fraught with conflict.

Karva's fist is still locked tight, Kato under her total control. One wrong move and he's dead.

She turns on me. Her gaze is so vicious I have to bite my tongue to stop myself from shaking. She waves her free arm and the mirage protecting the Heart drops. The Heart of Trutinor appears behind a perspex box. It's gory and beautiful, an enormous heart like yours or mine, only made of the purest white you've ever seen. Like clouds and heaven, like snow and milk. Despite being torn in half, it still beats. A hypnotic sound that fills the air, blood and essence and magic flow into the fountain beneath it.

Fuck.

Victor sneers and staggers toward it. Dorian steps in front of the fountain. Bo's figure solidifies. She moves in front of Victor, blocking his way. I slide in front of Karva.

"You don't have enough hands to control us all."

She hisses at me, then lunges with her free arm, grabbing me by the neck and lifting me into the air. My vision spots. Gray smatters across the room. I try to scream, but her fingers press my throat too tight. She slams me back down, my knee jars beneath me. I kick her feet out from under her and scramble to pin her between my legs, all while desperately scratching for air. I claw at her throat, her face pales. She shoves me off so hard I slam into the wall.

Victor steps back, his spine hits against the wall. We're side by side. Bo moves forward.

In the distance, thundering footsteps echo down the corridor outside. Bo's face breaks into a sneer. "Let's even things up a little, shall we?"

Angus Hathaway, Delphine Delacrois and Vega Throne bound into the room. Bo must have emergency called The Six from her pocket.

Chaos erupts. All three of them launch at Karva. Screams and roars tear through the room. Chunks of fur, blood spatters. It's too fast to see what's happening.

I run into the mash of bodies. Someone elbows me in the chest. I push and shove back. There are arms and feet flying everywhere. Bodies rolling away, grasping limbs as Karva inflicts endless pain on Delphine, Angus, and Vega. But she's only got one hand, the other is still fisted and controlling Kato. Someone drops to the floor screaming. I get a fist to my nose. I cry out. Blood spills down my chin as I blink tears away.

Then Delphine's on the floor, choking up blood. Vega follows suit and then so does Angus. *Shit.* Karva's back on her feet. In the background Bo's screaming at Victor, "I've done nothing but look out for you." Rage makes her figure ripple and contort. She's losing control, she's going to shift.

"ENOUGH!" Karva bellows and everyone freezes. "Let Victor drink from the Heart or Kato dies." She flicks her wrist and Kato cries out. Blood bubbles up and over his lips.

Bo's face hardens, her eyes steel. She looks at me.

Dorian's on the edge of the group. That's when I catch sight of his hand. Dangling from his fingers is a set of faraday handcuffs. One of The Six must have brought them. If I can get them over Karva's hand, she'll lose control of Kato.

Victor whimpers. Karva's attention wavers. A split second. A moment of hesitation, but it's enough.

I fire as much electricity into her chest as I can. Again and again until she's pinned against the wall. A cage of electricity holding her in place. Victor and Karva, right next to each other until the end. Bo appears next to me. In the corner, Kato's skin has paled to a pasty color.

Bo's sobbing as she glances from Kato to Victor. Dorian is behind me.

"Try it," Karva snarls, looking at Dorian's hand. "And he dies. You might have me pinned, but I still have him. Your choice."

Bo takes a deep shuddering breath and steps so close our legs touch.

"Do you trust me?" she says.

I falter. I've heard her say that before in my dreams. The words slip out before I can stop them.

"What do you mean?"

Her head snaps to face me, her expression as sharp as it is hard. "There's no time, Eden. Do you trust me?"

How is this happening all over again?

"I—" I say.

"This is the only way..."

Everything happens fast. She slides her arm to my leg. There's a scream. I don't know if it's Karva or Bo or Kato. Then there's a blade, and it's in Bo's hand.

The room quiets. Even the thudding of The Heart of Trutinor softens. A laugh ripples around the room. It's shrill and disconnected and it takes me a minute to realize it's coming from Bo. "I've tried to protect you. Look out for you, and you don't give a shit," she says.

I glance up at the mirrored wall and blink. I don't recognize her face. It's hard, and wild and full of sharp lines. People talk about these moments: the ones that define you. A part of me thought it would be the prophecy that took me to the edge, to some pivotal choice in my life. But it's not the big life-altering decisions that have the biggest impact. It's the small, daily ones that build over time, layer upon layer of hate and resentment. The throwaway comments, the shoves in the playground until suddenly it's not comments and shoves any more, but murdered dogs and broken arms. Then someone takes it too far and one gentle slip of a knife through pulpy flesh and the world changes. The games end, souls are scarred and fates are sealed.

One brother breaks a sister's heart. This is how lives end and wars start. I can't let Bo do this. She'll never forgive herself. But me? I love her enough I can let her go. If she hates me for killing her brother, it will save her Balancer.

Victor's head shakes, the hot stick of the room makes a line of sweat drip down my back. The thud, thud, thud of the Heart of Trutinor fills my ears.

Victor's saying something. I glance down, focusing on the shape of his crumbling lips.

"... You don't get to come back from this. This is forever Beatrice. You'll carry this scar with you in every lifetime."

"Bo," I say, "let me." I run my hand down her shaking arm until the blade is in my hand. Castor's words flit through my mind. Perhaps he was right. Sometimes you have to become a monster to kill a monster. If I have to be Bo's monster, so be it.

I slide around Bo so that she's in front of Karva and I'm in front of Victor. "Bo," I say, and give her a look. I hope she understands. I flick my eyes to Karva's hand, and Bo nods. When I focus on Victor, I'll lose control of the electricity cage holding Karva, unless she disarms that hand, Kato's done for.

"Please," Victor whimpers and slides to the floor. "I can't believe you're lowering yourself to killing me for revenge."

"You think I'm killing you for revenge? I'm not killing you for revenge. I'm killing you because you're a fucking plague. A parasite. All your existence does is cause pain and misery. You don't need to die. You need to cease to exist. You betrayed everyone who's ever loved you. Even your sister."

The perfect words form in my mouth. They curl around my tongue like poisonous berries, but when they come out, they taste sweet like nectar. "Any last words...?"

A shiver of pleasure rolls through my body as I lift his head off the ground. This is everything I wanted it to be. He is exactly where Trey was. Victor should have known better, the Balance has brought him full circle. He shivers under my grasp. Black tears roll down his cheeks. He knows this is the end. These words aren't mine. They're his. The same words he said to me a year ago as he tipped the knife and tore through Trey's neck. This is where it ends. Where he ends.

"Pl—" he stutters.

"Too late."

Everything happens simultaneously. Bo's body drops, shivering into wolf form as she pounces on Karva's hand, ripping it clean off. Dorian lunges and slaps the cuff over the other hand. I stab the Soul Scythe into Victor's throat. A carnal roar rips from my chest, reverberates around the room and pierces the rhythmic thuds.

One long second passes. Nothing happens. Our eyes are locked on each other. His wide. Bo's round, horrified. Mine cold, hard, victorious.

Silence beats through the room.

The Heart thuds.

Thuds.

Thuds.

No one moves. Until Kato drops to the floor. Karva screams as she realizes there's a blade hanging out of Victor's neck.

Victor's lips part, but just like Trey, he doesn't get any last words. Then he explodes in a cloud of matted gray flesh and decay-Dust. It plumes above me, showering my skin and body. I drop to the floor in the same place Victor was seconds ago, clutching the blade and holding my face in my hands.

Dorian touches my arm. "It's over."

Tears pour down my face.

"Bo, I'm sorry. I'm sorry."

I look up. She's cradling Kato, he's conscious, and she's showering him with kisses. Kato touches a bloodstained hand to her cheek. "I'm okay," he says. And that starts me crying all over again. Dorian sits next to me. His fingers curl around mine and squeeze. He pulls me into his arms, rocking me back and forth under a twirling flurry of ash and bone. Mottled black particles of rotten skin and bone fall from the air like snowflakes dancing in wind flurries. The ash and remains of the only person I've ever hated coat both of our skin and clothes. Is this some sort of karmic vengeance? I hated Victor so much I had to become him, break the most important promise I'd ever made. Between broken sobs, his ashes paint my skin gray. I get up, crawl over to Bo. At first, she gives me a hard stare.

This is it. I ruined it. I'll only ever be her monster, her brother's murderer. But then her face breaks and she's in my arms.

"It's okay," she sobs. "We're okay."

And then I'm crying too and we're holding each other and gripping on like we'll never let go. Eventually, we pull apart. Kato's sitting. The color has returned to his face at least.

Dorian hauls Karva to the side. She's unconscious from blood loss. He rips a sleeve off his jacket and uses it as a tourniquet to stem the bleeding at Karva's wrist. I slide the blade back into its holster and kneel by Vega to check for a pulse. "She's gone."

"FUCK," Bo shouts and then she slams her fists into the ground. "Fuck. Fuck. Fuck."

Dorian checks Angus and Delphine. "They're still breathing. We need help."

There's a rustle, footsteps, shuffle, stumble, and then a heaping thud. Someone's collapsed. I turn around, confused. No one else knows we're down here.

I blink. Scramble forward and haul the body onto its back.

For one infinite second, every atom of air evaporates from my body. The world expands and shrinks and expands again. *This isn't possible.*

My ears hollow, the roar of blood thumps through them. The room mutes and thunders all at the same time. Everything is backward and inside out. I can't breathe and yet every cell in my body is alive with pulsing static. My cheeks are wet. Drops of fat tears splash on the body's chest.

He's thin, skin sallow, hair lank and limp covering his face. A scar tracks from his Adam's apple around to his ear.

"Trey?" I whisper, and brush locks away from his face.

He's silent. Still. My blood runs icy. My arms slide under his armpits and I drag his body toward the fountain. Dorian races to my side and together we pull him up over the fountain ledge. He leans forward and plunges into the white fountain.

One second passes.

Three more seconds pass.

Then ten.

A knot tightens around my chest. He can't breathe under there. What the fuck did I do? He could hardly hold himself up and I let him drop into an infinite fountain.

I sink my arms into the blood, flinging them back and forth as I search for his body.

"Trey?" I scream. There's a rising bubble in my chest stealing my oxygen. My eyes sting. I can't lose him again.

A tingle lances through my arm. I glance down, my Binding Scar beats in time with the throbs. It crawls up my arm, into my chest, and through my whole body. I've felt this before. The cocktail of molten heat, liquid gold, and a soft peace that envelops my entire being. Pieces of me I'd lost, chunks that vanished and left holes I thought would never heal thicken and fill. I'm meshing back together.

I've found my missing puzzle piece.

My Binding.

Trey.

He surfaces, gasping for air. Bobs under the surface again.

I shriek, plunging my arms under the surface, reaching for him. I make contact and pull his head out.

"Dorian," I scream. He grabs Trey and together we pull him over the fountain ledge. Trey collapses on the floor. I wipe the glistening white blood off his face. Color pours into his cheeks, neck, arms. His body expands, torso building layers of muscle and tone. Even his eyes return to their familiar piercing blue.

"Are you...?" I say, my voice a whisper. "Alive?"

He nods. I'm not sure if I should scream or cry or puke. He grabs my arm and I help him into a sitting position. I have to do it, our silly ritual. I have to know it's real, that he's real, that this is real. So I place a shaking hand over his chest and lean my head down. His heart beats once, twice, three times. That's when I know. This is true. He is here, safe. I don't know how or why, but as my world tilts all over again, readjusting itself, realigning, one thought fills my mind, echoing over and over a crescendoing cry:

Trey is alive.

Trey is alive.

Trey is alive.

And then Bo's shriek cuts through everything.

BREAKING NEWS

"Good afternoon, Trutinor. This is Tarkin Tavas reporting for CogNews TV live in the South state outside the Luchelli mansion. We've had bizarre reports today. Eyewitness accounts from house staff reporting sightings of Fallon Luchelli senior. Yes, that's right, Trutinor, we've got an eyewitness account implying that Trey Luchelli is back from the dead."

Tarkin gestures off camera and the cameraman turns to a woman, a middle-aged Siren wearing the maroon and gold Luchelli house uniform.

"Madame Harker, could you tell me what happened earlier today?"

"I was just trying to tidy up. The foyer was a blinking mess. There was broken furniture and crap everywhere."

"And then what happened, madame?"

"Well, he just came through. As if nothing had happened. As if he hadn't died or nothing. Stumbled right through the foyer, he did."

"And what did you do?"

"Well, I screamed, didn't I! What would you have done if your master suddenly reappeared after he was meant to be dead?"

There's a ruckus behind Tarkin. The mansion doors slam open. A giant brown bear bolts out the door. Beatrice Dark and Eden East on his back.

"There you have it, ladies and gentlemen, Keepers of Trutinor. There appears to be some disturbance behind me."

Tarkin runs toward the bear, the camera judders and wobbles as the cameraman chases after Tarkin. Tarkin throws the cameraman a look back over his shoulder as he skids to a halt. There's muffled swearing. The cameraman follows the movement.

Spilling out of the mansion comes a man with brown curls, Delphine, a very bruised and bleeding Kato Luchelli. And then, Tarkin's mouth drops open. Trey Luchelli appears in the doorway.

Alive.

Tarkin drops the CogMic.

"RUN," screams Fallon East.

The cameraman swipes to follow the bear. On his back, Fallon Beatrice Dark convulses. Her figure flitting between forms. Tarkin turns back to the camera and draws his hand under his neck.

The scene goes dark, and the camera cuts out.

THIRTY

'The River of Souls is said to flow through the center of Obex. The river itself is comprised of the half-eaten souls discarded by Rozalyn. It is said if you venture too close, the souls that haunt the river will rip your soul from your body in a bid to restore themselves.'

Excerpt—The Book of Imbalance

EDEN

Bo's scream threads through the Heart of Trutinor's beating. Shrill, piercing cries laced between pounding thuds inside my chest.

Beat.

Scream.

Victor is dead.

Beat.

Scream.

Trey is alive.

Beat.

Scream.

Around me, Vega's dead wolf body lies splayed on the carpet, her head tilted at an odd angle. Angus groans beside Vega. Delphine clutches her ribs, her lip split and visible damage to one of her legs.

I look back at Trey.

He's here.

What the fuck. I don't know how he's here, but I don't care. He's alive.

In the corner, Kato is conscious. Dorian is securing Karva and tending to her wound, trying to stop her bleeding out.

"YOU," Trey says and lunges himself at Dorian.

Oh. Fuck.

"Trey, no," I bark. But it's too late. Trey throws his fist right at Dorian's face and Dorian does nothing to stop it. Dorian glances at me, a welt appearing on his cheekbone.

"Do you feel better?" Dorian says.

"No, you fucking son of a bitch," Trey replies and pulls his fist back to strike him again.

"I SAID STOP," I shout and launch an electricity rope around Trey's arm. "You were dead, Trey. DEAD."

Bo stands suddenly. A strangled sound erupts from her lips, and it sends shivers down my limbs. What little color she has in her face drains. She clutches her throat, gasps for air and then drops to the floor unconscious.

"SHIT," I scream. I glance at Trey, who's struggling to his feet. Kato pushes himself up and moves to Bo. He glances from Bo to Trey, his face deep with furrows, his voice high, strained. "Trey? What the fuck, TREY? I don't..." he shakes his head. "Eden? EDEN. HELP. FUCK. Bo's not breathing."

Who the hell do I help first?

"Go," Trey says. "Go help her." I hesitate, my soul screaming to hold him. Never let go. But I can't let Bo die.

"Dorian, what the hell is happening?" I bellow as I cross the room and drop to my knees by her side. He looks up from dragging Karva toward the fountain.

"It's the change. She's..." He looks back at the pile of Victor's ashes. "She's changing into a hybrid." He pulls Karva's arm over the fountain and dips it into the glimmering white liquid. He rubs Heart blood over the stump and it heals in front of me. Bo's body convulses on the floor. Her eyes roll back in her head.

"Give her some of the Heart blood," I say, running and scooping my arms underneath her.

"It won't work," Dorian says.

"Then what the fuck do we do?"

Kato shuffles up to brush Bo's hair away from her face. "Dorian, you're a Mermaid. Do something," he says, his voice is hoarse, dry.

Dorian runs a hand through his hair, a tremor behind his eyes. He's panicking.

"She needs to get to the ocean, and fast. It's the only thing that will help her," he says.

"That's a fifteen-minute walk from here. She won't make it."

Trey is standing, leaning against the fountain, his face is full of color, his body thick, toned, bronzed. He's really here. My mind is screaming and crying and bouncing, but there's no time to take in the enormity of what's going on.

Trey leans over into the fountain and scoops a handful of blood which he sips.

It gives me an idea. "Kato, drink from the fountain."

"Pardon?"

"JUST DO IT. Everyone needs to be healed. If we're healed we can get there faster."

He furrows his brow, but pushes himself to standing. Dorian helps him struggle to the fountain. He scoops a mouthful and swallows it. His head kicks back, a wave of gold washes over him. When he opens his eyes, they burn intense blue.

"Fuck me sideways," he says. "What is in that?"

Dorian snorts. "Pure power."

Kato shakes himself off, turns to Trey, who is also scooping another mouthful of blood out of the fountain.

"Brother?" Kato says. "Is it truly you?"

Trey breaks out into an enormous smile and pulls Kato an embrace. In my arms, Bo convulses again.

"Dorian, screw Karva. Tie her up and leave her. We don't have time. We need to help Bo."

Angus grunts from the floor, coughing and spluttering. He raises his hand. That's it. "Kato, Trey, help Angus and Delphine, make them drink. We can ride them to the ocean. It will be faster."

"V-Vega," Delphine stammers.

"It's too late," I say.

Delphine looks away, her eyes watery. She grips Kato's arm, and he helps her hop to the edge of the fountain. Once Delphine and Angus are healed, they shift. The room is considerably smaller, with a giant brown bear and a polar bear in here.

"Get her on Angus's back," I say.

"We need to take the Heart," Dorian says. "If Bo is in

transition, and Aurora makes landfall, Cecilia will know the banishment's broken. We don't have any more time. We have to take the Heart with us so we can join it to The Heart of Obex when Rozalyn returns."

I wipe my arm over my face. Everything is spiraling. I need a moment to stop and breathe and take in everything that's going on, but I can't. One deep breath, that's what I give myself. Inhale, exhale the panic and elation and fear that it's all in my head and Trey's not really back.

"Okay, Delphine, can you carry the Heart with us to the beach? Trey, help her disconnect the plinth and use the perspex box to carry it. Kato, Dorian, you come with me. I'll ride with Bo to the beach on the back of Angus."

"I'll call Castor en route," Dorian says, and then everyone bursts into a flurry of activity.

Five minutes later, Delphine is at the edge of the beach where the last of the city mansions peter out. The rest of The Six have arrived and they circle her in a defensive position. Angus pounds across the beach spraying sand and shells in the air. Dorian and Kato bring up the rear, having run behind us. And a moment later, Trey appears with Delphine's group.

He runs down the beach to meet us as Angus pulls to a stop where the sand darkens and the water ripples over the shore. Kato helps me down and between us we lay Bo on the sand. He slides his arms under her shoulders and I pick up her feet, ready to get her in the water. Trey puts his hands under her back for support.

"Kato, Trey, wait," Dorian says and puts his arms out to stop us from entering the water. "Not you. Land-based Mermaids are a different breed to sea-based ones. We've built relationships and truces. The ocean-Mers are still under Aurora's guidance. Until the banishment is broken, it's not safe for Sirens."

"I can't leave Eden on her own in the ocean. Bo's unconscious, she'll drown," Kato says.

"It's fine. I'm not letting you get attacked," I say.

"I'll go with you," Dorian says.

Trey opens his mouth, but Kato grabs his wrist and so he stays quiet. I slide my arms underneath Bo's armpits and drag her toward the shallows. Angus shifts back to Keeper form and helps me carry her into the ocean. When we're knee deep, he too steps back. He glares at the lapping water, his brow etched with lines. Dorian has stripped to his underwear and walked in up to his waist, his skin shimmers where it wants to change color.

"Be careful," Angus says and makes his way out of the water.

"She needs to be submerged," Dorian says, coming to help with Bo's legs.

Together, we drag her dead weight into the water. The cold bites my ankles the minute my feet splash through the waves. It penetrates through to my core. I'm shivering in seconds. But it doesn't matter, I have to save her.

As soon as we're in water deep enough, her body is submerged, and she stills. The convulsions stop and her limbs settle. It sends a spark of panic through me. Are we too late? Is she dead? But then I catch her face. Her expression softens, her jaw relaxes, she's no longer hurting, her face is serene. Her skin color shivers between white and silver, back to white and so it continues.

"Deeper," Dorian says.

"How far can you go? I thought the banishment kept you on land."

"Castor broke elements of the banishment for a select few rebels. I can go as far as she needs."

We pull her further into the red water. The ice-cold ocean licks up my thighs, stomach. It knocks the breath from my lungs and I have to grit my teeth to keep going. She's floating now. I lie back, kick my legs and swim her further. Dorian supports me, his tail propelling us through the water. My feet kick and circle to keep me afloat.

"We need to take her under," Dorian says.

Trey steps forward. I can just about make out the tight, stricken expression on his face from the shore. I take a deep breath. "Let's go."

We sink under the surface; I pull her under with me. Dorian keeps her under and I pray to Balance she has enough oxygen in her lungs she can survive. I kick and Dorian supports, dragging her deeper. The light dims, it's harder to see through the red liquid, the salt stings my eyes. The dimness reminds me of the tunnel to the rebel stronghold in the north. No wonder Dorian could see when it was so dark. Bo's body oscillates like she's going to shift. Only she doesn't. She convulses harder. Her neck undulates and then bursts, three gills slice through her neck. Her head drops back, her mouth opens, and a scream rips from her lungs. Even under the water, it makes me grasp my ears. Her body arches, her toes point, and then there's a burst of light from her body so bright, I recoil and have to cover my eyes. I wave my hand upward, hoping Dorian can see and swim to the surface to gasp lungfuls of oxygen. The beach is so much further than I thought; I didn't realize how far we'd drifted.

When I dive back under, I stiffen, pins and needles prickle my spine. I'm surrounded by Mermaids. There must be fifty, a hundred... maybe more? I swim in a circle. A thousand? Everywhere I look, silver faces, sharp teeth, long flowing hair drifting like smoke through the water. Dorian drops back. He puts an arm around my belly, swims me backward.

Three Mermaids are holding Bo, their hands beneath her, supporting her as she twitches and shudders. From their fingers, wisps of silver drift through the water, attaching themselves to Bo's limbs, stomach, face. The silver threads cocoon everywhere but around her gills. Her legs have vanished, and below her torso is a tail, black, shining and shimmering with silver. But then that too is cocooned in silver.

My eyes widen. Fuck. We did it. She's a Mermaid.

One Mermaid flicks her tail and swims up to me. I blink and she's in front of me. She shares the same silver hair the others do. But her face is familiar. She shares those same plump rouge lips that Castor and Bo have. Aurora?

She takes my arm and pulls me to the surface.

"Thank you," she says as Dorian pops up next to me.

"Your Highness." He inclines his head.

I'm shivering so hard I can't form words. So I incline my head. "Y-Your M-Majesty."

"To complete the transformation and break the banishment, Beatrice needs to be taken back on land. When she rouses back to consciousness, it will break the banishment and we will make landfall."

"O-okay." I take a deep breath and swim beside Bo as the Mermaids carry her as far as they can. Eventually, they all halt simultaneously. This must be the edge of the banishment. They push her into my arms and I surface, holding her under the chin and kick my legs as hard as I can. Dorian swims beside me, tugging both of us toward land.

One by one, Mermaids pop above the water, silver hair and faces. As their heads hit the warm air, color rushes into their skin, hair, eyes. Ten faces at first, then a hundred. More and more heads pop up, silent sentinels watching as I swim their savior back to the shallows and drag her out and onto the beach. The second my feet hit dry sand, Trey and Kato are at my side, helping to lift Bo back to safety. They lay her on the sand; the silver threads the Mermaids placed on her throb like a heartbeat. Dorian pulls his clothes back on beside me.

Kato leans down and checks for a pulse. "She's breathing. You did it. You fucking did it, East."

He's gripping my arms and swinging me around. Trey sticks a hand out. Kato lets me go and stands back. Trey grins and I leap into his arms. And now we're twirling and spinning and we collapse on the sand. We stay there, panting and smiling. He stares at me, a strange, peaceful expression drawn over his eyes.

"At last," he says and leans in to kiss me. It is everything. Our kiss is light and dark, loss and grief. It's warm and hard and full of love and pain and the world around us slows and stops, and for those few seconds, we are eternal and infinite and together.

Kato coughs and we pull apart and get up, dusting the sand offn. Kato turns to Dorian, grips his hands in his and pulls him into an embrace. "Thank you."

Dorian waves him off. I glance around, suddenly aware the beach is crammed full of people.

"Where the hell did they come from?" I say.

Keepers are everywhere. Dorian steps closer. "Castor arrived at the mansion and came straight here when he realized what was happening. His people are flooding the South as we speak. There's no time for war preparations. Cecilia will be aware the banishment is breaking. I suspect she'll be on her way here to stop us."

"Shit," I say.

Castor appears. He's pale, a sheen of sweat across his brow. He stoops beside Bo, checks her pulse, and brushes some of her hair away from her face.

"Beatrice will wake soon, and when she does, we need both blades ready for Aurora. Do you still have your piece?"

I touch my hip. It's safe and secure. "I do."

Trey moves to Castor's side. "I believe this is the other blade you're looking for. Rozalyn asked me to bring it," he says and unstraps a similar holster to the one on my thigh and hands over the blade.

"Thank you," Castor says and squeezes Trey's shoulder. "Stow it safe until Aurora makes landfall."

Bo makes another strangled sound, a shriek that cuts through the atmosphere. All of us clasp our hands to our heads. She arches back and the silver threads binding her body explode, and she falls limp.

The ocean rumbles and fizzes. It bubbles and spits like a cauldron. Red spray flies through the air and splatters the sand, our faces, drenches our clothes. The earth rolls and roars. I grab Castor to stay upright. One by one the Mermaids burst into shrieks and hollers, cries of joy and Siren songs curl through the air. Hundreds of Mermaids march forward through the deep waters. Closer, closer.

"THE BANISHMENT HAS FALLEN!" Castor roars, and his rebels burst into cheers and shouts of joy. Whistles, calls and Siren sounds fill the beach.

Bo gasps. I drop to the sand, take her in my arms. "You did it, you made it through."

Her eyes flutter open. Kato is by her side, kissing her

and holding her and stroking her head. She glances at me and smiles.

"It was... It was beautiful," she says.

"Kato, get her to the mansion. She needs to recover."

"What about you two?" he says to Trey and me. "I can't leave you to fight alone."

"We'll be fine. Just get her to safety. She needs to rest. I don't want Cecilia anywhere near her. GO."

Kato swings her into his arms, and she rests her head against his shoulder. They battle the swelling crowd, but I watch as he takes her off the beach and I breathe easier.

Beneath us, the ground shudders. It's no longer the same rumble I felt. It's erratic, sharper. I frown, turn to Castor.

"What's—" Trey starts.

In front of us, the sand rises, a mound, no, a body grows and forms.

"CECILIA," Castor roars. He turns to his rebels, barks commands. Dorian breaks off at a run to corral groups of Keepers.

Castor points and shouts. "PREPARE THE BATTAL-LIONS. READY MAGIC. ALPHA GROUP, TAKE THE HILL CREST. DELTA, SECURE AURORA."

The beach floods with more and more Keepers. This time, they're not rebels, not Mermaids—not our people. Their faces are blank, all wearing brainwashed emotions, under Cecilia's lure, her charm and compulsion, her delusions. Dressed in royal blue state symbols woven in gold, they march foot after foot onto the beach. Wands drawn, magic looping around their hands, their Shifted animal figures. Hundreds and hundreds of Keepers surround us until everywhere I look, the ground writhes with bodies.

I turn back to the water. Aurora advances on the shore.

Cecilia shakes off the remaining sand and screams, "CHARGE."

Chaos erupts, people slam into each other. Magic explodes and flies across the beach. Lightning bounces off the beachside mansions, bricks splinter and a torrent of marble covers the beach. Voices scream commands.

A group of uniformed Keepers advance on Delphine. She bristles, thumps her giant paws on the sand and roars, spittle spraying the advancing Keepers.

"PROTECT HER," I bellow. Dorian hears me bellowing and sends a group of Keepers running toward her.

A way down the beach, I spot Aurora. She's ten feet away from making landfall.

Eight.

Six.

Cecilia screeches, her eyes blaze, her sheer porcelain exterior cracks and she runs at Aurora.

"No. We need Aurora to open the barrier," Castor shouts.

"Trey, give me the blade. We need to get them both to Aurora."

He slips the blade into my hand and I take the other one out. "Cover me," I say, and call to Castor, "Cover Trey. I have to get her the blades."

Castor waves his hands, pointing, directing, bellowing over the clash of magic on magic, fists on skin and the crunching cries of bones breaking and final breaths being drawn. Around me, bodies are dropping to the sand. Limbs are torn from torsos. Heads ripped from bodies. The beach stains red, blood running into the waves and eddies and turning the ocean darker.

We're losing. We need more Keepers.

I run.

I push harder than I ever have. My feet pound into the sand, my arms swing until my muscles throb. Cecilia roars. I'm punched in the back and then I'm drifting through the air, arms flailing. The blades are thrown from my grasp and tumble forward. My body is wrapped in electricity. But not mine. It sears hot, drilling into my skin and bone. Cecilia.

I land on my hip. Cecilia's on top of me, hissing and spitting and punching. I cover my face, my ribs, but it's not enough. She's too fast. Her fingernails grip my shoulder and shake, and then she sinks her nails into my muscle. I scream, a reverberant ringing that scratches my insides as it bellows out.

The vault shudders. And this time, I let it crack right open. I can't fail. Not now, not this close. I will not let her win and for all the times I've been afraid, this time I let it all go. All the pain, the emotions, the heartache and loss. I let the vault break for Trey, for my mother and father, for Titus and Nyx. I let it burst. The veil of crimson drops. I pump electricity through my hands and it ricochets off the sand and pushes me back upright. And then I grab her arms and flood electricity into her. She recoils, releasing my shoulder, and backs away.

She throws a punch. I block. But her other hand comes at me. She wallops my mouth and my lip splits. I spit blood on the floor and lunge for her face, my hands ablaze with lightning. She flails hitting out at me, but I pump harder. Faster. I throw her to the sand and dive for the blades, dodging threads of Cecilia's magic as I roll and pick them up.

Blood drips down my arm and chin, but I refuse to stop. I turn on her and fire everything I have, lightning, fire, water. I throw my arms up, calling to the atmosphere, drawing everything I can. My body thrums with power. It builds and builds until I swear I'll rupture. When I can't take it anymore, I funnel it straight into Cecilia.

She screams. But she doesn't go down. It's not enough. I have to get Obex open. We need Rozalyn.

Trey appears and steps in front of me. "GO," he says. "I've got her."

Cecilia's eyes narrow, a darkness settles over her expression that will haunt me forever. My chest tightens. What if he's not strong enough? What if I'm not? What if he dies all over again before we've had a chance to be together?

He snaps around. "I said go." And this time, his eyes are maroon too. He opened the vault. "There's no time. GO."

So I do. I turn and run, and I don't stop until I'm skidding through the sand in front of Aurora. I shove the blades in her hands. She stops, her toes and feet still buried in sand and shells and water.

She breathes deep, takes my hand as she wobbles. "So many lifetimes I've waited."

She steps once, twice, and then she's onto dry sand. A biting cry rips through the beach as she waves her arm forward. Mermaids holler and charge onto the beach. Hundreds and hundreds of Mermaids. Water splashes and soaks me as they rush past, slamming into soldiers.

I touch her arm. "We have to merge the blades, we have to get Obex open now."

She's different now. Instead of silver hair, it's raven black, long, wet curls draped over her back, her eyes are deep lake green and her skin as smooth and pure as marble.

She takes the blades, in the same hand she's missing a finger. There's a smooth stump where the bones once connected. She kneels on the sand, splays her hand out and holds the blades together. She sucks in an enormous breath and pushes down, carving the nub of the stump off. I gag and have to shove my hand over my mouth to stop from being sick.

She pushes and slices until a second fleshy lump separates from her hand. Then she raises her hands over the blades, blood dripping down her arm. Her eyes roll back and she sings. It worms its way into my head. Her sound is eerie. A melody, as enchanting as it is dangerous, carries through the air, wrapping both of us and the blades in haunting tones that shiver and claw their way inside my soul. The blades and stump of finger rise from the sand and hover in the air.

But I can't watch. There are Keepers charging toward us. I stand back, fire bolts of electricity. Reaching up, the clouds stir as I pull atoms and lightning down. The sky darkens. A boom of thunder rolls above us and then I fling my arms at the oncoming attack, firing bolt after bolt into bodies. I throw fire balls and spiraling water spurts wrapped in electricity at the oncoming Keepers. One of Cecilia's soldiers breaks through. She kicks out. I dodge her leg and throw a punch that connects with her face.

"Hurry," I shout, wiping my bleeding arm on my pants.

"It's done," Aurora says and hands me a blade three times as long as it was. It shimmers and glitters. She smears her blood over it. "Now get to the boy and tear the world open. Start in the sand and draw open a door. Go. Run. I have your back."

So I do. Aurora runs behind me, flinging her arms at attackers who halt and grasp their heads and shriek. I reach Trey and grab hold of him. He's bleeding from his thigh and nose.

"Hello, Aunty," Aurora says.

Cecilia screeches, and they both run at each other.

When their bodies slam into each other, the air cracks, the ground shunts and I trip and smash into the sand, toppling Trey. He's up before me and drags me standing and toward the group protecting Delphine and the Heart. Which is considerably smaller than it was.

"Hurry." I push Trey on, running faster.

Finally, we reach Delphine and together, my hand on Trey's, we hold the blade and start in the sand, carving a door through air. It fizzes and fissures appear. Deep maroon light seeps through the cuts we made. It casts sharp shadows on the sand.

Castor appears at my side. "Move back," he says. "QUICK."

We dive out of the way. The air-door balloons. Red light swells in the frame. Obex, finally pouring into our world. The door judders, rattles and then...

"DOWN," Castor bellows.

Everyone drops as the door explodes. A sound so deep and jarring, I swear my ribs crack. My hands press against my ears. A cloud of red light, steam and fractured tatters of atmosphere scatter across the beach. Steam hisses and screeches its way into Trutinor from the doorway. But it's not really a doorway anymore. It's a giant wound in the air, in the fabric of the universe.

The sand vibrates, particles rise and hover around us, vibrating. Trutinor knows Obex is here, and it's calling to its soul mate. I push myself up, but the rumbling sand beneath my feet knocks me back down. My heart thunders in my chest. I'm consumed by panic. Did we do the right thing?

Then, the steam clears and I realize what we're looking at. A woman stands up. Behind her lies a throne made of bones.

Rozalyn.

She smiles. It's terrifying. My rib cage tightens as I face a grin filled with spikes. Her mouth forms a murderous smile as she dusts her white corset dress down and steps down off the throne.

She appears in the middle of the shredded doorway, her blood-red eyes a patchwork of emotion as she inhales the Trutinor air, and says, "At last."

And then she steps into Trutinor.

THIRTY-ONE

*'No one is sure of the origins of **The Heart of Trutinor**. But ancient lore passed down from the Dryads suggest **The First and Last Fallons** pulled Trutinor's beating heart from the very center of the earth early in their life. The Dryads imply that this is how they gained their excess of power and took control of Trutinor.'*

Excerpt—The Lost Scriptures

EDEN

The doorway burns brighter, the edges fray, fracture, splinter into a web of cracks. They peel and tear and chunk by chunk; the cracks split the sky as far and wide as I can see. And the world rips open. Obex stands disconnected, a darkened city floating above the ocean, above the beach, a world of darkness and demons unleashed on Trutinor.

Twilight streams in from Obex, pouring its muted light onto the beach. Thousands of demons stand waiting. Rozalyn takes another tentative step into Trutinor, inhales deep. Her eyes scan the beach. She finds Cecilia and sneers. She turns back to Obex. "BRING ME THE HEART."

"DELPHINE," I bellow. A crowd of Keepers circling Delphine edges closer to us.

In front of Delphine, Hermia stands, a blade smeared in red drawn. Her orange eyes smolder with fury. She's covered in blood splatter, her face lacerated. It's the first time I really believe she used to work as an assassin. Hermia stands in front of the group as the demons bringing the Heart inch closer to us.

The Heart of Obex appears in the tear, and at the front is a strange short demon with uneven horns, one of which pusses.

"Hermia, quick."

Hermia and the demon both stop short. Their eyes bulge, Hermia stumbles, then gathers herself and runs faster toward him. I catch sight of Trey and he's grinning so broadly that it lights up his entire face.

"It's Bellamy," he shouts over the roar of battle.

Trey leaps up and runs into Obex to grab the abandoned trolley holding the Obex Heart-half. For a second, my back tingles watching Trey run into the twilight. But as fast as it tingles, my body moves on autopilot. I grab the box from Delphine, and Trey and I and run at each other.

Cecilia is screeching, roaring and bellowing commands at her army. Sending floods of Keepers toward us. I won't make it.

Something smashes into me, and I stumble and hit the

sand. A Keeper in a blue uniform pummels my body and yanks me onto my back to straddle me. I raise my palms, ready to defend, but someone rips her off me and plunges a knife through her chest. The soldier collapses, but not before slashing out with a blade that slices across my arm. I glance at the Keeper—no, demon—who stopped the soldier and all the air whooshes out of my lungs.

Eve.

There's a beat. A moment of recognition. She nods. "Go. I'll cover." And then she runs, swinging her blade into the sea of Keepers making a path for me. I scramble up, grab the trolley, and go.

My eyes cast over Hermia and Bellamy and the battle, the screams and cries, the broken bodies and magic flying around us, drown into silence as the two of them crash into each other, one soul mate reunited with another. Time stops for them as they grip hold of each other, their fingers indenting skin. I swear magic reverberates around them.

But I can't stand and watch. We have to merge the Hearts.

"Stand back," Rozalyn shouts. "Lift the lids, let the Hearts connect."

The pounding roars through my ears as both sides of the heart thrum and thump in time together.

Behind me, Cecilia is screaming.

"HURRY," Rozalyn bellows. She commands a hoard of demons who rush past me and slam Cecilia into the ground.

I push the trolley, Trey shoves his, and then, like a magnet, the heart halves lock on and draw us together of their own volition. As the two sides merge, white light bursts from the rapidly closing seam. Where our hands hold the hearts, layers and layers of magical threads, black, green, silver, maroon, blue and lilac, peel off the heart in sync with the thud, thud, beat. The threads connect to our arms. It burns and pulses as it enters my body and surges into my system. Honey and silk flow through my veins, my senses alive, and then it needles, gentle at first, then it sears and peaks as raw magic cascades into my system.

"I can't take it," I shout. But Trey trudges around the Heart and grips hold of my hand.

"We can. We Will. Together."

Power courses through our bodies. The world is bright and loud and it consumes us. Everything vibrates and spasms, but Trey never lets go. Never leaves. The world speckles. I realize this must be why we had to Inherit, why our parents died. This is more power than a body should be able to hold. I swear I'm coming apart. My insides stretching, ripping. This is worse than when Trey died.

We're both on our knees, wrapped in ribbons of magic, our voices hoarse from screaming. My vision fades. This is it. We're dying. And then, just as suddenly, it's over.

"We," I breathe, "made it."

Trey is panting. I'm breathing just as deep. My body thrums with the excess of power, all my senses alive, buzzing like they had a hit of adrenaline.

"We have it all," Rozalyn says. "The blood, the blade and the bodies. Now we attack. DEMONS, CHARGE."

Rozalyn scans the beach until her eyes settle on a cluster of Keepers with Cecilia in the middle. Her eyes narrow, her lip curls, and she runs full speed at her sister. They smash into each other, and a thunderous crack like a bomb exploding plumes out. The backfire throws Keepers outward. Bodies crumple to the ground, bouncing into each other.

I glance at Trey. Terror lines my brow. This is the Obex

battle repeating over again. I cannot watch him die. Not again.

Cecilia and Rozalyn throw sorcery, fire, and lightning. They dance and spin and dive and jump. Fists crush bone, skin dapples red and black. Within seconds, both of them are battered, bruised, and broken. But still they fight. I'm holding the blade in my hand, but there's no way I can get between them to use it.

"We need to get closer if we want to finish this," I say to Trey.

I run down the beach, dodging and jumping figures and magic as it flies past my head and chest. Trey runs behind me. I sprint until my lungs sear. But every time Cecilia and Rozalyn smash into each other, the ricochets flatten us. I weave around people, scanning the beach. And then I find Aurora fighting back to back with Castor. I sprint harder.

"We need you. Can you two provide cover for us?"

"When you're close, I can control them," Trey says. "That should give you enough time to get between them."

"No. Not after Obex. Not again. You could die," I say, my voice stricken.

"And so could you. If you get that close, what's to say she won't turn on you instead of gunning for her sister? We can't take the risk."

"You can," Castor says. "You're stronger now you've absorbed the power of the Heart. Dig deep. Embrace. All. Of. Your. Power. This is what you were born for."

Around my arms are laces and threads of wispy smoke patterns.

"You were always meant to be here, in this moment, fulfilling a destiny to end all others. You have to try," Castor says.

I grab Trey's chin and pull him around to face me, and

kiss him hard. As hard as if it were the first and last time, as if it were a lifetime of kisses and love captured in one moment on the lips.

"I love you, Trey, in this lifetime."

"And all the lifetimes to come," he finishes. And then I break away, moving deeper inside the circle. This time it's me leaving, not him. Behind us, around us, hundreds of Mermaids trudge in circles defending us. We move as one, sprinting across the beach as the circle tightens. The closer we get, the harder Cecilia's army fights. Demons join the charge, protecting the Mermaids. Spittle, blood and pincers hack and chop at soldiers. Crackled roars and guttural cries fill my ears, but inch by inch we edge closer. And then the circle halts and breaks. There they are.

Two sisters.

Two gods.

The first and last of our kind.

Cecilia and Rozalyn.

I slide my gaze back to Trey. A calm descends over me, a stillness and completeness I haven't felt since I was first Bound to him. The noise of the battle quiets until the only thing I hear is the hollow rattle of my breath and the beating of the complete Heart of Trutinor.

"Let it all go. Don't be afraid," I shout back at him.

His eyes fall on mine. He takes a deep breath and maroon descends over his pupils. I shut my eyes, listen to the beat, beat, beat.

The vault rattles, trembles, and then it falls away completely, and I let it consume me. My body thrums and pulses, surging with the power from the Heart, the prophecy and the Imbalance. I grip the blade and run.

Aurora screams instructions, Castor shouts at the rebels left alive to move into defensive positions.

Cecilia catches me approaching and launches a fireball in my way. When I bat it off, she spreads her fingers and flicks her wrist at the sand. Loops of thickening sand scratch and pull at my legs. One tightens around my shin. I stumble as it tightens, harder and harder, until the bone crunches and I'm thrown down. My leg fractured. I roll onto my front and throw up. The pain is acute, but I'm too close to stop.

Rozalyn swipes the air, and the sand falls away. Around me demons crush skulls, Mermaids tear into soldiers, but still Cecilia's army keeps coming.

I hobble closer.

Closer.

Trey appears opposite me. Cecilia hesitates, flicking her gaze at him. It's enough. Trey locks on, his blood-red eyes blazing as he raises his hands and focuses all his power on Cecilia. She stumbles, falls. But she's back up in seconds and Trey loses his grip on her. Rozalyn charges, grabs her sister by the neck. They spin, joined hands on throats, fists punching jaws, nails and teeth and magic. I pace behind and around them. They're moving so fast I can't get a clean shot at Cecilia.

"DO IT," Rozalyn says.

Cecilia roars, raises her hand and aims at me, and then freezes. Behind her, Trey stands with both his hands pointed at her. Blood drips from his nose. It wells under his eyes. Even with all the power of the Heart and vault, it's still too much. I can't lose him again. I move, hopping, dragging, trudging as fast as I can. My eyes watering as my leg screams with pain. Blade in hand, I sprint and I don't stop; I don't think, I just keep going. The air tugs at my essence, willing me to draw on it. So I do. I pull and tug and absorb every single atom of static and electricity. From the sand and ocean, from fish and bodies. More and more until bodies drop to the sand, collateral damage. But it's not enough so I keep going. Drawing from the sky, the earth, and I fire it all into the twirling sisters. It encases all three of us in the brightest cage of lightning I've ever seen. It blinds and scorches my eyes, my head throbs, my ears ring, my nose drips blood onto the sand. But I can't stop. The sisters' movement's slow, both of them under Trey's control.

"NOW," he bellows.

"I CAN'T, I'LL GET ROZALYN,"

Rozalyn snaps to face me as she ducks under Cecilia's fist. Her gaze is so fierce, so tired. An infinite exhaustion laces through her expression and penetrates all the way to my soul, and I realize. The blade, the blood and the bodies... bodies plural. Castor's words filter through my head. She knew all along killing her sister would mean killing her too. There was never any other way.

"EDEN," Trey screams, "I CAN'T HOLD THEM MUCH LONGER."

I step forward.

"NOW," Rozalyn says and throws herself at Cecilia, wrapping her arms around her sister. I raise the blade and with all the strength I have left, I thrust it right through the middle of them both.

Cecilia's face stills, widens, she lays one final ferocious glare on me and then both sisters explode in a rainbow of matting ash that rises and billows and then the Dust falls to the earth. Only this time there is no pulse of magic as it touches our skin. Everything stops. Bodies, sound, power. Outstretched arms bereft of magic. Lightning fizzles out, fires peter to embers, and the whole beach descends into a quiet that's as silent as death and shadows.

THIRTY-TWO

'Every new beginning comes from some other beginning's end.'

Seneca, human philosopher

EDEN

The first noises come from Cecilia's soldiers. Quiet whimpers, the groans of injuries and intakes of breath as each soldier realizes they're no longer under Cecilia's compulsion.

Trey appears by my side along with Castor and Aurora. They lift me to the beach edge where a swarm of Dryads appears. Aurora and Castor return to the beach, lifting and carrying wounded Keepers to the waiting Dryads for healing.

One elderly Dryad, with an array of speckled silver twigs for hair, kneels beside my leg and pulls out a pouch of herbs and liquids. His bark-colored hands move over my leg, I open my mouth to scream and he pops a ball of herbs in. I lie back, dizzy, sleepy, and awash with warmth and cinnamon dissolving into my taste buds.

My eyes snap open as Trey brushes hair away from my face. I'm wrapped in his arms, warm, safe.

"You're awake." He smiles and kisses my forehead. "Thank Balance."

"How long was I out?" I say.

"Not long. Fifteen minutes, maybe." He fusses over me, checking my temperature, checking my leg, the cuts I've accrued.

When he's satisfied, he continues. "The Dryad said he rapid-healed the bone break. You'll have to go to the hospital to make sure it's set okay and for follow-up, and for more painkillers, but you'll be okay for now because whatever he gave you was strong enough to last a few hours."

He holds out a hand and I stand, tentatively, testing my foot and leg, testing a little weight. A bit more. It aches like a bitch, but it's not agonizing anymore. Trey picks up a long stick from the sand.

"The Dryad grew this and snapped it off to help you walk temporarily on the beach."

"Great, thank you." I take the cane and goosebumps rush over my arms. Dorian.

I glance across the sand, scanning. Everywhere I look are acres of motionless bodies, groaning Keepers, and standing alone in the center is the Heart. It beats loud and constant, whole now at last. But I don't see Dorian.

"I...I—" I start.

"You want to look for him?" Trey finishes.

I swallow, buying myself time. This is not really the

time or place for this conversation, but equally, I'm not going to lie to Trey.

"We..." I start and falter.

"I know you slept together," Trey says, his words cold, blunt. "Rozalyn... She... actually, never mind."

Acrid bile creeps up my throat. My gut swirls and churns, and then I get angry. "What do you want me to say? I thought you were dead."

Maroon flashes over Trey's eyes.

"I was dead. I didn't... For godsake, I'm not having a go. I don't want to argue about this. But it's not exactly easy knowing you slept with someone else."

"AND WHAT ABOUT YOU? Don't even try and tell me you didn't sleep with Eve."

"That's not..." Trey falls silent. "Fine. Yes, I did. I'm sorry, okay. I was dead, and I'd lost hope and had no idea if I would ever see you again. It's not... Look, I'm not judging, fuck, I'm not guilt-free. We both messed up here."

I dig my foot into the sand, hunting for the right words. They're not between the grains and I can't find them in myself. It's a train wreck.

"I figured you'd slept with her when I saw you in the pub..." I suck in a breath, trying to bite down tears prickling the backs of my eyes.

"I'm sorry, I wish I could take it back," he says.

"I'm sorry, too. I would never. If I'd known you'd come home..."

He pulls me into his arms, rubbing his hand over my head. And then he leans back. "Do you... do you love him?"

"God no. No. You are the only person I have ever loved. Will ever love. It was always you. But he... Dorian was something else. He was independent of my history, a safe space, protection while I healed. And he was also an addict.

So he understood what I was going through in a way no one else did."

I pause, because the realization hits me, I didn't love Dorian. "But you love Eve."

He doesn't talk for an age. But eventually he says, "Yes, I love her. She was in my life for years. But I'm not in love with her and I never have been. She was there through the hardest moments in my life. But I've never been in love with her."

"We've both hurt each other. But right now, the only thing I care about is the fact we have each other back. We're both alive. Together. Nothing else matters. Not today anyway."

He leans down, his warm breath blending with mine. "I love you, Eden, in this lifetime..."

"... and all the lifetimes to come."

And then he kisses me and the world, the beach, the moans from wounded Keepers, the thumping Heart. Everything disappears as I sink into his arms and warmth and scent.

When I finally pull away, my hand slips to the temporary cane. "We should look for them. Both of them."

Trey frowns. "Really?"

"Really."

So we do. We traipse up the shore, scanning bodies and faces. We ask Dryads and Mermaids, but we don't find Dorian anywhere.

Eve, though, we do find.

As we near the middle of the beach, the Heart of Trutinor pumps an echoing beat amid an ocean of standing figures.

"They're not Keepers," I whisper to Trey.

"No," he says, taking my hand. "That's an enormous crowd of demons."

Hundreds of them, all crowding around the beating Heart. We step closer, a narrow tunnel peels open for us to squeeze through.

A skeletal-looking demon walks toward the Heart. He has no eyes, just a skull and yet he appears to have an expression hewn from awe or inspiration, or, I don't know what.

"Pest?" Trey says.

Trey knows the demon?

"Pest? What are you doing? Hey, man, be careful."

But it's too late. Pest reaches out, his forehead furrowed as he gazes in wonder at the Heart. Behind and around him, dozens more demons lumber closer, inch by inch toward the Heart.

"What's going o—" I start. But Pest's fingers make contact and it's like a detonation.

A shower of light and gold swells over his body. It reminds me of Nyx, and I bite down a sob as the sweetest aureate note I've ever heard rings out over the beach. Nyx exploded. This is not an explosion, it's a soft billow. The waves of light throb around Pest. Brighter and brighter, he blooms, light merging into him until he is whole. The note his body sings fills me with a strange glistening joy that hums and vibrates my insides. Slowly, pieces of him melt and fade until he is the purest golden light, and only his face remains—it holds the most serene expression. The note blossoms, trilling around us until finally, Pest's skull-eyes close and his face disintegrates into light and nothingness.

"What was that?" I whisper.

"I... I think he finally completed his soul and moved on," Trey says.

So we stand hand in hand as one by one, dozens of demons plod toward the Heart. One after another, they lay their fingers on the pulpy, pumping flesh and their souls sing their final melody.

Trey turns to me, his voice low beneath the harmonies the souls are singing. "When I was in Obex, I ran a fight club trying to recruit demons for Rozalyn. The price of joining was a fight. The winner took a piece of the loser's soul. It was a bid to get the demons to complete their soul sufficiently enough they could move on. But when parts of their souls were torn, the shrieking would cripple every one of us in the club. It was horrific. And yet, this, this is the most peaceful music I've ever heard."

It lasted half an hour. And we stood hand in hand the entire time, as light flourished and burgeoned and music floated through the breeze.

After the last demon touched the Heart, there was only a girl with gray skin and a limp golden plait left. Trey stiffens under my grip. But we'd seen her when we approached the clustered demons. I knew this was coming.

Eve looks different from earlier, much bloodier and more bruised. She'd caused me so much pain over the years. Even in death, she'd dug her claws into Trey. And yet they'd spent so long together. She was there for him when I couldn't be. Just like Dorian was there for me.

I don't want to let him go to her; I want to keep him all to myself. I've only just got him back. But letting him go is the right thing to do. If she touches the Heart, she's gone forever, she'll move on to her next life and the pain she's caused us can fade. Whatever history they have, however much Trey and I have messed up, I can't take a last goodbye away from them. Aren't we all the product of our histories? I scan the beach again, searching for Dorian, wishing I could thank him, make sure he's okay, say a final goodbye. But he's nowhere.

"It's okay," I say. "We both have a lot to talk about. We've both made mistakes, but we have time to deal with it. She doesn't. You should say goodbye."

"Are you sure?" he says. "I..."

My hand slips into his. "I love you. I will always love you and we can get through this. There is no mess we can't fix."

He places a kiss on my cheek. "Thank you." Then he paces across to where she's standing. "Eve?"

She draws in a sharp breath. "Trey?" Her face is cut, her legs are bleeding, there's a gash on her arm, but she flings herself at him. My jaw flexes. This is okay. I am fine. We're alive, we're together, and now we're going to rebuild our world. I can let him say goodbye.

When she lets go of him, she catches my eye. "I'm so sorry," she mouths. "For everything."

I give her a soft smile. I don't have to like her, but I can at least forgive her. The only thing hatred ever does is poison the owner. So that's what I do. I forgive her and wave goodbye. She nods at me, and then her fingers slip to the Heart's surface. There's a flash of light and a deep, humble note. Trey slouches to the sand, his shoulders droop. I go to him. There isn't anything I can say. She's gone for real this time, but to a new life, her soul whole, with a chance to live again. I guess that doesn't make the loss any easier. So I choose not to say anything. I just wrap my arms around him and stay there until he's ready to move.

I don't know how much time passes, but we stay there until Kato reappears, his eyes and face are streaked with grime and tears. It's this that makes me rush to my feet and stagger toward him, my chest vice tight.

"Is it Bo? OMG, KATO, IS IT BO?" I say, my voice high and shrill.

"No. She's... Bo's okay. But you need to... I have to show you."

We walk a hundred meters down the beach. But I realized before we arrived what was wrong. There's a crinkled flash of orange. Ice splinters through my body, my fingers numb, my throat dry.

"No." I run, throw the cane to the sand and hobble as fast as the pounding ache in my leg will allow. Trey runs beside me. Kato too. Then we're all kneeling beside them.

Hermia. Bellamy. Hand in hand at last.

Their broken bodies lie unnaturally still, sand covers one of her feet and half an arm. Her fiery eyes have dulled and lifelessly stare at the sky. A sob rips from my chest. I adore her. I want her here, alive, breathing. It's selfish, I know, because this—I reach down and stroke their clasped hands—is everything she wanted. A millennium separated, but at last, in death, she found her soul mate again. Now they can rest united for eternity. I squeeze their clasped hands and pray their love stretches through the thousand years they missed. I close her eyelids. "May you find each other in all your lifetimes to come." And then I'm sobbing in Trey's arms and Kato is in the middle of us and we're all crying together. We cry because she's gone, cry because Cecilia is finally dead, but more than anything we cry because Trey is finally alive.

Hours later, after helping to clear the beach for as long as I could before needing painkillers, after helping place Hermia's and Bellamy's bodies in the arms of Dryads to take to the morgue, after visiting Bo, receiving another checkup from a Dryad, finally, Trey and I are alone. Home.

In his mansion, together.

He dims the light in his bedroom, closes the curtains and walks into his bathroom, running the freestanding bath. It's huge with room for both of us. After a minute or two, bubbles fill the tub and I am desperate to get naked and climb in. He holds out his hand and I take it and he leads me into the bathroom.

"We have so much to talk about," he says. He looks down, his cheeks flushed.

"We do. But we can't change what's happened. We can only move forward together, build a new future. Whatever that looks like."

He pulls me in by the waist, wrapping his arms around me.

"It looks like us, together, forever. Living in peace with a gaggle of kids. A bar. A cabin by the lake..."

I raise an eyebrow, knowing exactly which cabin and what he's referring to.

"Trey...?" I whisper.

"Yes?"

I lean in, place a soft kiss on his lips. "Stop talking and take my clothes off. We need a bath."

He sucks in a breath, his fingers tighten on my waist. I smile, knowing I can do that to him.

Gentle against my various injuries, he pulls off my top, helps me out of my pants, underwear. He strips himself, and then he climbs into the bath and helps me in.

I sit with my back to his chest as he caresses my skin and

rubs soap and bubbles over my body. Then we swap and I do the same to him. When we're clean, he slides his hand through the water to hold mine.

"We should talk," he says.

"We will. But right now, I just want to be with you."

I pull him close. "Kiss me."

He does. He kisses me like it's the first time, the last time. He kisses me like he's making up for the thousands of kisses we've missed. His breath is hot and heavy. My skin erupts in goosebumps in the wake where his fingers caress me. He moves carefully and lies on top of me, slipping a hand under my back, trailing soft lips over my chest, my breasts, my nipples.

"I want you," I breathe into his ear. He knows it. He's already hard against my thigh.

"Are you sure?" he mumbles into my skin.

"I'm sure."

He grabs my bum and pulls us upright until I'm straddled his lap. Water splashes over the side of the tub. I giggle and then gasp as he pulls me close and slides himself inside me. Water floods the floor. Neither of us care because this... this time, being together, moving as one, loving each other is everything.

It's months of yearning and pain and loss. He doesn't even try to hold back his emotions or his Siren powers. They crash into me, a swarming flourish of heat and honeyed salt and cool silvered mint. All of it, mine and his. A swell of emotion balloons inside me and spills between us. It makes me gasp and moan. His Siren essence takes it in and pushes it back out and it rolls over me, into me, around me.

Tears and grief and love and relief. It builds and builds. The smell of his skin, frankincense, and golden summers. There's a deep, lingering taste of smoked cherry of lust and love. Beneath it, a slice of ice slowly disintegrates, as does the fear that I'd lost him forever. The thud of our pulses. It's overwhelming and intense, and I drink it, and him, and us in.

His hands worship my body. My hand clings to his neck, fingers locked in his hair. I lose myself in him, in our motion, in the panting of our breath, the beating of our pulses, in our union. His mouth and tongue roam my skin, exploring me like I'm new. Like he's never seen me before and he's desperate to consume me. Like I'm his entire universe, and I believe it. I feel it as he pulls me tighter and we move in slow, rhythmic waves. His tongue glides over my breasts and it makes me gasp, pushes me over the edge until my fingers dig into his back and a thousand glittering tingles course through me, through him, through our clasped hands and locked lips.

When it's over, and half the bath water is on the tiles, we collapse in the shallow waters laughing, and kissing and crying. And knowing that whatever happens next, we'll be okay. We found our way back to each other and this time, we're never letting go.

THIRTY-THREE

'We are the makers of our own fate.'

The new Laws of Trutinor

EDEN'S EPILOGUE

Four Weeks Later

In the wake of The Battle of the Hearts, as Tarkin Tavas called it, Trutinor was broken. Literally, physically, emotionally, and magically. It took two weeks before Obex settled and the land shifted to reincorporate it and then another week for the Heart of Trutinor to heal enough that we regained our powers. I'm sure Guild Sorcerers will speculate for years on the hows and whys. I like to think that Trutinor was finding its own Balance again, readjusting to its piece of missing soul. It's enough of a jolt for anyone, let alone a city-sized shift. We can cut the Heart some slack for needing a break.

The sky, though, hasn't quite recovered. Not that anyone minds. Now, reds permanently streak the clouds, a scar from Obex, if you like. It's kind of beautiful.

Those two weeks without magic were long and confused. The Dryads were the only ones with any power left. I guess because they're connected to the land in a way we're not. Those weeks were filled with so much mourning before we could put our lives back together. The soldiers left alive from Cecilia's army were taken to Dryad City Hospital and taken through a program to rid them of any remaining compulsion. The Heart itself was taken to the Guild of Sorcerers for study and examination. I suspect eventually it will come back to the South.

For three days, we cleared the beach. We found more loved ones. Arden had ended up in the battle, his broken body found under a soldier's corpse. It hurt to find him, but I hope he is now at rest with Tilley and Ren.

The old laws dictated that the Balance would crumble and dissolve if a line of Fallons were to end without an heir. After Ren died in the Libra Legion attack, Arden was the last remaining Sorcerer. But the Balance, it seems, remains unaffected. The entire West state mourned the loss of their beloved leader for two weeks. Even now, a month later, the streets are full of flowers and wands and gifts to the lost line of Winkworth's.

As a result of Arden's death, and the Battle of the Hearts, Cecilia was revealed for the fraud she was, controlling Trutinor with lies and compulsion. When you live as long as she did, she only had to wait for generational memory to forget what was real and true, and her lies penetrated the next generation.

A week ago, when the new Council formed, Israel and I were asked to join. We agreed mutually it was best for all that we should step down. Instead, we're both choosing to live a quieter life outside the public eye. Maddison still hasn't recovered from losing Victor the first time, let alone Cassian. While the council is still forming, rumor has it Aurora will be the head. I think it's an important show of faith. If we want a new world, different from what Cecilia created, then we all need to be equal and the Mermaids need to be integrated back into society at all levels. It makes sense.

Bo and I are talking. Our friendship has always born the scars of too much loss and too much heartache. But we've stayed friends through it all, we are connected by the very things that have tried to force us apart, by the awful choices we've had to make and the battles we've had to fight. Despite all of that, she was, is, and always will be my best friend, no matter what.

She's embracing her new hybrid status. Being the first Shifter-Mermaid has made her quite the celebrity. Aurora taught her a few things already and promises once the Council is settled to teach her all about her new Mer-self. Bo's talking about giving up The Six and the army. She's enjoying learning about Mermaid life and her hybrid ability. I wonder if she'll end up an academic. Her relationship with Castor is strained. Likewise, with Israel. It's a lot for all of them. Bo blames Castor for Victor's death, even though it was my hand that ended him. I suspect, eventually, they'll settle into a relationship. She was far too curious about him before the war not to give him a second chance.

Now Hermia has gone, Kato's decided to finish out Stratera Academy after all. He's going to reopen their shop in the East once he completes his studies. And is talking about some new techno design thing. A new style of CogTrackers that he thinks is going to sweep Trutinor. I smile and nod at him to avoid the regular and lengthy conversations he likes to bore me with over the engineering details he's putting into the Trackers. I try not to listen. What I did appreciate, though, is that he's decided once the shop reopens to name it Endlesquire and Co. A fitting tribute to Hermia.

Karva has been locked in Datch prison. She survived losing her hand, but she's not doing so well. I hear on news reports she's on end-of-life care. Nothing the Dryads are doing is helping. They can't understand because she's Cecilia's daughter. She should be practically immortal. The romantic in me thinks she's dying of a broken heart. The scientist thinks it has to be something to do with the way she crossed through the Door of Fates.

So many people were lost in the battle. Alongside the thousands of dead, there were several hundred who went missing.

Dorian was one of them.

I searched for days, weeks. Trey helped me. We talked as we combed the beach. I told him what happened between me and Dorian. He told me everything that happened with Eve, too. It hurts, he hurts, we're hurting. But we're working on it. We were under exceptional circumstances, and life is complicated. That doesn't change the fact we love each other. Dorian provided a safe space for me to heal while Trey was dead and Eve was part of Trey's life for the best part of half a decade. We're soul mates, but that doesn't mean we don't need other people.

Yesterday, exactly a month after the battle, I found his

cane washed up in the shallows. The Council had already recorded him as dead; lost in the battle, but it wasn't enough. I wasn't satisfied. So Trey took me to the Binding Chamber last night. It took us three hours, but eventually we found him and Pax. Both their heads were grayed out.

Even though he's gone, sometimes I walk along the beach and hope to find him swimming in the water. I never really got to thank him for everything he did for me. Sometimes I like to imagine he went back to sea, found a beautiful Mermaid and had half a dozen Mer-babies and lived a new life filled with the joy he never got. Another part of me is glad he was finally reunited with Pax. I'll never forget him or the debt I owe him. Perhaps one day in this life or the next, I'll be able to say thank you.

As for Trey and me, Trey has decided that now there's a new Council and they're bringing in a new governing system, he's not needed for public life, so he's going to focus on the bar. He's going into business with Felicia, and the pair of them have plans to turn half of Siren city into a nightclub strip. I can just imagine in a couple of years' time it will become some central district in Trutinor for nights out, posh dinners and Tarkin bloody Tavas's paparazzi antics. I guess we'll see how successful they can make it.

Felicia, I'm pleased to say, has finally forgiven me too, though occasionally I'd find an insect leg in my drink but only because I'd asked for a strong one.

Sheridan and I are growing closer. After extensive research with no results about my dreams, she turned to genealogy. It seems a few generations back there was a powerful scryer and I've inherited some of her abilities—a genetic throwback, if you like.

Which brings me back to now. A month after the battle, now that magic is flowing back into the lungs of Keepers, and the nation is healing, I've been invited to talk to Trutinor on CogNews TV as one of their last broadcasts.

Tarkin Tavas hands me the CogMic.

I step up to the plinth and clear my throat. "Good afternoon, Trutinor. In the wake of the most devastating battle in our history, The Battle of The Hearts, Trutinor will need time to heal. For centuries we have been lied to, defrauded, controlled and manipulated and we shall stand for it no longer. With the passing of the First and Last Fallons, we are no longer bound to Balance law, or any law for that matter. Our future is unknown. At last, our destiny is our own. I cannot tell you what Trutinor will look like tomorrow, next week or next month. But we will be free. No longer will we be under the reign of a dictator. We will live free, make our own laws and governments. We will remake Trutinor as we see fit. Never again will anyone be forced to be Bound to a soul mate they haven't chosen. Those choices will rest in your hands. Today, tomorrow and for the rest of our infinite lives, we will be the makers of our own fate."

THIRTY-FOUR

'Without fate, every day is a second chance.'

New Trutinor Proverb

TREY'S EPILOGUE

I've never been to France, let alone Paris. It's hot here. A dry kind of heat, more like the desert than the South.

There's a mix of smells in the air. Warm sweetbreads and the sour tang of wine and beer. Peppered along the streets are small metal tables outside cafes and restaurants, all of them full of people smiling, drinking and smoking.

"Next street," Bo says. Next to her, Kato strolls with his hand in hers. His face has healed from where Karva hurt him. He has a nice scar across his cheek to match the one on his brow. He was livid at first, but then a gaggle of Siren girls fawned over him and said how brave and strong he must have been and he promptly got over having another scar. Beatrice, however, lost her shit at him. It made me laugh. They never change. Squabbling and bickering. But my god is it good to hear again.

I glance to my side, Eden's grinning at the two of them as well. I pull her back, take out the battered journal from my back pocket. I've wanted to give this to her for a while. It explains everything, what happened before, my time in Obex. We've forgiven each other, but I don't want to keep my memories alone anymore. Sharing them with the journal healed me so much I can't help but wonder if sharing them with Eden will, too.

"What is it?" she says.

"A journal. I wrote it while I was in Obex. I wasn't sure how or even if I should give it to you."

"Are you sure you want me to read it?"

I nod, pull her into a hug and say, "I can't believe you convinced me to come here."

She squirms out of my grasp and tuts at me. "Don't start. You know as well as I do, this isn't just for you. It's for Kato too. You got a second chance at life. So you can give her one too."

I flex my jaw. She has me there. That's exactly how she convinced me, too. She slides the journal into her pocket and her hand back in mine.

White vintage buildings line the streets. The scent of warm pastries fills the air and makes me hungry. We turn according to Bo's directions and then they come to a halt. Bo and Kato pour over the CogTracker map, arguing over which "right" was right.

Eden steps in front of them, squints, draws a sharp breath.

"I see her."

Across the road, there's a small bakery and cafe.

Outside, chic white-metal tables line the front of the shop. The awning is down, providing much-needed shadow. The branded signage reads:

LUCHELLI BAKES

A woman comes outside holding a tray of coffees and cupcakes. She keeps the door open with her foot for a customer to leave. Eden surges forward. Kato looks up, startles, and follows. Bo and I bring up the rear.

The woman's hair is long, thick and wavy. Her skin has that familiar Siren tan. When she glances up, there's no mistaking the piercing blue eyes shining back at me.

She gasps. Drops the tray. It crashes to the pavement, shattering mugs and spraying cupcakes across the street. Her hands clasp her mouth, tears stream down her cheeks as she falls to her knees.

Kato steps forward, his hand outstretched. "Mom?"

BREAKING NEWS

"This is Tarkin Tavas reporting for CogNews TV for the last time. In light of The Battle of the Hearts, the disruption to Trutinor and Obex, CogNews has decided to close its doors and reopen with a different mission. From next week, CogNews will be rebranded under new management. We're launching Fateless TV, where no destiny is ever pre-determined.

We'll be bringing you the latest in hot predictions, news of the latest trend of "FreeBinding" Celebrity gossip and Fallon pregnancies. Fear not, beloved viewers, you're not losing award-winning reporter Tarkin Tavas just yet.

No. We will be back, bigger, better and even bolder on your CogScreens.

Although no one knows what tomorrow will look like, or what their future will hold, or how we will remake Trutinor. What we do know is that we must live and love and appreciate the moments of joy and freedom we find every day.

This is Tarkin Tavas signing off from CogNews TV for the final time.

May you forever carve your own destinies."

AUTHOR'S NOTE

Some books, like children, are sent to try us. Other books are little cherubs that fall from your literary loins at a rapid rate of knots and dance across the page like the Bolshoi Ballet. And then there are the books that... well, they're more like the spawn of Satan mixed with an apocalypse. They're a millennium of childhood nightmares and a plague of locusts rolled into one.

This book was the latter.

I'm sure I'm supposed to say lovely things about writing and how magical this book was and blah, blah, blah. And some days it was those things. But also, I don't want to lie.

This book nearly killed me. It nearly killed my fiction career. It riddled me with doubt and anxiety, fears and worries. And yet, that doesn't make me love it any less. I slayed the dragon.

Keepers, the first book in the series, was rewritten three times from scratch. I literally threw the entire manuscript in the bin twice. But that's okay, I was learning to write. Each book was better than the last. I knew it, felt it and could see the development. It was a process.

But then Victor was one of those cherub-like books falling onto the page in six swift months with only a minor hiccup about the location the first chapter was set in.

Victor was published in 2018.

As I write this, it's 2022. Four years. That's how long this book took. It's unfathomable to me that a book should take so long. Especially after I was on such a roll.

I was going to give you a lengthy explanation of why it took so long, but I'm not sure it matters now. It's done. The series is complete.

What I do want to say is, this was hard. Really, really hard. There were times I thought I'd never write fiction again. But I'm also not one for quitting or letting things beat me. So I picked up the pen and tried again. And again. And again.

There is something about doing "hard" things—that when you finally complete them, it's sweeter, more momentous, more significant, more delicious.

Finishing *Trey* was a literal infusion of ecstasy and relief. Never have I been prouder of completing a book.

Writing will always be a journey, and *Trey*—actually, the entire series—taught me so much. The art of persistence, problem solving, grit, dedication. It showed me that no matter how stuck, how blocked or how tied in knots I am, I can still finish a book.

It also showed me that—in the words of Glennon Doyle —I can do hard things. This book marks the end of a twenty-one year journey. Eden came to me when I was nine years old and being bullied. She kept a lonely nine-year-old company as she wove stories of magic and electricity. I can't believe it's over.

This was always going to be the first series I wrote. It had to be. I owed it to Eden. It's almost as if it were fated.

I guess now, like Eden, my literary destiny is my own. I'm excited, I'm scared, but more than anything, I'm filled with the buzz of opportunity. It's time to dance with the scattered motes of possibility that lie just beyond the horizon.

I hope you'll join me.

Sacha Black,

16th February, 2022

ACKNOWLEDGMENTS

First, I need to thank you, my wonderful readers, for sticking with me while this series took an unprecedented amount of time to complete. I appreciate you more than you know.

Jackie Mackenzie-Dodds, thank you for the tour of a lifetime behind the scenes of the greatest museum in the world. I still can't believe floor five point five exists! I will never, ever forget that day.

To Chloe and Atlas, the loves of my life, thank you for cheering me on from the sidelines, continuing to support me, for secretly reading the book in the mornings and for threatening to send a certain arch-nemesis politician a letter of loving devotion if I didn't finish the book.

To the Helens. Helen Glynn Jones, I'm not sure you realized what you took on all those years ago when you agreed to CP for me, but I'm deeply grateful for all the drafts you've read and re-read. For the #NivvyPushtons you got me through, the #vagkicks you gave and the #LitO's you inspired. You've been there through them all. We finally made it!

Helen Scheuerer, who burns as long and hard as I do. Thank you for picking up the series last minute and racing through it to give me the reassurance I needed. Thank you for keeping me accountable, for the daily voice memos of joy and for always being there to talk about work, business, and dreams. We will win.

To Katlyn Duncan, our relator circle is everything. Your consistent execution keeps me on the straight and narrow, keeps me striving to be half as machine-like as you. You are a queen of delivery, and I appreciate your strengths more than you know.

To JP, who took an hour out of his day to help me brainstorm my way out of the most significant plot-block I've ever had, thank you for having an amazing #ideation brain.

Thank you to my amazing Patrons who keep me on my toes, fill the community with warmth and support, occasionally deride me, wind me up, poke the competition beast and generally antagonize me... I adore you. All of you. Thank you for the continued love.

To Elli, for your savage coaching, I am indebted. Your brutal truths, your unwavering belief, your wonderfully quiet nature and the wild fear I have of disappointing you. You got me through this. You made me finish. For that, I owe you everything. Thank you.

Finish the complete series now...

The Eden East Novels:

- Book 1 - Keepers
- Book 2 - Victor
- Book 3 - Trey
- Book 4 - Sirens (a short bonus novella set in Obex)

ABOUT THE AUTHOR

Sacha Black has five obsessions; words, expensive shoes, conspiracy theories, self-improvement, and breaking the rules. She also has the mind of a perpetual sixteen-year-old, only with slightly less drama and slightly more bills.

Sacha writes books about people with magical powers, sapphic fiction for teens, and other books about the art of writing. She lives in Cambridgeshire, England, with her wife and genius, giant of a son.

When she's not writing, she can be found laughing inappropriately loud, blogging, sniffing musty old books, fangirling film and TV soundtracks, or thinking up new ways to break the rules.

www.sachablack.co.uk

instagram.com/sachablackauthor
facebook.com/sachablackauthor
amazon.com/Sacha-Black/e/B072BQ2M-P7/ref=sr_tc_2_0?qid=1533912504&sr=8-2-ent